Praise for *Five Odd Honors*

"There's something for almost everyone here: urban fantasy, ancient legends, flawed characters and outstanding ones, treachery, redemption, hope, despair. The disparate strands of this one could easily have escaped the author's control but they're all managed well and shaped toward the conclusion. It's really hard to compare this to anything else as it borrows selectively from so many different sources. Try it. You'll like it."

—Don D'Ammassa, *Fantasy Reviews*

"Lindskold maintains a focus on Chinese folklore and interpersonal connection, and her characters work through their problems in dialogue as often as action. Urban fantasy fans looking for something a little more mellow will enjoy this foray."

—*Publishers Weekly*

"A superb thriller." —*Baryon* magazine

"The author demonstrates a talent for creating believable characters, while her gentle humor adds depth and credence to a tale drawn from Chinese culture. Should appeal to fans of Charles de Lint's urban fantasies." —*Library Journal*

"A delightful romp through a mythical tradition not often encount

Revu

TOR BOOKS BY JANE LINDSKOLD

Through Wolf's Eyes

Wolf's Head, Wolf's Heart

The Dragon of Despair

Wolf Captured

Wolf Hunting

Wolf's Blood

The Buried Pyramid

Child of a Rainless Year

Thirteen Orphans

Nine Gates

Five Odd Honors

FIVE ODD HONORS

JANE LINDSKOLD

五奇榮譽

TOR®
fantasy

A TOM DOHERTY ASSOCIATES BOOK
NEW YORK

This is a work of fiction. All of the characters, organizations, and events portrayed in this novel are either products of the author's imagination or are used fictitiously.

FIVE ODD HONORS

Copyright © 2010 by Jane Lindskold

All rights reserved.

A Tor Book
Published by Tom Doherty Associates, LLC
175 Fifth Avenue
New York, NY 10010

www.tor-forge.com

Tor® is a registered trademark of Tom Doherty Associates, LLC.

ISBN 978-0-7653-5623-9

First Edition: May 2010
First Mass Market Edition: May 2011

Printed in the United States of America

0 9 8 7 6 5 4 3 2 1

For Jim
From a Tiger to her Dragon

ACKNOWLEDGMENTS

Many thanks to those who read this and assured me that weird was the only way the story would work. These include: Jim Moore, Bobbi Wolf, Phyllis White, and Yvonne Coats. My editor, Melissa Singer, gave the manuscript lots of her time. My agent, Kay McCauley, kept my spirits up.

Special thanks to those readers who have contacted me to share their responses to the earlier books in this series.

FIVE ODD
HONORS

PROLOGUE

Brenda Morris sat down at her computer, her fingers flying as she wrote a letter she knew she'd never be permitted to send.

"Dear Shannon,

"In your last e-mail, you sort of yelled at me for not staying in touch better this summer. No. I haven't gotten stuck-up working for a movie star. Nothing like it.

"It's just that, well, there's so damn much I'm not allowed to talk about, and it's the stuff that I really want to talk about. Take Pearl—my 'famous boss' as you called her. No. Go back further. Start with my dad hauling me out here to California to introduce me to a guy it turns out he's known since they were both, like, ten. Maybe younger. I'm still trying to work all of this out. Take getting to that guy's office—his name is Albert Yu and he's famous, too, in a really weird way—and finding it trashed. And Albert Yu's missing. And when we finally find him, well, he's still sort of missing. And soon my dad is, too . . .

"Then there's finding out that Dad talks Chinese like a native, and that this skill is perfectly normal compared with the fact that he's a sorcerer of a real obscure sort. And so's Pearl. And so's Albert. And . . . Jeez . . . so am I, at least a little. Yeah. This summer, I'm interning in magic and self-defense.

"Hell. Can you see why I can't talk about it?

"You said you wanted me to tell you all about the people I've been meeting, the things I've been doing, that you already know I make a great chocolate mousse, thank you very much. Tell you the good stuff.

"Okay. How about this? I've met a white tiger the size of a house. No, I'm not exaggerating. His name's Pai Hu. I've talked to dragons and turned into a rat. Really.

"I've made some new friends, and seen them bleeding, half crazy with terror. I've been cut by a sword. I've seen one of my new friends, a really cool old man named Waking Lizard, sprawled, deadddddddddddddddddddd"

Brenda's hand stuck on the keyboard, that final letter stuttering out like her own heartbeat, as she remembered the horrible realization that victory tasted a whole lot like defeat.

She didn't realize she was crying until the hot, wet drops hit the backs of her hands.

"Shannon," she said aloud, her voice tight with tears. "I wish I could tell you, but I can't. I can't. I can't even tell you about the guy I . . . I can't. I'm sorry."

Brenda touched a few keys, let the words shine bright, then struck them away to nothingness, wishing, just a little, that all her problems could be erased so easily.

I

Thundering Heaven has betrayed us," the ghost of Loyal Wind reported, his voice tight with suppressed fury.

He who when alive had been the Horse manifested much as he had in the prime of life: a tall man, his shining black hair cut close to a well-shaped head. The styling of that hair showed some vanity for, although it was worn short, the sideburns were long and neatly squared. He wore a full mustache and a small chin beard. Loyal Wind's clothing was simple, a long tunic, trousers, and riding boots, but the fabric was the best, the embroidered trim sumptuous.

The one to whom he spoke, Nine Ducks, she who in life had been the Ox, was nothing like him. Even in death, where the choice of appearance reflected the spirit's mental state more than any fidelity to the life lived, Nine Ducks manifested as an old woman, bent and leaning on a cane.

Appearance of age notwithstanding, Nine Ducks possessed a tremendous vitality of spirit. She was attired in a shenyi—the long, full-sleeved robe praised by the philosopher K'ung for embodying a unique combination of functionality and symbolic import. The elaborate embroideries that covered the golden-yellow fabric invoked luck, prosperity, and longevity.

"Thundering Heaven has betrayed us?" she said. "How?"

"He has taken Bent Bamboo, the Monkey, into his keeping."

"Is Thundering Heaven holding the Monkey prisoner?"

Loyal Wind frowned. "I am not certain. Thundering Heaven may simply have made certain that the Monkey would hear only one version of recent events. For whatever reason, the Monkey will not see me. Without his cooperation, I cannot reach him."

"And without the Monkey," Nine Ducks said, straightening, although she still leaned upon her cane, "we cannot move forward with our plans to open the gates into the Lands Born from Smoke and Sacrifice. Why would Thundering Heaven do this? Surely he does not wish our exile to be extended. Surely a hundred years and more is enough."

"Thundering Heaven is complex," Loyal Wind replied in a tone that indicated he did not approve of such complexity. "Or so I have been told. Debating Thundering Heaven's motivations can wait. Among the living, our allies include the Rat, the Tiger, the Hare, the Dragon, the Rooster, the Pig, and the Dog. Among the dead, you and I—Horse and Ox—have agreed to join forces with the living. Even so, if we are to open the final gate into the Lands, we must have the Snake, the Ram, and the Monkey."

Nine Ducks nodded. "And among the living, these three are useless to us. We must have the cooperation of the dead."

"Yes."

Loyal Wind extended one callused hand. Where nothing had been before, there stood a powerfully muscled chestnut stallion, strength and swiftness singing from every line. The stallion was caparisoned for battle. As Loyal Wind swung into the saddle with easy grace, the ghost's attire shifted to match the warlike gear worn by his steed.

"The living must be informed about this turn of events," Loyal Wind announced, looking down at Nine Ducks. "I have a connection to them which I can exploit to make contact, even though they have not summoned me."

"Very well. You tell the living," replied Nine Ducks, pushing herself to her feet with her cane. "I will warn the dead."

☆

Brenda Morris was growing accustomed to having really odd dreams, but this one was about to get star billing.

She'd been half reclining on the grassy bank bordering a dancing, laughing stream. A handsome young man was seated next to her.

The young man's eyes were wide, round, and exactly the color of freshly opened spring leaves. His hair, the red-gold of dark honey, was curly, cut just long enough to look untamed without being in the least feminine. He had a wonderful mouth, full-lipped and sensuous. A moment before, he had been singing.

At least Brenda heard music: robust and rhythmic as any rock-and-roll piece, but flavored with harps and flutes rather than electric guitar and drums. She didn't know what you called this type of music, but she knew she liked it. She also couldn't remember the name of the young man who was sitting next to her, but she felt fairly certain he was about to kiss her, and she liked that, too.

Brenda felt a little odd about how much she hoped

the young man with the green eyes and the red-gold hair would kiss her.

This was a dream. Certainly it was all right to let a man kiss you in a dream, even if . . . you loved another man? Something like that.

For a moment Brenda had a vision of that other young man, the memory of his face suspended between her and the youth with green eyes. This face had slanting, almond-shaped eyes, dark and serious. It was framed by silky black hair worn as long as her own, caught back with a leather tie.

This second man was as handsome as the green-eyed youth of her dream, but far less real. Brenda couldn't even remember his name.

The young man with the red-gold hair cupped Brenda's cheek in one of his musician's hands. There was an urgency in the brilliant green of his gaze, an urgency Brenda didn't think was entirely related to the kiss his lips still shaped.

Something was buzzing in her ear.

Brenda shook her head, moving out of reach of that cupping hand. She smelled horses. Sweaty horses. Hay and manure.

What had happened to the stream? Where was the grassy bank? Suddenly, Brenda was sitting upright on a straw bale, the freshly cut straw a brighter gold than the hair of the young man who sat next to her, bolt upright and looking distinctly uncomfortable. A moment ago he'd been wearing . . .

A cap-sleeved tunic? Yes! He'd been dressed like a page or young squire from that book of Arthurian tales her grandmother Elaine had loved to read aloud when Brenda had been too small to read for herself.

Now the young man wore denim coveralls and a short-sleeved, red-plaid cotton shirt. The music in the background blended temple bells and brass chimes incongruously with banjo and fiddle. The green-eyed youth no longer looked as if he were about to kiss Brenda. Now his expression was distinctly annoyed.

A chestnut horse had thrust its head in over the half-open door. Then a man stood there instead, a Chinese man with a full mustache and very short beard. He was wearing ornate armor and a helmet upon which a pair of the longest plumes from a pheasant's tail were set. These caught a faint breeze, giving the Chinese man an illusion of motion although he stood perfectly still.

Brenda recognized the new arrival at once.

"Loyal Wind! What are you doing here? For that matter, what am I doing here? I was sitting on a stream bank. There was a . . ."

She looked around. The young man with the green eyes had vanished like the dream he had been.

"Why am I in a barn?" Brenda concluded, not really wanting to explain that she'd been sitting on the riverbank with a young man who was not the dark-eyed, black-haired young man whose name she could now remember perfectly.

Flying Claw. His name was Flying Claw.

Loyal Wind chose to answer her last question. "Perhaps you are in a barn, Brenda Morris, because I am the Horse, and where else would you expect to find a horse?"

"In a parking lot," Brenda muttered.

Loyal Wind looked startled, and Brenda hastened to explain.

"A joke some little kids I knew told over and over. They had just discovered knock-knock jokes, but they didn't understand the logic behind them . . . Oh, never mind. What's going on? What are you doing in my dream?"

The barn was gone now. Brenda and Loyal Wind

were standing, facing each other on a dry and barren steppe. Cliffs could be seen in the distance, burnt-orange, barren of all but greyish scrub growth in shadowed crevices.

"I am a bit surprised to find myself in your dream," Loyal Wind admitted. "I sought to bring a message to one of the Thirteen Orphans. I had thought my desire would connect me to Deborah or Riprap since they were among the Orphans who traveled to the Nine Yellow Springs under my guidance. Still, you took part in that journey as well. The Rat is the sign opposed to the Horse on the wheel. There is a strong attraction between opposites."

"But I am not the Rat," Brenda protested. "That's my dad."

She caught herself rationalizing aloud.

"I know, I know. Dad didn't go on that journey, and so maybe that's the reason you reached me and not him. Maybe the others are both awake. Is it easier for you to contact someone who is asleep?"

"Infinitely," Loyal Wind said, and Brenda could tell that, for him at least, this explained the anomaly. She made a mental note to find out how late Deborah and Riprap had slept.

But Loyal Wind was speaking.

"I have come to bring the Orphans and their allies news of ill omen. You recall that when last we met, I agreed to journey through the Hells until I found the ghosts of the Thirteen Orphans—especially of those four of whom we had need—then seek to win them to our cause?"

"Yes." Brenda nodded. "We've been wondering how you were doing. Quite a few days have gone by since we parted. We've all been recovering, but recently Righteous Drum has started hinting that perhaps we should try some more traditional summons."

Quite a few days, Brenda thought. *Well, just five. And I, for one, have been glad for them. What happened at the end of Tiger's Road . . . I've needed time to think, to adjust.*

Loyal Wind, however, took Brenda's comment as a reprimand. He answered with stiff, military exactitude.

"You do realize that the afterlife is vast, far vaster than the worlds of the living, and to locate five spirits—not all of whom recalled me fondly—"

"Yes. Yes," Brenda cut in. "I'm sorry if I seemed unappreciative. Please, tell me what you learned."

Loyal Wind seemed appeased, but his words continued to hold the stiff tone of a report from scout to headquarters. "I located Nine Ducks, the Ox, first. I related to her the heroic tales of the dangers undergone in order to link the Nine Gates to the Nine Yellow Springs. This proved sufficient to win her to our cause."

Brenda remembered that Nine Ducks had been halfway won over already, but nodded understanding and approval.

"Next in order on the wheel is the Snake," Loyal Wind went on, "but as the Snake is not as greatly needed as the other two, I decided to leave Gentle Smoke for later. Equally, the Ram, my yin counterpart, was likely to be easy to convince—or so I judged, given that in life Copper Gong was fierce in her desire to return to the Lands. Thus, next I went searching for the Monkey."

"And did he refuse?" Brenda prompted when Loyal Wind fell silent.

"Worse. I could not find Bent Bamboo at all—or rather, when I did, his trail blended with and then ended in that of another of the Exiles, one whom I had not sought."

"You're procrastinating," Brenda said. "Get on with

it. I don't want this dream to end like dreams do in those stupid books where the dreamer gets woken up right before she learns something vital."

Loyal Wind's expression became vaguely disapproving, and Brenda remembered that in the strict hierarchy the Horse had been trained in, he would have expected more respect from a junior. Well, if he wanted abject respect, he shouldn't have come breaking up her dream—especially when she was about to get kissed.

"Where the signs showed me that I should find Bent Bamboo, the Monkey," Loyal Wind continued, "instead I found Thundering Heaven, who was once the Tiger. Fierce and defiant, Thundering Heaven awaited me before the dark mouth of a sheltered cave. I knew without asking that the Monkey was within, and that unless I fought Thundering Heaven, I could not pass into that place."

"So you came to report," Brenda said. "Smart."

Loyal Wind looked slightly embarrassed. "Actually, I was considering charging forth and challenging Thundering Heaven when I felt Nine Ducks seeking to contact me. Upon hearing her voice, I realized the wisdom in letting someone else know the situation before I confronted the Tiger, for Thundering Heaven manifested—even as did I—as a man in his prime."

"And Tigers," said Brenda, who had learned a bit in the almost three months since her world had turned so inside out and upside down that she took having conversations in dreams with ghosts of men who had died more than a hundred years before somewhat for granted, "are the best solo fighters of all the twelve signs, although Horses are the finest battle commanders."

"Precisely," Loyal Wind said, obviously mollified regarding her earlier impertinence by this recognition of his prowess. "I discussed what I had learned with Nine Ducks. We resolved that I would come and tell the living of this turn of events, while she would seek out and warn the others among the dead."

"And my job," Brenda said, "will be to pass on your news to the others. I wonder what time it is?"

As if in answer, an explosion of raucous rock-and-roll shattered the dream into fragments. Loyal Wind and the stable didn't so much vanish as never had been. Brenda sat bolt upright in bed.

"Good timing," she muttered, untangling herself from the sheets and padding barefoot across the room to where the alarm clock was positioned on the farthest edge of the small desk beneath the window.

No more stream bank. No more barn. No more handsome green-eyed squire. No more Chinese ghost. Just the comfortable bedroom in San Jose that was increasingly coming to feel like her own.

Slamming her hand onto the alarm clock's "off" button, Brenda thought again about that letter she'd wanted to write Shannon. So much had happened since they'd parted at USC that May, promising to stay in touch.

It's late July now, Brenda thought, going into the bathroom. She moved a pink plastic pony with a silky nylon mane and tail to the back of the toilet so she could reach her toothbrush. *No. August.*

I accept sharing a bathroom with a two-and-a-half-year-old and her mom, whereas at home I'd have my own bathroom, and even in the dorm I only had to share with one other person.

Brenda stripped out of the oversize tee shirt she wore instead of a nightie and adjusted the shower water. There was no noise from the door that led into the other bedroom, but then there wouldn't be. Nissa Nita and her daughter, Lani, would have risen around six A.M. Most of the household consisted of early risers, but Brenda (and Deborah, who had a room upstairs) had negotiated to be permitted to sleep until at least eight.

Brenda felt the slight shift in water pressure that told her that Deborah had just turned on a shower upstairs. She hurried to get her long, brown-black hair rinsed. Pearl had put in all new plumbing just the year before, but that didn't mean the hot water didn't run out—not in a household consisting of four adult women, three adult men, and one child.

Pearl's carrying us all, Brenda thought as she turned off the water. She considered her "famous boss" as she toweled off.

Pearl Bright had been a child actress, a contemporary and sometime costar of Shirley Temple. Now silver-haired, her petite form in excellent condition, her face carrying age lines with dignity, Pearl bore little resemblance to the child who sang and danced her way through the old films that were rapidly becoming Lani's favorites.

However, Pearl Bright was far from a spent "has been." Her mother had invested Pearl's earnings well. These days, Pearl managed a modest financial empire and indulged in philanthropy, all the while maintaining very active connections to the entertainment world.

Pearl has me, Riprap, and Nissa on her payroll as interns. I don't know if she's paying Des anything. I'm not sure about Deborah. How much longer can Pearl afford to keep employing us? How much longer can any of us continue to interrupt the lives we left behind? Classes will begin soon. I can register online, maybe make excuses for starting the semester late, but eventually I'm going to have to show up in the flesh.

Brenda dressed that flesh in lightweight trousers of off-white natural cotton and a matching sleeveless top

embroidered with dark purple irises. Bare feet would
be fine for now, especially since Brenda didn't think
she'd be going much of anywhere for a while.

*Not with what I've got to tell them, but who should
I tell?*

Brenda's long hair, wet from the shower, couldn't be
taken care of as casually as the rest of her. Brenda
toweled her hair mostly dry, combed out the tangles,
then worked a quick, loose braid, tying off the end
with a ribbon that matched the irises on her shirt.

All the while, Brenda rehearsed the details of Loyal
Wind's message, making sure she hadn't forgotten anything, dreading the reaction to what she must report.

Dreading one reaction more than the rest.

The kitchen clock was showing eight-thirty when
Brenda came downstairs. "Kitchen" was almost a misnomer, for the long room at the back of the house
combined kitchen, informal dining area, and family
room. This interconnected area was one of the most
frequented in the house. Brenda was not disappointed
in her expectation that she would find most of her
housemates there.

Strawberry blond Nissa Nita, pretty and round-
figured—maybe even a bit plump—sat at one end of
the table, counting round loops of oat cereal into her
daughter's mouth.

Lani—fair as her mother and sharing the same startling shade of turquoise in her eyes, but too full of
energy to be any rounder than a healthy two-and-
a-half-year-old should be—was going along with the
game, but Brenda knew Lani well enough to know
that the little girl's cooperation wouldn't last much
longer. Sometimes it seemed to Brenda that Lani survived on air and sunlight rather than normal caloric
intake.

Down the table a few seats, the newspaper's baseball statistics folded neatly in front of him, sat a member of the household whom no one would ever imagine subsisted on sunlight.

Charles Adolphus—never called anything but Riprap—was a big black man who, before the affairs of the Thirteen Orphans had drawn him from his life in Denver, Colorado, had worked as a bouncer nights and a coach by day. Somewhere in there he must have slept, but Brenda wasn't sure when. He certainly didn't seem to sleep much now.

Riprap was working his way through a large bowl of granola topped with milk and fresh peaches, but Brenda would have bet large sums of money that this was at least the man's second meal of the day. He'd probably been up for hours, gone for a run, then lifted weights in the makeshift weight room he'd put together in the basement.

Brenda moved into the kitchen proper and found Desperate Lee stirring something in a pot set over a very low gas flame. Des was somewhere in his late thirties, making him older than Nissa, who was only a few years older than Brenda herself, or Riprap, who was in his late twenties.

Even in a household of rather unusual people, Des stood out. Taller than average and so lean that he seemed even taller, Des was ethnically Chinese, although a native Californian—as had been his parents before him. Des wore his black hair in a style popular at the time of the California gold rush: forehead shaven, dark hair trailing in a tightly braided queue that fell to the middle of his back. His long mustache and wispy chin-beard were a match for the hairstyle.

Des looked up as Brenda came into the kitchen and smiled warmly, showing off cheekbones a supermodel would envy. He was dressed in a bathrobe of dark red brocade so ornate it could have easily passed as street wear.

"Morning, Brenda. I've just about finished a batch of congee. Would you like a bowl?"

Brenda had been thinking about breakfasting on bacon, eggs, and toast, chasing it all with strong coffee. One of the few good things about her own lean build was that she could eat anything and never show it—but she'd rather come to like congee for breakfast, especially when it was fresh. The thick rice porridge wasn't too unlike grits. For Brenda, who had been raised in South Carolina, something warm and mushy for breakfast qualified as comfort food.

"Sure, Des. Thanks. Is that green tea in the pot?"

"Just finished brewing," Des assured her with a purist's fervor.

"I'll pour," Brenda said, and did so. Black coffee's bitterness didn't go well with the pickled vegetables she knew Des would serve with the congee.

"Where's Pearl?"

"In her office with Shen," Des said. "She was up early this morning. They both were."

Brenda heard a faint note of reproof in Des's voice, and swallowed a sigh. Pearl and Shen were both in their seventies, and Brenda guessed that if anyone should have needed to sleep in it was the old folks. Still, she'd noticed both Pearl and Shen seemed to need less sleep than she did—or at least not as much all at once.

Brenda suspected that Des's reproof had nothing to do with Brenda's sleeping in. Although the events of five days ago had bought them some time, they all were aware that the fate of the Thirteen Orphans was far from resolved.

"I'm going to need to talk to Pearl," Brenda said. "Or maybe she's the last person I should talk to. I'm not sure."

Nissa spoke from the other room. "Breni, what do you mean? I know you haven't had your coffee, but must you speak in riddles?"

Brenda took her bowl and teacup to the table, and plunked unceremoniously into a chair across from Rip-rap. He'd pushed the baseball stats to one side, but continued eating without pause, his velvet brown eyes inquisitive and alert.

Lowering her voice, Brenda said, "What I've got to talk about has to do with Pearl's father, Thundering Heaven. Ever since I woke up, I've been trying to decide whether Pearl needs to know—at least right off. You know how she is about her dad."

Nods from everyone but Lani. The little girl had eaten her fill of cereal and was now sprawled on the family room carpet playing with some mismatched toys. Lani alone was oblivious to the tension Brenda's words had raised.

"Thundering Heaven?" Des repeated. He'd carried his own bowl to the table, and now sat stirring pickled eggplant into the thick rice gruel. "How could you learn anything to do with Thundering Heaven?"

Concisely, Brenda told them about her dream—leaving out the bit about the squire with the green eyes. Her fantasies, she felt, were a private matter. Just as she had not bothered to disbelieve Loyal Wind showing up in her dream, so no one here wasted energy telling Brenda, "Don't worry. It was only a dream."

They'd profited from her dreams before this.

Moreover, those seated around this table had walked through the jaws of the White Tiger of the West, had trod the grass of worlds that could not exist. Each had long ago surrendered the right to dissuade themselves that there was only one way of judging reality.

"Thundering Heaven," Nissa said when Brenda finished. "I can see why you wondered if you should say anything to Pearl. That fine lady does have some serious problems about her daddy."

Riprap nodded. "And for good reason. Thundering Heaven treated Pearl pretty badly when her only crime was being born a woman."

"A female Tiger," Des corrected with pedantic firmness. "In the system within which Thundering Heaven had been educated, he hadn't just fathered a daughter, he'd fathered an abomination. Pearl was born late in her father's life. From what my grandmother told me, Thundering Heaven wondered if having a daughter thrust upon him as his heir was his punishment for not attending more promptly to his duties to assure the line of the Tiger."

"Why Thundering Heaven felt as he did doesn't change anything," Nissa said. "What matters is what Brenda just told us. Loyal Wind says that Thundering Heaven is working against us. If Thundering Heaven keeps the Monkey from us, we have little hope of opening the final gate into the Lands."

Brenda nodded. Her teacup was empty, and when she rose to refill it, she added another glop of congee to her bowl.

"So what do we do?" she asked. "Do we tell Pearl, or do we see what we can learn on our own?"

"Tell Pearl," Riprap replied instantly. "Then stand back and watch the fur fly."

Des nodded. "I agree. I've known Pearl since I was a boy. She has never liked being treated as anything less than the Tiger she is. Who are we to protect her from something she is going to need to learn eventually?"

"But does she?" Nissa said. Although a strict and fair parent to Lani, Nissa was far less inclined to confrontation than the rest of them. "Perhaps we can deal with this situation without Pearl having to learn what Thundering Heaven has done."

"Nice idea," Riprap said, "but you know as well as the rest of us what price Thundering Heaven is going to insist on if we want access to his prisoner."

Brenda dropped her spoon into her bowl, the congee suddenly heavy in her gut. She knew she'd suspected this from the moment Loyal Wind had told her his message, knew she'd suspected, but hadn't wanted to admit it to herself.

"He's going to insist that Pearl renounce the Tiger."

II

The remaining tea in the pot had grown cold, so Pearl and Shen headed toward the hum of conversation in the kitchen. Brenda Morris was speaking, but Pearl, thinking over what she and Shen had been discussing, did not really register anything until the word "tiger" caught her attention.

"Was someone talking about me," she said merrily as she entered the kitchen, "or was some other Tiger under discussion?"

It was an open secret in the household that Brenda had a bad crush on Flying Claw, the Tiger who had come from the Lands Born from Smoke and Sacrifice. What was less certain was whether the young man returned Brenda's feelings or was as indifferent as he sometimes seemed.

Pearl's entering line did not meet with the response she had expected. Instead of smirks and perhaps a blush tinting the warm ivory of Brenda's cheek with rose, on the faces of the four seated around the long table she read guilty embarrassment.

"So you *were* talking about me," Pearl said. "Would you mind . . ."

The steady rhythm of solid footsteps on the stair interrupted Pearl. Deborah Van Bergenstein called out, "Don't start without me!"

So Pearl held her question, eager as she was to learn what had made the others look so uncomfortable. She turned to Shen.

"We came in here for tea. Shall I put water on?"

Shen Kung was the closest in age of those present to Pearl herself. Like her, he was well past seventy. They had been occasional playmates in childhood, friends thereafter. In the weeks since his arrival from New York City, Shen had been more physically active than he had been for years. Pearl liked to think that, overall, the effect of his more active life had been beneficial.

Although Shen's hair was more white than brown, and nothing would ever remove the seams and lines that years of close work as a calligrapher and gem cutter had put on his face, his eyes were more lively, his laughter came more easily. He was even moving with more vigor, doubtless because he was getting more exercise.

"Let me put on the tea water," Shen said. "The doctor said you shouldn't be using that hand."

He gestured to where Pearl's right hand hung encased in a cast slung against her chest.

"I can fill a teapot with one hand," Pearl protested.

Shen gently pushed her to one side. "You use the right hand as a brace. I've been watching."

Pearl let Shen take over. Her broken hand was healing—well, at least it no longer throbbed—and she didn't want her frustration with the restrictions that came with it to set back the process.

Deborah entered at that moment.

Solidly built, of average height, Deborah was somewhere in her late sixties. Her hair was cut short, and showed about equal parts brown and grey. Once she knew you, her smile could be warm and grandmotherly, but beneath that affable exterior was a very strong personality. As Deborah herself liked to say, no matter how domestic Pigs might be, boar spears had been invented because pigs had another side.

Deborah brought with her a bustle of good mornings and queries after how everyone had slept. As Deborah took her own seat at the long table, Pearl could feel the atmosphere in the room calm.

The kettle was beginning to rumble its way to a boil when Pearl turned to Brenda.

"Is there something you need to tell me?"

Brenda met Pearl's gaze. In the younger woman, Pearl saw a little of herself at that age. Brenda was taller, but both of them were small-figured rather than voluptuous. Pearl's mother had been Hungarian, while Brenda's was mostly Irish, but in both the ivory skin and a certain almond shape to the eyes made the contribution from the Far East undeniable.

Brenda drew in a deep breath. "I had a dream right before I woke up. Loyal Wind asked me to relay a message. Thundering Heaven—the ghost of your father—has decided to take a part in matters, and I don't think he means us well."

Without her years of training as an actress, Pearl wasn't certain she could have managed the controlled and encouraging nod she gave the younger woman. Certainly, from the reactions of everyone else in the room, they had expected a much more unpleasant response.

"Go on," Pearl said. "What has that old Tiger done?"

Brenda gave her report, ending with, "I'm sorry I

don't know more, but my alarm clock went off right then. Still, I don't think Loyal Wind had much more to add."

Des leaned forward. "Did Loyal Wind indicate what he planned to do after you spoke?"

Brenda shook her head. "No, but I did get the impression that he'd decided that going after Thundering Heaven by himself would be a bad idea."

Riprap had risen to pour himself a tumbler of milk. He called from the kitchen.

"Can ghosts kill ghosts? I mean, they're both dead already."

Shen, who in his education as the Dragon had studied many esoteric matters, replied, "That's a good point. I think the answer is both yes and no. Yes, they could fight to the equivalent of death, but that death would not be permanent. However, it might take a great deal of time for the defeated ghost to re-form. Loyal Wind is wise to take care."

Pearl nodded. "We need Loyal Wind far more than we need Thundering Heaven. We have our Tiger."

Her words were a challenge, and she knew it. No one had brought up why Thundering Heaven would have involved himself in their plans, because everyone knew—or suspected they knew.

"Shall I say it aloud?" Pearl asked. When no one uttered a sound, she went on. "Twelve of our ancestors were exiled from the Lands Born from Smoke and Sacrifice. We have contracted with our new allies from those same lands to help them return home. However, our analysis indicates that the final gate cannot be opened, the final bridge built, except by twelve who are affiliated with the Twelve Earthly Branches as our ancestors were."

Pearl stopped and sipped from the tea Shen had brought her.

Des, perhaps seeking to relieve her from talking about an unpleasant subject, took over.

"But over a century has passed since the Exile, and over that time, various of the branches have lost contact with the lore of the Lands. Seven can be counted on, but five have fallen away. Rather than undertaking the near-impossible task of training those five, we had decided to ask five of the original twelve to resume their roles and assist us in opening the way to the Lands."

Pearl was determined to speak the final lines herself. "Now it seems that my father—who never liked having me as his successor—has decided to turn the situation to his advantage. He will make me agree to let him be the Tiger. In return, we will have access to the Monkey. Is that how you all interpret the situation?"

Heads fair and dark inclined in agreement.

Nissa said, "But I suppose we had better ask Thundering Heaven what he wants, hadn't we? Just in case we're wrong."

Silence met Nissa's statement, then Pearl nodded slowly. "I suppose we should, but I don't think I am the one who should do the asking."

"And the question should not be a leading one," Shen added, "in case we end up accusing Thundering Heaven of something he has not contemplated."

"Let Loyal Wind do the asking," Pearl said. "I, for one, have no desire to journey into the afterlife any sooner than I must."

"If Loyal Wind agrees to speak with Thundering Heaven, his doing so will save us a great deal of time," Des agreed. "Travel through the afterlife is time-consuming for the living. Since Brenda reports that Nine Ducks has agreed to support our mission, perhaps she could accompany Loyal Wind as a witness."

"And backup," Riprap added. "If Thundering Heaven has captured the Monkey, we don't want to give him an opportunity to add the Horse to his menagerie."

Nissa asked, "Do we tell our allies about this latest development or do we wait?"

"Wait," Pearl said decisively, and was glad to see Des and Shen both nod immediate agreement. "Let us see what Loyal Wind and Nine Ducks learn from my father. At this point, all we would do is worry our allies, and invite empty speculation."

"I can agree with that," Nissa said, and the other two apprentices nodded.

Shen sighed and pushed himself to his feet. "I'll work the summoning ritual and speak with Loyal Wind. Horse's partner is Ram. We don't have the Ram. If Brenda would assist me, since Loyal Wind seems to have found an affinity with her, I believe our summons would be stronger."

Brenda nodded and rose from the table, her motions containing an easy grace Pearl remembered her own limbs once holding.

"Sure, Shen," Brenda said. "I'm done with breakfast. Let me put my dishes in the dishwasher."

Shen and Brenda left the room together, heading for Pearl's office, where an ancestor shrine had become a more or less permanent fixture. Pearl thought about her father's choice of captive—or ally—if he had in fact managed to convince the Monkey to join him in opposing the current Orphans.

Monkey sat in opposition to Tiger on the zodiac wheel, a strange choice for an ally, but sometimes opposition provided a far stronger link than a more randomly chosen sign.

Rabbit, Tiger's partner sign, would have been of little use to Thundering Heaven as a hostage because the

Rabbit's line—currently represented by Nissa Nita—had been one of the few to never stray from fidelity.

Pearl got up from the table, managing strength if not Brenda's easy grace, and turned to Riprap.

"If you're done with your breakfast, young man, I wonder if you would care to join me outside for a bit of weapons practice? For some reason, I have a great deal of nervous energy to work off—and I think I need to practice using my left hand."

☆

Loyal Wind rose along the incense of summoning and listened to Shen Kung's request.

"I will do as you ask," he said. "How shall I send news of what I have learned? I cannot manifest in the world of the living without help, and I am reluctant to once again interrupt someone's dreams."

Brenda Morris shrugged her slim shoulders. "I don't mind. It was just a dream. This is a lot more important. Still, it would be a pain if you had to wait until night to find someone in the right frame of mind."

"I agree," Shen said. "I have no plans for today that should take me far from here. At the beginning of each hour, I will meditate for a few moments upon the Horse. That should make it easy for Loyal Wind to contact me."

"Better meditate on both the Horse and the Ox," Brenda said, with what Loyal Wind thought was somewhat less than proper consideration for his feelings, "just in case Loyal Wind isn't in a position to contact you."

She looked at Loyal Wind with those strange eyes that were rounder than those of a person should be, yet still held some of the shape of her long-ago ancestry. Brenda's expression was serious, and he realized that she had been perfectly aware that he might be angered by her words.

"No offense, Loyal Wind," Brenda continued, "but if I've learned anything this summer, it is that the one thing to include in any plan is that plan going wrong."

"No campaign plan survives first contact with the enemy," Shen said in a soft voice. "Von Clausewitz. It's not a bad thing to remember."

"I will remember it," Loyal Wind agreed. "I will."

After he left the living, Loyal Wind located Nine Ducks. Since the Ox was interested in what he had to say to her, this proved quite easy. If Nine Ducks had been actively blocking him, Loyal Wind might have had to search for days—or even months or years.

This gave Loyal Wind food for thought. He shared his conjecture with Nine Ducks when he found her. She was seated in a garden pavilion, contemplating the antics of a small flock of her namesake birds as they grubbed in the mud beneath the shallow waters of a lake whose surface was so still that the ducks seemed to dive into their own reflections.

"That is interesting," Nine Ducks replied. "So you wonder if Thundering Heaven meant you to learn that he had Bent Bamboo in his care."

"I do," Loyal Wind agreed. "Or if not me, perhaps one of the Orphans. After all, if—as we all believe— Thundering Heaven's goal is not so much to stop us from reopening the way into the Lands as to force Pearl Bright to renounce her connection to the Tiger, then he must have wanted to be found."

"Yes. Otherwise, he would have had to issue a challenge, and that would have put him in a weaker position."

"What is Thundering Heaven like?" Loyal Wind

asked. "You know I was the first of the Exiles to die. After my death, I paid little attention to the affairs of the living. When I died, Thundering Heaven was a young man, somewhat brash, but certainly without this bitterness of character everyone seems to take for granted."

Nine Ducks fell silent, considering. "I cannot speak of Thundering Heaven without speaking of things that may cause you pain, Loyal Wind."

"Speak. I am learning to accept that choices I made when I myself was in pain caused others harm."

"Very well." Nine Ducks fell into thoughtful reverie, reviewing events from nearly a century before.

Loyal Wind did not attempt to speed her along. Time had a certain fluidity in the afterlife. Events in the world of the living were not so urgent that a minute or two would matter. Indeed, if they were, nothing either of them could do would change things in the least.

At last, Nine Ducks began. "When we were exiled from the Lands, Thundering Heaven had been appointed the Tiger for only a short time, his predecessor having been killed in the early stages of our downfall. At the time of our exile, friends of Thundering Heaven's family attempted to appeal his exile on the grounds that Thundering Heaven's crimes were not equivalent to our own . . . and that, being young, he could be taught new loyalties."

"I remember," Loyal Wind said. "I think that appeal might have been granted, for Thundering Heaven's family was a powerful one, but Thundering Heaven himself refused to be shown mercy."

"For two reasons," Nine Ducks agreed. "First of all, Thundering Heaven would not renounce his chosen allegiance, never mind that it was of short duration. Second, Thundering Heaven wanted to assure his family's protection. He said that if he—and they on his behalf—accepted the new emperor's pardon, then they would become supplicants. However, if he accepted exile with the rest of us, then, although the family would be forced to bear the stain of having a traitor listed among their ranks, their property and persons would be safe."

"Noble," Loyal Wind said, "if impulsive and brash. What changed him?"

"You, in part," Nine Ducks replied.

Loyal Wind knew what was coming next, but forced himself to listen.

"I am certain you recall," Nine Ducks began, "how after we were forced to accept that our exile might extend beyond the natural life spans of at least some of our number—for some of us were of advanced years—we took steps to assure that what we had brought with us from the Lands would not be reacquired by our enemies upon our deaths.

"Therefore, we bound the Twelve Earthly Branches, one each to the biological lineages of each of the Twelve Exiles: the First Branch to the Rat, the Second Branch to the Ox, and so on. Our next task was to assure ourselves of heirs. I was already past the age for bearing children, so I adopted a Chinese child."

"Your Hua," Loyal Wind said, hearing Nine Ducks's voice catch, and wishing to give her a chance to recover.

Or perhaps to delay her, he thought, *before she must speak of my own shameful behavior.*

"My Hua," Nine Ducks continued. "The male Exiles did not face the problems the females did, for a man may father a child long after a woman's days for bearing have passed. You, Loyal Wind, took the easiest course, associating yourself with several women of easy virtue, women who could be bought or who were bored enough to smile upon the advances of a not unhandsome face.

"Your reasons for pursuing your duty in such a detached manner were not without merit. You sought not to give your heart to another, because your heart was already taken by Water Cloud, our Rooster. You and your beloved could not risk bearing a child together, lest the route of the Branches become confused, but I believe you thought that once the route of inheritance was secured, you could again become lovers."

Loyal Wind could not bear this dry narration of his pain. His own voice came harsh and rough from his throat when he spoke.

"Yes. I loved Water Cloud. I thought she loved me. She had said she did, but her manner of fulfilling her own obligation to provide an heir made me doubt. I had thought she might follow in your course, and adopt a deserving Chinese child. At worst, I thought she might wait until her body was ripe and offer herself anonymously to some man. I did not think she would go so far as to prostitute herself to one of our enemies."

Nine Ducks leaned forward in her chair and patted his hand. "Perhaps, Water Cloud, the Rooster, already realized what was being murmured about my Hua, how Hua bore no blood-tie to the Lands, and that this would not only prevent her from returning, but also would prevent the rest of us as well. Perhaps Water Cloud sought to strengthen our tie to the Lands, giving her heir both father and mother who carried the link.

"Whatever Water Cloud's reason, you did not react in a reasonable fashion. Instead, when you knew what she had done, and that she carried a child who all the auguries showed would inherit her affiliation, you sought . . ."

Nine Ducks looked directly at Loyal Wind, her old eyes compassionate. "To me, at least, your reasons for acting as you did have always been as murky as were those of your lady love. You sought out your rival, but did so in such a fashion that—despite being our war leader—your own death was almost assured. Did you seek his death or your own?"

"My own," Loyal Wind said, his breath coming in a rough rasp. "I can no longer deny it. My own. I could not face a future where even if Water Cloud and I were free to be lovers, I would be forced to face that the child she dandled was the child of my enemy, that the child I would teach as my heir was the lightly gotten work of a sordid night. The future was black in my eyes, and so I sought an ending."

Nine Ducks nodded. "And found only an eternity of exile, for the wheel seems stalled for those of us from the Lands, stalled until we can resolve matters we set awry."

Loyal Wind looked sharply at the older woman. It seemed to him that her words referred to something more than merely the exile of the Thirteen Orphans from the Lands Born from Smoke and Sacrifice. He considered asking, but, fearing that his own cowardly desire to avoid learning how his suicide had played a part in the corruption of Thundering Heaven was behind the thought, he did not.

That can wait, he thought. *If we do not assemble the Twelve Exiles once more, we cannot take any step toward setting matters right.*

Aloud, he said, "You brought up my actions in light of how they shaped Thundering Heaven. Come to the point. What I did was long ago, and is fixed in time."

Nine Ducks agreed. "That is so. Thundering Heaven was the one who found your body. As he carried its broken length back to our camp so that the proper rites might be performed, I suspect he contemplated our changed situation.

"Here we were, but five years into our exile. Already one of our number was dead. Moreover, the one who had died was our war leader. Yet that war leader had not died in noble battle or leading the way in some perilous action. He had died foolishly, for no greater reason than to spite a woman—a woman, who if only he had considered the matter, was not worthy of such devotion."

"Must you rub it in?" Loyal Wind said with what mildness he could manage. "I assure you, I have had many long years to contemplate the selfishness of my action."

"I do not seek to renew your bitterness, Loyal Wind," Nine Ducks said softly, yet without the least yielding. "I seek to show you how matters seemed to Thundering Heaven."

"Quite bleak."

"And all the bleaker because, although Thundering Heaven was young and of the age that, had his life taken a more usual course, his parents would have been urging him to wed a first wife, he had been seeking a perfect bride to bear the next Tiger. He had dismissed your casual getting of an heir and the methods adopted by some of the other older men as appropriate to your years. If you did not father your heir quickly, you might not live long enough to train him."

"Ouch. Do you know this or are you guessing?"

"I lived for nearly forty years after the Exile," Nine Ducks said, "and although Thundering Heaven and I were never heart's companions, still we had a long association with each other. He did not tell me, but I think my guesses are accurate."

"So I disappointed him twice—as a suicide and as a romantic. Anything else?"

"Yes. I believe that at the time of your death Thundering Heaven had begun to court a young lady of good breeding, if not of wealth. Had we stayed in that place, he might have won her, but your actions made it necessary for us to move on. Newly soured on romance, Thundering Heaven made no effort to convince his lady fair to accompany us. He left her, but I believe her image in his heart kept him from any serious romantic entanglement for many years to come."

"Thundering Heaven did marry, though," Loyal Wind protested. "Pearl is not some chance-gotten child."

"Oh, Thundering Heaven did marry," Nine Ducks agreed. "Twice. His first marriage was after we were all settled in the United States, after some of us had begun to give up our hopes of returning to the Lands. Tea Rose was Chinese, but born in the United States. I think Thundering Heaven loved her very much, but the marriage was without children.

"I have never been certain what happened to Tea Rose after Thundering Heaven divorced her. After that divorce, Thundering Heaven surprised us all by marrying a woman who was not Chinese. She was a Hungarian Jew named Edna . . . I forget her last name. His choice was very strange, but the marriage produced several children."

"Why were you surprised when he married this Hungarian woman? By that time, others of the Exiles had married those of other races."

"I suppose it was because Thundering Heaven had been among those who had not ventured much outside of the Chinese enclaves. He made a rather poor living for himself teaching various martial arts, learned both

Cantonese and Mandarin well enough to pass as a native speaker, but never learned more English than he needed to get by."

"I can see why you were surprised," Loyal Wind said. "And Thundering Heaven finally fathered his heir on this woman?"

"Yes. Thundering Heaven was disappointed when his first child proved to be a girl. Initially, he was not concerned when auguries showed Pearl was to be his heir. He was confident that when he fathered a son, the Tiger would place his paw firmly on that son's back."

"But it didn't happen."

"No. To make matters worse, Pearl was truly an extraordinary child. Edna saw this and made sure that as soon as the little girl could walk she was tutored in song and dance. Pearl loved both the lessons and the attention. That joy lit her from within, and it was no wonder that—despite her obvious Oriental heritage— she began to win roles on stage and screen. The family prospered under Edna's careful management of the extra income."

"And Thundering Heaven had yet another reason to resent the child."

"That is so. Thundering Heaven fathered two sons, but the Fourth Earthly Branch knew where its best interest lay, and the Tiger never shifted his earlier choice. Thundering Heaven tutored the girl, at first reluctantly, then with an almost ruthless intensity, as if seeking to prove she could not possibly perform as he demanded. He died when she was in her late teens, hoping, I firmly believe, to the very end that Pearl would not inherit."

"You were dead by then," Loyal Wind said with the callousness of one to whom death is not anything but a change of address.

"I was," Nine Ducks agreed, "for many years, but my good Hua continued to make offerings to my spirit not only at the New Year and on Ching Ming, but weekly. I heard the family news in great detail until Hua's death."

Loyal Wind nodded. He knew the difficulties that had followed Hua, and the part her treatment had played in the dissolution of purpose among the Thirteen Orphans, but his thoughts were on present problems.

"So this bitter Tiger has decided to act against us," he said. "I am glad I asked you what to expect. Despite my glimpse of Thundering Heaven when I was tracking the Monkey, I think I expected to meet with the young man I had known before my death."

"But now you will not?"

"Now," Loyal Wind said, thinking himself garbed in armor and with his favorite weapons near to hand, "I will go prepared to deal with an angry Tiger, one who would gladly eat even his own young."

"And I will go with you," Nine Ducks said, rising from her chair and shaking out the skirts of her golden-yellow robes. "I may be an old Ox, but my horns are still sharp, and I have not forgotten how to gore."

☆

When she came out of the office, Brenda heard the clash of sword against staff and knew Pearl and Riprap were still hard at practice.

Brenda knew she wasn't much of a fighter. Her inclination was to believe physical violence should be a last resort, but recent events had told her the only thing likely to come from that attitude was her own injury or death—or worse, the injury or death of someone she failed to help in time.

I wonder if Des wants to practice?

Des Lee, however, had gone out on one of his mysterious errands. Nissa was available, and when she learned what Brenda intended she put down the book of Chinese mythology she'd been studying and sprang to her feet.

There were times Brenda tended to forget that Nissa Nita was only three or so years older than she was. Their lives had been so different, what with Nissa becoming pregnant when she was about Brenda's age, that Brenda always thought of Nissa as a lot older.

Today, however, as Nissa almost ran to join her, Brenda realized that they could have been in the same college classes, if Nissa had maybe had some requirement to take or Brenda had been taking a higher-level elective.

"Where's Lani?" Brenda asked automatically.

"With Des. He's going to drop her at Joanne's for a singing lesson, then pick her up on his way back. What kind of practice did you have in mind?"

"Well, I wasn't completely happy with how I handled the bracelets there at the end of the Tiger's Road," Brenda said, referring to the conflict in which Pearl's hand might not have been broken if Brenda had been better prepared.

"You did better than I did," Nissa said. "I never even got into the fight. I wasn't even there to help the wounded, like I was supposed to."

"So we both could use some practice," Brenda said. "I don't think anyone would complain if we expended some bracelets. We could even practice with dummies, just to get the moves right."

"I'm for it." Nissa moved to a window. "Pearl and Riprap are slowing down. I bet they'll be quitting soon. Why don't we go out and use the patio?"

Ten minutes later found them out on the brick-surfaced patio beneath the shade of a ramada over-grown with grapevines heavy with several varieties of grapes.

Riprap was seated in one of the chairs in the shade, alternating between sipping from a tall tumbler of water and mopping sweat off his face.

"Pearl is in a mood," he said. "Man, did she ever push—off-hand made no difference. If I'd closed my eyes, I would have thought I was fighting Flying Claw."

Given that Flying Claw was in his early twenties and in perfect physical condition, this said a lot.

Nissa grinned. "If you'd closed your eyes while fighting either one of them, you'd have been flat on your butt, fellow. Now, Brenda and I came out here to practice. Are you going to let us get on with it?"

"I'll just sit here in the shade, ma'am," Riprap said, drawling his words like a cowboy in an old western, "and admire your technique."

Brenda grimaced, but there was no sense in asking Riprap to leave. The man was not only their fellow student, but he had spent years as a coach. If he had anything to say about their technique, it would likely be useful. The two women ignored him, and took places across the patio from each other.

Brenda and Nissa had brought out an assortment of amulet bracelets. These resembled nothing so much as fourteen mah-jong tiles strung together with elastic into rather chunky bracelets.

Resemblance was deceptive. Unlike the jewelry they resembled, these tiles were made from polymer clay, each tile shaped by hand and carefully etched with the various symbols: bamboo, dots, characters, winds, and dragons. When created with appropriate concentration, the tiles stored within them a single spell that could be released upon the destruction of the bracelet.

There had been a time when Brenda, exhausted

from the expenditure of both ch'i and concentration that went into each bracelet, had tried to envision willingly destroying her handiwork. That reluctance had vanished the first time one of those stored spells had intervened between her and danger. Now she broke the amulets willingly, and longed for the days when she could summon and direct ch'i without the need for an intermediary.

"Nissa," Brenda began, "you said you wanted to work on getting your defenses up fast. Why don't we start there?"

In reply, Nissa lightly touched her left wrist where an amulet bracelet rested.

"I'm waiting."

Brenda reached behind her back and came out with a Japanese bokken, a sword-shaped piece of polished wood, that she had stuffed in her belt when Nissa wasn't looking.

"You can't wait," Brenda said, drawing and coming at Nissa, the bokken upraised to strike.

Brenda had no skill with a sword, but the bokken was well balanced and felt natural in her hand. She'd had ample opportunity to watch real swordplay over the last couple of months, and came at Nissa as if she knew what she was doing.

Her act wouldn't have fooled a real fencer, but it flustered Nissa. She fumbled at her wrist for the bracelet, but hadn't slammed it down to summon the protective spell within before Brenda had brought the bokken against her waist.

Brenda pulled the stroke so that the polished wood only touched Nissa's side.

"Damn!" Nissa swore softly. "That would have been right through me. Step back and come at me again."

"Right." Brenda skipped back several paces. Then, again without warning, she charged forward.

This time Nissa did much better. She hooked the amulet bracelet with the fingers of her right hand and threw it down hard against the bricks. The polymer clay tiles exploded into dust. Brenda felt the ch'i released into the surroundings. She didn't pause, but continued her charge, bringing the "blade" of the bokken in at Nissa's head.

Nissa ducked, but Brenda had been ready for this and adjusted her blow on a downward slant. This time she didn't pull her stroke, and the bokken hit against the Dragon's Tail spell Nissa had released.

The sensation was rather like hitting a punching bag. The surface Brenda struck against yielded, but not much. Brenda yelped as the force of her own strike reverberated up her arms.

Over on the side, Riprap laughed, although not in the least unkindly.

"Stings, doesn't it? You don't get the same bounce if you're using an edged weapon, but still you feel the resistance."

Riprap rose, and came over to join them.

"Nissa, you shouldn't have ducked. That's a waste of motion. The Dragon's Tail is wrapped around you, and you're pretty safe unless your opponent is using something like fire or gas or liquid poison. You knew Brenda just had that bokken. You should have been working on your countermove."

"But it's hard to strike out of a Dragon's Tail," Nissa protested. "What could I do?"

"A counter spell. Dragon's Breath, for example. Or you could have turned tail and run. A Dragon's Tail blocks, but it doesn't leave you immune to, say, having a net tossed over you."

"I didn't want to hurt Breni," Nissa said. "She doesn't have a protective spell up."

"You could have mimed tossing another bracelet,"

Riprap said relentlessly. "Go through the routine again. This time trust that Brenda's bokken is going to get nowhere near your pretty head."

Nissa stuck her tongue out at him, but she followed instructions. So did Brenda.

They'd worked up a sweat to match Riprap's own by the time Nissa's Dragon's Tail gave up beneath repeated pummels and they decided to call it quits.

As they headed inside, Brenda glanced up. She caught a glimpse of Pearl standing at the window, looking out. Brenda waved, but Pearl did not respond. Clearly, she was seeing nothing present, and Brenda was very glad.

Pearl's expression had been very fierce.

III

Thundering Heaven!" Loyal Wind yelled. "Come forth. I would speak with you."

His challenge bugled across the open field, but only its echo from the rocks of the Tiger's cave came as reply.

"Field" was something of a misnomer, for the area at whose farther edge the Horse stood was nothing but hard-packed dirt. A field, yes, but a killing field whose only crop was the promise of death.

Loyal Wind called again, more loudly.

"Go away!" came an answering shout. "You're not the one I wish to see."

The voice sounded hollow, but did not reverberate from the rock. Spoken from within the cave, then.

A dark shadow stood against the grey of the rock

face. Standing within that shadow . . . Yes. A darker figure, man-shaped, holding fear within its outline.

Had Loyal Wind been other than himself, he might have backed away, but Loyal Wind had faced more than his own death. He had confronted and admitted his own shameful part in that death. Fear had little power over him.

He stepped out into the killing field, muttering a charm that would keep him safe in case the creature within decided to launch a missile attack. Such preventative measures did not indicate that he feared— or so Loyal Wind told himself—but doubt whispered beneath his breastbone.

"Thundering Heaven," Loyal Wind repeated, and tried to keep the note of challenge from his voice. "Come forth. I want to ask you a question."

The dark shape of fear took a step forward and, illuminated in the harsh, directionless light that hung over the killing field, became Thundering Heaven.

He was older than when last Loyal Wind had seen him: a man in his prime, strong, heavily muscled, yet lithe and graceful, powerful, as a tiger given human form must be. Thundering Heaven's jet-black hair was caught up in a knot near the nape of his neck. He was clad in a green tunic over green trousers, the fabric dyed so dark a hue that his clothing showed as muddy black except where the light hit them.

Thundering Heaven's features were handsome, although, coarsened by age and exposure, they no longer held the heart-stopping masculine beauty that made his great-nephew, Flying Claw, seem more like a work of art come to life than a living man. Yet the resemblance between them could still be seen. Loyal Wind understood how Pearl Bright could have caught a glimpse of the one and known the nature of the other.

"You have a question for me," Thundering Heaven said, stopping in his advance as soon as he was out into full light. "Ask then."

"I have traced Bent Bamboo, the Monkey, here," Loyal Wind said. "I have news for him—good news. Steps are being taken to finally end our exile."

"But you need his help to achieve this admirable goal," Thundering Heaven sneered. "Don't ask how I know. I do. Living and dead must join forces if this exile is to end soon enough to benefit those who—in all justice—should be viewed as our enemies."

"They are not enemies," Loyal Wind said. "Peace has been made between us, peace confirmed by loyalty when confronted by considerable danger. Surely we, who have been exiles ourselves, understand the desire to return home. Moreover, the exile will not end only for them. Our new allies have sworn that upon their return they will rescind our sentence. All will be as we wished."

"Will it?" Thundering Heaven asked the question first as one who meditates over a philosophical conundrum. Then he repeated it with mockery in his voice. "Will it? They promise, but can they keep their promise?"

"I believe they will," Loyal Wind said.

"But why should I?" Thundering Heaven smiled a very unkind smile. "Ah, what I believe does not interest you. You do not want my assistance. You came here not for me, but for Bent Bamboo, the Monkey, who is my guest."

"Guest?" Loyal Wind asked. "Then why does Bent Bamboo not come forward to speak to me? We were once comrades."

"Perhaps he does not wish to speak to a comrade who betrayed him," Thundering Heaven said slyly.

But Loyal Wind was beyond where such comments could sting him.

"If so, then bring Bent Bamboo forth so that I may apologize. When my apologies are made, I will explain to him what has happened in the world of the living, and how, with his aid, all can be right again."

"I have already told him," Thundering Heaven said. "And I now come to tell you that Bent Bamboo is not interested in your proposition."

"Let me ask him myself!" Loyal Wind replied, not bothering to keep the note of challenge from his voice. "Let me hear his answer."

But Thundering Heaven replied as if he had not heard.

"Bent Bamboo is not interested in your proposition unless . . ."

He paused, drawing out the words, but Loyal Wind did not think that what Thundering Heaven had to say would surprise him. He met the other's gaze and found madness glittering like flaws in broken obsidian.

" . . . Unless the offer is made to both of us. Then Bent Bamboo will sever the tie that binds his neglectful heir to the Monkey and take on the mantle again. And, since dead can serve your needs as easily as can the living, Pearl will renounce her scandalous connection to the Tiger. Then I will take up my rightful place among the Twelve."

"Pearl Bright is the Tiger," Loyal Wind said. "Proven and confirmed in that role by Pai Hu, the White Tiger of the West, himself. She has not forgotten her place nor neglected her training as my own heir has done. We do not—"

He bit off the hasty words, but Thundering Heaven finished them with a slow, ugly grin.

"You do not need me. You have a Tiger—two Tigers if one includes our enemy turned ally, Flying Claw. What you need is a Monkey, but I have the Monkey."

"Then Bent Bamboo is your prisoner!"

"He is my guest. I assure you. He does not wish to see you."

"Only because you have poisoned his thoughts."

But Loyal Wind doubted that this was completely true. Bent Bamboo had been the least interested of all the Twelve in returning to the Lands, just as Copper Gong, the Ram, had been the most driven by her yearning to return. Thundering Heaven had picked his target well. Perhaps Bent Bamboo truly didn't care about rescinding their exile.

No. Loyal Wind refused to believe that. From what the others had told him, Bent Bamboo had changed near the end of his life. He had been a good father to his young heir, but . . .

Thundering Heaven was speaking. "Surely if honoring promises made to enemies—and I am struck by the peculiarity of making promises to a defeated foe—means so much to Pearl, then she will be happy to assist in any way possible. Bring her my message. If she is loyal to your goal of reopening a way into the Lands, soon you will have both the original Monkey and the original Tiger to speed your plans to fruition."

"Let me talk with Bent Bamboo," Loyal Wind countered. "Let me hear his support of this plan from his own lips."

"Are you saying you don't trust me?" Thundering Heaven taunted. "Yet you trust others not nearly so worthy. Leave your emotional assessments out of the matter. Who would serve your purpose better? Surely not an old woman who is well past her prime, who was tutored in an attenuated version of the lore of the

Lands, and who, until recently, never used her skills either with sword or spell in combat.

"Why would you prefer her to me? I have seen war. I have fought in personal combat. I know the Lands and belong to them as Pearl never could. Moreover, I have shed the restrictions of a living body. If I so choose, I can be anything I was in life."

Loyal Wind found himself almost persuaded. What Thundering Heaven said did make sense. Perhaps Bent Bamboo, the Monkey, who had not had Loyal Wind's opportunity to know and appreciate the strengths and versatility of the living Orphans, might indeed have been persuaded to back Thundering Heaven.

But then why does Bent Bamboo himself not come forth and tell me? Loyal Wind thought. *Monkeys have never been known for holding their chatter. If Bent Bamboo truly is Thundering Heaven's ally, then he should be at the Tiger's side.*

Therefore, Bent Bamboo is a prisoner, not an ally. If I can but free the Monkey, defeat Thundering Heaven, then all will be as we desire.

Without allowing time for further consideration, lest Thundering Heaven read his changed resolve in the lines of his body, Loyal Wind advanced.

"I must see Bent Bamboo for myself," he said, "and assure myself that he is free and cooperating with you voluntarily. If he is, I will accept my defeat, but if he is a prisoner, I owe him—"

"As he is my guest," Thundering Heaven retorted, drawing a blade he had not been wearing a moment before, "I owe him privacy within my home."

The sword was not Treaty, the blade Thundering Heaven had created, for that sword had not died with its owner, but had been inherited by Pearl. Loyal Wind felt a moment of gratitude for this, for Treaty had a strange way of awakening when binding agreements were threatened. If Thundering Heaven and Bent Bamboo had indeed made a pact . . .

Loyal Wind had come to this meeting armed and in armor. Now he took advantage of his kinship with the Horse and willed himself mounted upon his chestnut steed, Proud Gamble. His horseman's saber remained in its sheath at his belt. Instead he manifested a giau-chiz, the horseman's long spear.

Loyal Wind knew some might view this choice of weapon as unsportsmanlike, but he had lost any illusion that there was fairness in either love or war. Tigers were superlative hand-to-hand fighters, and to rob himself of any advantage would be mere foolishness.

Giau-chiz blocked and parried sword. Loyal Wind managed his long weapon with such dexterity that he scored a long, narrow cut across the outer edge of Thundering Heaven's upper arm when Thundering Heaven did not manage a complete parry.

Yet, even as blood poured down his arm, Thundering Heaven manifested neither armor nor shield. His dark eyes glittered with mad intensity as he changed his attack. At the cost of another wound—this one to the top of his shoulder near the neck, gliding down over his back—Thundering Heaven ducked within the reach of the giau-chiz and ran to close the distance between them.

With that move, Loyal Wind was effectively disarmed. He shouted to Proud Gamble, commanding his steed to back up. Dropping his giau-chiz, Loyal Wind drew his curved cavalry sword. The blade was heavy, edged on one side only, equally able when wielded by skilled hands to parry an attack or inflict a nasty wound.

Thundering Heaven had taken advantage of Loyal Wind's retreat to manifest armor for himself. Blood leaked from beneath the metal-embossed leather plates.

Thundering Heaven seemed to glory in the gore, wearing it as a savage might have worn garish war paint, grinning ferociously as he advanced on Loyal Wind.

Mounted, Loyal Wind had the advantage of height, but Thundering Heaven gained that of mobility. Moreover, Thundering Heaven's sword was slightly longer than Loyal Wind's, giving him the advantage of reach as well. He demonstrated this by slashing out and nicking Proud Gamble on the side of his neck.

The charm Loyal Wind had cast upon himself before entering the field did not automatically extend to his mount. He cursed his lack of foresight. Of course, Thundering Heaven would go for the horse. He was a tiger.

Proud Gamble screamed in pain, but he did not shy as a more usual horse would have done. In exile, Thundering Heaven had created the blade Treaty. Water Cloud had created the Rooster's Talons. The Exile Rat had created an abacus that permitted him to calculate arcane matters as a more usual abacus sped along the calculation of wealth.

Loyal Wind had created no such tool. Instead, in the chestnut stallion, Proud Gamble, he had created the perfect warhorse, brave and calculating, infused with almost human intelligence and understanding of the fighting arts. Into Proud Gamble, Loyal Wind had fused something of himself, in addition to memories of the best and bravest horses he had known as a mounted warrior.

When Loyal Wind had died, Proud Gamble had come with him into death. Perhaps this was because the steed was in some sense an extension of Loyal Wind. Perhaps it was because at the time of his death Loyal Wind was obsessed with himself and his own pains and gave little thought to the child heir he was leaving behind. For whatever reason, unlike Thundering Heaven who must make do with a secondary weapon, Loyal Wind augmented his abilities with the ideal weapon of his choice.

This, then, Loyal Wind calculated, gave him an advantage over Thundering Heaven, an advantage the other could not match.

Proud Gamble knew that if he shied or fled, this would give the enemy an advantage. He knew the weight of his iron-shod hooves and how they could crush bone, render muscle into bloody pulp. This understanding went beyond the rote training of a warhorse to comprehension of the tactics involved, but even with this magical enhancement, Proud Gamble was not a human general, any more than the sword Treaty was a diplomat.

The stallion reared, seeking both to bring his rider clear of any danger from Thundering Heaven's sword and to bring the power of his front hooves into play. He reared, and, as the tiger seeing the soft underbelly of his prey exposed strikes, so Thundering Heaven struck.

A tiger might have been foiled by the armor that protected some of Proud Gamble's underbelly, but for all the glittering insanity in his eyes, Thundering Heaven had full possession of his human intellect.

His blow did not strike harmlessly against armor, but sliced deeply, cutting through the chestnut stallion's hide and hair, ripping through muscle and into gut. Proud Gamble screamed. Although he attempted to bring down his hooves in a killing blow, some essential muscle or sinew had been severed and the strike fell short.

As Thundering Heaven's blade cut into Proud Gamble's belly, Loyal Wind realized that what he had believed was his advantage was, in this battle at least, a disadvantage. He had created the chestnut stallion to be an extension of his abilities. Somehow, Thundering Heaven was exploiting that link, making the stallion's pain and debilitating weakness Loyal Wind's own.

Through the pain, Loyal Wind suddenly grasped something of the nature of the blade Thundering Heaven wielded in Treaty's place.

"The sword," he gasped.

"Its name is Soul Slicer," Thundering Heaven said, laughing as he sliced the air with the finely honed blade. "Philosophers teach that our souls have at least two parts, some argue for more, but even the most ignorant peasant knows of the hun and po souls. With Soul Slicer I can render a ghost into partially aware fragments. And, of course, I can transform the living into the dead."

Loyal Wind felt Proud Gamble stumble as Thundering Heaven made another lightning-quick strike.

Throwing his weight onto his arms, Loyal Wind balanced himself against the chestnut stallion's withers and heaved himself from the saddle before he could be crushed beneath the falling horse's bulk. Thundering Heaven's second blow had been to Proud Gamble's right foreleg. Now Loyal Wind's own right arm ached with an echo of the horse's pain.

Limping from the force of his landing, Loyal Wind dragged himself to stand between Proud Gamble and further attack. He brought his sword around to block Thundering Heaven's next blow, but a tearing pain in his gut made him slower than he should have been. Loyal Wind knew he was not bleeding, that nothing had actually cut him, but the pain was exquisitely real.

Loyal Wind parried Thundering Heaven's attack, but he was aware that he had only succeeded because the Tiger was playing with him. Being already dead,

Loyal Wind could not die, but he thought that what Thundering Heaven intended for him would be worse than death.

Dissolution.

Rendering into fragments that would vaguely remember who and what he had been, and that might take centuries to consolidate once more—if ever they did.

By contrast, death had been a mere transition of states.

Behind Loyal Wind, on the packed dirt, Proud Gamble was blowing red-tinged froth. Blood pooled from numerous wounds, sinking into the dry, packed dirt, making it a sticky, tacky mud.

Loyal Wind felt his own ch'i draining away, his protective spells fading to nothing. Before his ch'i was completely gone, he stretched his awareness along the thread that bound him to Proud Gamble. The stallion might be a magical construct, but its suffering was all too real.

Leaving himself unguarded, Loyal Wind snapped the bond. The chestnut horse ceased to breathe, ceased to suffer. Tears welled in Loyal Wind's eyes, blurring them so that although he could see the flash of silver grey that meant Soul Slicer was descending upon him, that his own dissolution was imminent, he was unable to effectively block the attack.

He fell to the bloodied ground, determined that although he might weep, he would not scream.

Soul Slicer cut the air, but the blade did not strike Loyal Wind. A barrier flashed between him and the descending blade. The ground shook as if in grumbled protest at being fed so much blood. A glossy, blue-black flank filled Loyal Wind's vision.

Loyal Wind smelled rank cattle sweat, saw the triangular head and the curving horns of a water buffalo. Nine Ducks, the Ox, had come to his rescue.

Loyal Wind could sense the protective spells that surrounded her, and knew then who had cast the barrier that had saved him.

Proud Gamble's pain was fading from his limbs, but Loyal Wind still felt incredibly weak. With a certain shamed gratitude, for if he had not given in to impulse, he would not have needed rescue, he heard Nine Ducks speak.

"Get away, Loyal Wind," she said, her voice coming from between the water buffalo's lips. "I'll cover your retreat."

She spoke then to Thundering Heaven.

"There was a tale told when I was a girl, about a farmer who left his prized water buffalo to graze near a rice paddy while he returned to his hut for his midday meal. A short time later, a neighbor who farmed a nearby plot rushed in, chattering almost incoherently about the enormous tiger that had attacked him while he worked in his field, and how he had only escaped by the merest chance.

"The farmer grabbed a spear and ran to defend his prized buffalo, but when he arrived, the buffalo was grazing peacefully and the tiger was nowhere to be found. Nervously, the farmer came closer, hoping his neighbor had been exaggerating. Then, a few feet away from where the buffalo grazed he noticed a patch of cropped grass, dark with blood and adorned with fragments of black and orange and white fur.

"All that remained to prove that this mess had once been a tiger were the teeth and claws. The rest had been trampled to pulp."

Loyal Wind had been backing away while Nine Ducks told this story. The Tiger was trembling with barely suppressed rage, but he was no fool. The protections the Ox had erected around herself would take time to break down. While the Tiger sought to do so, Nine Ducks would not be standing patiently watching.

There might well be another bloody stain on the killing field when she was finished.

"I merely sought to protect my guest from unwelcome intrusion," Thundering Heaven said, wiping Soul Slicer's blade on his trousers, then stepping back so that he was between them and the entrance to the cave. "Do you seek to enter here?"

Nine Ducks considered, angling her head side to side so that the light glinted off her curving horns.

"I would like to speak with my old friend, Bent Bamboo."

"I speak for him," Thundering Heaven said, his arrogance returning. "I have told Loyal Wind the conditions under which Bent Bamboo would cooperate with your plans."

"I heard," Nine Ducks said. "Very well. I don't believe those are Bent Bamboo's terms, but I believe they are yours, and that you have placed yourself between us and the Monkey. Given what you claim that sword of yours can do, I can believe why he agreed to support your agenda."

"Then we understand each other," Thundering Heaven growled.

"I understand you," Nine Ducks said, turning her back on the Tiger and walking away, her tuft-tipped tail swinging lazily side to side. "But don't make the mistake of thinking you understand me. It might be your last mistake."

Loyal Wind admired Nine Ducks's courage as she sauntered over to him, never glancing back at the angry Tiger behind her. True, she was armored in heavy protective spells, but that did not mean she was immune to harm. Was she taunting the Tiger deliberately? Seeking, perhaps, to draw him away from the entrance to the cave?

Loyal Wind thought she was, and braced himself in case Thundering Heaven took the bait. However, the Tiger was too experienced a campaigner to give in to the rage that was apparent in every line of his body.

"Let's go," Nine Ducks said when she stood beside Loyal Wind. "We cannot achieve anything more here."

Loyal Wind agreed. When they had returned to Nine Ducks's pavilion alongside the lake, he accepted tea and refreshments.

"I'm sorry I didn't reach you sooner," Nine Ducks said. "The two of you shifted so quickly from debate to battle that I nearly did not have enough time to set my protections and come to your aid. Tell me, is Proud Gamble gone forever?"

Loyal Wind swallowed his tea around the hard lump that formed in his throat.

"Quite possibly. At the very least, I will need to recreate him. I lost so much ch'i in that encounter. . . . Where do you think Thundering Heaven acquired that sword? Surely he did not craft it himself."

"You forget," Nine Ducks replied. "Thundering Heaven is not the young man you remember. By the time he died, he was in his early seventies. Unlike many of us, who gradually shifted at least some of our attention to our daily lives, Thundering Heaven had done little with his life but perfect his knowledge of the fighting arts—and he did not neglect the arcane branches of those arts. It is quite possible he created that sword, but whether he did so in life or in death, I cannot say."

Loyal Wind shook his head slowly. "I don't know. I felt . . . I don't know what it was I felt, but there was something there, something horrible. I suppose it could have been Thundering Heaven himself, but if so his nature has become corrupted beyond anything I could recognize."

"I saw madness in his eyes," Nine Ducks replied, her voice soft. "Whatever else Thundering Heaven was when he died, I do not think he was insane. What will you do next?"

"I will report to Shen Kung," Loyal Wind said, "and ask whether he wishes to tell Pearl Bright of her father's ultimatum, or whether he wishes me to do so."

"Do you have the strength to make the contact?"

"You saved me before my ch'i drained completely away," Loyal Wind said. "It will not be difficult to make the contact. Shen said he would be waiting."

"Very well," Nine Ducks said. "Away with you. Our time may be infinite, but the same is not true for our mortal associates."

Loyal Wind rose to his feet and made a rather awkward bow.

"I owe you my continued existence, Nine Ducks. If there is anything I can do in return . . ."

The old woman looked up at him.

"There is."

"Name it."

"Stay away from Thundering Heaven. Next time he'll be ready for both of us. He may be ready for an army."

"I pity Pearl," Loyal Wind said.

"Perhaps," Nine Ducks said softly. "But I believe I also pity Thundering Heaven."

IV

From the expression on Shen's face when he came out of Pearl's office several hours later, anyone could have guessed that Loyal Wind's report had been anything but good.

Brenda had to admire Pearl for her poise. As Shen started to speak, Pearl held up her right hand in a gesture that was almost regal.

"Why don't we call Colm Lodge and see if Righteous Drum, Honey Dream, and Flying Claw can spare some time? That way Shen only has to give his report once. Moreover, we won't need to entertain the same speculations twice, but can move directly into a plan of campaign."

Despite her eagerness to have her suspicions about what Loyal Wind had learned confirmed, Brenda joined her voice to those murmuring agreement. Pearl did have a point. If the Orphans shared any trait, it was the ability to talk any issue nearly to death—and the Landers deserved a fresh shot at the problem.

Besides, Brenda had thought she wouldn't have a chance to see Flying Claw today. Now her heart lifted at the prospect.

Riprap asked, "Want me to call Colm Lodge?"

"Yes," Pearl said. "Tell them we'll be over in about a half hour. I'll call Albert and see if he can meet us there."

They took two vehicles, since the lot of them would have squeezed the seating in the van to its limits. Lani stayed behind with Wang, Pearl's gardener, freeing Nissa to be merely the Rabbit, not also the Bunny's Mom.

"I want Lani to learn about the Orphans naturally," Nissa said with a light laugh, "but asking a two-and-a-half-year-old to sit through a meeting is anything but natural."

Colm Lodge was another of Pearl's properties. Unlike the house in the Rose Garden district in which Pearl lived, Colm Lodge was set on several acres of land and included a horse stable and associated outbuildings. The acreage made it relatively private—a very good thing, given the oddity of Pearl's latest tenants.

There were six of them: five men and one woman. Any of the residents of the adjoining estates probably assumed the tenants were from China, for three of them spoke no English, and the other three preferred to speak Chinese except when absolutely necessary. In fact, without a very carefully tailored translation spell that made it possible for Brenda, Nissa, and Riprap to understand Chinese, someone—probably Des, because he loved such word games—would have constantly been employed interpreting between the groups.

However, it's a good thing that no one around here speaks Chinese, Brenda thought. *Otherwise, the neighbors would quickly realize what an odd form of the language Pearl's tenants speak. Their lack of information regarding current events, both here and in China, also would be certain to raise eyebrows.*

When the vehicles disgorged their passengers at the top of an elegant circular driveway, the front door of Colm Lodge was opened by Righteous Drum. The Dragon from the Lands was a somewhat stout, middle-aged Chinese gentleman dressed in a pale yellow polo shirt and khaki trousers. The shirt's sleeve hung empty at the right shoulder, a visible reminder of how dangerous their situation had become.

Righteous Drum's hair was cut short, in the modern

style, and he was clean shaven. Brenda personally thought Righteous Drum looked a lot like Chairman Mao, and no matter how many times Riprap—who had a thing about precision—pointed out to her all the ways the description didn't match, Brenda stubbornly stuck to it.

Maybe it has as much to do with how Righteous Drum carries himself. I mean, any other guy his age would look really dumb, always dressing in shades of yellow, but Righteous Drum carries it off. He's got that poise that says, "I'm a person of consequence," or something.

"Righteous Drum," Pearl said as she mounted the short flight of steps that led to the front door. She spoke the Chinese of the Lands. "Thank you for accepting this invasion. We apologize for giving you such short notice."

Righteous Drum smiled graciously, and opened the door wider.

"We expected some sort of visit today," he replied in the same language, "especially when Riprap phoned to inform us that your household would not be joining ours for practice. Come in. Have you eaten?"

Brenda knew this last was a traditional Chinese greeting, and knew the proper response was to state that she had. Therefore, even though some wonderful odors drifting from the back of the house made her stomach rumble, she joined the others in saying she was well fed.

"Even so," Righteous Drum said, and a twinkle in his eyes made Brenda wonder just how good his hearing might be, "my daughter, Honey Dream, is setting out a few refreshments and a variety of beverages. This household hopes you will avail yourselves of our hospitality."

He gestured in the direction of the large formal living

room that was set to one side of the entry foyer. Extra chairs had been brought in from other parts of the house. Brenda counted seating for eleven, and Righteous Drum answered the unspoken question.

"When your phone call came, I had the impression that we might be discussing sensitive matters. I thought that perhaps it would be best if the three who until very recently were our prisoners were not admitted into conferences that, after all, are related to matters of the Twelve."

Pearl nodded, and no one else objected.

Brenda thought "The Twelve" was a rather loose way of describing their company, for the Orphans counted their full number as thirteen. She, technically, was not even one of those thirteen, since her father, Gaheris Morris, was still alive and still actively the Rat.

But Gaheris, as soon as the battle of Tiger's Road was concluded, had departed San Jose. He ran his own business, Unique Wonders, and seemed to feel everything would fall apart if he wasn't on hand to meet with clients.

Brenda joined Riprap and Nissa, who were heading out into the kitchen. Helping out had been the rule in the Morris household, and although Pearl still had her gardening service and maid service call at both residences, most of the time they all did for themselves. Matters were too sensitive—too flat-out weird—to permit outsiders easy, unsupervised access.

In the kitchen they found Honey Dream. Honey Dream did not resemble her father, Righteous Drum, in the least. In age, she was probably somewhere between Brenda and Nissa. Slender as the Snake that was her affiliate, Honey Dream managed to be voluptuous as well.

The red tee shirt she wore had a deeply scooped

neckline, embellished with lacy beadwork flowers in contrasting crystal. Honey Dream wore shorts that were not as short as some Brenda had seen her wear, but that nonetheless admirably displayed the length of her legs. One bare ankle was looped with a tattoo of a small snake. Honey Dream's long, ink-black hair was caught up in what looked like a casual style, but Brenda had tried something like it, and knew how difficult it was to pull off. To Brenda, that hairstyle gave away the effort Honey Dream had put into her appearance.

As always, Honey Dream's sensuous physicality made Brenda all too aware that she herself was nearly as flat-chested and narrow-hipped as a boy. She swallowed a sigh and reached for one of the trays of dainties that stood on a counter waiting to be carried into the next room.

"Thanks, Brenda," Honey Dream said, and those two words emphasized more than anything else that one thing had changed about Honey Dream. Unhappily, for Brenda's recurring insecurities, if anything the change made the other woman more lovely.

Gone was Honey Dream's prickly arrogance, replaced by something almost approaching humility. Honey Dream, perhaps more than any of them, had been tested by recent events. The solicitude with which she brought Righteous Drum his tea and a little plate of delicacies showed that Honey Dream had not yet forgotten how recently she had thought her father dead.

Riprap had stepped into a back pantry, and now he emerged carrying trays of glasses. He was accompanied by Flying Claw, the Tiger of this group, and the subject of a great deal of heady daydreaming on Brenda's part.

Flying Claw was a counterpart for Honey Dream's

physical beauty, but there was nothing in the least feminine about him. He was neither as tall nor as obviously muscular as Riprap, but Brenda had seen Flying Claw hold his own and then some against the much larger man—and not only because Flying Claw had trained in fighting arts since he was a small child. There was strength in the young Tiger, as well as beauty, and grace to balance the strength.

Unlike Righteous Drum, who had cut his hair better to blend into modern America, Flying Claw still wore his hair long, nearly as long as that of any of the young women. Today he had it caught back with a series of silver pony tail holders that were ornamental even as they kept his hair from getting in his face. Brenda suspected Des's hand in the choice of jewelry. The Rooster had a distinct sense of style, and had taken it upon himself to act as buyer and fashion consultant for the strangers.

Brenda knew that Flying Claw was related to Pearl—a not-so-distant cousin—and that physically he resembled Pearl's father, Thundering Heaven, the source of their current problem.

I wonder if Pearl's going to get all prickly with Flying Claw again, Brenda thought, glancing over at the older woman anxiously. *She's only just barely started treating him like he's human. Now that I think about it, I wonder how Flying Claw's going to take the news about Thundering Heaven. I mean, Pearl's dad was his idol, the whole reason he studied to become a Tiger. This could be really bad.*

A knock at the front door announced Albert Yu. Like Des Lee, Albert's heritage was ethnically Chinese, and like Des, Albert was something of a flamboyant figure, although in a completely different fashion.

Des wore his hair and beard like those of a Chinese immigrant of a hundred or so years ago. If Albert resembled anything out of Chinese history, it was the idea of the exotic Orient as embodied by the stage magician. His dark hair was worn long enough to cover the top of his collar. His chin beard and full mustache were neatly trimmed yet saturnine, just a little wicked. Today, as most times Brenda had seen him, Albert wore a neat business suit. His only concession to the early August heat was the absense of a jacket and a slight loosening of his tie.

Brenda thought that, despite his neat attire, Albert looked rather haggard.

And no wonder. Albert is trying to run his fancy chocolate business, but unlike Dad he doesn't keep cutting out on us. He's really serious about being the leader of the Thirteen Orphans, but in a way, he's like me. He has a place, but he doesn't. I mean, there were twelve exiles, each tied to the zodiac. He's the Cat, descendant of a kid who himself was a son of an emperor who got overthrown. What good is an emperor without an empire—who hasn't had an empire for three generations?

Brenda knew some of her thoughts were colored by her father's rivalry with Albert—a rivalry that dated back to when they were both boys. She also knew she was reacting to the fact that—unlike Gaheris Morris—Albert was here. He had a job. He had his own business, but he was here. By comparison, her own dad fell short.

Although with Albert's arrival their company was technically complete, every chair filled, still they all felt the absence of Waking Lizard.

But that rascally old Monkey won't be joining us, Brenda thought sadly. *He won't be here to puncture Righteous Drum's pomposity with a casual "Drummy" or pull the best of the egg rolls right out from Riprap's fingers with a dart of those long fingers. Damn. I hope*

I don't start crying. . . . Somebody had better start talking or I think I'm going to lose it.

Perhaps sensitive to the prevailing tension, Albert assumed the role of informal chairman with a natural assumption of leadership that wasn't in the least offensive.

"Shen, will you tell us what Loyal Wind reported?"

"Nine Ducks, actually," Shen said. "Loyal Wind began the report, but he was weaker than he had wanted to believe, and Nine Ducks took over. You see, it seems that Loyal Wind's meeting with Thundering Heaven went a bit out of control. Loyal Wind, well, he overstepped himself."

Shen then proceeded to recount with just the right mixture of dry fact and sensational detail the encounter between the three ghosts.

Brenda listened with a mingling of anger and dismay. Yes, they had all expected Thundering Heaven's ultimatum, but this . . . Despite everything Pearl had said about her father, despite everything Thundering Heaven's callous dismissal of his daughter and heir had implied about him, she had not expected him to be so vicious.

Shen finished by relating Nine Ducks's assertion that she believed that given time Loyal Wind would recover from his injuries. Silence fell, broken only by the sound of melting ice cubes shifting in the pitcher of lemonade.

Then Albert asked the question they were all thinking.

"Well, Aunt Pearl. How do you think we should respond to Thundering Heaven's ultimatum?"

Pearl was parting her lips to give what was doubtlessly a carefully considered reply when she was interrupted from a very unlikely corner.

Springing to his feet, his silver-ringed hair snapping behind him like a tiger's tail, Flying Claw almost snarled the words, "There is only one answer that is acceptable. Pearl is your Tiger. Nothing must change that. Nothing!"

Brenda was astonished at the ferocity of the young man's words. Until very recently, Pearl had been far from kind to Flying Claw. True, Pearl had never been precisely cruel, but Brenda felt Pearl had done little enough to earn this loyalty. Judging from the expressions on the faces of several of those present—Pearl herself included—Brenda was not the only one to think so.

"I," Pearl said into the startled silence, "feel rather the same way. However, before we accede to my wishes, I do think Thundering Heaven made at least one very valid point. You must consider that he might very well be a far stronger Tiger than I. I am not a young woman. Sometimes, especially early on a rainy morning when my arthritis is acting up, I would even admit to being a rather elderly Tiger. Freed as he is from the limitations of the flesh, Thundering Heaven would be far stronger than I am, far more versatile."

"Stronger," Riprap replied, flexing his own strong hands so that the muscles corded and rippled in his arms, "but more versatile? I'm not so sure about that. And judging from how Thundering Heaven treated Loyal Wind, I'm not certain he'd be as wise. What Thundering Heaven did was ugly, really ugly, especially when you consider he attacked someone he claimed to wish to ally himself alongside. There's something really wrong there."

"'Wrong,'" said Shen Kung as if tasting the word. "That's exactly what I've been thinking since Loyal Wind and Nine Ducks contacted me. There's something very wrong here. Righteous Drum, what is the lore of the Lands regarding the spiritual nature of ghosts? I seem to recall that it is connected to the nature of the soul."

"That is correct," Righteous Drum said. "The soul has two primary parts: the hun and po souls."

Shen inclined his head, inviting the other to continue. Brenda was impressed by Shen's diplomacy. Shen and Righteous Drum were both Dragons—considered to be both the most scholarly and the most magical of the Twelve. This was not a contradiction, for in Chinese lore, scholarship and magic went hand in hand. Knowledge literally was power.

But Brenda had already figured out that knowledge was not the same as wisdom, and that therefore the likelihood of competition between the two Dragons was quite high.

Shen was the elder, with many more years of study behind him, but Righteous Drum—himself a man of mature years—had shown himself very aware that his studies, if of lesser duration, had taken place within the very libraries from which Shen's teachers had brought away only memories.

Righteous Drum accepted Shen's invitation to continue. "The hun soul is the soul that is associated with intellectual achievements and the higher emotions. The po soul is associated with the more bestial urges and the baser emotions. Upon death, so we are taught, the hun soul departs the body through an opening at the top of the skull. On rare occasions, the po soul may cling to the body until decomposition sets in, and, in rarer cases, even thereafter. That is why fresh graves are places to approach with caution."

Brenda leaned forward, intent on a contradiction. "But like Riprap said, something is wrong here. Really wrong. I mean, Thundering Heaven is acting like you said a po soul would act: angry, raging, out of control."

"Not completely out of control," Shen corrected gently. "From what I was told, Thundering Heaven did a very good job of presenting an intellectual argument as to why he should take over as Tiger. A po soul—as I understand the lore—would never have stopped to talk."

"Not only that," Righteous Drum agreed, "it wouldn't be able to talk. Speech is one of the higher functions."

After making his declaration, Flying Claw had remained standing. Now he looked over at Pearl, something like desperation twisting his handsome features. Brenda's heart ached at his pain. For a moment, Flying Claw had looked more like Foster—the amnesiac he had been when she had first gotten to know him, all lost and confused—than like the warrior he was.

"Honored Aunt," Flying Claw said, somewhat awkwardly giving Pearl a title of relationship that, while not strictly accurate, reflected the new accord between them, "I know Thundering Heaven was not the most gentle of fathers to you, but is this how he truly was?"

Anger and sorrow touched Pearl's features, and Brenda thought that Pearl looked as if she wanted to say, "Yes. Underneath. Beneath the proper front he showed to most people, my father really was that vicious," but honesty won out over old wounds. Pearl shook her head.

"No. He wasn't. My father could be cold and harsh. He could be unkind, but he was not a raging killer, nor was he a monster. As far as I know, Thundering Heaven never used his blade except in defense of himself or of those he had sworn to protect. He was a hard father, but he did not beat me beyond what anyone of that time would have considered acceptable—and even when he was angry, he usually did not need my mother to convince him that added training would be a more useful punishment than violence."

Flying Claw looked relieved.

And no wonder, Brenda thought. *By his own account, Flying Claw idolized Thundering Heaven—not the man, but the reputation he left behind him in the Lands. Because of Thundering Heaven, Flying Claw trained from childhood in the hope of someday becoming the Tiger in his turn.*

Nissa's soft Virginia drawl broke in. "I'm sorry if I'm getting away from the point, but there's something else that's been puzzling me. Where did Thundering Heaven get that sword—Soul Slicer, I think he called it? Is it a traditional weapon or something like that?"

"I've never heard of a sword called Soul Slicer," Des said, and his comment had weight because with the possible exception of Shen, he was the most fanatical of their number about obscure elements of Chinese myth and legend. "Have any one of you? Does Soul Slicer belong to the lore of the Lands?"

Heads shook all around.

"So where," Nissa persisted, "did Thundering Heaven get that sword? Can ghosts just conjure things like that, the way they can change their bodies?"

"I do not believe so," Righteous Drum said. "Ghosts—even hun ghosts—are limited to what they brought with them from the world of the living. That is why offerings to the dead are so important. The gifts of the living—food and money and even clothing and other luxuries—sustain the dead. Without these offerings, the dead are doomed to become hungry ghosts who in their desperate need are yet another threat to the living."

Riprap looked over at Pearl. "I don't suppose you gave Thundering Heaven anything like that sword, did you? As a substitute for Treaty, maybe?"

"No." Pearl went on, answering a question Riprap clearly wanted to ask, but knew would be impolite. "Nor did I repay him in death for his lack of kindness to me in life by neglecting the proper offerings. Twice a year, on New Year and Ching Ming, my brothers and I have made the proper offerings—both of money and of paper representations of items our father might need to make him comfortable in the afterlife. My brothers started the custom of making offerings in October—on or near to the date of our father's actual birthday—a very American touch, since the Chinese don't usually celebrate birthdays. Still, it's a nice gesture."

"And would your brothers have given Thundering Heaven anything like Soul Slicer?" Riprap persisted.

"No," Pearl said. "To my father's undying resentment, my brothers did not have a trace of magical ability in their veins. They couldn't even work a simple charm. They grew up interesting hybrids: Chinese Jews. Both went into finance, and both did very well."

"So your brothers go through the motions," Riprap said, satisfied but obviously disappointed. "That's it."

"I'm afraid so," Pearl said. "I don't think we'll find the origin of Soul Slicer in their actions."

Albert frowned. "Thundering Heaven's actions are very peculiar for a ghost—at least for a ghost in the Chinese tradition. I wonder if Thundering Heaven lived long enough in the United States to adopt some European ideas about the undead. Wrathful yet calculating creatures like vampires are common enough in European traditions."

"That doesn't seem likely," Pearl said. "My father may have married a woman of Hungarian Jewish descent, but he remained adamantly, proudly, a Chinese of the Lands until his death. I'm not sure he would have known what a vampire was—a chiang shih, yes, but not a vampire in the European tradition."

Deborah rose and refilled her glass of lemonade. "So we have a ghost who is not acting at all as a ghost should behave, bearing a sword that is a puzzle all in itself—a sword that seems particularly suited for battling other ghosts. Shen, did Loyal Wind happen to mention if that magical horse of his had ever been injured before—and if, when it was, had he felt the injury himself? Something about how you recounted the battle made me think this connection between him and his horse had been unusual."

Shen nodded. "I thought the same thing, but didn't want to interrupt the flow of the narrative to clarify that point. Yes. Loyal Wind's horse had been injured before this, but never before had Loyal Wind himself felt the injury."

Brenda frowned, feeling her brow crease with thought. "Had Loyal Wind gotten into fights, well, since he died? I mean, maybe this is a ghost sort of thing and has nothing to do with Thundering Heaven."

"I asked Nine Ducks that, too," Shen said. "Loyal Wind has apparently been busy since his death, seeking to redeem himself for his failures in life. I won't go into details, but there are ample battles in which a noble warrior might involve himself, even in death."

Albert cleared his throat. "Despite Flying Claw's adamant opposition, we still have not resolved the first question—or rather Pearl has not. How do you choose to respond to Thundering Heaven's ultimatum?"

Pearl answered with admirable directness. "If ever I had been tempted to surrender my place as Tiger to Thundering Heaven," she said, "our recent discussion of the peculiarities in his behavior would make me doubt the wisdom of that choice. However, I will be frank. I have no desire to cease being the Tiger, but I also have no desire to have my stubbornness stand as a barrier between ourselves and our success."

"Fairly spoken," Albert agreed. "Does anyone have any suggestion how we can get Bent Bamboo away from Thundering Heaven if Pearl doesn't surrender to the Exile Tiger's demand?"

"One course," Pearl replied promptly, "would be for me to offer to fight Thundering Heaven to win the Monkey's freedom—with Thundering Heaven's taking over as the Tiger if he defeats me."

"But, Pearl," Deborah objected, "your sword hand is broken. How could you fight?"

Pearl quirked a half smile, and Brenda knew the Tiger had anticipated this protest.

"If we fight, it would be in the afterlife, and I do not believe my physical impediments would carry over. If they do, well, perhaps I can manage with my left hand. As Riprap saw today, I am not too bad with my off-hand."

"I'll agree with that," Riprap said, but Brenda didn't think he was completely happy about having to agree. As the Dog, Riprap's urge was to protect, not to let someone else take the risks.

"However," Pearl said, "I should note that it's not at all certain that Thundering Heaven would accept my challenge."

Brenda asked, "Why wouldn't he? I mean, Thundering Heaven sounds arrogant enough to believe he'd win without much effort. We know he might not have such an easy time beating you, but does he?"

"He might not decide to take the risk of losing," Pearl replied. "Or he might simply prefer to have us continue in the role of supplicants."

"Well, then," Albert said with a slow smile that Brenda thought didn't look very friendly at all, "we'll just have to make certain our proposal is worded so that Thundering Heaven will accept—that is, if you really want to do this, Aunt Pearl."

"I do," Pearl said firmly. "Do we have any alternatives?"

"We could have some of our ghostly allies go after Thundering Heaven," Des said immediately.

Pearl shook her head. "No. We nearly lost Loyal Wind that way. We would have if Nine Ducks hadn't stepped in. Thundering Heaven will be expecting a group assault—I know I would. And I know how I'd oppose it."

"Bring Bent Bamboo out to join the fight," Riprap said with the same analytical rapidity he brought to the lessons he shared with Brenda and Nissa. "Our side would be hampered by the desire not to harm the Monkey both because we need him, and because we suspect he's been duped. Bent Bamboo probably wouldn't feel the same, not if Thundering Heaven primed him right."

"Exactly," Pearl said with an approving nod. "The same objection holds to some or all of the living making the journey to join the dead. Not only would we lose time, but we'd have to fight against the very person we want to rescue."

"And there's Soul Slicer," Nissa reminded. "It seems to do some really nasty things to ghosts. I have a feeling that its powers would work even better against the living. Our two souls are still in us, I mean."

"Interesting point," Righteous Drum said, and Pearl was pleased to see that the Dragon from the Lands was impressed by these acute insights from one who, just a few months ago, had known very little about magic or Chinese philosophy.

He'd better be impressed by her, Brenda thought grimly. *He's relying on her—on all of us—to get him home.*

Deborah, resignation warring with the unhappiness that had been her first reaction to Pearl's statement, cut in with a sigh. "And we don't have time to go find and train the boy who is the living incarnation of the Monkey. If we delayed that long, not only are we likely to have trouble from the enemies Righteous Drum and his friends left behind them in the Lands, but there are plenty of people in this world who are uncomfortable enough with the situation that they might decide to involve themselves in our business. I don't like it, but I think Pearl's right."

Albert glanced at the very expensive gold watch he wore on his right wrist. "It's getting late in the day. The Double Hour of the Rooster is nearly upon us. Des, why don't you and Shen come back with me to Pearl's house, and we'll set things up to contact Nine Ducks."

"I need to go back, too," Nissa said. "Lani's going to be missing me."

Brenda vacillated. Part of her wanted to stay here and see if Flying Claw might want to talk or something, but despite the fact that she was beginning to think he might actually like her—or maybe because of that—she was reluctant to thrust herself forward. Then there was the sly smile she'd seen Honey Dream give her, like the other woman could read her thoughts.

"I'll come with you," Brenda said. "The snacks were great, but we should probably put some dinner together."

Matters ended up with all of Pearl's household returning, with one addition. Flying Claw had been speaking to Shen and now he addressed the company at large.

"In the Lands," he said, "we have a ritual for challenging the established holder of a Branch affiliation. Because of my own training, I know the ritual for a challenge between Tigers. Perhaps this would be of some use."

Pearl smiled at him. "Thank you, nephew. I believe it might be. Thundering Heaven will have a lot more trouble refusing to fight me if we present the challenge to him with proper ritual flourish. Can you come to my house and tutor me in the details?"

"Gladly."

Brenda felt her heart leap at the thought that Flying Claw would be coming "home" with them. Immediately, she scolded herself.

He's coming to help Pearl, not to spend time with you.

But rationality didn't change her feelings a bit. She still felt ridiculously happy.

V

None of the living—not even Des and Shen, who stood as guards when Albert, through the intermediary of Nine Ducks, issued Pearl's challenge—would ever know exactly what Albert Yu said to Thundering Heaven to make the Exile Tiger accept their terms.

By the end of the Double Hour of the Rooster—about seven in the evening—Pearl's household had all assembled in the family room. Albert, looking more weary than ever, gave them the news.

"Thundering Heaven has accepted, but he's not giving you much time to prepare, Aunt Pearl. He insists that if you two are to meet, the meeting must take place at this next Double Hour of the Tiger. The meeting will take place within the traditional challenge format. I had no choice but to accept on your behalf, but I will admit, I only had a hazy idea what I might be getting you into. I hope Flying Claw has been able to fill you in on the details."

Riprap rose angrily to his feet from his seat at the table where he'd been eating a slice of pie.

"Double Hour of the Tiger!" Riprap protested. "That's three in the morning! Pearl's already been up all day. She'll hardly get any sleep."

Pearl favored the strong young man with a dry smile. "I believe meditation will serve me far better than sleep. We are fortunate Thundering Heaven accepted my challenge at all. I am not going to risk a postponement."

Pearl turned her attention to Albert. "Flying Claw has briefed me, and I am willing to accept a challenge within the traditional forms. However, there are few enough hours for me to gather my ch'i. If you all would excuse me . . ."

"Of course," Albert said, echoed by the rest. Concern showed in tone and expression as it did not in the matter-of-fact words.

Shen reached out to snag Pearl's hand as she went by him.

"Ming-Ming, if I can assist . . ."

She shook her head. "Help Flying Claw ready the altar. I'll be down at two-thirty."

Pearl turned and headed, not for her office, which was too filled with distractions, but for her rooms on the second floor of the house. She had her own suite there, including a private bathroom, and now, more than ever, she felt a need for privacy.

Initially, she could not settle into meditation. Restlessly, she paced back and forth in the space between the foot of her bed and her dresser. Back and forth, barefoot on the thick Persian carpet she had bought herself twenty years ago, and that still held its jewel tones, as bright as on the day she'd fallen in love with the edge of a pattern peeking out of a heap of carpets on a dealer's showroom floor.

Pearl let herself pace, using the motion to slowly calm her roiled nerves, as she had done years ago before stepping out on a stage or before a camera.

Forth and back. Pearl moved to a comfortable reading chair, let her head relax against the padded rest. Raised her feet on the ottoman. Without looking, she tugged the nearby light off, knowing exactly where she would find the chain.

She sought relaxation, muscle group by muscle group, starting with her feet, moving up her legs, into her torso. She located the flow of ch'i moving within her, sought to facilitate the various threads. Imagined that the ch'i was a stream within her, a sparkling ribbon, golden, as sunlight on clear water is the color of light.

Breathed deeply, slowly, regularly. With each pass through her, down each limb, up and around, through heart and lungs, liver and spleen, stomach and intestines, the shimmering stream became brighter, shedding the poisons of exhaustion and nervous energy, collecting the ch'i pocketed in little nooks of dream and vision throughout her mind and body.

The stream moved through Pearl Bright, collecting force and reaching out beyond her to touch the greater flow of ch'i that moved through her house. Feng shui was old news to Pearl by the time "fung shew-ee" became the hottest new trend in New Age home decorating. Her house could have served as a textbook example of how to maximize good energies and minimize bad.

Now Pearl connected her personal stream to that greater river, cycling this environmental ch'i into herself, creating reservoirs. She concentrated on building an image of the Tiger she would most like to be, for when she crossed to do battle with Thundering Heaven she must cease being Pearl Bright and become wholly the Tiger.

Pearl saw the concern on her associates' faces transform into something like awe as she descended the stairs to the ground floor. All the residents of her household, except for Lani, who would have gone to bed hours ago, were present, as was Flying Claw. Each of them evinced signs of having drunk too much coffee or tea in an effort to stay awake and alert until this late hour.

Nissa had a reddish smudge on one cheek that showed she, at least, had probably dozed in some awkward position, head resting against fist or perhaps against the headrest of a chair.

Pearl had pulled herself from meditation a half hour before, taken a quick shower, and done an abbreviated tai-chi routine to limber up bones and muscles that, beneath honest assessment, did not need limbering.

Her entire body was humming with stored ch'i, so much so that Pearl entertained the fancy that the elaborate shenyi she now wore, elegantly embroidered with symbols of luck and prosperity, as well as with countless representations of the Tiger in all his moods, floated around her aura instead of hanging against her physical form.

"Are the preparations made?" Pearl asked, smiling benificently at them all, but granting special attention to Flying Claw and Shen, who would have done most of the work.

"They are," Shen said. As she came close to him, he said in a soft whisper, "You look fantastic, Pearl."

"Thank you, my friend."

The furniture in Pearl's office had been rearranged.

Her desk had been slid back to make more floor space. Sufficient chairs for the assembled company had been arrayed in this open area.

The most comfortable of the chairs, a twin to the reading chair in Pearl's bedroom, had been placed close to the altar that dominated one end of the room. Someone had draped the chair with a piece of green fabric. Pearl recognized the top from a sheet set, but the drape did add a touch of elegance to what would otherwise have been a prosaic setting, so she restrained the flippant comment she might otherwise have made.

The altar at the far end of the room now included various items related to the Tiger, including photos of herself and of Thundering Heaven. The red tapers that usually stood at each corner had been replaced with ones in a vibrant emerald green.

"Everyone wanted to stay with you," Albert said almost apologetically, indicating the circle of chairs. He'd changed from his suit to casual trousers and a short-sleeved sports shirt. "I tried to tell them we couldn't be of any help, and we might be a distraction, so the choice is yours."

"Anyone who wishes to do so can stay," Pearl said. "I will not be distracted, and if people want to watch me sleeping in an armchair, then I don't mind. I'll even admit to being touched by your concern."

Flying Claw stepped forward. He wore the same jeans and tee shirt as he had earlier, and carried no weapons. Nonetheless, he managed to give the impression of being girded for battle.

"Those of us from the Lands," he said formally, speaking careful English, "wish to extend our wishes for good luck."

"Thank you," Pearl replied. "Now, the Double Hour of the Tiger is nearly upon us. Let me go forth."

Nissa stepped forward to settle Pearl in the chair.

"The Rabbit is the Tiger's partner," she said, "so Flying Claw said I should help light the incense and strike the bells."

"By all means," Pearl said, amused despite herself. She could imagine the conversation. Nissa's voice: bright, alert, alive with concern.

"Is there anything I can do to help? I feel I should. Pearl's risking herself for all of us."

And Flying Claw kindly manufacturing this bit of business. Certainly there had been nothing like it in the briefing he had given her earlier.

What Flying Claw had told Pearl had been much less elaborate and much more frightening.

Pearl let the words run through her head as she settled herself in the chair.

"This is a battle between Tigers, so tigers you must be. The ability to manifest a tiger form is necessary, so that manifestation in itself is the first part of the test. Afterward . . ." He had shrugged and tried not to look concerned. *"Tigers, especially male tigers, do not share their territory. You must defend yours against one who would take it from you."*

Pearl relaxed into the chair and began the process of separating her spirit from her body. Astral projection, as the practice was dubbed in Western magical traditions, was not new to her. Although the magic of the Thirteen Orphans included it among its practices, there was no simple spell to facilitate the separation, no simple sequence through which she could run and "Hey, presto. Here's the body. Here's the soul."

Pearl thought this was because the process of separation must, by definition, be unique for each person. What could be more personal than finding what was the essense of oneself and then sending it forth? This could not be done without a very strong sense of who that self was.

Fresh from hours of meditation, Pearl did not find the process of separation unduly difficult. More difficult was shaping that self into a tiger. A superficial shaping, an image of the self as the animal self, was not too hard to manage. Even Brenda and Nissa had done this, and, despite Nissa's Rabbit affiliation, they were hardly more than apprentices.

What Pearl needed was one step beyond. Nissa and Brenda had only shaped the form of their animal. Pearl must shape not only the tiger's body, but its soul as well. When she had done so, that body and soul would be as key and passport into the domain she must defend—a domain that was one and the same as her right to be the Tiger.

Within the interior of her mind, Pearl found and recognized the soul that was and would always be Pearl Bright, no matter what changes were made to her body.

Next, she twisted that self—herself—around, reshaping, losing hands, gaining paws, stretching her spine, extending and adding, so that she came to possess a long and lashing tail.

With the addition of the tail, Pearl's orientation changed, her center of gravity running parallel to the ground beneath her, no longer struggling to remain upright against the ground's pull.

Tigers have binocular vision, so what Pearl saw did not change, but her range of color changed subtly: not to black and white, as most humans believe "animals" see, but within a more narrow scope, with different emphasis. Darkness no longer seemed an impediment, and every flicker of motion was noted and registered.

Pearl's wide, damp nose caught new scents, her hearing became momentarily painful in its acuity. Then her brain adjusted to being a tiger's brain and accepted the sharpness of both scent and hearing as normal, processing the information and sending it to her as a comprehensible image.

Most curious of all—more curious than the loss of height or the fact that Pearl's wonderfully flexible body was completely covered in thick fur—was that she had gained extra senses. One of these was the tactile extension granted by her long, marvelously flexible whiskers. The other was the odd blending of taste and smell granted by the vomeronasal organ, a net of specialized cells on the roof of her mouth.

The vomeronasal organ could operate passively, like all sense organs, but its particular sensory abilities were enhanced when Pearl curled back her lips and drew air into her mouth, tasting it as a wine connoisseur might a rare and unusual vintage. She breathed in now and caught faintly, distant and a touch rank, the odor of a male tiger.

In nature, the territory of a female tiger may overlap that of several male tigers. Additionally, tigresses will share territory with their cubs, even when those cubs are two or three years old. Male tigers are far more exclusive in their choice of co-residents. A dozen leopards sharing their territory will not bother them, but a single rival tiger crossing over is a deadly challenge.

In this thick and tangled jungle where Pearl now opened tiger's eyes and surveyed her domain, Pearl's instincts were those of a male tiger, for in the Chinese zodiac, the tiger is the most yang of all the signs, and although yang is not the same as male, the essense of male is very much yang.

Thus, when Pearl Bright scented the presence of a male tiger, she considered whether or not to announce her presence.

Flying Claw had raised the matter in his briefing.

"Since you are not the challenger, there is no need for you to make your presence known. However, there are those who feel that failure to do so indicates cowardice."

Pearl had replied, "It seems to me that refraining from announcing myself would indicate prudence. Why give away my location before I must?"

However, now that Pearl's heart beat strong and steady in a tiger's chest, the issue did not seem so simple. She sniffed the air again, and the scent of that other tiger annoyed her. Lifting her head and drawing in breath, she roared.

A tiger's roar is an impressive sound, loud enough to carry three miles. Pearl listened to the reverberating rumble fade, then roared again. Why not? It felt good.

Then she set out to find the invader, noting with some disdain that although he was the challenger, he had not chosen to roar in turn.

Despite having a sense of smell far keener than a human's, a tiger does not hunt by scent as does a wolf or dog. Sight and sound are far more important to a tiger—those senses and the strange combination of scent and taste granted by the vomeronasal organ. Pearl's mind—human intellect meshing with the instincts and training of the tiger—sought to use all of these senses to their best advantage. Yet, she found herself at war with emotional—or perhaps merely hormonal—urges from the tiger's body.

Her territory had been invaded. She was angry. Enraged. Threatened. Her primary desire was to find the invader and show him just who was the biggest, strongest, most dangerous tiger in all these jungles. Her intellect fought an increasingly futile battle against these tigerish impulses.

In vain did Pearl warn herself that this invader tiger

was no more a simple animal than she was herself. This tiger embodied Thundering Heaven, a man who had devoted himself with exclusive fanaticism to the arts of war, the arts he believed made him most suited to be the Tiger.

There had been no acting in the theater for him, no standing on her mark before movie cameras, no long years of mostly rote physical training, training pursued because it was customary, because it helped her keep a trim figure well past menopause.

Pearl's intellect knew all of this, but the tiger she had become knew its own strength, gloried in the flexible power of bones and muscle and sinew, felt the sharpness of fangs with a tongue that could rasp through skin and scour flesh. The tiger felt her/his weight as paws left deep pug marks in the damp jungle soil.

This tiger Pearl had become knew only that there was an invader, and that the invader must be dealt with. Clamoring with increasing futility from the depths of a mind striped red and white with fury and angry heat, Pearl felt the tiger taking charge, and wondered—from the depth of her doubts of her own abilities to win against Thundering Heaven in a purely physical contest—if the domination of the tiger might not be best.

Thus the Tiger prowled deeper into the jungle, and the fragmenting threads that were Pearl Bright took note of what a strange jungle this was, a thing the Tiger, confident that this was his realm, did not note.

Amid the thick-boled, vine-shrouded, broad-leafed trees that were what Pearl would have expected a jungle to contain were elements distinctly anomalous. Roses intertwined with jungle vines, their flowers recognizable as modern hybrids: the dark red of Don Juan, the butterscotch of Jactan, the cream-edged-with-rose of Handel.

Once Pearl noticed the climbing roses, she became aware of the presence of shrub roses as well: hybrid teas neat and perfectly mannered despite their keeping company with broad-leafed bananas, thick stands of bamboo, and other, less recognizable jungle foliage. The messy profusion of floribunda and polyantha blossoms seemed perfectly in place in the verdant confusion.

The Tiger growled. He had not noticed the roses except as fleeting perfume impeding his ability to read the trail. However, he noticed something far more important.

Slashed bark on the trunk of a forest ancient, strips curling down fresh and bright, sap beading in the new wound, showed where the invader had left his mark. Pearl reared onto her hind legs, and extended long claws to cross his mark with her own. She was not able to reach quite as high as the invader had done, but to her satisfaction, her claws scored far deeper.

Alongside the claw-marked tree was what at first glance looked like another tree trunk. It was broader and straighter, a far better choice for a marking post, and Pearl idly wondered why her opponent had not chosen it. She reached to mark it as her own, but when her paw touched it, she felt it move.

Dropping to her haunches, Pearl sniffed. With her first intake of breath, she realized that this was no tree trunk but a plaster column, overgrown with moss and twined with vines and roses.

She shook her head and coughed, voicing confusion. Raising her head and looking around, she now noted other such columns. They were arrayed in a semicircle around a raised dais of considerable size. There was something familiar about the place, a familiarity that had nothing to do with her Tiger's life.

In a moment, Pearl remembered. This was a stage set from one of her greater successes as a child actress. She had played a slave girl in ancient Rome, a talented child who had soothed the broken heart of a lovely patrician woman who still mourned a child lost to her some years before. Of course, by the end of the movie, Pearl's character had been proven to be that missing child—reported dead of fever, but actually stolen away by pirates.

Pearl had spent hours on this particular set, practicing and then filming complex song and dance routines that later would be intercut with shots of the admiring (and decadent) Romans.

Unsettled, Pearl paced away from the vine-grown memory, but this last recognition had returned some balance between her mind and that of the Tiger, as if the beast realized that additional help would be needed to navigate these hunting grounds.

Even as Pearl searched for the invader tiger's pug marks, his scent posts, and noted the eerie silence that marked the jungle folk holding their collective breaths lest the hunting tiger take note of them, Pearl took in other unusual landmarks.

There were traces of stage sets—usually from productions notable for some achievement on her part: a starring role, a flamboyant dance, a poignant song. There were fragments of the life Pearl had lived: the bedroom window from her first apartment canted between two trees, a favorite end table set neatly in the middle of a stream, a window box bright with purple and white petunias, a dress neatly arrayed on a hanger, a pair of ballet shoes, an antique teacup.

Seeing these things anchored Pearl in herself, confirmed her in a dual nature in which the animal elements of the tiger were no longer dominant. This was *her* territory. She was the Tiger. She—Pearl Bright—specifically and uniquely her.

Pearl was caught up in the realization of what this strange landscape might mean when there was a snarl behind her. The snarl became a blur of orange striped with sun and shadow, then a bright slice of pain in the vicinity of the back of her neck.

Pearl ducked, jerking the skin of her neck scruff loose before the fangs that sought a solid hold could fasten tightly. She knew full well that a tiger's favorite hold is on the scruff. If powerful jaws cannot break the neck vertebrae beneath, then, with a slight readjustment, a crushing grip can suffocate the victim.

She ripped herself free, seeing the blood that welled forth sparkle in the air like liquid rubies as she spun and attacked her yet unseen opponent.

Fingernails like claws had been a cliche of the "bad girl" when Pearl had been younger. Even now she often made a quiet statement of her formidible feminity by painting her long, perfect nails a deep scarlet. But in reality fingernails are nothing like claws.

Fingernails do not slide from sheaths within the toes as Pearl's did now. She pivoted on her hind legs, reveling in the flexibilty of a torso that would let her strike directly behind even though the lower portion of her body was still oriented forward.

Fingernails are not curved like hooks, nor are they sharp and thick enough to rake through a dense fur coat and draw blood from beneath the hide. Claws are and claws can. Pearl saw the flash of ivory fangs as the tiger who had attacked her snarled and sprang backward.

But her attacker did not retreat. Neither did she. Snarling, he reared onto his back legs, swiping out with his right paw in feint and challenge. Pearl noted the reach of that slashing paw. It confirmed what she had noted at the signpost tree. Her opponent was larger than she was, his reach greater.

Pearl dared hope she was the stronger, but she could not be certain, not until they grappled. Grappling was not a test she was eager to make, for if she guessed wrong, she might not come away alive from that deadly embrace.

Tail lashing, Pearl struck back—right paw, left paw, right—gauging her opponent by his reactions, seeing if he could be led.

Despite the blood that darkened his fur where her claws had cut, he was unfazed. Pearl flattened her ears and snarled at the confidence he exuded. He had no doubt who would win this match. He was even playing with her, aware of her uncertainties.

Raw anger powered her next blow.

When Pearl struck there was nothing of the test about it. Her opponent—Thundering Heaven, she suddenly remembered—her father, Thundering Heaven, grown sure of his superior reach, did not dodge in time. Pearl caught him solidly on the side of his head, cutting into an ear. It was not a deep cut, but beads of blood dripped from the dark ear tip to stain the white fur of the spot that dotted the back of his ear, dripped into the white face ruff below.

Thundering Heaven snarled and lashed out at Pearl, but she was ready for his counterattack and sprang backward. He lunged, rearing up to take advantage of his greater size, springing forward. She leapt to one side, trying to get an angle from which she could reach his vulnerable hindquarters. He scooted them out of her reach, reorienting with incredible swiftness.

They sparred, occasionally drawing blood, but neither doing more than scoring the other's coat. Eventually, on each, golden orange fur acquired added stripes of muddy, dark red, stripes that, trickling into the white fur of ruff and underbelly, marked the course of a wound in vivid scarlet.

They snarled, chuffed, and hissed as they fought. Soon both were panting, foam and saliva dripping from open mouths. They were well enough matched—her greater dexterity eliminating the advantage of his greater size and weight, both of them skilled in combat—that Pearl began to feel the battle could go on forever.

Or at least until one of them made a mistake, and as they grew weary, one of them was certain to make that mistake. Thus far she had avoided close combat, where forepaws would grip shoulders and rear paw would rake belly and flanks. Yet that moment was approaching, for soon neither of them would have the strength to dodge. Close combat—and mortal wounds—would be inevitable.

As Pearl slashed out with her right paw, lunging to bring her fangs to bear at an apparently open spot on her opponent's right shoulder, she forced herself to consider.

Pearl tried to remember the location of the ruins of the theater where once she had sung and danced the role of a Roman slave. She had been circling back to take another look at those ruins when Thundering Heaven had sprung upon her. They shouldn't be far away.

Pearl waited until Thundering Heaven was rearing back to bat at her again with paws that were beginning to slow in the rapidity of their blows—but then so were her own. This time, instead of blocking and counterattacking, she wheeled and began to run.

Pearl knew the danger of this tactic, for tigers prefer to spring on their prey from behind, so much so that the sight of a face apparently staring at them—as in a mask worn on the backside of the head—has been known to dissuade even a confirmed man-eater from attacking.

Pearl had no mask. Indeed, the sight of her apparently fleeing should give Thundering Heaven the renewed strength of confidence.

Yes. He was giving chase. She ran harder.

Even on the damp ground of the jungle, Pearl could hear him coming after her, hear the dull thuds of his paws hitting the ground. She ran, long body stretching out with each leap, rear legs gathering in behind to push off almost before they touched. Panic at what would happen if Thundering Heaven should come close enough to leap onto her back gave Pearl the added speed she needed to stay just that far ahead.

Mossy green over glimmering white, the pillars of the stage set showed against the browner trunks of the natural trees, obvious now that Pearl knew what she was looking for. She did not dare slow, but ran near to one of the pillars, cornering like a horse on a barrel racing course, close but not too close. She wove in and out of the pillars, thinking crazily of Little Black Sambo with the tiger chasing him, racing round and round the tree until at last the tiger turned into butter.

Pearl cut closer, closer, not quite touching but feeling her fur brush against the moss-covered, vine-shrouded plaster. Her control was perfect, that of a dancer who could perform complexly choreographed routines, that of an actress who always kept within her spot. Then it happened.

Thundering Heaven—larger than she was, made furious by having his prey in reach but ever just out of reach—cut too close to one of the pillars. Had the pillars been the trees they resembled, this would not have mattered. He maybe would have bruised a rib, but would have come on hardly hindered.

But these were not trees, but plaster pillars. A full-grown tiger can weigh more than six hundred pounds, and Thundering Heaven was a very large tiger indeed, a very large tiger running with all the strength of his powerful hind legs.

Thundering Heaven crashed into the pillar, and the pillar broke. The upper part swayed and snapped, falling heavily to smash not onto Thundering Heaven—that would have been too much luck—but into the next nearest pillar.

Pearl, hearing the thud of impact, the snarl of rage and indignation that burst from Thundering Heaven as the "tree" broke, dared wheel about.

She saw her attacker momentarily halted, ears and whiskers twitching in every direction as he sought a clear path out of the rain of falling plaster.

Plaster is neither rock nor wood, but heavily packed, sodden with drifting mist, it is not insignificant either. Moreover, not just one but several pillars were falling.

Pearl stood on her hind legs and pushed with her forepaws against the nearest intact pillar. She shoved hard and the pillar toppled, bringing with it another pillar, for a mesh of vines had grown between, netting them together.

It was a sensational sight, but Pearl knew this mess of falling plaster was only a distraction. She had regained some of her wind. Now, while Thundering Heaven was distracted, she did the one thing Flying Claw had not told her was essential to winning this battle.

Had not told her, because he could not have known.

With a surge of ch'i, Pearl forced herself back into her human shape. The jungle had told her what each Tiger must learn for herself—or himself—the secret that each Tiger will not tell even the most beloved apprentice.

Yes. To be the Tiger, and to maintain your place as the Tiger, you must be able to shape a tiger and to hold your own in a fight in that form.

But you are also human. It must be both as a human and as a tiger that you confront your challenger. Let the tiger alone rule and even the best fighter may well lose, for the challenger will come at you with all the fresh, raw arrogance of the tiger's form—a form that, in anticipation of this battle, he will have practiced to perfection. Let the human alone rule, and you will never have the strength to wear down your opponent.

So Pearl stood as a human while the slobbering, snarling, bleeding, plaster-coated tiger that was her father's ghost paced up to her.

She raised her hands and shaped the Tiger's wind, the wind of the east-northeast, and caused it to place a barrier between them.

Then she did the little spell called Dragon's Breath and from it sent forth a gust of flame to scorch the whiskers of the tiger that was Thundering Heaven.

And somewhere in the back of her mind Pearl heard her mother's voice reading from *The Jungle Book*, about how the hunter Buldeo had bent to scorch Sher Khan's whiskers, because if you don't scorch his whiskers the tiger's ghost will haunt you. Overhearing, her father had commented that the kuei—the ghosts of those the tiger killed—are far worse than any tiger's ghost.

"Back," Pearl said, and Thundering Heaven's bloodied ears flattened against his head at the sound of her human voice. "Leave this place, or I will begin to fight you in all earnest."

Pearl had expended a bit of the ch'i she had stored before coming to answer this challenge, but she still maintained ample reserves. She used some now, so that she might augment her senses both to match those of the tiger and to see things arcane as well as natural, for she did not trust Thundering Heaven not to attempt to fool her with some spell of his own.

Thundering Heaven's aura held the brilliant shades of anger and fury. The colors of intellect and rationality were present, but pale within that raging storm. He crouched close to the earth. His ears were pinned back and his fur was tousled as he tested the barrier made by the east-northeast wind.

Pearl studied him, wondering if this creature possessed even the intellect to talk to her.

"Take your human form," she commanded, adding as a goad, "if you can manage to do so that is. If you do not, I will force you into it."

The crouching tiger snarled. The angry aura dampened slightly and the intellect flared as Thundering Heaven retook his human form.

The transformation was swift, but for the briefest moment, Pearl clearly saw something that nearly shocked her into losing control over her spells. A woman's form, spectral and wraithlike, stood behind Thundering Heaven.

Malice flowed from the woman like cold wind sweeping off a glacier. Then the woman vanished—but feeling that lingering chill, Pearl did not think the specter was gone.

Pearl seized the moment her father needed to orient himself to enhance her protective spells. A wind alone could not protect her from the malice she had felt. Who was Thundering Heaven's strange ally? Pearl had not recognized her.

But neither did Thundering Heaven seem aware of

her. He now stood on his own human feet. Unlike Pearl, who had healed herself in the act of accepting her dual nature, he remained battered, blood seeping from various wounds, his mien cringing, but Pearl had no doubt that if his ears had been able to move, they would have been pinned back and a defiant snarl would have twisted his features.

"Do you admit yourself fairly beaten?" Pearl demanded of Thundering Heaven. "Or must we continue this ridiculous battle?"

Thundering Heaven had appeared to Loyal Wind and Nine Ducks as a warrior in his prime, but looking beyond his wounds Pearl saw that to her he had manifested as he had looked when she was a rebellious young woman in her early teens, and he, although past his prime, still a powerful disciplinarian.

She wondered if this was a conscious choice, if he sought to intimidate her with old memories, or if this was simply how he saw himself in relation to her.

If Thundering Heaven was hoping to intimidate, the form was not a bad choice, for Pearl's skin prickled with goose bumps of remembered fear when his familiar voice spoke.

"Fairly beaten?" he said. "Beaten, certainly, but could you hold your own if you let that wind drop?"

"That is not the point," Pearl said. "I will not let this wind drop, nor release any of my other protections. They are my right as the Tiger, as much mine as claws or fangs. Why shouldn't I use them?"

"Would you fight me spell to spell?" Thundering Heaven snarled.

"Would you?" she replied with insulting mildness.

"No," he said, and the one word was like a tiger's chuff. "No. Not with me worn, and you in your glory. I thought you would fight this fairly."

"I have," Pearl said. "I am the Tiger and this is my

jungle. No warrior fights with fists when he can raise a sword. Now. Will you honor your agreement and surrender Bent Bamboo, the Monkey, to me, or must I continue to batter you?"

"I will," Thundering Heaven said, and the words were pulled from him in halting cadence, "give Bent Bamboo the Monkey to you—or rather I will let his ghost come to meet with you. But convincing him to take up your cause . . ."

Thundering Heaven laughed, and it was an ugly sound.

"That will be your problem."

VI

Loyal Wind and Nine Ducks found Bent Bamboo, the Monkey, waiting for them in the little bit of paradise that was to him as the pavilion by the lake was to Nine Ducks.

Given the philandering that had defined the earlier years of the Monkey's life, Loyal Wind would have expected Bent Bamboo to find his ideal afterlife in a pleasure palace or perhaps in a garden where lovely women outnumbered the flowers.

Instead, when they entered Bent Bamboo's chosen domain, they found themselves in a drugstore soda fountain. The only available seats were at the long counter. There were ample empty stools. Down at the end of a counter a man wearing a drab brown uniform was sipping a cola and flirting with a waitress as she scooped ice cream into various curvilinear glasses.

Backing the counter, occupying both booths and small, round wire-legged tables, were young people.

Most seemed to be about high school–aged, on the threshold of adulthood, very much enjoying their ability to show their independence.

One young couple sipped something frothy and very pink from a single tall, fluted glass. Four young men in a booth laughed loudly over something a shy, bespectacled young man had said as he paused by their table. A rosy blush crept over the speaker's face, but he didn't seem entirely displeased. Down by the register, a girl hardly large enough to see over the counter dug in a little purse for coins to settle her bill.

Loyal Wind had died in mainland China, so in life he had never been inside such a place, but he had maintained an awareness of the world of the living. After some consideration, he decided the soda fountain might be just right for a Monkey—a place of easy socializing, of physical indulgence, even of casual carnality.

None of those gathered in this busy establishment seemed to notice the man and woman who had just taken their seats at the counter, not even though Loyal Wind wore leather armor adorned with highly polished metal studs and a pheasant tail–plumed helmet, and Nine Ducks a heavily—even overly—embroidered yellow shenyi.

Only one person noticed them, a counterman clad in white trousers, white shirt, and white shoes. He looked about twenty-five, just a little older than the majority of his customers. His most notable features were large ears that stuck out like jug handles from the sides of his head and wistful brown eyes that were far too sad and old for his youthful face. A white paper hat perched on his short-cropped black hair, maintaining its place in defiance of both logic and gravity.

When the counterman turned, Loyal Wind was not in the least surprised to recognize Bent Bamboo, the

Monkey. Bent Bamboo ambled over to them, his gait loose-limbed and slack, then gave the counter in front of them a few lazy swipes with a damp rag.

"I suppose," Bent Bamboo said in a tone of voice that would have been more appropriate if he were asking for their order, "this is where you tell me just how badly I've screwed everything up, not just in listening to Thundering Heaven, although anyone in their right mind could see the glint of madness in his eyes, but as far back as when we made our initial pact, and then later when I led you to believe that the wrong boy was my new heir apparent."

Nine Ducks looked at the Monkey, her expression holding sorrow rather than anger. "I suppose we could, but since you've figured it out for yourself that would be a waste of energy. Why don't we talk about whether you're willing to join with us in our new venture, in our chance to make it all right again?"

"You mean this idea," Bent Bamboo said, "that you have about some of us resuming our association with our Branches, taking them onto ourselves so that the Ninth Gate can be opened and the Exiles—both more recent and the original Thirteen—return home again."

"That idea," Nine Ducks agreed mildly. "Do you have a problem with that?"

"Lots," Bent Bamboo said. He turned away from them and went to fetch two glasses of ice water from the prep area behind him. "For one, how is that going to solve the problem of the Earthly Branches being split between the Lands Born from Smoke and Sacrifice and the Land of the Burning? Have the living realized that merely opening the Ninth Gate will not be sufficient, that this will not cause the Branches to rejoin? Are the newcomers from the Lands—Righteous Drum and all—prepared to accept this?"

Loyal Wind sipped his water, deciding this was Bent Bamboo's way of fulfilling the traditional offering of food to a guest. The water tasted very good: crisp, clean, and bright, like a handful of newly fallen snow.

Keeping his voice low—for he could not quite believe that the chattering people around them were simply adornments of a lonely ghost's fantasy—Loyal Wind replied. "The Orphans—at least those who have remained aware of their heritage to some extent—are aware that simply opening the gate will not solve the problem. They have promised that, if necessary, they will do what they can to put their new allies in power again. In turn, the new allies seem resigned to accepting that the Earthly Branches are split and will remain so."

Bent Bamboo had listened politely. Now he returned to the service counter. When he turned to face them, he set before each a cut crystal dish of sherbet hued in brilliant shades of yellow, orange, red, and vibrant, unrealistic green. The confection smelled vividly of tangy fruit juices. Loyal Wind reached for his spoon without hesitation.

If there was one good thing about being dead, it was that no one could poison you.

"So there is an understanding for after the Ninth Gate has been opened," Bent Bamboo said heavily. "That's good. From what Thundering Heaven hinted when he was convincing me to join his side, the balance of power has shifted since Righteous Drum took his two young associates off on what was supposed to be a quick jaunt."

Loyal Wind wanted to know more, but he also didn't want to seem surprised. "We have had some indication of this, from prisoners our living associates took when they were attacked. Also, Waking Lizard . . ."

"The Monkey who died," Bent Bamboo said, his tones even more gloomy.

"Waking Lizard spoke of strange weapons and new tactics," Loyal Wind went on. "However, he was the first to admit that he was no warrior, and could do little more than repeat secondhand what he had heard their Horse—"

"Who also died," Bent Bamboo interrupted, *sotto voce*.

"—had said before what would be his final battle."

"Died," Nine Ducks said, tasting the word far more thoughtfully than she had the sherbet she had been spooning up with quiet enthusiasm. "Have you encountered either Waking Lizard or this other Horse here in the afterlife? Waking Lizard is likely still working his way through the intricacies of judgment and adjustment. . . ."

"Monkeys are not entered in the judges' books," Bent Bamboo said, "or so the legends say."

Nine Ducks ignored him. "But that Horse . . . I wonder. Now that I consider, probably he is also still caught up in transition. Not more than a few months can have passed since his death. So much has happened in so little time."

Loyal Wind felt Nine Ducks was forgetting their purpose in seeking out Bent Bamboo.

"Those others are no longer essential," he said. "What is essential is learning whether or not Bent Bamboo will join us in helping to open the final gate."

"Am I the last holdout?" Bent Bamboo asked.

"You are," Nine Ducks said. "I have been speaking with the others. Even Gentle Smoke, the Snake, whose heir lives but is very elderly, and therefore unfit to make this journey, has agreed to temporarily retake her hold on the Sixth Earthly Branch and assist us."

"Temporarily," said Bent Bamboo slowly. "So that's

all we get out of this—to turn a key in a lock, then go back to our afterlives?"

"We had better hope we can do that much," Nine Ducks said bluntly. "The Earthly Branches have clung to their association with the living, shunning the dead. The plan the Orphans have come up with assumes that we will be able to reassociate ourselves."

"So it's not certain," Bent Bamboo said. A slow smile spread over features that had been somber. "Well, nothing like a challenge. Count me in."

☆

"Who was that woman?" Brenda asked the morning following Pearl's battle against Thundering Heaven.

Morning was something of an exaggeration. After sitting up so late, just about everyone in the household had slept in. It was closer to lunch by the time everyone had assembled around the long table.

Their number had been augmented by two. Des had driven over to Colm Lodge, briefed Righteous Drum and Honey Dream, and then brought them back to Pearl's house.

Brenda marveled that Des could have done this—and not because he'd managed to remain clear-eyed and alert despite the late night they'd all had. Des, like the Rooster, awoke alert and with a clear head.

No, what made her head ring as if her hold on reality was shaking was that all of them had been witness to Pearl's response to Thundering Heaven's challenge. All of them but one: Flying Claw claimed to have seen nothing other than his companions drifting into a light trance, leaving him to sit alone, aware that momentous events were occurring but unable to witness them.

Last night, they'd told Flying Claw enough to assure him that Pearl was the victor. Then they had all stumbled to their beds, more exhausted than their late vigil merited. Clearly, the contact with Pearl's vision had drained their personal ch'i.

Crowded together into their shared bathroom, brushing their teeth and hair, Nissa and Brenda had speculated why Flying Claw alone hadn't shared in the vision.

"Maybe it's because he's a Tiger, and couldn't know the secret of the Tiger's test," Brenda had said, patting back a yawn.

"Maybe it's because he's not an Orphan," Nissa said, adding hastily as Brenda, too tired to hide how this statement wounded her fragile sense of belonging, started to protest. "I mean one of us, one of our tradition. Stop being a pill, Breni. You're not the Rat. You never let us forget it. However, you are Gaheris's heir apparent. You are one of us."

"I know," Brenda said around her toothbrush. She leaned into Nissa, in a sort of sloppy hug. She spat out toothpaste and wondered if she had the energy to rinse her mouth. "I'm an idiot. I'm sorry. I'm too tired to figure out anything complex now."

"In the morning," Nissa agreed. "That will be soon enough. It had better be."

So now it was morning, and if Brenda didn't feel exactly chipper, she didn't feel much more groggy than she usually did before her first cup of coffee.

She poured that coffee, and grabbed a large chunk of pecan coffee cake from one of a series of bakery boxes set on the counter. It was after she'd drunk half the coffee and was heading back for a container of yogurt that she asked her question.

"So," Brenda repeated, pulling her head out of the refrigerator in case everyone hadn't heard. "Who was that woman?"

"Woman?" Righteous Drum asked. He glanced over

at Des with vague indignation. "You didn't tell us about any woman other than Pearl herself."

"I didn't," Des said, "because I hadn't had a chance to ask anyone else if they'd seen her. I mean, it was just a split second, there at the end, right after Pearl forced Thundering Heaven to take back his human form. Is that what you're talking about, Brenda?"

Brenda nodded, her mouth full of raspberry yogurt. It tasted amazingly good, better than usual, and from this she deduced that even after eight hours' sleep she was still suffering from mild ch'i depletion. Apparently, one didn't ride along on someone else's vision without paying a price.

For a moment, Brenda felt a touch indignant. Pearl, sitting there at the end of the table, looked fine, but then she'd stored up a ton of ch'i beforehand. Why hadn't the rest of them been warned that their vigil might turn into something more? Why hadn't they been told to prepare?

Because, moron, Brenda answered herself, *they didn't know. The Orphans have always passed their connection to the Branches along by a biological inheritance chain. This was the first challenge any of us has ever had to face.*

She grinned to herself. *And Pearl met that challenge just fine.*

Des had been polling their assembled company. It turned out that everyone had seen the woman—or wraith, as Riprap insisted on calling her, saying what he'd seen had looked female only by virtue of some gut instinct.

"I mean, what I saw did not look like a woman," Riprap clarified. "Skinny, translucent, almost transparent. Long hair flying all over the place. A really nasty expression, like she wanted to eat Pearl's liver."

Everyone nodded, and Pearl added, "I also had the

distinct impression that the wraith was female. I don't know why, but I feel firmly convinced that was so."

"So we weren't," Nissa said, looking up from the crayon-scrawled piece of paper Lani had just thrust into her hands, "seeing part of Thundering Heaven—maybe his po ghost, I mean."

"I drawed a ghost," Lani said. "A pink one. A girl ghost."

Nissa nodded. "That you did, Bunny. Go draw us a boy ghost, okay?"

Righteous Drum had been considering. "I don't think so. There is nothing in our tradition to account for such a thing."

"A mystery," Shen said, "and one we should not forget. However, before we get sidetracked, I want to tell you all that Loyal Wind has been in touch. Bent Bamboo, the Monkey, will join us. Nine Ducks has secured the cooperation of Copper Gong, the Ram, and Gentle Smoke, the Snake."

"So with the addition of the five ghosts, we have a full company," Pearl said. "The Thirteen Orphans can at last be assembled."

"If," Shen said, glancing with a touch of apprehension at Des, "we can convince their affiliate Branches to join with ghosts."

Brenda knew why Shen had looked at Des. From the start, Des had been the least enthusiastic about this plan, largely because he had a healthy distaste for what he insisted on referring to as necromancy.

But Des only inclined his head in a small, reassuring nod.

"I'm all right with it, Shen. What's the plan?"

"We never did quite work out the precise details," Shen said, "since doing so seemed a waste of time until we knew if we could convince the ghosts to cooperate. How shall we begin?"

Honey Dream, quiet, suspiciously passive—at least to Brenda's way of thinking—to this point, spoke. Like the rest of her, Honey Dream's voice was lovely, even if she was inclined to get a little bit too much into the Snake thing and hiss on her s's.

"In anticipation of Pearl's success," Honey Dream said, "last night my father and I reviewed possible ways to enable the ghosts to resume their bonds with the appropriate Earthly Branches. We have a few thoughts."

Righteous Drum took over. "Although our research of late has focused on the setting of the Nine Gates, Shen has been gracious enough to tell us something of the magic by which the Earthly Branches were bound to their specific holders."

Brenda saw Pearl give Shen a sharp, almost admonishing, look.

And no wonder, Brenda thought, covering her inclination to grin at Shen's surprised expression with a quick spoonful of yogurt. *Shen seems to have overlooked how easily that information could be turned against us—that Righteous Drum came here expressly to separate the Earthly Branches from their holders.*

But since Pearl didn't say anything, Righteous Drum had the option to overlook her unspoken criticism and continue.

"The spell used has been codified under the All Pair Honors. The pattern of pairs will be somewhat different for each of the five ghosts. In order to break the binding tie, we will then work the sequence in reverse."

Honey Dream opened a notebook and leafed through it quickly, showing five pages, each with their own neat notations. Since the writing was in Chinese, it meant nothing to Brenda, but several others of those gathered nodded as they read what was written there.

"We have worked out," Honey Dream said, "what we think would be the most auspicious sequencing of pairs from among the Winds and Dragons—what you term the Honors suits. We would desire that you confirm our calculations."

But, Brenda thought a trace maliciously, even though Honey Dream hadn't done a thing to deserve it, *you bet we'll all agree that you and your daddy have been brilliant. I'm okay with that, actually. I certainly couldn't have done it.*

"Fine," Des said, "so we can release the tie between the Earthly Branch and its living affiliate. Great. How do we convince it to bind with a ghost? My understanding is that, in your tradition as well as ours, the tie has always been with a living person."

"True," Righteous Drum agreed. "Therefore, we must, if only for a short time, resurrect the dead."

"What?"

Brenda wasn't sure who made that exclamation. It might even have been her, because suddenly everyone was talking at once.

"Summoning the dead is bad enough," Des said, his voice rising above the babble, "but this? This is all wrong. Not only is it against nature, it could get us in a lot of trouble with the indigenous magical traditions. Pearl's already had some polite queries about the Orphans' mah-jong sets."

No one needed to ask why. Somehow—Brenda suspected a very nasty woman named Tracy Frye had contributed to the rumors—the indigenous magical traditions had learned that the Orphans' mah-jong sets were made from bone and bamboo. That in itself was not a problem—almost all the old mah-jong sets were made from bone and bamboo. The problem here was that the bone was not cattle shin bone, as was more common, but human bone—taken from the corpse of the appropriate member of the original Thirteen Orphans.

Righteous Drum waited for the babble to calm down a bit. Now he spoke, his tones those of a professor giving a lecture.

"I do not know what your tradition holds, Desperate Lee," he said very formally, "but in our own, there are many tales where the judges of the underworld have permitted a ghost to return as one of the living in order to set right some matter that only they could facilitate."

Des slumped a little, but Brenda could tell he was still very uncomfortable.

"I know, I know. The story of the disloyal friend and the stolen money. Or those tales of the faithful son or daughter who returns to serve the needs of an elderly parent even after death. But this talk of raising the dead makes my skin crawl. . . ."

"Des," Riprap said, "we're not talking zombies here." He looked quickly at the others. "I mean, I don't think we are, are we?"

Righteous Drum and Honey Dream both looked puzzled. Brenda guessed that there wasn't enough of a connection between zombies—which were Caribbean, weren't they? Or did they come from New Orleans?— and whatever the closest thing was in Chinese culture for the spell to translate.

Flying Claw, who by virtue of his time as "Foster" had been exposed to a wider variety of American culture, clarified. "Zombies. Kuei Hsien. Or something close to that. Mindless walking dead."

Righteous Drum shook his head. "No, Riprap, that is not what we intend. Mindless dead would not serve our purpose at all. Indeed, the body matters little in this case. It is the spirit and permission for the spirit to function in the world of the living that matters."

Riprap looked at Des. "Any problem?"

Des sighed. "I'll try to relax. Righteous Drum, do you have a procedure in mind for achieving this resurrection?"

Righteous Drum nodded. "Yes. We must appeal to the judges of the underworld for permission for the spirits to return. We will base our appeal on the grounds that these five Exiles have unfinished business that only they can appropriately resolve."

Brenda spoke up. "Do you think they'll listen? These judges, I mean."

"Yes," Righteous Drum said. "Especially since what we say is only the truth. Also, there is the issue of the disrupted balance created by our presence in this world when we belong in the other. The judges are very concerned with order. In the tradition of the Lands, order or the lack thereof could be said to matter as much or more than those more elusive terms 'good' and 'evil' that are so often tossed about in this society."

Deborah nodded. "I can see that. I doubt Brenda and the other apprentices have been exposed to the teaching of the great Chinese philosophers, but a common thread running through many of their works is that of maintaining the social order. If society is ordered, then justice will automatically follow. If society is not ordered, then chaos—and the abuses of justice that thrive in a chaotic society—will follow."

"I can see that," Des said, "for the Confucians and related philosophers—and of course for the Legalists, but does that really apply to the Taoists?"

"It does," Deborah said firmly. "The yin-yang symbol is very important to Taoist philosophy. What does that stand for other than an ordered universe where all traits are balanced?"

"All right," Des agreed. "I was thinking about all the varied and contradictory stories that come out of the Taoist tradition, but looked at the way you do, you're right."

"Valuing order makes sense, I guess," Brenda said, thinking of long discussions she'd had with her friends in the dorm about what was the difference between a soldier killing in a time of war and the same person doing the exact same thing for personal reasons. One was a just act, the other murder.

But the poor sap ends up dead just the same, Brenda thought.

"So do we talk to the judges first or second?" Riprap said, ever practical. "I mean, if we release the ties between the Earthly Branches and the heirs before we find out if the judges will let the ghosts join us, then haven't we created more problems?"

Albert nodded, a decisive snap of his head that Brenda just knew would have driven her dad up the wall.

If Dad bothered to be here, she thought, then banished the impulse to feel annoyed. Gaheris Morris would be here when they needed him. Did they really need one more voice around the breakfast table?

"I think Riprap has a point," Albert said. "First we speak to the judges. Then we arrange to release and reassociate the Earthly Branches. Finally, we pass through the Nine Gates and reopen the way into the Lands Born from Smoke and Sacrifice."

"How do we speak to these judges?" Nissa asked. "Last time we had to send people to the underworld the journey took days—and a couple of those who went nearly got killed along the way."

Righteous Drum smiled, which Brenda thought was very brave of him, given that he was one of the ones who'd almost died.

Of course, I was the other one, she thought, *but I*

was too dumb to realize how bad things were until the very end.

"We made friends on that other journey," Righteous Drum said, "and those friends will help us now. The Nine Yellow Springs consider themselves 'men' or family with us. They will permit those we choose to speak for us to make the journey swiftly and easily."

"That's good," Nissa said. "I guess. When are whoever is going planning to leave?"

"Tomorrow at the earliest," Pearl said firmly. "We all need to rest from the events of last night."

"Tomorrow," Righteous Drum agreed, "should be soon enough."

"So who will speak for us?" Albert said. "I will go, of course. This appeal should be made by the emperor in person—even if I am an uncrowned emperor without a throne. How large an entourage would be appropriate? Any suggestions as to who I should include?"

"An entourage of three or four would be all that would be needed." Honey Dream spoke with the assurance of an authority on such matters. Brenda remembered that as the Snake, Honey Dream would have been trained in court etiquette and procedure—even if Brenda often had found Honey Dream less than perfectly tactful in day-to-day matters. "The judges will more likely be impressed by the gravity of your argument than by mere numbers."

"Very well," Albert said.

Honey Dream went on. "The ghosts should join you. In this circumstance, they will be the ones on whose behalf you are making petition, so they wouldn't really count as part of your entourage. For the same reason, I am not sure whether any of us from the Lands should be part of the contingent. We, too, are seeking aid, and therefore could be considered petitioners."

Albert nodded and sat for a moment deep in thought,

his elegant finger stroking along the line of his neat beard.

"Shen," Albert said finally. "I'll want you. The residents of the House of Mystery are skilled in both magical and courtly matters. Since our Snake will be represented by a ghost, and Honey Dream thinks she had better stand down, you're our best choice—especially since this transition between living and dead is a highly magical matter, and magic is the Dragon's specialty."

Albert glanced at Righteous Drum. The other Dragon inclined his head in unspoken agreement. Shen nodded his acceptance, waiting, Brenda noted, until he was certain he would not offend his counterpart.

Honey Dream could take lessons from Shen on how to make diplomacy look effortless, Brenda thought.

Albert went on.

"Since we are seeking to expand our number, I think I also want a representative of the House of Expansion. That would be the Tiger or the Rabbit. Pearl, you have seniority among the Orphans, so even though Tigers are not known for diplomacy, I should take you. The Chinese culture respects age."

Pearl nodded. "I'll come, present my old grey head for inspection, and keep my mouth shut."

Nissa looked distinctly relieved.

Brenda would have liked to take bets on whether Pearl really would keep her mouth shut, but Albert's thoughtful gaze was scanning the assembly. Brenda felt her heart race, even though she knew she wasn't likely to be chosen. Even so, a competitive part of her wanted to wave her hand in the air and shout, "Choose me! Choose me!"

Albert was thinking aloud. "With the Tiger we have a representative of the House of Expansion. With the Dragon, we represent the House of Mystery. Since this is a matter of reuniting sundered families, and restoring sundered familial bonds, I think my last representative should be from the House of Family. Riprap, I know you're brave and valiant, but with Pearl along, we don't need more of those particular qualities. I think the Pig would be the best choice. Domestic ideal. Deborah?"

"I will be at your side," she said, pointedly ignoring Riprap's frown. Clearly he didn't think choosing an older woman over him was a good idea, and Deborah responded to his unspoken protest. "I don't think it hurts that, like Shen and Pearl, I'm definitely among the senior citizens. Our young emperor will be supported by his elders."

"I'm hardly young," Albert protested mildly, fingering traces of silver in his beard, "but I'm vain enough to appreciate the designation. Does anyone wish to make alternate suggestions?"

His question was primarily directed toward the three from the Lands. Flying Claw immediately shook his head. Honey Dream and Righteous Drum gave the matter thoughtful consideration.

"I think you have chosen wisely," Righteous Drum said. "In fact, if you wish one of us to accompany you in the role of petitioner, then I would agree."

Albert considered. "If one of you came, I'd like to take Honey Dream, because she'll be able to give us advice on court etiquette. However, I'll leave which of you comes up to you, since your petition is secondary."

Honey Dream inclined her head with a studied grace. Brenda looked, but she didn't seem in the least miffed that her father had just contradicted her advice, however mildly.

"If I am needed," she said, "I will come."

"We'll do some auguries," Albert said, "and check the advantages and disadvantages. We're going to need to do auguries in any case, in order to ascertain the best date and hour for our departure. When we know that, we'll contact the ghosts."

The group around the table began to disperse, the Dragons, Des, and Honey Dream joining Albert in Pearl's office to work the auguries. Pearl, apparently more drained by her battle than Brenda had realized, excused herself to get some more rest.

Nissa's attention had been claimed by Lani, and Deborah was patiently explaining to Riprap why he hadn't been overlooked, and why—even if the entourage could be as large as four—he didn't need to insist on accompanying them.

A little embarrassed, hearing her own "Choose me!" in Riprap's intensity, Brenda slipped out of the kitchen onto the back patio. She heard soft footsteps behind her and looked to see Flying Claw on her heels.

"Want to go for a walk?" he asked, and his smile—shy and yet friendly—made her heart sing and removed the slight sting of imagined rejection. "I have always enjoyed walking with you."

"I'd love to," she said.

So close, but so far from, "I love you."

VII

With the blessings of the Nine Yellow Springs, the First Gate carried Albert Yu and his small entourage directly to the underworld.

Their initial step had carried them over the threshold of the pine door from which the gate had been made and deep into the heart of a cloud of fine particles. Pearl had felt the sting of the swirling dust against the skin of her face and hands—the only part of her skin her elaborate ceremonial shenyi left exposed.

As suddenly as it had arisen, the dust cloud dropped, momentarily fragmenting frozen sunlight, before vanishing entirely.

Pearl gripped the hilt of her sword, Treaty, and looked about her. There had been arguments—there were always arguments and debates when the Thirteen Orphans made a plan—about the rightness of carrying weapons before Yen-lo Wang.

"But I am the Tiger," Pearl had said, thrusting the sword into its sheath as if daring anyone to remove it, "and a Tiger is never without her fangs and claws."

No one had taken her challenge, and Pearl noted with a quiet smile that Shen carried at his belt the iron pen case that, like the Lama in Kipling's *Kim*, he could use to do more than merely hold his pens, brushes, and ink. She wouldn't be in the least surprised to learn that Albert and Deborah also carried weapons.

"Seems," Deborah said, looking around as she smoothed down the skirts of her shimmering black shenyi with a restless gesture that showed she didn't wear long skirts very often, "that someone is waiting for us over there. Several someones . . . I recognize Loyal Wind from our trip to find the Nine Yellow Springs, so I'd guess the others must be our remaining ghosts."

Honey Dream, who had accompanied them after a series of intricate auguries had shown her presence could possibly be beneficial, said, "You're right. The old woman standing next to Loyal Wind is Nine Ducks. She looks much happier than she did the last time I saw her."

Honey Dream raised her voice slightly and called, "Greetings, Grandmother Ox. As a representative of three barred from their homelands without even the polite formality of an exile, I thank you and your associates for your assistance in our journey home."

Nine Ducks smiled as she came forward, hands outstretched in familial greeting. As with all their company, the Ox was attired in a shenyi, the color of the fabric—in her case yellow—appropriate for her Earthly Branch affiliation. The embroidered designs showed not only the Ox in various poses—reclining, grazing, charging—but also various emblems invoking long life, good luck, happiness, and prosperity.

Behind Nine Ducks, in the order of their zodiac signs on the wheel, came the ghosts of three people. Two of them—the Snake and the Monkey—had died shortly before Pearl's birth. The third, the Ram, had been one of the grand old ladies who ruled over various gatherings.

First came Gentle Smoke, the original Snake of the Thirteen Orphans. Gentle Smoke had been in her late seventies when she had died, but now she chose to appear much as she had at the time of the Exile—as a woman in her late forties.

How odd, Pearl thought. *She looks so young, yet all the stories I heard about her when I was growing up stressed her advanced age at the time of the Exile— how fearing that menopause would rob her of her ability to bear an heir Gentle Smoke had seduced a local lord and made him father of her children.*

Gentle Smoke was no va-va-voom beauty like her counterpart, Honey Dream. Small and very slim, she moved with almost boneless grace. Her features were elegant. The fashion in which she wore her glossy dark hair—pulled back from her face and gathered in an elaborate double-bun style—emphasized perfect cheekbones and a full-lipped mouth the damask hue of a newly opened rosebud.

Yes. No great beauty, Pearl thought, *but a woman to*

make a man look twice and dream disquieting dreams. Combine this with a Snake's supple tongue and no man, no matter how happily married, could long resist. And marital fidelity was not considered a necessity for a man.

Gentle Smoke bowed before Albert as would a highly ranked counselor before the emperor. The rest of them she offered a bewitching smile.

"Thank you for remembering me on all the feast days, especially when my granddaughter was forced by age to fail in her duties. I will gladly join in this venture—especially since an almost accidental side effect has been the awakening of my great granddaughter to her heritage."

And so assuring that you and your family will not lack for offerings in the future, Pearl thought.

When Gentle Smoke stepped back, Loyal Wind stepped forward and bowed before Albert. Pearl noticed that Loyal Wind's bow was noticeably deeper than the carefully measured courtesy Gentle Smoke had offered. His greeting to the rest was also more humble.

He is still hurting. Aware of his failures more than where he has succeeded, Pearl thought. *Good in some ways, but dangerous in others.*

"Your Imperial Majesty," Loyal Wind said to Albert, "we have met after a fashion, when you summoned me into your presence."

Albert inclined his head and graciously bowed in return. "I remember you, Loyal Wind, and thank you for the many times in these past few days you have come to our aid."

Loyal Wind looked pleased. He gestured to one side. "May I present my partner on the Wheel? This is Copper Gong, the Ram."

He motioned forward a very resolute looking woman

clad in a sunflower yellow shenyi. Copper Gong was apparently in her mid thirties, although Pearl knew she had been almost eighty when she died. Apparently, like Gentle Smoke, Copper Gong was tightly focused on that time in her life when the Exile was new, and return home her greatest desire. Unlike Gentle Smoke, Copper Gong wore her hair simply, in a tight twist, eschewing any sense of feminine delicacy.

Copper Gong offered Albert a stiff bow.

"At last our descendants are set upon reopening our way into the Lands. I must apologize that my own lineage has fallen short of expectations, and offer my own services in their place."

"Thank you," Albert said.

Bent Bamboo, the Monkey, was the last to step forward and offer his bow before the emperor. There was no trace of the counterman at the ice cream parlor now, nor did Bent Bamboo seem to be dwelling on lost youth. He presented himself as a man of mature years, some silver in his hair, but not in the least decrepit.

His bearing was very formal, but laugh lines around his mouth and eyes showed his more playful side. Pearl felt a pang of sorrow at the thought of Waking Lizard, the Monkey from the Lands, and wondered where in the journey of transition from Life into Death that brave, merry, and curiously wise old Monkey was. All their auguries had been able to tell them was that on this journey, at least, they were not likely to meet Waking Lizard.

The judges of the underworld had better be kind to you, Waking Lizard, Pearl thought fiercely. *Or I for one will be back to speak very sternly to them.*

"Now that our company is assembled," Albert said, "does anyone have any idea where we will find Yen-lo Wang?"

Gentle Smoke raised her arm and pointed with a

perfectly manicured fingernail before letting her sleeve fall modestly over her hand. "I see the gates of the palace of the Fifth Hell where Yen-lo keeps his court."

Pearl turned and looked in the direction Gentle Smoke had indicated. A rounded gateway was there, solid and yet somehow inviting passage through a thick, gently undulating wall of white masonry.

"How odd," Pearl muttered. "I could have sworn there was no gate there a moment ago, not even the wall."

Shen grinned at her. "I could have sworn that one step back—two at the most—I was standing in front of a completely average unfinished pine door set up in the middle of that little warehouse of yours. Forget it, Ming-Ming. The rules we're used to don't apply here."

Albert had been listening. Now he nodded, shifted his shoulders to settle the fall of his shenyi, and made a little shooing motion with his hands to direct each member of the company—living or ghost—to their appropriate position in his entourage.

"Aunt Pearl, you take point. Uncle Shen and Deborah, you flank me about a pace behind. Petitioners, arrange yourselves as you see fit. Let's not keep Yen-lo Wang waiting."

As Pearl led the way toward the arching gateway, its shape almost perfectly round except for the flat area at the open bottom, she considered what she knew about Yen-lo Wang.

There were many judges in the afterlife, a heritage of the varied and often contradictory tradition that the Taoists had adapted from their competitors—if not precisely rivals—the comparatively latecomer Buddhists.

This Yen-lo Wang whom they were seeking was thought by many scholars to be one and the same as

Yama of the Hindus. Indeed, the judges of the various hells were often referred to jointly as the Yama Kings.

The Orphans had chosen to make their appeal to Yen-lo Wang, rather than to one of his numerous associates, because of a tradition that held that at one time Yen-lo Wang had been the highest ranking of all the judges, until the gods had noticed that Yen-lo Wang too often took pity on his human subjects, granting the guilty lighter penalties and elevating some of the more extraordinary to posts as demi-deities within his administration.

The three from the Lands also had been familiar with this tradition regarding Yen-lo Wang, a fact which seemed promising, for sometimes the traditions of the Lands Born from Smoke and Sacrifice and those of the Land of the Burning did not overlap—a thing that had frequently distracted Shen and Righteous Drum in the course of their research. Discrepancies occurred most often regarding those strange beasts and stranger spirits who were classified under the general term "hsien" in Chinese.

Hsien, Pearl thought. *Spirits or fairies or demons or immortals, and sometimes all of these, depending on the translator and his or her cultural bias. Sometimes, from the way the Landers speak of them, I've had the impression that hsien are as common in the Lands as bathing suits on a summer beach. I wonder if they are more like fairies or demons?*

Pearl had reached the rounded doorway. The gates stood invitingly open, swung inward as if to point them in the right direction. Try as she might, Pearl couldn't recall if this had been the case when Gentle Smoke had first directed their attention to the gateway.

Carefully, without trying to look too suspicious of this good fortune, Pearl checked for guards or porters.

None were evident.

"That's strange," Shen said softly. "Most traditions hold that Yen-lo Wang's court will be guarded and at the very least bribes must be offered in order to gain entry."

"Maybe," Deborah said in an equally soft voice, "we'll run into the guards further in. Maybe this is just some sort of general entrance."

"Maybe," Albert agreed, but he sounded as if he expected trouble any minute.

They passed through the gate into the type of garden the Chinese loved beyond all others: a representation of Nature so stylized that it seemed more natural than the genuine article. Shrubs, trees, flowers, statuary, rocks, and even walls were all arranged to give the impression of vast space, verdant greenery, and potential surprises around every bend. Pearl's own garden was designed in a similar fashion. As she led the way along what was clearly the main walkway, she admired the artistry.

She itched to turn down this inviting path to see what lay at the end or to pause to read the short poem elegantly calligraphied on a piece of painted wood. However, Pearl was not the Tiger for nothing. She knew that the unmoving goat in the middle of a forest glade might be, in reality, the tethered bait of a trap.

So although tempted, Pearl didn't pause, didn't stray. With every measured pace, she kept alert to the possible wandering of those she led.

Everyone stayed close, however, perhaps goaded into wariness by the element that was markedly missing from the scene.

"I've seen fish," Deborah said at last. "I've seen more types of birds than I can name. There are butterflies everywhere, dragonflies, too. I heard small dogs yapping a while back. I'm sure I saw a golden-brown monkey climbing a fruit tree, but where are the people?"

"There should be gardeners at least," Shen agreed. "The human element is as natural to a Chinese garden as are flowers and decorative statuary."

They had passed through yet another undefended passageway as he spoke, and now Honey Dream, who walked a few paces behind Deborah, cried out.

"There! Over there, among the azaleas. I saw a man."

Pearl glanced in the direction Honey Dream indicated, years of training the only thing that kept her from scowling that a girl Snake might see more than a mature Tiger. Then Pearl relaxed.

The man Honey Dream had seen was indeed standing near a thicket of magnificent pink azaleas, but he was in the act of emerging from a small building neatly framed by the shrub, closing the doorway behind him.

The man was dressed as a minor court functionary, wearing a drab olive robe whose only adornments were deep borders at the sleeves. His long beard was liberally streaked with white. His headdress was black fabric shaped in a fashion that Pearl knew would tell the knowledgeable—of which she was not one—his precise place in the bureaucracy.

"Our first challenge," she murmured, and fought her inner Tiger's urge to lay her hand on Treaty's hilt and snarl.

That wouldn't help, Pearl chided herself. *Pretend you're at some government office. You wouldn't expect that pulling a gun there would speed you along—at least not in the right direction.*

The functionary startled Pearl by stepping into the path and greeting them with a perfectly meaningless, perfectly courteous smile.

"The unrecognized emperor, Albert Yu, and his associates? You are expected. Please, follow me."

The functionary turned in the direction of a wide, four-lobed opening in the wall, a door after the plum-blossom fashion. Carved stone steps made passing over the lintel easy to manage with perfect grace, even when wearing long robes.

Pearl glanced back and saw her own surprise at the official's welcome mirrored on faces living and dead. Albert inclined his head slightly.

"We mustn't keep Yen-lo Wang waiting, Tiger. Proceed."

Pearl stepped gracefully over the curved lintel of the plum blossom door, following the functionary with a measured tread. The others followed suit. There was a quickly swallowed profanity as Deborah fumbled with her skirts, but otherwise the only sounds were the staccato notes of birdsong and the slight crunching of gravel beneath their feet.

They passed along avenues lined with plum trees and stands of bamboo. Decorative beds of chrysanthemums or elaborate pots of orchids accented these taller plants. Plum blossom, orchid, bamboo, and chrysanthemum were known to the Chinese as the "gentlemen of the garden." It was certainly no coincidence that these were the same plants most often represented on the "flower and season" tiles of a mah-jong set.

We haven't had time to teach the apprentices so many of the finer workings, Pearl thought. *We have had so little time to prepare. Crisis to crisis, besieged on all sides.*

She smiled ruefully to herself as she stepped after the functionary through yet another plum blossom door.

Or we had nearly a hundred years in which to prepare, and are now paying for our procrastination.

After they passed through this second door, more humans began to take their rightful place in the landscape. Courtiers in brilliant and complex robes that

Pearl was certain would have set Des to muttering about anachronisms. Sages in simple attire, gathered in quiet discussion in a picturesque grove. Scholars seated at open-air desks, poring over long scrolls and taking notes with neatly tipped brushes.

Last, and for Pearl most important, there were soldiers, resplendent in elaborate armor, each of whom glanced at the functionary, read messages in the deep borders of his olive green sleeves, and then let their company pass without challenge.

Other than the guards, none of the humans gave their company more than passing notice. They did not ignore them, only politely averted their gaze from improper interest in another's business.

The functionary led the way up a rise from which a palace was now visible. The palace was nestled into a hollow of a south-facing hill that overlooked an almost perfectly oval lake upon whose dark blue waters pleasure barges sported. The light laughter of women and sounds of lutes, flutes, and the higher see-saw notes of the two-stringed violin were carried to their ears by a sportive breeze.

When they had all mounted to this vantage, the functionary paused to allow them a moment to admire the perfection of the landscaping, then set off along a road that rounded the lake and led toward the palace.

The palace possessed many doors and open windows, some screened with beautifully carved lattices. The building was topped with curved pagoda-style roofs built from blue-green tile that contrasted nicely with the pale beige of the exterior walls and the red accents painted around the doors and windows. The roof tiles rose in pleasing asymmetry, as if the wavelets on the lake below had taken on solid form and risen to crown the building.

The sense that the palace might have as easily been at the bottom of the sea was enhanced by the carp and dragons set along the cornices—an old charm against earthquakes, for everyone knows that earthquakes come from the motion of dragons, and it is hoped that the dragon will mistake the carvings for her children, and therefore avoid harming the building by impetuous motion.

"If this is hell," Albert muttered, "I might just be ready to die."

"Afterlife," Shen corrected softly, "and I'm astonished. From my studies, I had expected Yen-lo Wang's court to be less a place of leisure, more formal, more austere."

If the functionary in the olive green robes heard this, he did not react. He led them up a broad path toward the largest of the curve-topped doors.

Their shoes no longer crunched on gravel, but tapped against slightly roughened marble tile laid in intricate patterns and etched with auspicious signs and symbols.

Auspicious for whom? Pearl wondered. *The judge or the to-be-judged?*

Within the palace the air breathed the pleasant coolness that reminds one that one has been out beneath the sun. Liveried servants hurried forward, offering them iced drinks and moist towels with which to wipe their faces.

Pearl accepted a towel gladly, but—remembering both the Greeks' Persephone and Chinese tales about fishermen who dined in the dragon king's palace beneath the ocean, only to return home to find that, like Rip Van Winkle, time had passed them by—she only mimed sipping from the thin golden goblet.

Glancing at her living companions, she saw that they were following suit, but that the five ghosts were drinking deeply.

After all, she thought, *what do they have to lose?*

When he saw they were all refreshed, the functionary in the olive-drab robe motioned for them to follow him once more.

"This way," he said politely, indicating wide double doors at the far end of the entry chamber. "Yen-lo Wang awaits you."

This time the functionary stepped to one side and let them pass through unescorted.

Pearl drew in a deep breath, adjusted her already perfect posture, and walked through the door.

As she entered the room the murmur of voices and scratching of pens stilled, so that the people within seemed a part of the ornate furnishings.

The audience chamber was vast, the floor tiled in enormous squares of a highly polished golden-brown stone. A wainscot of contrasting ice-blue bricks, bordered at the chair rail level in dark mahogany, provided a contrast. Above the rail the walls were painted a warm umber. From a red screen accented in blue, cream, and bronze hung banners embroidered with clouds and dragons.

Pearl had the impression the chamber had been very busy a moment before, but now clerks and ministers, flunkies and scribes raised hundreds of pairs of eyes to study the new arrivals. Chief among those who turned a critical gaze upon them was the one they had come to see: Yen-lo Wang, King of the Fifth Hell, judge of the dead.

Yen-lo Wang sat in a chair upon a raised dais set in the center of the back third of the room. At least Pearl assumed he sat on some sort of chair or throne. His robes, styled like those of an emperor, many-layered and elaborate, hid his seat and most of the dais as well. On his head he wore an elaborate headdress that Pearl thought was a crown of some sort, one that left his face—adorned with a neat goatee and long but nicely barbered mustache—open to view.

Pearl was glad. She'd never much liked the square-brimmed headdress with its curtains of pearls or tiny gemstones front and back that emperors were shown wearing in so many of the old paintings. Those curtains were meant to shield the eyes of the Son of Heaven from seeing anything ugly, but in Pearl's less than humble opinion, the more ugliness rulers saw, the more prepared they would be for the responsibilities of rulership.

When they had all entered the room, Albert spoke softly: "Time for me to earn my keep, Pearl," and stepped around her to take the lead.

Albert knelt and performed the kowtow, touching his forehead lightly against the polished surface of the floor nine times—the highly formal three times three kowtow. Honey Dream had offered the argument that since an emperor technically outranked a king—even a king of hell—Albert was offering a terrific show of humility by kowtowing at all and only need offer three touches, but Albert had overruled her.

"I haven't ever seen a situation where you get in trouble for being *too* polite," he'd said. "This is a king whose help we're seeking, and neither I nor my ancestors ever were emperors in fact, only in theory."

When Yen-lo Wang motioned for Albert to rise, Albert did so with admirable grace, demonstrating that although he spent most of his time selling expensive chocolates, he hadn't forgotten his physical training.

Albert then spoke traditional greetings in appropriately flowery cadences. Pearl found herself impressed.

Albert has taken his role so seriously, she thought proudly. *Maybe we're lucky the Exile extended until he could represent us rather than his father or grandfather.*

At Yen-lo Wang's request, Albert presented his entourage and the six supplicants. The kowtow proved a challenge for stout Deborah. Shen's stiff old knees didn't like all that bending and groveling much either. Pearl did her best not to act smug as she went through the motions without even a popping knee joint.

For the ghosts and for young and supple Honey Dream none of these formalities offered any problems. The grace and exactitude of their obeisances did much to erase any bad impression that might have been left by the more awkward members of the company.

Yen-lo Wang surveyed them all thoughtfully, then spoke. "You come to me with a request."

Albert inclined his head in acknowledgment. "We do, Yen-lo Wang. We ask that these five who have entered your keeping be permitted to return to the state of the living, so that they may again take upon themselves their affiliation to the Earthly Branches they once embodied. This will enable the Ninth Gate between the Lands Born from Smoke and Sacrifice and the Land of the Burning to be opened so that three who were barred from their homeland may return."

"This is all you desire from me?"

"Yes, great Yen-lo Wang."

Yen-lo Wang asked more questions, which Albert answered adroitly, always emphasizing the dead's need to carry out a vow they had taken when alive. He carefully avoided the question of whether the Exiles were perhaps violating an earlier vow by trying to return to the Lands, even after death. To Pearl's surprise Yen-lo Wang himself never raised the matter.

Instead, the judge of the Fifth Hell turned his attention to the six supplicants. First he asked Honey Dream how she, Righteous Drum, and Flying Claw had come to be barred from their homeland. Pearl knew Yen-lo Wang had to be perfectly aware of the situation, but guessed he was seeing what spin Honey Dream would put on the matter.

The young Snake spoke well, with none of the flashes of temper she often demonstrated when her personal desires were involved.

After questioning Honey Dream, Yen-lo Wang cross-examined the five ghosts. Copper Gong, the Ram, was passionate about her desire to fulfill her own ancient vow of finding a way to have the Exile legally remitted. The other four, although less fervent, spoke of duty and responsibility.

At last, Yen-lo Wang leaned back in his throne and motioned that they were to all wait while he deliberated. Once or twice he held out a hand and a clerk ran forward with a transcript of the spoken testimony. Other times he requested a particular scroll of the teaching of some philosopher or called a clerk to brief him regarding a case that might offer precedent.

Pearl schooled herself to the waiting stillness she had learned long ago as an actress, when rehearsals—especially once she graduated to film—seemed to consist mostly of waiting while some light or camera was joggled into place. She caught Deborah glancing longingly at the chairs neatly arrayed behind the table where underclerks busily wrote up heavens knew what complicated assessment of the situation, but the Pig did not move from her stance. Shen had slumped slightly, but as his expression was thoughtful and intent, this might have been as much because he was distracted as because he was tired.

When Yen-lo Wang at last addressed them, Pearl nearly jumped, then mentally chided herself for permitting herself to be caught off guard.

"I will grant your request," Yen-lo Wang said without preamble. "There are precedents, and the need is great. Indeed, as the Ninth Gate cannot be opened except by the entirety of the Thirteen Orphans, and so many of the Thirteen Orphans have fallen away from their training and thus would not be available to participate, one might say the participation of those who are now my subjects is vital if this goal is to be achieved within the lifetimes of Honey Dream and her associates. However, my granting of the ghosts' liberty will extend only for as long as is necessary, no longer."

"Thank you, your August Majesty," Albert said, not bothering to conceal his relief. Pearl, who knew Albert well, saw something else beneath the relief, a touch of confusion or surprise.

That expression vanished almost as soon as she noticed it, but she thought Yen-lo Wang had noted it as well.

Effusive and appropriate thanks were offered on all sides. Then the olive-drab-clad functionary stepped from the crowd of his fellows to lead them from the palace.

He guided them through the gardens as well, coming at last to the gate through which they had entered Yen-lo Wang's precincts. There, a short distance away, stood their pine door, both prosaic and extraordinary as it stood alone amid a swirl of mist.

When Albert turned to thank the functionary, the man had vanished.

"I think it's time to go," Albert said.

When they were all—ghosts included—back in the warehouse, Pearl turned to Albert.

"Yen-lo Wang asked a tremendous number of questions, but even so, that went too easily. He didn't even ask for a particular gift or sacrifice in return for permitting the ghosts to be re-embodied."

No one disagreed.

"I noticed," Albert said. "The great judge of the Fifth Hell seemed worried. In turn, that makes me very, very worried indeed."

VIII

Yen-lo Wang's granting permission for the five dead to re-enter the world of the living launched a new stage in their preparations.

Over the next several days, Brenda grew accustomed to the sound of chanting and the scent of incense coming from Pearl's office where the re-embodiment of each of the five ghosts was taking place at a rate of one per day.

Sounds and smells were about all Brenda got out of it, because, since she wasn't the Rat, there wasn't really a role for her in the various rituals. Even Gaheris Morris showed up, since the Rat is Ox's partner on the zodiac wheel and stands in opposition to the Horse.

Not being needed for the rituals didn't mean Brenda wasn't busy. Early every morning, she joined whoever was going over to Colm Lodge for physical training. Later in the day, she'd either make an amulet bracelet or work with Des on some aspect of her magical training. Often she did both, since Des, as the Rooster, was only needed for one of the re-embodiment rituals—that of his partner the Monkey—and with two Dragons in their company, Des's knowledge of magical lore was not as much in demand.

There were always routine chores that had to be done: meals to be prepared, runs to the grocery store, shuttling people back and forth between Colm Lodge and Pearl's house, and dozens of other tasks. Brenda threw herself into these, often in the company of Nissa or Riprap.

Due to a quirk in which families had remained faithful and which had fallen away, the three apprentices were rarely needed for the rituals. Their partners on the wheel—the Tiger and the Pig—were both more magically sophisticated and were better choices to stand in for the Houses of Expansion and Family when needed. Their opposites—the Rooster and the Dragon— were not among those who needed to be reincarnated.

"Reincarnation," Brenda said to Nissa one afternoon when they were coming back from a trip to the grocery store, "isn't quite the right word for what we're doing, is it? More like re-embodiment."

Nissa swiveled from where she'd been leaning into the backseat so that she could retrieve Lani's new favorite toy—a plush bunny wearing a many-pocketed vest, a gift from Gaheris Morris—from where her daughter had dropped it on the floor.

"Re-embodiment," Nissa agreed. "I'm glad we're almost done. Even with Colm Lodge to hold the overflow, there are five more mouths to feed, five more odd people to explain. Pearl's already stretching the truth with the answers she's given to Dr. Pike so that he can disseminate them to the various members of the indigenous magical traditions who remain overly curious about our business."

"Nosey," Brenda agreed, thinking of Franklin Deng and Tracy Frye.

"And Pearl and Albert are stretching their bank accounts to feed and clothe everyone," Brenda added, with what she immediately knew everyone would say was a Rattish concern for money.

"But the rejoining," Nissa said, bending and retrieving

the toy—"Next time, Vesty-Bunny stays on the floor, Lani—of the 'ghosts' with the various branches is working."

Brenda heard an implied question in Nissa's inflection, and answered. "That's what Dad says. Since the Ox is partnered with the Rat, he could sense the switch—especially since he was 'listening' for it."

"Tomorrow," Nissa said, "they'll be done. Bent Bamboo, the Monkey, is the last. After that, we go through the Nine Gates and it's over."

Or is it? Brenda thought, knowing Nissa was talking confidently to ease apprehensions they all had. Returning the three to the Lands Born from Smoke and Sacrifice wouldn't do much good if their enemies were still in power—enemies who had already shown themselves to be willing to cross the guardian domains to go after what they wanted.

Aloud, Brenda said, "Where is Lani staying while we're away?"

"Joanne is having a singing and dancing workshop," Nissa said, "and she says Lani can stay with her if we're—uh—late getting back. Lani's looking forward to going to Joanne's, aren't you?"

In the rearview mirror of the car, Brenda caught a glimpse of Lani looking preternaturally serious for a moment, before brightening her face into a smile.

"I'm gonna have fun!" Lani said. "We're gon' learn a frog-hop dance. An' eat cake an' hotdogs."

Lani's being brave, Brenda thought. *She knows something's up, and she's pretending she doesn't. What if something happens to us? What if we don't come back?*

Luckily, they were now at Pearl's house. Threading the car through the tightly packed, narrow streets provided sufficient distraction and grounding in a reality that did not involve re-embodied ghosts and mystical realms that Brenda could manage to put her fears from her.

But the next morning, when her alarm clock went off at the beginning of the Double Hour of the Dragon—that is, seven in the morning—the nervousness was back.

No one except for Gaheris Morris had argued that Brenda shouldn't be part of their company through the Nine Gates. Brenda had been glad that her dad cared about her safety, but equally glad that he didn't win out.

"Brenda is part of our company," Righteous Drum had insisted. "She was the one who rescued me, and among those who fought along the Tiger's Road. The guardians of the four directions consider themselves in her debt and the Nine Yellow Springs sing her praises."

"And," Honey Dream had added with a slight return of her former waspishness toward Brenda, "Brenda is weird. She breaks the rules without knowing she's doing so. We might need that peculiar flexibility."

So Brenda rose and headed for the shower. She and Nissa had worked out a schedule the night before. Nissa was already up, dressed, and gone, driving Lani to Joanne's.

Brenda was standing head down, plaiting her hair into a single, heavy braid, accented with a purple ribbon, when there was a soft rap at her bedroom door.

"I'm decent!" she called.

The door swung open, and Des came in carrying a small bundle of black fabric.

"I have a present for you," he said. "Actually, from me and Flying Claw."

Brenda straightened. "What?"

"I'd noticed," Des said, "that you seemed to feel

rather underdressed during our last venture beyond the gates."

Brenda, who had indeed felt that jeans and a shirt, while sturdy and comfortable, didn't quite fit in when just about everyone else was wearing an embroidered shenyi, had to agree.

"After I was delegated the job of getting ceremonial wear for Nissa and Riprap," Des said, referring to a discussion that had occurred soon after the Tiger's Road venture, "Flying Claw came to me. He said he thought you deserved something, too. I agreed."

Brenda's gaze stole over to the neatly folded bundle; she couldn't get the slightest hint about what it contained except that much of it was black. That made sense. Black was the Rat's color.

Des was going on, "As you must have noticed by now, the ceremonial costume traditionally worn by the Thirteen Orphans is the shenyi, which dates back at least to the Ch'in dynasty. When I went to measure Riprap for his shenyi, he pitched a fit, said he'd be no use to anyone if he had to wear long skirts—that he didn't even wear a bathrobe that came lower than the middle of his calf. After putting him in a robe—even finding one his size was a challenge—I had to agree. I spoke with Shen and Albert, and we decided that training Riprap to walk in skirts could wait. I was given permission to modify the costume."

Brenda thought she could guess where this was heading, and didn't know whether she felt insulted or relieved. In the end, she decided on relieved. She had worn long skirts to a couple of proms and to her graduation, but that didn't exactly qualify her as graceful or at ease.

Still, a single word squeezed out, "Nissa?"

"I tested her, and she qualified for a shenyi," Des said. "However, I had to argue Deborah into wearing hers. Once she learned Riprap was going to get a trouser suit, Deborah had lots of reasons why she needed one, too."

"But you talked her around?"

"Pearl did. Deborah has had her shenyi for years, and charms have a way of accumulating power over time. That tipped the balance, but you might have noticed Deborah's been wearing her shenyi a few hours every day, just to get used to it."

Brenda had, but had dismissed it, figuring that the Pig was simply helping out with some aspect of the many arcane rituals that had filled the last several days.

Brenda accepted the bundle, not hiding her eagerness.

"So this is my 'trouser suit'?"

"Unfold it," Des said, with pardonable pride. "I swiped a pair of your jeans and one of your more tailored shirts so the seamstress could use them to estimate your size. The outfit isn't skin-tight by any means, but I think . . ."

Brenda let the comfortable flow of his words, discussing fabric, sizing, the question of precisely how long to make the tunic, go by without comment.

Black proved to be the color of only the trousers—and only of the upper part to the knees at that. Below the knees, the fabric was divided in equal bands of what Brenda now knew were the remaining significant colors: green, red, white, and yellow—this last more closely a shimmering gold. Each band was of equal size, and divided by a slim border of black like the border between panes of a stained glass window.

The tunic was an orchestral celebration of the five colors, the pieces fitted together in what Brenda knew were significant patterns. There was a billowing white cloud she knew represented luck, and an elaborate scarlet chrysanthemum she remembered indicated a wish for a long life. There were others, smaller, that she couldn't immediately recognize, but suspected invoked similar blessings.

After all, Brenda thought, fingering the soft, satiny fabric reverently, *of the five blessings, luck and longevity are going to matter a lot more than prosperity, happiness, and wealth. On the other hand, maybe happiness would be a good thing.*

"You had this made?" she said, looking at the elaborate garment and remembering something in the flow of Des's words.

"That's right. Friend of mine. Does costume work. She's absolutely brilliant—and fast. Has to be, what with the first dress rehearsal usually leading to half the costumes on some productions being torn apart and reworked because they look lousy from the floor. Want to try it on?"

"You bet!"

Des moved as if to go out the door, then paused. "I forgot to show you Flying Claw's contribution. Look at the end of each sleeve and the cuffs of the trousers."

"You mean that little green leaf?" she said after a moment's inspection.

"That's it." Des grinned. "He says it's a variation on the bamboo—a charm for longevity, especially geared for clothing. It doesn't make it invulnerable or anything. Think of it as magical spray that helps the fabric resist stains and snags. Apparently Tigers are pretty hard on their clothes."

Des slipped out the door on that line, and Brenda was left staring at the delicately embroidered leaf.

"Great," she said to the empty air. "Apparently, my friends not only think I'm too clumsy to get along in a skirt, but a slob who'll tear up my clothes as well."

Still, she felt quite happy as she pulled off her jeans and tee shirt, and donned the new clothing. Both top and bottom fit wonderfully. Des's friend had apparently followed the traditional form of the loose trousers and tunic, but hadn't felt she needed to do so slavishly. Unlike the clothing shown in many pictures Brenda had seen from the years when the California gold rush had brought large numbers of Chinese into the United States, neither tunic nor trousers were baggy. They weren't form-fitting by any stretch of the imagination, but she didn't feel as if she was wearing a satin flour sack either.

As a final touch, Brenda coiled her braid into a loose knot at the back of her head, and hung at her waist the carved stone frog charm Des had given her before their first venture into the guardian domains.

First, she thought. *This makes the third—or is it fourth?—trip. Whatever, I'm certainly not ready to take it all for granted.*

☆

Reunited with the Horse.

Loyal Wind closed his eyes and shivered with delight. One of the Orphans had told him that in a legend from one of the cultures of the Land of the Burning, the Horse was said to be the wind condensed into living form. Loyal Wind thought that image was nicely poetic, but every right-thinking person knew that the Horse was an embodiment of Fire.

Loyal Wind burned with that fire now, and until it had been restored to him, he had not realized how much he had longed for its warmth.

Now, as the Horse, he carried Flying Claw, the young Tiger of the Lands, ahead of the rest, scouting the location of each of the Nine Gates, making certain that there were no difficulties.

Since eight of the nine gates had been created as a gift by the rulers of the guardian domains, no trouble was expected.

But we did not expect Thundering Heaven to turn against us, and the question of where that strange sword of his came from remains unanswered. And if that is disquieting, even more so is the sense that there are questions we lack even the information to ask.

The gates were not difficult to locate. Flying Claw's "brother Tiger," the great White Tiger of the West, Pai Hu, had given a small blessing to the two Tigers in their company. Both Pearl Bright and Flying Claw could feel the direction of the next gate as soon as they passed into the appropriate section of the guardian domains. Pearl was guiding the larger part of the group, letting her restless younger counterpart range ahead.

That main group was indeed large, for in addition to the Thirteen Orphans it included Honey Dream, Thorn, Shackles, and Twentyseven-Ten.

These last three were uneasy allies, as Loyal Wind saw matters, but he had reviewed the treaties that bound them to service, and thought they would remain faithful to the letter of these documents. He would remain watchful to assure they remained faithful to the spirit as well.

The guardians had not set the gates side by side. In most cases they had even gone to some trouble to conceal them from casual detection. In a few cases—as when the Vermillion Bird of the South set the Second Gate high on a cliff face—reaching the gate offered some difficulty.

Initially, Loyal Wind wondered if this challenge had been intentional, or if the Vermillion Bird had not considered the near impossibility of mere humans reaching a gate set within a sheer rock wall. When they found that the Dark Warrior had placed the Fourth Gate on an island in the middle of a deep, still lake, Loyal Wind ceased to wonder. The four guardians remained edgy.

The challenges increased in difficulty the farther they progressed, and Loyal Wind knew he himself should be more nervous, but the dual joys of being permitted to once again cross into the land of the living, and of being reunited with the Horse made him feel as if he had joined the Eight Immortals in one of their unending drinking bouts, experiencing all the delights of wine without the complication of a hangover.

After many hours of travel, they reached the Ninth Gate. This was set in the domain of Ch'ing Lung, the Azure Dragon of the East, and Ch'ing Lung had made certain that not even the most clever of his denizens would interfere with it.

As the Tiger is the lord of all the land animals, so the Dragon is the lord of the waters. Yet the element specifically associated with the direction east is wood.

"It's where?" asked Shen Kung, hurrying up to join them, the other Dragon, Righteous Drum, only a pace behind.

"There," Flying Claw said, pointing into the depths of a lake. "Loyal Wind and I circled the lake several times so I could triangulate. At first I thought the gate was on the other side of the lake, but it's there, in the depths, in the midst of that clump of trees."

"Trees?" Des Lee said. "Don't you mean seaweed or kelp or something?"

"Take a look," Flying Claw said. "It looks like a forest to me."

"You're right," the Rooster said. "Trees. Deciduous mostly, with a tasteful scattering of evergreens."

Loyal Wind had shifted back into his human form after their scouting was concluded. Now he offered his own observations.

"We have seen nothing move there, not even the trees."

"Like they're frozen?" Brenda Morris asked.

"Like that," Flying Claw agreed.

"So," said Pearl, her hand resting lightly on the hilt of her sword, "it's not like we have monsters to fight."

"No," Nissa Nita said, shivering a little like a frightened rabbit, "we just have to figure out how to get down there without drowning."

"Easy enough," Brenda said. She turned to Shen Kung and Righteous Drum. "We can do what we did before. I mean, Dragons can extend the ability to breathe water to those they carry—and this time we won't be doing anything that should exhaust anyone."

Righteous Drum nodded. "An elegant solution, and precisely the one I suspect Ch'ing Lung expected us to employ."

"Wait," Pearl Bright said. "Before we start ferrying ourselves down there, there's something that needs to be done. If we are to be able to cross into the Lands— that is, if we need to—the Exile must be rescinded. Even if we aren't needed there—and I for one hope we will not be—then the Exile still must be rescinded so that the original Thirteen will be free to return to the Lands."

Honey Dream reached into the sleeve of her shenyi and extracted an ivory scroll case.

"I have the ritual here," she said. "Gentle Smoke was a tremendous help in the design."

Standing side by side, as they were now, Loyal Wind found himself thinking how very different the two Snakes were. Honey Dream was the more impulsive, the more temperamental. By contrast, Gentle Smoke, smiling softly now at the compliment her younger associate had paid her, was practically the embodiment of the diplomatic truth that sometimes it was wisest to be overlooked until one must strike.

"I was pleased to assist," Gentle Smoke said. "My training in the laws and rites of the Lands Born from Smoke and Sacrifice is a bit outdated, perhaps, but not so much as to be useless. After the Exile, I found myself thinking what a great deal of time I had spent committing to memory what was now unnecessary information. I must say I was pleased to be proven wrong."

Honey Dream gave a quick smile of appreciation. "Far from useless. Far from."

The younger Snake resumed her authoritative manner.

"Line up," Honey Dream ordered, "in the position of your place on the zodiac wheel. Albert, you stand in the center."

The Thirteen Orphans, living and dead, did as instructed, leaving Brenda Morris, looking slightly forlorn, off to one side.

"Now," Honey Dream said, "link arms. No, don't hold hands." This to Bent Bamboo, who with a return of his more usual lasciviousness had grabbed Copper Gong's hand very firmly in his.

There was shuffling and nervous laughter as they did this, variations of height and size making for some awkward combinations. When they were all in place, Honey Dream nodded approval.

"I know this will be awkward, but without losing your current connection, extend your hands and fingers—lower arms, too, if you can manage it—toward Albert Yu. That connects him to the whole. Gentle

Smoke and I were uncertain whether his exile needed to be rescinded, since the stolen child never formally agreed to exile, but we thought we shouldn't leave that to chance. Albert, extend your arms toward the others, but don't touch anyone in particular. Now revolve slowly, so that you are not aligning yourself with any one person."

The dignified Albert Yu did so, but Loyal Wind heard him mutter, "I feel like an idiot," and Pearl Bright softly hush him.

Honey Dream now turned to her father and Flying Claw.

"We rehearsed this several times already. We read the words on the scroll together."

Three voices—two deep and masculine, one melodiously feminine—began, "As the affiliates of the Earthly Branches, legally chosen, our bonds sealed, we assert our right and our duty to rescind . . ."

Loyal Wind became aware that he was hearing something other than the stately progress of those measured words "exile accepted," "exile revoked." Something like a wind rushed in his ears, or perhaps it was the racing sound of a bonfire newly lit and crackling toward the heavens. Air rushed and snapped. Bonds that had been sealed around his soul, always felt, but for the sake of sanity nearly forgotten, loosened, loosened, then slipped away entirely.

Tears coursed down Loyal Wind's cheeks, blurring his vision, but he did not break the circle of linked arms to wipe them away.

Even when the ritual had been worked that enabled him to pass out of the afterlife into the world of the living, even when the Horse had come back to him, and he had ridden once again filled with the Celestial Flame, Loyal Wind had not felt such joy, such a sense of being complete in himself.

He gloried in the sensation, and through the rush of wind and fire heard three voices raised in final salutation: "Now, your long journey is ended. We welcome you home once more."

Loyal Wind let his arms drop from those of Gentle Smoke and Copper Gong. He wiped his sleeve across his eyes, mopping away the haze of tears. He saw the others—even those who had never been to the Lands, even Brenda Morris, who was not the Rat in truth, doing the same.

Typically, it was Pearl Bright, always so careful to guard her warmer emotions, who first got hold of herself.

"Well, that seems to have worked. Beautifully done, Honey Dream. Now, shall we see about getting ourselves to the bottom of the lake?"

The two Dragons took themselves off to one side where they could divest themselves of their robes and change their forms. Everyone had stored extra ch'i in anticipation of this journey, and Righteous Drum applied just a bit extra to provide himself with the means of propelling himself not too clumsily despite his missing forelimb into the waters of the lake.

"I want to be one of the first down," Riprap said. "I'm tired of being useless."

"I'll go as well," Albert Yu said. "I would like an opportunity to compose myself."

"Do we need to take our clothes off?" Riprap said, fingering the deep golden yellow trouser suit he wore.

"No need," Righteous Drum said from where he rested in the shallows. "As long as you remain in contact with us, you will stay dry."

"But at the bottom?" Riprap said doubtfully.

Shen Kung, distinguishable from Righteous Drum only by virtue of possessing all his limbs, replied, "I wouldn't be concerned. I think that Ch'ing Lung will have made provisions for breathing and other matters of physical comfort in the location of the gate. After all, he would know that we all must assemble there in order to open the gate back into the Lands."

"And if he didn't?" Riprap said, not argumentatively, but with that thoroughness Loyal Wind had come to expect of him.

"Then we shall adapt our plans," Shen said. "Come along."

But the Dragons' trust in Ch'ing Lung's forethought proved merited. The Ninth Gate was enclosed within a translucent bubble that held air and was sized to accommodate their entire party—twenty in all—without strain.

Shen and Honey Dream were busy with ink brushes, marking an elaborate zodiac wheel on the beautiful double-paneled polished mahogany door, which was the physical manifestation of the Ninth Gate.

Loyal Wind felt anticipation building, anticipation that sang in harmony with the joy that had filled him when the Exile was rescinded. Even after death, when all barriers should have been lifted, the Exile had persisted. Not one of the Exiles' ghosts could see the Lands, nor feel the offerings that Righteous Drum had assured them had continued to be offered by those whose lives and property had been preserved by the Exiles' sacrifice.

And in just a few moments . . .

Righteous Drum was deep in conversation with a spirit Loyal Wind could only faintly perceive—a chiao, also often called a marsh dragon. The chiao was similar to the traditional *lung*, but had a somewhat smaller head and neck, and possessed no horns. The colors that adorned its scales were quite spectacular: its flanks in brilliant yellow, its breast sunset red, its back striped in shades of green.

This chiao had been a particular friend of Righteous Drum in more peaceful days in the Lands, a research associate of sorts, one of those who had helped Righteous Drum and his original allies set the foundations for the bridge that had carried them from the Lands into the Land of the Burning.

Loyal Wind silently urged the others.

Hurry! Hurry! I have waited over a hundred years for this moment. Suddenly each breath is too long to wait. Why are you taking so long? The gate stands. Surely the four Guardians who created the gates would not have erred. Hurry!

His expression still troubled, Righteous Drum turned away from his conversation with the chiao and addressed the twenty people who waited.

"My friend assures me that the Ninth Gate will open. Further, he assures me that it has not been detected by our enemies."

"Father," Honey Dream said, "this is all good news. Why are you so troubled?"

"Chiao—*lung* in general—do not perceive the world quite as we do, therefore I cannot precisely say. My friend speaks of unrest within the bones of the earth itself, of disruptions within what is and what should be. I sought clarification, but all I could gather was that we should be extremely cautious. Something is very wrong."

Pearl Bright, the studied tranquility of her features giving away that she, too, was impatient to have this final ordeal ended, said softly, "But we could have guessed as much from what we learned from our newest allies." She inclined her head politely at Twentyseven-Ten, Thorn, and Shackles. "We saw things at the end of the Tiger's Road that remain unexplained. Then, too, there was Yen-lo Wang's peculiar cooperativeness, against all expectation. Here is one more confirmation."

Des Lee shifted his shoulders within his ceremonial shenyi as if loosening them for action.

"Pearl's right. Delaying won't tell us anything. Let's open the gate."

Albert Yu glanced at Righteous Drum, and only when the Dragon nodded agreement did he move to the front of the gathered group.

"We rehearsed this back at Pearl's," Albert said. "One at a time, each in order of your place on the wheel, place your hand on the appropriate mark on the door. Then take the brush, write your name, and sign within the space. Step away quickly so the next can follow. I will open the door."

"I still think . . ." Riprap began.

"No," Albert said. "We settled that earlier. Danger or not, this is my place. My ancestor alone did not agree to exile. Moreover, it's about time one of my family started acting like a leader."

Riprap shrugged, but judging from the glances he exchanged with Flying Claw, both young men were agreed that if they were attacked, their first job would be getting Albert out of the way and themselves through first.

Loyal Wind didn't disagree with their feelings. Indeed, he might have been conspiring with them, except that three would crowd the available space.

He decided instead to keep a careful eye on Twentyseven-Ten, Shackles, and Thorn, for these three were the least reliable of their company. True, they had sworn oaths, but oaths—even those magically enforced—had been broken in the past. He noticed that Brenda Morris was also watching those three, and smiled.

She'd be a good Rat someday.

Then an odd thought hit him. The Orphans had taken their affiliations with the twelve Earthly Branches with them when they had been exiled. Two parallel series of associations had developed over time. What would happen now that the Exile was about to end? Would those separate associations continue? And who would have prior claim? Those truly of the Lands or these hybrids from elsewhere?

Unease welled within Loyal Wind, but it was too late to ask questions, even if he had wanted to do so. The Houses of Construction and Expansion had made their marks. Gentle Smoke was finishing for the House of Mystery. It was his turn, as the first member of the House of Gender. He stepped up and wrote his name, then beneath it the sign for Horse.

He handed the brush to Copper Gong, stepped back and watched her quickly write her name and sign. The brush went to Bent Bamboo, then to Des Lee, to Rip-rap, and finally to Deborah Van Bergenstein. The Pig finished writing her sign, handed the ink brush to Shen Kung, who methodically began to stir the bristles in a cup of water he held ready. His gaze never left Albert Yu as the Cat strode forward.

Mien lordly, head held high, Albert Yu laid his hand on the door pulls. The inked characters flared with light. Although each had been written in black ink, now they shone with the colors associated with each of the twelve branches.

Beneath Albert's hands, the doors moved easily, so easily that Albert had to let go of one side or be inelegantly stretched between the panels. The Cat stepped gracefully to the right, and when he was wholly clear, a brilliant flash of white light lit the space.

Despite its brilliance, this light did not blind, but revealed. And seeing what it revealed, Loyal Wind shouted in shock and dismay.

Nor was his voice the only one to do so.

IX

Pearl heard someone shout.

Perhaps Pearl herself had been the one who had spoken, but what would she have said? What could anyone have said?

The vista exposed by the opening of the Ninth Gate defied the mind's ability to impose order.

Take the elements of a classic Chinese landscape painting: a placid lake, a rocky hillside, twisted trees, flowering shrubs, mountains in the background, a pagoda or little shrine to draw focus to the foreground.

Now render this landscape not in usual blue-blacks and greys of more or less diluted ink, but in the vivid colors of the natural world. Emphasis on vivid. These were ur-colors, primal and forceful: pinks that played cymbals, greens as salty as fresh tears, blues that smelled of wintergreen and orange blossom, purples that tickled your skin like fluff from a dandelion.

The painter of this scene must have been the bastard son or daughter or perhaps hermaphroditic hybrid of Salvador Dalí and M. C. Escher. Orientations were askew. Half the mountain range pointed quite correctly toward the heavens, but each distinct element of the other fifty percent seemed to be choosing its own orientation at whim: down, up, side to side, shifting just as you thought you had the hang of it.

The lake surface bulged out then retracted, a shimmering nacreous soap bubble that won't quite burst. That's probably a good thing, because there's something in that bubble, something that seemed to be trying to get out. Light glinted from razor-edged claws.

That pagoda housed something that was eating the

flowering shrub, regurgitating the petals in a confetti rainbow that scatters itself on the rocks and sticks there—but only for a moment, because the rocks they are a'rolling.

The entire scene is unfixed. It spins and twists, each moment revealing some new aspect until there is nothing left but the idea that once there was something in front of your eyes that resembled a classic Chinese ink brush painting, while what you're looking at now resembles nothing so much as a paint box that has had water, oil, and a smattering of insects (don't forget spiders, ants, and centipedes) spilled in it, and they're all walking in different directions.

Some of them are walking right toward you.

"Back!" a voice yelled, and Pearl was astonished to realize that it was her own. "Get back! Something is wrong. Somehow the guardians must have oriented the Ninth Gate incorrectly. This cannot be the Lands."

For reassurance she glanced at those from the Lands, because if they were looking at this scene as if it were old home week, then the Lands of her ancestors was a lot stranger than Pearl imagined.

But Righteous Drum, Honey Dream, and Flying Claw all looked shocked. Stunned, even—as did Twentyseven-Ten, Thorn, and Shackles.

"Keep moving away," Pearl commanded, and felt unreasonably pleased that her voice sounded something like normal.

Everyone obeyed—although no one turned their backs on that twisting, swirling vista.

The space beneath the waters that held the Ninth Gate stretched to accommodate their retreat—a good thing, for if it had not, the next arrival would certainly not have had room to join them.

A gigantic white tiger appeared in the space between the cluster of frightened and confused humans and the open Ninth Gate. He was a very large tiger, and his presence effectively blocked the chaotic vista behind him.

Normally the arrival of a gigantic white tiger in a tightly confined space would have been a reason for panic. This time, although the sight of Pai Hu, the White Tiger of the West, filled Pearl with awe and a healthy amount of terror, what she overwhelmingly felt was a wash of relief.

"I must inform you," Pai Hu said in a voice that held more of growl than purr in rumbling bass notes, "that neither I nor any of the other three guardians erred when setting up the Ninth Gate. As you requested, this gate opens into the Lands Born from Smoke and Sacrifice—as they have been transformed by the actions of those who now rule."

Silence met Pai Hu's announcement, silence broken only by the sounds of the colors blossoming and singing softly on the other side of the Ninth Gate.

Then Flying Claw said very softly, "So is our home completely gone? Are our families destroyed?"

Pai Hu twitched his ears, distracted by the strange sounds coming from the gate. "I do not know, little cousin. My realm is one of the interstitial lands—a land between and of the border, related yet distinct. I have no personal knowledge of what goes on within the Lands."

"Ah," Flying Claw said. His handsome face was stern and set, but Pearl saw the wet brilliance of involuntary tears in his dark eyes.

"Yet," Pai Hu continued, "I believe—and this is belief only—that the chaos you see through this gate is not the whole of what is within. We—my fellow guardians and I—have consulted with hsien whose dwelling places are more intimately related to the Lands. They admit that their contact to the Lands is dimmed—as if a fog has arisen—but even through that fog they sense something of the Lands they knew."

"Hsien?" Des Lee said, a note of question in his voice. "You wouldn't be referring to an entity such as Yen-lo Wang, would you, great and honored guardian of the West?"

"I might," said Hu Pai, "and do. As you and your associates have noted before, death connects all places."

"But what has happened?" Honey Dream asked, her usually melodious voice tight and shrill. "Did you choose some place where this storm rages in order to draw our attention to the changes?"

"We chose the location your father requested," Pai Hu said, the faintest note of reprimand sharpening his words. "A place where he said he had associations with a certain chiao from whom he hoped to gain knowledge."

"Great Guardian of the West," Righteous Drum said, "forgive my daughter her foolish words. I have spoken to that very chiao and from that alone she should have known the gate was set in the correct location. She is young and overwhelmed."

"For good reason," Pai Hu replied. "This is a sight to overwhelm more than youth—my fellow guardians and I are deeply concerned."

"But you didn't warn us," Gaheris Morris said sharply. "Why not?"

Pai Hu turned a level amber gaze on Gaheris, and Pearl remembered that the Tiger had no reason to love the Rat. Gaheris obviously realized he'd been completely out of line.

"I'm sorry," he said, lowering himself quickly despite his formal robes, and kowtowing to the White Tiger. "I guess Honey Dream isn't the only one who is panicked. I thought we were nearly done. I thought this was almost over and now . . . this."

"This," Pai Hu repeated, and the twitch of his whiskers gave Gaheris permission to rise. "Yes. What will you do now, Orphans and allies? Do you continue on, or do we seal the Nine Gates?"

"We go on," said Flying Claw without hesitation. Only after speaking did he look at the others. "At least I will go on—if I can figure out how one progresses through a landscape that mutates underfoot. As I see it, my responsibilities are twofold. First, I owe our allies in the Land of the Burning some idea as to whether they can expect further aggression from the Lands Born from Smoke and Sacrifice. Second, I owe those I left behind—allies and family both—what small aid I can offer."

Righteous Drum forced out a dry laugh. "Eloquent, especially for a young Tiger. I could not have put matters more clearly myself."

Honey Dream inclined her head in agreement, and moved a little closer to her father—and to Flying Claw, Pearl noted with mild amusement.

The three who had been prisoners—Twentyseven-Ten, Thorn, and Shackles—were a little slower to agree. Pearl understood why. Their loyalties must be soundly divided at this moment. They were the only survivors of a much larger force that had come after the Orphans and their allies. Initially kept as prisoners, they were given an opportunity to earn their way home if they joined in the battle on Tiger's Road. They had done so, and one of their number had died. Now these three must be wondering what would happen when they returned to the Lands. Where did their best interests lie?

Twentyseven-Ten said, "Certainly nothing but a very restricted life awaits us in the Land of the Burning.

Whatever has gone awry, through that door are the graves of our ancestors."

Thorn and Shackles nodded.

"Sure," Thorn said. "Why not? You can count on me."

"Me, too," Shackles said.

"And the rest of us," said Riprap. The big, black man looked almost angry. "Are we going to just leave them like this: 'Well, go on, have fun storming the castle,' all that stuff? I thought we'd agreed to help them?"

"We have done so," Albert said mildly, but his was the mildness of a leader who does not expect to be interrupted. "We have aided in the creation of a gate back to the Lands—something they were not able to manage for themselves."

Riprap started to speak—shout, more likely, Pearl thought—but Albert held up his hand.

Brenda cut in. "Wait. Albert, I mean, you were still, well, out of it, when Waking Lizard arrived. Soon after, Flying Claw and Honey Dream told us the bridge had been destroyed. What I'm trying to say is that you were there after we started working on the treaty, but not at first, so you can't remember that we didn't just talk about giving them sanctuary and getting them home. We decided that sitting around and waiting to be got at wasn't something any of us wanted. We pretty much promised to go after their enemies if they could use our help."

Brenda gestured almost helplessly toward the still open Ninth Gate. "And it sure looks to me as if they could use our help."

"A reckless agreement," Gaheris Morris said, "but one I agreed to, since it had been the price of my freedom. I'll keep my part of it now."

He glowered at his daughter. "But you, young lady,

whatever the rest of us do, this is the end of the road for you."

☆

Brenda stared at her father in disbelief.

"What do you mean?" she cried. "I signed that treaty, just like the rest of you."

"And I never liked that you were made to sign," Dad said firmly. "I said so at the time, but I let Auntie Pearl and Uncle Shen talk me around. They said you'd signed the first treaty, that your signing the second one was just a formality."

Gaheris Morris paused, then added a touch maliciously, "They said you made Righteous Drum nervous, and that if you didn't sign he'd likely refuse . . . as if he had a choice. But I let myself be talked around, because I was assured your participation wouldn't matter. Well, now that I see what's out there, I'm saying you're not going anywhere into that."

He waved an arm in the direction of the Ninth Gate, and found himself facing Pai Hu's unblinking amber gaze.

"Is this the time or place for a family dispute?" the White Tiger of the West said with what Brenda was certain was deceptive mildness. "The Ninth Gate is open, and decisions must be made."

Nissa, silent to this point except when she had to speak some ritual phrase, now turned to Brenda.

"Breni, Pai Hu is right." She turned the force of her startlingly turquoise eyes on Gaheris Morris. "I'm not even sure you're wrong, Gaheris, but I do think you picked a bad time to start a family quarrel."

"Would you want Lani—" Brenda's father began, but Nissa made a shooing gesture with one hand and turned her attention to the larger group.

"Pai Hu, Shen, Righteous Drum, clarify a point for me. Is this opening of the Ninth Gate a one-time deal? I had the impression that in setting up the Nine Gates we were creating the means for us to go freely—if in a somewhat roundabout fashion—between the Lands and our world. Do we need to make final decisions here and now about who goes where when?"

"Only if you wish the gate permanently sealed immediately," Pai Hu replied. "We four guardians are not reneging on our agreement with you to permit Nine Gates to be used by you—and your allies—to go between the Land of the Burning and the Lands Born from Smoke and Sacrifice. We will, however, not permit any others than this immediate group to use them—at least not without considerable consideration."

"Understood," Nissa said.

Brenda was impressed. Nissa could be so quiet, so mild, that much of the time you forgot the underlying strength of her personality, but Nissa hadn't managed to be a single mom, to keep secret just who Lani's father was, to both go to college and work, and keep up with a bunch of other activities, because she was a pushover. Nissa had started out behind Brenda and Riprap in magical training, but even with Lani as a constant distraction, she'd caught up—and in some areas, Brenda knew, she'd surpassed her classmates.

At this moment, Nissa looked much as she had on the night she'd told Pearl that unless things changed in how a young man then called Foster was treated, she was packing up and heading home to Virginia—and no one had called her bluff, because they knew it was no bluff.

Now Nissa turned to Flying Claw. "Flying Claw, are you determined to go charging into that mess?"

"Someone should scout," he said, and Brenda felt

her heart do a funny flip-flop at his lopsided grin, rueful, aware of his own impulsiveness. "I thought I would be a good choice."

"You're right," Nissa said, "but to scout—not to get yourself killed."

Bent Bamboo stepped forward.

"I've heard a great deal about how, despite having called himself a coward, my fellow Monkey, Waking Lizard, showed courage in battle. Let me rise to the mark he has set and be the first to pass through the Ninth Gate." He swung around, loose-limbed and rubber-jointed, to face the assembly of Orphans and allies. "Don't worry. I'm just going to see what it feels like over there."

There were various murmurs of agreement and a few encouraging words. Brenda looked at Flying Claw and Riprap, now standing side by side. Both were leaning slightly forward, as if they couldn't wait for their chance.

And me, she thought. *Am I really angry at Dad for protecting me? Do I really want to go into that— whatever that is?*

Pai Hu had moved to permit access to the Ninth Gate. Somehow, without making a fuss, he had become smaller and now was only the size of a really big "normal" tiger.

A normal tiger, Brenda thought, *with a sort of aura that means no one in their right mind would mistake him for anything but a god. Or spirit. Or hsien . . .*

She stilled her mental babbling, knowing it as a symptom of nervousness, and concentrated on Bent Bamboo.

The Monkey had taken out his weapon. Like Waking Lizard he preferred a staff to a sword or spear. Brenda wondered if there was something traditional about Monkeys and staffs.

Standing in front of the open Ninth Gate, he probed over the threshold with the foot of his staff.

"Feels solid," he said, "even if the 'grass' is a really interesting shade of puce. I'm going to put a foot over."

"Wait!" Riprap called, moving forward as he uncoiled a length of rope that had hung from his pack. "It may feel solid, but the way the scene keeps changing . . ."

Bent Bamboo didn't protest. Brenda guessed that Monkeys didn't have the warrior pride of Tigers or Horses.

Riprap didn't just loop the rope around Bent Bamboo's waist, but rigged a simple harness that passed over his shoulders and around his waist, his hands moving with quick efficiency.

"Learned a few things taking my Scouts rock climbing," he explained matter-of-factly. "Okay. I'm your anchor. Go for it."

Riprap stepped back a few paces. He flashed a grin of thanks when Flying Claw took up his own hold on the rope, never mind that Riprap both outweighed and outmassed the Tiger.

Don't turn down help when it's offered, Brenda thought. *Pride goeth before a tumble. Damn, I wish Dad . . .*

Brenda forced her thoughts away from her father. Bent Bamboo had stepped through the Ninth Gate. Against the screaming, shifting colors, strangely he, not the weird landscape, was what ended up looking less real.

Like someone took a cut-out from a magazine and superimposed it on a painting. Somehow the painting looks more real.

Bent Bamboo narrated every step. "It feels like moss underfoot. Wet moss, just on the dry side of squishy. Or like walking on clouds, not that I've ever done that—not like the Stone Monkey."

I've got to look that story up, Brenda thought. *Waking Lizard talked about a Stone Monkey, too. I wonder if that's the same as the Monkey King I read about.*

"There's water here," Bent Bamboo went on. "Or at least it flows like water and is in a streambed of sorts. It looks like tangerine juice."

He bent down and cupped some in his hand. Before anyone could warn him, he took a quick sip.

"Tastes like water. And, no, don't fuss at me about the risk I'll drink poison. If we're going to travel through here, we can carry food, but carrying sufficient water would be too heavy. We can always boil water before drinking. That should remove most taints. That raises another question."

Bent Bamboo walked back to the Ninth Gate. "Riprap, you have any matches? Piece of paper or kindling?"

Riprap, of course, had both. He handed a book of matches and a candle stub to Bent Bamboo.

Bent Bamboo lit a match and then the wick of the candle. Although the candle didn't change in any way, remaining—like Bent Bamboo himself—sort of photo-realistic amid surreal surroundings, the flame burned normal reddish orange only for a moment. Then it shifted and began to burn a really horrid green.

"Interesting," Righteous Drum said. "What we bring with us remains untouched—at least in the short term—but the elements become one with their environment."

"So we should be able to travel there," Des said. "I wonder, since the elements seem to belong to the Lands, if we'll be in any danger breathing the air. Will it transform us? Gradually change us into whatever that is?"

"But air," Righteous Drum reminded him sententiously, "is not an element—not in our tradition. Even so, I see your point."

"We could wear gas masks, I suppose," Des said, "carry oxygen, but in the end . . ."

Bent Bamboo had set the candle on a rock—a rock that cooperatively stayed in one place after he did so—and continued questing about, ranging farther and farther from the gate while Riprap patiently played out his safety line.

"I don't feel strange," the Monkey called back. "Or any stranger than usual. In any case, we know we're going to risk it, so why argue?"

"I agree," Loyal Wind said.

The other three former ghosts voiced their agreement as well.

Copper Gong added, "I think we 'ghosts' should be among the scouts. We are familiar with the Lands. In one sense at least, we have less to lose."

Gentle Smoke turned from where she had been studying the constantly shifting landscape. "Having resided in the afterlife for a good many years, we have another advantage as well. Shifting landscapes and places that don't make 'sense' in the usual way will not bother us nearly as much."

"Very well," Albert said. "However, I think you should take with you a few of the 'living.' There may be things you are vulnerable to that we would not be."

"I'll go," Riprap cut in rapidly. "I may not be the hottest when it comes to magic, but I can take amulet bracelets. I'm good in a fight, and I have some odd skills that might come in useful."

Flying Claw spoke up. "I will go as well."

"Why you?" Righteous Drum said sternly. "I had intended to lead this expedition."

"And I'm not leaving my father," Honey Dream said.

Unspoken was *Not with him still adjusting to having lost an arm.*

Flying Claw shook his head, and Brenda was impressed by his decisiveness. She'd seen him in battle, but never really as a commander.

"No, Righteous Drum," Flying Claw said. "We are forming a scouting party. Already our numbers are sufficient to draw unwelcome attention. Remain in the Land of the Burning until we bring back information. Prepare magics against our probable need to go into battle."

Albert said mildly, "Righteous Drum, Flying Claw does have a point. I'm certain we could all argue why we need to go along, but probably a smaller group will have a better chance of success."

"Flying Claw speaks wisely," Righteous Drum agreed with a sigh. "Very well."

Twentyseven-Ten spoke, his tone of voice so polite that it managed to be insulting. "And so my comrades and I will be kept from the Lands even longer? I thought that the entire reason for taking us on this journey was because we were going home at last."

"Circumstances have turned out," Albert said, gesturing toward the swirling landscape on the other side of the Ninth Gate, "rather differently than we intended."

Pearl added, her words a silky snarl, "Consider that we are doing you a kindness, my young friend. If the scouting group encounters your former associates, you might find your loyalties strained in dangerous directions. Best that others scout first, so you will be protected from undue influences."

Twentyseven-Ten—so like Flying Claw in some elements of appearance and bearing, but coarsened, like a photo run through a low resolution scanner—narrowed his eyes with unspoken resentment, then nodded.

"Very well," he said stiffly, "but don't forget that our alliance with you was based upon the promise that we could return home."

Pearl looked at him, and Brenda shivered a little at the naked contempt in the Tiger's eyes.

"Fine. Just let me know when you want to return to being a prisoner. I'd be happy to arrange it—and this time the cells might not be so comfortable."

X

A group of seven was still large enough to be quite noticeable, and the ghosts immediately took steps to make their number less obvious. Loyal Wind changed himself into a chestnut horse that closely resembled his "deceased" magical companion, Proud Gamble. Nine Ducks took on her strong, solid ox form.

"We shall serve as mounts," Loyal Wind said to Flying Claw and Riprap.

Riprap grinned. "Okay. I'll go with that. Flying Claw, you've ridden on Loyal Wind before. If Ms. Nine Ducks doesn't mind my weight . . ."

"A feather," the Ox replied, "but you might find my spine rather sharp. Do you have a blanket in that pack of yours?"

They worked out a makeshift saddle and Riprap hoisted himself astride.

Gentle Smoke, the Snake, said, "If I shift my form, I can ride on one of your arms or perhaps around your neck."

Riprap shrugged. "Sure enough, ma'am. I'm not queasy about snakes, and seems to me I might need telling about what's what here. This is a very strange place indeed."

"Strange for me, too," Flying Claw assured him. "Copper Gong, would you care to ride behind me?"

The Ram shook her head. "No. I think I would prefer that none of us are too heavily burdened. If I take my animal form, and Bent Bamboo his, then I will be able to carry him."

Bent Bamboo chortled. Loyal Wind thought the Monkey was about to say something lewd, but perhaps remembering that even female Rams have horns—and quite solid horns at that—Bent Bamboo politely excused himself. When he returned, his shape was that of a long-armed, squat-bodied monkey, with a tail so short as to be almost nonexistent. He carried his clothing in his arms.

Conversation was minimal as they traveled, for adjusting to the peculiarities of their constantly changing surroundings took all their attention.

Flying Claw was taking the journey seriously. Repeatedly as they moved on, he took an elaborate compass similar to those used for feng shui readings from his pack and noted their progress on a makeshift map. After they had hiked for a few hours in more or less a straight line, he asked them to halt while he took another reading.

"At last," Flying Claw said, relief lighting his face, "I have located Center."

"Center is important," Riprap said, showing something of a student's eagerness to display his knowledge. "Des told us that the ideogram for China is the same as that for Center. Did you expect not to find Center?"

Flying Claw gestured at the chaotic, shifting landscape that still surrounded them.

"I had tried several times and failed. I was beginning to wonder if somehow it was gone. Removal of the center, the hub on which the other four directions turn, seemed quite possible given all of these other changes."

"Center," Copper Gong said, lipping idly at a bit of rust-purple grass. "The location of the Jade Petal throne, the prize of a hundred, even a thousand battles. Should we head there or avoid it? If our enemies survive, that is likely to be their base."

"Eventually," Flying Claw said, sliding his compass into a forest green brocade drawstring bag before putting it in its case, "we may need to go to the Center. However, I agree with Copper Gong that it is unlikely to be a safe location for us. I would prefer to scout the fringes, see if we can learn anything from the inhabitants, and then spiral in when we know more."

"Inhabitants," lisped Gentle Smoke from where she hung in her snake form about Riprap's neck and shoulders. "We have seen none living thus far."

☆

After their return from the Ninth Gate, despite all the persuasion Pearl and Shen had turned on him, Gaheris Morris had kept to his threat to take Brenda away. He must have pulled some strings—or miracle of miracles, paid full price for two plane tickets—and by the next day he and Brenda were gone.

The day following the Morrises' departure, the scouting party returned. Their report was not encouraging. They had found no humans. Those few hsien they met couldn't tell them anything about how and why the Lands had been so tremendously altered.

"We're going to need to go back," Riprap said firmly, "and penetrate more deeply, see what we can learn."

There had been considerable discussion about this and how best such a search could be conducted. In the end, the group of seven had been augmented by one. Des Lee had all but begged to go along.

"They'll need magical support," Des began.

"What about the former ghosts?" Pearl said, rather more sharply than she had intended. "They have magic."

"Do they?" Des countered. "I've talked to them. Internal abilities, like shifting shape, still seem to work, but Nine Ducks told me that she has found storing ch'i for later use more difficult. She hopes it's simply that she's out of practice."

"Why you?" Pearl pressed.

"Face it," Des said. "Righteous Drum who, as I am the first to admit, would be the logical choice, simply isn't up to the job. Too much of his magic relies on gestures he can no longer make. If he needs to rely on written charms, well, then, I'm more versatile."

Shen joined the discussion. "How about Honey Dream?"

Des glanced at the Snake. "Honey Dream has already said she won't leave her father."

Pearl thought, judging from the look that flitted across Honey Dream's face, that the young woman might be regretting that statement.

When the scouts had returned, Flying Claw had clearly been saddened—even upset—to find that Brenda had already departed. Clearly, Honey Dream would have liked to take this opportunity to renew her own pursuit of the young man, when Brenda would not be there to offer competition, but having proclaimed her filial piety so loudly, she could not without her motives seeming suspicious.

Shen nodded. "As the other Dragon, I know I'd be a logical choice, but frankly the events of these past few weeks have brought home to me that I'm simply not up to rough and tumble. I'm a good theoretician, but not a fighter."

Pearl had thought about offering to go, but hesitated. Colm Lodge and the house in the Rose Garden were her properties, their residents her responsibility. And, although her broken hand was healing nicely, it was still not ready for use.

Moreover, earlier that day she had received a very discreetly worded note from Dr. Broderick Pike. The note had indicated that some people left unnamed— but Pearl didn't doubt that Franklin Deng was one of them—had expressed concern as to the continued possible threat from the Lands. No. As much as she wanted to do so, Pearl couldn't leave now, not merely to serve as a scout—and Des really would be a good choice.

After a day to rest and gather gear, the scouting party had departed once more, promising to check in daily if at all possible.

"Although it might not be," Des had confided to Pearl. "I have a feeling that the erratic state of ch'i in the Lands is going to make direct magical communication difficult. We may need to relay messages through Righteous Drum's friend the chiao, and then impose on one of the rulers of the guardian domains."

"Pai Hu should be willing," Pearl said, "as a favor between Tigers. He has not forgotten that if we had not intervened, he would not be in a position to help anyone."

Des nodded. "That was my impression, too. I'd place a healthy bet the two events—that attack on the guardians and the current condition of the Lands— are connected."

"And that would be a bet I would decline," Pearl said, "but I cannot work out the connection."

"Well, maybe we'll learn something," Des said. "We'd better."

The day after the scouting party left, Deborah and Shen came to Pearl's office shortly after breakfast.

"If you and Albert don't mind," Deborah began, "I'd like to go home to Michigan—at least until I'm needed for something definite."

"And Umeko has been making noises," Shen said, "asking if she should consider herself widowed. We have been gone quite a while—five weeks."

Pearl nodded. After Gaheris's departure with Brenda, then the scouting party's initial, indefinite report, both she and Albert had expected something like this. Unlike Des and Riprap—both of whom held jobs that paid the rent, but didn't exactly tie them down—Deborah and Shen had homes and families.

Deborah's husband was a placid, home-loving workaholic who was probably getting along fine without Deborah, but Shen's wife had a hotter, more artistic temperament.

And it wasn't that long ago that Umeko believed Shen had suffered a stroke so severe as to alter his memory. I don't blame her for wanting him back.

Within a few days, Shen and Deborah had departed.

Albert returned to his home in San Francisco. Although he called regularly, Pearl sensed he was somewhat relieved to give at least some attention to his home life and the business of Your Chocolatier.

Honey Dream and Righteous Drum continued to reside at Colm Lodge with Twentyseven-Ten, Thorn, and Shackles. Daily workout sessions continued.

Righteous Drum was working hard at schooling his body into alternate means of casting spells. Pearl knew that he was also struggling to learn to write well enough with his remaining arm to make the ink-brushed charms that served those from the Lands as the amulet bracelets did the Orphans.

Honey Dream, aware of her father's basic defenselessness, had busied herself writing charms and spells for his use. As the days passed, she began to look thinner, a bit transparent even, and Pearl felt she must warn her to take care.

"You won't be any good to anyone if your ch'i is so depleted that you cannot cast a spell. What if the scouts were to return at this very minute, telling us the time to act is now?"

Honey Dream rubbed at her eyes with the heels of her hands. "Then I would go, as you would. But with each day that passes, I believe less this will be the case. I think we face a siege of our patience rather than a drastic emergency."

Pearl had to agree. Des had kept true to his promise to report, but as he had feared, direct magical communication was impossible.

When the scouts changed their orientation toward Center, they learned that the worst chaos was near the borders. However, this did not mean they were treading familiar terrain, only that up and down seemed willing to remain basically constant, and the most violent violations of sanity had ceased.

The scouts had met few occupants in these altered Lands, and those they did meet were largely so confused that even carrying on a conversation with them was a challenge. All those they had met had been spirits tied in one way or another to some physical feature—elemental spirits or the genus of a particular mountain or waterway.

No wonder they're confused, given that chaos has undermined the very bedrock in which they had taken root.

Even though Des's reports held little useful information, those who had remained at home all waited anxiously for them. When the Double Hour of the Tiger came, Pearl would go to her household shrine and humbly beg Pai Hu to relate if he had heard anything from the scouts.

Between scheduled reports, they felt an even greater sense of tension, for communication out of order would mean something had gone horribly wrong.

Although this uncomfortable sense of expectancy was as an extra tenant, Pearl could not believe how empty her house seemed. Nissa and Lani still provided company, thank heavens, but after the noisy group who had gathered around the long table in the family room, sharing meals, playing games when other duties permitted, there were times when those who remained seemed to rattle about.

After a week, Pearl made a decision.

"Nissa, where's Lani?"

"Wang just got here. Lani is out 'helping' him with some pruning."

"I was wondering . . ." Pearl realized she was more nervous than she had been when she went to accept Thundering Heaven's challenge. "That is . . . Please, sit down. There's something I'd like to talk to you about."

Nissa looked both astonished and somewhat uncomfortable, but nodded. "Here," she said, gesturing around the kitchen family room area, "or in your office?"

"Here's fine," Pearl said, sinking into her favorite easy chair.

Almost immediately, Amala, one of her two cats, leapt up into her lap. When Nissa took the matching chair, grey Bonaventure claimed her lap for his own.

"Nissa, I have a proposal for you," Pearl said. "I realize you've been gone from home for a while, and must be, like the others, considering how much longer you should stay."

Nissa's gaze dropped, and Pearl knew she was right.

"I had been—" Nissa began, but Pearl interrupted.

"I have a proposal for you," she repeated. "Would you consider permanent relocation to San Jose?"

Nissa blinked. Pearl raced on, eager to get her arguments in before Nissa could decline. The Nita family was clannish in the extreme, the daughters of Nikki Nita living together on a sprawling piece of land in the Blue Ridge Mountains of Virginia.

Pearl wasn't certain Nissa could pull herself away from that clan, and felt somewhat selfish for even attempting to persuade her to do so. During the three months that Nissa had been in California, the young woman had called one or the other of her sisters pretty much daily, and Pearl suspected that e-mail added details and had kept the ties that bound pretty tight.

"I've enjoyed having company in the house," Pearl said. "Real company, not just interns who stay for a few months and then move on. Oh, many of them stay in touch, but it's not the same as what I've felt since all of you came piling in last May. My brothers have children, and I suppose I could try to guilt one of them to come and stay with old auntie—especially if I hinted that inheritance might come their way—but I'd never know if a smile was for real or just in the hope of keeping the old bitch sweet."

Nissa was looking pole-axed, but Pearl surged on.

"There's one other thing. With you and Lani here, I could relax. I've had to hide the part of my life that's tied up with magic, with the affairs of the Orphans. You want Lani to know her heritage, so there would be nothing to hide."

Nissa started to say something, but Pearl held up one hand.

"Please. I know I'm being imperious, but I want

you to know that I do have things to offer you in exchange for your giving up living with your family. For one, we've all said a lot about how the Dragon and the Snake—members of the House of Mystery—are very magical signs. Less has been said about the Rabbit, but in Chinese tradition the Rabbit is the creature who pounds out the potions of immortality up there on the Moon. The Rabbit is actually a very magical sign, and I could teach you—"

This time Nissa managed to interrupt.

"Pearl! Listen."

Pearl stopped with some difficulty. She'd rehearsed her proposal as she would have a part in a play, and she hadn't even gotten to the financial and educational incentives, but there was something in Nissa's expression—part amused, part alarmed—that made Pearl stop.

"Pearl, I'm really grateful that you brought this up. Nancy and Nina have both been after me to come back in time for Lani to adjust before I need to start classes in the fall."

Pearl nodded. Nissa was studying to become a pharmacist, and had, in fact, given up the chance to take a course during the summer term to attend to the Orphans' business.

"I've been uncomfortable with how reluctant I've been to go back," Nissa went on. "I mean, I've changed over these last three months. I know that magic works. I've been places. . . . You've been out to the family land. You know what it's like. My sisters are good people—none better—but they're into all that back-to-earth stuff: organic foods, home schooling kids, natural medicines. I've never been quite as into that."

Again, Pearl nodded. Now she didn't have any trouble keeping her mouth shut. This was going far better than she had dared hope.

Nissa nervously twisted a lock of fair hair around one finger as she continued. "Nancy's beau is seriously into New Age stuff—crystals especially. He can get really pushy. I could just see myself getting fed up and telling him off, telling him he doesn't know anything, or worse, that I know better."

A wry grin lit Nissa's face. "I'm not always prudent. You may not believe it, but I've always realized that at some point I'd probably have to move. I mean, our town supports one pharmacist already, and that's all we need. The rest can be done by assistants like me. If I finish—when I finish—my degree, I would either have to continue as an assistant and hope Bob retired early, which he's not likely to do, or move.

"Then there's Lani. Right now it doesn't matter to her that she doesn't have a dad around, but she's not stupid, and some of the older kids, well, they've been saying a few things that aren't exactly kind."

Pearl could imagine. Lani was probably the result of a one-night stand—an accident that had occurred even though Nissa had been on the pill. "Pill Virgin" might be an affectionate nickname between adults, but children would make cruel comments.

"I'd like to explain to Lani in my own time, in my own way, that just because I was dumb doesn't mean I didn't want her, that I don't love her as much— maybe more—than I could any 'planned' child. She's my gift-of-God baby, and I don't want anyone to sour that. So that was another reason I'd been thinking about moving."

Pearl said hesitantly, "So you'd consider moving here? I could help with arrangements. I've done a little research into schools, and there are plenty of places where you could continue your degree. Dr. Andersen would be of help when you are ready to find a job. I have no desire to cut your feet out from under you and make you my dependent."

"Thanks. . . ." Nissa grinned, suddenly relaxed. "That's good. I wouldn't want to find myself in the place of that hypothetical niece or nephew. If Lani and I could take over the whole suite we're sharing with Brenda now—eventually, I mean—then I think we'd be very comfortable. I could use my room as a bedroom and office of sorts, and Lani would have a nice play area."

Pearl nodded. "And I was thinking that . . ."

That easily, the matter was settled between them. Pearl flat-out refused to let Nissa pay rent, pointing out that the house had been paid for long ago and that maintenance would have to be dealt with in any case.

Nissa agreed, but insisted that she would chip in for groceries and household supplies.

Pearl agreed, although she didn't feel this was at all necessary. She was quite well off, rich even, and despite her Chinese upbringing and her fondness for her brothers and their children, felt no requirement to refrain from spending what she had earned in order to leave them a considerable inheritance.

Besides, Pearl thought. *Nissa is family in a way, too. Our ancestors may have thought of themselves as Orphans, but they were very odd Orphans, with very strong bonds.*

Pearl smiled as Lani came barreling in through the back door, her hands full of newly cut roses. As she accepted her makeshift bouquet, Pearl realized she was happy, happier than she had been in a long, long time—maybe almost forever.

XI

Just over two weeks had passed since Gaheris Morris had laid down the law regarding his daughter's continued participation in matters related to the Thirteen Orphans.

Brenda had hardly spoken to her father the entire flight back to South Carolina, but when her mom met them at the Greenville/Spartanburg Airport, Brenda couldn't keep up her sulk. Keely McAnally was so clearly pleased to see her only daughter that Brenda would have felt like a complete heel to shun her.

Mother and daughter had spent a great week together, shopping to get Brenda what she'd need for her return to college, visiting the various grandparents, watching the boys play soccer and baseball, talking about everything under the sun—although Brenda had been forced to be a bit inventive about exactly what her internship with Pearl Bright had involved.

Brenda's younger brothers, Dylan and Thomas, had eventually decided they could show their big sister they were glad to see her. The water balloon fight in the backyard one hot sticky night was just about perfect.

Gaheris was often off at work. Dutifully, he reported to Brenda about the progress the scouts were making in the Lands. The news was always the same. No significant change.

She called Nissa a couple of times, but the three-hour time difference made connecting hard. Even when they could talk, there was so much they weren't allowed to talk about except in the most circumlocutious manner.

Increasingly, the summer of magic and weird wonder began to feel rather unreal.

Other than wishing she knew more about what was going on in the Lands, Brenda enjoyed her time at home. She honestly regretted when she had to go downstate and resume her life as a resident student at USC. She might have asked to transfer somewhere closer to home, but she knew it was too late in the school year, and that her parents would never agree.

Despite Gaheris's notorious penny-pinching, he had agreed with Keely that there was one place where cutting corners was not in order. Although USC's upstate campus at Greenville/Spartanburg would have been close enough to home for Brenda to commute, both her parents had wanted Brenda to have the whole college experience. That included sharing dorm rooms with strangers and not having her parents quite near enough to solve all her problems for her.

Gaheris did complain that cell phones made it far easier than it had been in his day for a college student to run to Mom or Dad for help. He probably would have cut Brenda's cell phone contract if he hadn't gotten a better deal on it than he could have gotten for a land line in her room.

Teaching me to be independent, Brenda thought a trace ruefully as she strapped tape onto the boxes she was taking with her. *Dad couldn't have had the least idea just how much this summer was going to force me to learn to think for myself.*

Despite being a bit sad when they unloaded the last box, took her out to an early dinner, then hopped in the van for the drive home without her, Brenda couldn't help but feel a sense of anticipation at being back at USC.

Brenda had enjoyed her first year on campus. Her

preassigned roommate hadn't been too much of a horror—a bit more of a party girl than Brenda was, but they got on well enough. This year, Brenda was going to room with Shannon, the best of her new college friends. They'd corresponded over the summer via e-mail, with Brenda giving Shannon the highly edited version of her internship.

Lately, she'd talked about the pretend internship so much that it was beginning to seem almost as real as what she'd been through. Only the amulet bracelets—one for Dragon's Tail, one for Dragon's Breath—that she wore on each wrist provided a constant reminder of how real it all had been.

Shannon wasn't in their shared room when Brenda returned after dinner with her folks.

Not quite in the mood to seek company, Brenda put the leftovers from dinner into the little fridge, then set about unpacking her most necessary clothing. She'd just finished stacking her panties when she heard a key rattling in the lock.

Turning, Brenda saw Shannon coming in, accompanied by a very tall, carrot-haired, freckled young man. They were giggling and speaking in clumsy Gaelic.

Brenda had met Shannon at a club devoted to things Irish: the Gaelic language, folk dancing, history, literature, and even less serious things like food and (very under the table, since technically only the seniors and the graduate students could legally imbibe alcoholic beverages) drink.

They'd ended up sitting next to each other during a reading from Synge's *Playboy of the Western World*, stifling giggles since half the people seemed determined to read in what they fancied was an Irish brogue, while the other half stuck to their own—largely Southern accented—modern American English. By the end of the "performance," although they hadn't shared a word, they were well on the way to being fast friends.

Neither of them exactly knew what they wanted to major in, and that had helped, too, since they found themselves taking mostly the same required general courses. Then their shared fondness for fantasy fiction—and some science fiction, too—had cemented the bond.

So Brenda wasn't surprised that Shannon's male companion looked as Irish as only an Irish American could. Shannon's crushes always ran that way, and usually lasted until her male companion learned Shannon was as serious about her Irish Catholicism as they wished she was not.

"This is Dermott," Shannon said with a wave of her hand. "I met him at church this summer and told him all about the club."

Promising, promising, Brenda thought, offering Dermott her hand, and seeing his mild look of surprise that Shannon's friend from the Celtic Culture Club looked not in the least Irish.

"And this," Shannon said, motioning to someone Brenda hadn't seen because he was standing behind Dermott, "is a new transfer student. Dr. McGee asked if I could pick him up from the airport. He's from Ireland."

Brenda could have guessed this from the combination of "transfer student" and "Dr. McGee" since the latter was the sponsor of the Celtic Culture Club.

The transfer student eased himself into the room around Dermott—who finally remembered to stand to one side.

"My name," the newcomer said, in a voice touched with just the faintest music of an Irish accent, "is Parnell. You must be Brenda. Shannon's been telling us all about you."

Brenda blinked. Parnell was only slightly taller than average height, but something about him made tall, brilliantly colored Dermott seem pale and washed out. Parnell's medium length curls were a dark blond, but when the sunlight drifting through the window caught his hair, it shone the red-gold of honey. He had a good build, neither thickset nor thin, but definitely athletic. Yet what caught Brenda's attention were his eyes, large and of a clear leaf green.

"Have I met you before?" she blurted before she could think.

"In your dreams." Shannon giggled. "I told you. We just picked him up from the airport."

"In your dreams," Parnell agreed with a faint smile. He had a very nice mouth. "Lovely phrase. You must have kissed the Blarney stone, Shannon."

Shannon, who was also fair, with wheat-colored hair she wore in a thick braid, and a curvaceous figure that Brenda had envied until Shannon had confessed how often she had back aches, colored right up to her hairline.

Dermott cut in. "We're going out for coffee," he said, reaching out and taking Shannon's hand with a proprietary air. "And then we're going to walk around campus and show Parnell where some of the buildings are. Want to come along?"

"Absolutely," Brenda said, dropping the lid on her suitcase closed. "Let me grab my bag."

In your dreams . . .

☆

Loyal Wind was concentrating on the footing over a particularly rocky spot when he heard Riprap say in a choked voice, "Tell me I'm not hallucinating, but I see an old man over there, on that lake. He's gliding over the water. . . ."

Loyal Wind flicked an ear back and heard Riprap fumbling with the binoculars he wore around his neck.

"And he's balancing on what looks like a crutch—a metal crutch?"

"I see him, too," Des said, his voice tight with excitement, excitement that was quite merited given that this was the first time they'd seen anyone even vaguely approaching human in all their days of travel. "Powers above and below, could that be who I think it is?"

Flying Claw shifted his weight—Loyal Wind felt the grip of his knees and turned to bring them to where they could both see the lake they had been skirting for the last several days.

"If you mean Li T'ieh Kuai, Li of the Iron Crutch," Flying Claw said, and although the young man tried to keep his tones laconic, a thrill of emotion colored the words, "yes, that is who I think I see as well."

"Li of the Iron Crutch," Des repeated. "One of the Eight Immortals. Is he real here then?"

Horse, Ox, and Ram, along with their various passengers, had moved toward the lake. Now Bent Bamboo said, "If by 'real' you mean, are the Eight Immortals said to dwell in the Lands—along with dragons, ghosts, and various hsien—the answer is yes. If you mean is such an encounter common, not in the least."

Gentle Smoke's hissing Snake voice came from where she currently hung about Riprap's neck.

"My teacher claimed to have seen several of the Immortals once. Han Hsiang Tzu, the flute player, was performing in the marketplace. Everyone was dancing or singing, and Lan Ts'ai Ho had spilled the flowers from his basket onto the pavement and was using the basket to collect coins from the audience."

"Li of the Iron Crutch," Riprap said. "I'll ask later who that is, and why I should be impressed. What I want to know now is do you think we can flag him down and maybe learn something about what happened here? None of the hsien we've spoken with have been anything but confused. That looks like one purposeful old man."

"We can try," Loyal Wind said, slowing and shrugging his skin to tell Flying Claw he should dismount, "but if Li doesn't wish to stop, I don't see what we can do. We don't have any means of traveling over water."

Flying Claw swung down, and in a moment Loyal Wind was a man again. He accepted both the binoculars Flying Claw offered him and a pair of loose trousers. Donning the latter, he raised the binoculars and focused in on the distant shape now receding over the waters of the lake.

Riprap was waving a piece of cloth—a bandana, he'd called it—back and forth and bellowing loudly, "Mr. Li! Mr. Li! Please, come back. We'd very much like to talk to you."

He paused for breath and said, "Or is it Mr. Iron Crutch?"

"No, Li is correct," Gentle Smoke assured him. "Try again. I think he was turning."

Riprap resumed his polite call. This time Flying Claw and Loyal Wind joined in. Bent Bamboo added some surprisingly loud calls, given that they came from his monkey chest. Copper Gong bleated.

"Undignified," she admitted in a pause, "but I think we must catch his curiosity."

"Well," Des said with a laugh, "we're a pretty curious group."

Nine Ducks had divested herself of her passengers

and was in the process of returning to her human form. Des had helped remove the luggage the Ox had carried, and was now digging through his pack. Raising his head, he added his voice to the general clamor.

"Please, Honored Li, we would be able to entertain you. We have a small amount of wine. . . ."

Loyal Wind had the binoculars to his eyes, and saw the wake cut through the waters by the iron crutch change angle and shift direction.

"He's coming toward us! Good thinking, Des. Do you really have some wine?"

"I hope he likes California merlot," Des said. "I brought a bottle, well, just in case we needed to bribe someone or get them drunk."

"Explains why," Nine Ducks said, straightening her hastily donned shenyi and brushing her hair into order, "your pack was so heavy. Here I thought the weight was the lamp oil and water purification systems and medicines you insisted on hauling along."

"Li is definitely coming in to shore," Flying Claw said. "We should prepare."

He bustled around, spreading one of the blankets from his bedroll. Des was removing a wine bottle and some collapsible drinking glasses from his pack.

"I hope," he muttered, "one bottle is enough. From what I recall, the Eight Immortals liked their wine."

Riprap said, "Why is this Li traveling on a crutch—an iron crutch, if I understood what you said a moment ago?"

"He's crippled," Copper Gong said, as if that was something any idiot should know. "Cripples use crutches."

"But not," Riprap said with heavy patience, "to go surfing. In fact, my usual experience is that metal poles sink—and that an iron crutch would be awfully heavy anyhow."

"Don't stress over it," Des advised. "Worry more about us running out of wine, okay?"

"For now," Riprap said, glancing to where their guest was about to bring his unlikely vessel to shore. "For now."

Riprap squared his shoulders and, with Flying Claw and Loyal Wind, headed down to meet their guest. Seen up close, Li proved to be an old man, balding, resoundingly ugly, clad in the casually wrapped robes of a Taoist scholar. "Old" was probably the wrong word for him, for although Li's skin was wrinkled and his bright eyes set within wreaths of lines, there was an aura about him that defied the weariness and illness associated with age, transforming them into a pure vitality.

"A man made of polished obsidian," said Li in a voice that was high-pitched, but not in the least effeminate. "An obsidian man who smells like a Dog. A Tiger who walks on two legs, and a half-naked Horse. Indeed, I am glad I decided to accept your invitation. Did I hear a Rooster crow that there was wine?"

"Imported," said Des, walking forward and offering a small cup, "from a very far land."

"From a land where Fire transforms," said Li, "into Earth and from there into Water, Wood, and Metal. Yes. I never thought I would drink such a rare vintage. Truly, this is a wine to be savored."

Li sipped the wine, leaning on his iron crutch, surveying the group assembled to meet him. All had resumed their human shapes, but even so they were a motley group. Des and Riprap wore the clothing of their homeland. The three women and Bent Bamboo wore shenyi. Loyal Wind, responding to that "half naked" comment, quickly pulled on a rumpled tunic. Flying Claw wore armor.

"A curious party of traveling companions," said Li, returning the cup to Des with a slight inclination of his head. "Nearly as strange as myself and my fellows, although we have had many more years to cultivate eccentricity."

He leaned on his crutch and limped with a certain ease that spoke of his familiarity with that form of locomotion. When he came to the blanket Flying Claw had spread, he eased himself onto the ground and raised his hand in anticipation of the cup of wine Des was already handing to him.

"An excellent vintage," Li said. "Will no one join me?"

Nine Ducks smiled. "I am making tea," she said, indicating a small spirit stove where, true to her place as a member of the House of Construction, she already had a small kettle heating. "You are welcome to join me."

"Ah, I will stay with the wine," Li said. "Please, make yourselves comfortable. I should ask why you wished to talk with me, but truly that would only be a formality."

"You seem to know something of us," Des said cautiously, "enough to give some of us one of our names."

"Ox, Tiger, Snake, Horse, Ram, Monkey, Rooster, Dog . . ." Li said. "Dangerous names to bear in this Land at this time. When you are sniffed out, take care."

"Does everyone here have your ability to sniff?" Riprap asked.

"A good question from a Dog," Li said approvingly. "No. Everyone does not, but then those who hunt you will not be everyone—only some rather dangerous people."

"Who?" Copper Gong began, then she stopped herself with visible effort. "Please, Honored Li. What has happened? Some of us have been away from the Lands for many years, but from what we have been told, these changes are relatively new."

"They are," Li agreed. "Only a few months old, but that is long enough to feel as if they have lasted forever."

He held up his cup. Wordlessly, Des refilled it.

"Let me see, how to begin?" Li said, shifting his crippled leg into a more comfortable position. "Perhaps with the fall of the last emperor to sit upon the Jade Petal Throne.

"As all of you . . ." Li glanced at Riprap and Des, then amended his words. "As most of you know, although the Lands consist of many and varied kingdoms, there is one kingdom that, especially in matters of magic, is considered the most important. This is the Jade Kingdom Under Heaven. The ruler who sits on the Jade Petal Throne is considered the greatest emperor of the Lands. He—or occasionally she—is advised by the human incarnations of the twelve signs of the zodiac, human embodiments of the Twelve Earthly Branches.

"In an ideal universe, this high emperor would be just and his advisors wise. In fact, this has rarely been the case. The right to sit upon the Jade Petal Throne is highly contested, and a catalog of dynasties that have ruled the Jade Kingdom Under Heaven reads like a mongrel's pedigree.

"But those of us who reside in the Lands grew accustomed to this. Especially for the hsien, which human backside warmed the smooth, cold stone of the Jade Petal Throne hardly mattered. Dragons, ghosts, spirits, demons, and supernatural creatures of all sorts—including immortals such as myself and my seven associates—went about our long and interesting lives, aware of the changes of rulership as mortals are aware of changes in the weather—inconvenient at times, but rarely lasting long enough to make a notable difference.

"Something like a hundred years ago, the Lands began to change. The battles contesting the right to hold the Jade Petal Throne became more violent. Emperors hardly had time to be fit for their coronation robes before they were displaced and those robes became shrouds. I cannot say I paid much attention, but one of my associates, Ts'ao Kuo Chu, has some interest in law and related matters. He commented that the power of the twelve advisors and the Twelve Branches had been attenuated and stability thereby threatened."

Loyal Wind exchanged glances with his associates. They knew perfectly well why this had happened, for when the twelve advisors had become the Twelve Exiles, they had arranged to maintain their connection to the Earthly Branches. They hadn't known if this would weaken the Earthly Branches in the Lands, but they had known this was a possibility.

And we didn't mind one bit, Loyal Wind thought, trying to decide whether or not he felt guilty about it. *We hoped that if there was weakening, that we might be able to return home—either by invitation or because we could exploit the link.*

Judging from the ironic twinkle in Li's shining eyes, he was perfectly aware of who his audience was, and that he was telling them a tale intimately connected to their own lives.

"Then," Li said thoughtfully, "a short while ago, things went completely wrong. I was sitting with my associates in a pavilion on one of the Fortunate Isles. We have resided there for quite a long time, gotten it arranged to our satisfaction—you know, pavilions angled to catch the morning sun and the afternoon breezes, convenient streams in which to cool the wine. . . ."

He held out his cup and Des poured in a bit more wine. Loyal Wind saw the Rooster stare into the neck of the bottle and frown, heft it as if trying to surreptitiously judge how much it contained, then frown again.

Bet it's nearly as full as when they started, Loyal Wind thought. *Li of the Iron Crutch wouldn't want to run out of wine while telling a good story.*

Li sipped his wine, nodded thanks to Des, and went on.

"There was this sensation. . . . I don't know how to describe it except that simultaneously I felt squeezed and shoved. A wind was blowing with terrible force, howling in my ears. Yet when I looked around me I noticed that nothing on the Fortunate Isles was affected. Not a blossom was dislodged from its tree. Those leaves that shifted did so as if beneath the pleasant caress of the lightest breeze.

"Maybe leaves and grass and flowers weren't affected, but I certainly was being blown. If I wasn't nearly bald already, I think the very hairs would have been blown from my head. A good thing my crutch is iron, otherwise it might have been swept from my grasp. I held on to my crutch as if it was an anchor. Then, blown and pushed and squeezed, I found myself shoved right off our chosen Fortunate Isle—or the island pulled out from under me.

"I went tumbling ass over tea kettle, and when at last I was no longer being squeezed and blown and pulled I came to a stop here. Or I should say, not here precisely, as in on this lakeshore, but in this changed world."

Li of the Iron Crutch gestured around him, at a sky that was streaked lime and violet, at grass that was a nice shade of pale pink, at the waters of a lake that, very strangely in contrast, were a clear and lucid blue flecked with small whitecaps.

"How long ago was this?" Copper Gong asked.

"Time is not something I am accustomed to measuring, dear lady," Li said, "having reached a portion of my life where I am blessedly without appointments. Moreover, it is difficult to measure here. The sun rises and sets, true, night follows day, or day night, but sometimes I'm not sure I can tell the difference."

They all nodded. They'd noticed the phenomenon themselves. Had Des not equipped several of their number with mechanical timepieces and reminded them to keep these wound, they might have been in a similar predicament themselves.

Even so, Loyal Wind thought, *I doubt if those watches are keeping accurate time. There was that night when the sky glowed indigo and the stars seemed so near that we could see their colors and hear them sing. Time seemed to move faster then.*

"Well," Copper Gong said resignedly, "it couldn't hurt to ask. Do you have any idea what caused the storm that drove you from your island?"

"And have you reunited with your associates?" Flying Claw asked anxiously.

Loyal Wind knew the young man was thinking of his own family and that of Righteous Drum and Honey Dream. Thus far, they had seen nothing of any human community.

"I do not have any idea what caused the storm," Li said. "I do know that my associates and I were far from the only inhabitants of the Lands to be disrupted. I have met numerous hsien—lesser deities, immortals, creatures of land and sea—who report having encountered a similar storm. I have also located my associates."

He smiled at Flying Claw, appreciating the young man's concern. "Their tales are similar to mine. We have dispersed throughout these altered Lands, seeking our island home, but none of us has found it. We have found other islands, empty palaces, deserted gardens, statues, but our own beloved Fortunate Isles, where the Queen Mother of the West has held her tranquil reign, those have been swept beyond our reach—or perhaps we beyond them."

Gentle Smoke asked the question Flying Claw was too polite to press. "Is there any place where there are settlements of mortals? We have been traveling for many days in various directions, and we have not seen even the smallest village."

Li scrubbed at the lobe of one ear with a long finger.

"I have not seen any," he admitted slowly, "but there is a feature of these changed Lands that you have not yet encountered."

Whereas when the immortal had told of his own adventures he had seemed cheerful, even enthusiastic, now his expression grew serious and the words came slowly.

"Please, sir," Riprap said. "Tell us about it."

Li frowned. "If you move toward the Center, you will find a forest, a forest unlike any I have ever seen or heard described. It is lifeless. Beneath the feet is drab grey rock—featureless rock without grain or strata or pattern. The surface is neither smooth nor rough, but is so hard that each step on it jolts through one's bones—at least if they are old bones like mine.

"From this grey soil grow trees made entirely of stone, wind-polished so that the browns and whites and greys and pale blues of the stone shine in the sun.

"Above this expanse of stone is sky, white sky ungraced by a single cloud. My understanding is that this forest is about two days deep if one crosses in a straight line—I did not do so, but I spoke to a hsien who did. And crossing in a straight line is difficult in a forest. The hsien to whom I spoke said it took her more like three days, and her feet were bruised from the passage."

Li of the Iron Crutch fell silent. Again, Riprap prompted him.

"And on the farther side, closer to the Center?"

"There is a wall of water, water falling straight down from a sky that holds not a single cloud. The hsien to whom I spoke could not penetrate this wall. She tried, but in two steps she was nearly drowned.

"She was rescued by a dragon who had crossed the watery zone. The dragon said that the wall of water was as high as the sky and easily as wide as the stone forest. As the dragon swam through the water wall, although breathing underwater offered no challenge to one of his kind, the force of the falling water beat upon his frame ceaselessly, pummeling him to the marrow in his bones."

Again Li paused. This time Loyal Wind himself prompted, "Honored Li, on the other side of the wall of water, what did the dragon find?"

"The dragon found a sea of fire, not molten lava but living flame, rising and falling as would waves of water. This sea was interrupted by little islands, coals of fire, each as large as a house.

"Heat billowed up from the coals, making the very air melt and rasp against the throat whenever one drew breath. The dragon went no farther, nor did the dragon find anyone who had dared cross that fiery sea. When the dragon had recovered a little of his strength—and he found this very difficult since these regions seemed singularly devoid of ch'i—the dragon retreated."

"And found the hsien," Flying Claw said, "and rescued her."

"Yes," Li said. "She was a little mountain spirit, very delicate, like a wisp of milkweed."

"No humans lived in these places?" Flying Claw asked.

"Not that either the mountain spirit or the dragon saw," Li of the Iron Crutch replied.

Flying Claw spoke as if thinking aloud. "And no people here, and this strange barrier between us and the Center—where the humans might be."

"Are you thinking," Riprap said, "what I think you're thinking?"

"That we should try to cross the stone forest, then swim through the wall of water, go over the fire and learn what is beyond?" Flying Claw said. "I am. We have known from the start that it is likely we must reach the Center, for at the Center is the Jade Kingdom Under Heaven."

"Yeah," Riprap admitted. "That's what I figured you were saying. Well, we're not equipped for such a trip. We're going to need to hit headquarters first."

Li of the Iron Crutch smiled sagely at them. Despite the fact that, by Loyal Wind's estimation, the immortal had now drunk at least enough wine to fill two bottles—if not three—of the size Des held, he seemed unimpaired beyond a certain rosy glow.

The immortal rose from the blanket, leaning against his iron crutch, and smiling benignly at them all.

"If you find our island," he said, "could you return it? We rather miss it, you know. It has been our home for quite a long time."

"By all means," Flying Claw said solemnly. "Regaining our homes is what this is all about, isn't it?"

Is it? Loyal Wind thought as he readied himself to return to his horse form.

A bit of doggerel he'd heard Riprap recite one day came back to him, slightly altered.

Ours not to reason why. Ours just to do . . . then die.

XII

Nissa flew back to Virginia with Lani soon after she and Pearl had settled the matter of their relocation.

"It'll be easier to explain to my sisters in person why I'm moving," Nissa said. "For one thing, they won't have several days to sit around thinking about ways to convince me to come home. For another, they won't have the sentimental argument—'but you've forgotten how lovely and perfect things are here.' It'll also be easier to speak with administrators at my college about transcripts."

Despite these decisive assertions that Nissa planned to come back, Pearl found staying cheerful very hard as she waved good-bye at the airport security gate.

I wonder how long until I get a call asking if I'd please ship back the things she and Lani left, Pearl wondered as she drove away from the airport. *Family can be so very persuasive. How will Nissa feel once she sees Lani running around with her cousins, part of a happy, noisy mob?*

So absorbed was Pearl in her thoughts that initially she didn't pay much attention when her town car began first to vibrate, then to shake.

"What the . . ." she said aloud, quickly glancing over the dashboard, checking various gauges. Nothing was running too hot or too cold. The gas gauge showed full and none of the warning lights glowed.

The car continued to shake. Pearl looked around. None of the other cars on this relatively quiet road seemed to be experiencing any difficulty.

Not an earthquake, then.

Pearl pulled off at a strip mall devoted to various

professional offices: two lawyers, an insurance agency, a travel agency, and a dentist. All the businesses were closed for the day. Nissa had opted for an evening flight in the hope that Lani would sleep through much of the trip.

After pulling into one of the parking spaces, Pearl shut off the car's engine. The shaking persisted. Frowning, she reached for her cell phone and was only mildly surprised when she found herself in a dead zone.

Pearl's pulse quickened as she tried to school her ch'i to shape All Green, a spell that would permit her to see magical workings. Although All Green was considered quite a difficult spell by the three apprentices—since it involved altering one's own aura, not summoning something already present as in Dragon's Tail or Dragon's Breath—Pearl considered All Green a routine working. It was one she had done almost daily when she was a young woman studying under Thundering Heaven.

Today, however, Pearl could not line up the images in her mind. The bamboo twisted, yellowed, and dried. The pair of green dragons—an image of increase, usually almost too ready to form in the company of vegetative bamboo—now refused to take shape.

The town car continued to shake. Pearl fumbled for the door handle. Her fingers were so weak that she could hardly wrap them around the latch. With a colossal effort, she unlatched the door. Leaning against it, she shoved.

The heavy door hardly moved. For once Pearl regretted her fondness for big cars, regretted letting her chauffeur go, regretted not having Nissa take a cab to the airport. Her chest was beginning to ache, pins and needles shooting up her arms, through her blood. Her head throbbed.

Even so, Pearl was a stubborn woman. Moreover,

she was quite strong for one of both slight frame and advanced years. She shoved her shoulder and upper body against the door. The town car was well maintained. This time the door swung out. Pearl hauled her feet around and half fell from the car.

Grabbing at the upper edge of the car door, Pearl pulled herself mostly upright. The pressure in her chest was growing more intense, the prickles spreading to her legs, growing to burning intensity in her arms. Her head was pounding so hard that she could barely remember her name, much less something as complex as how to hit the emergency numbers programmed into her cell phone.

If they'd reach anyone.

I'm having a heart attack, Pearl thought, dragging herself a few steps away from the car. *No great surprise, given how I've been pushing myself.*

She looked back at the sleek, dark blue bulk of the town car. Perhaps she'd had more success with the All Green than she had thought, for what she saw was a faint double image. One was of the town car sloppily parked over three spaces. The other was of the same car vibrating like a cartoon character that had walked into a wall.

"Boing!" Pearl said, and giggled shrilly. "Boing!"

The shaking had spread to her legs. She managed to sit more or less decorously on the nearest curb, glad in some illogical part of her mind that she'd worn a pants suit, not a dress. She'd hate for the paramedics to find her crumpled over with her underwear showing, her stockings bunched up and full of runs.

Sitting up was proving to be too much of an effort. Breathing hurt. Pearl couldn't feel her feet or hands. How did she want them to find her? Flat on her back, or curled on her side? Curled would look better, like a sleeping child.

I never got my will rewritten to make sure Nissa benefited. I hope my brothers aren't too greedy, that they'll be guided by the letter I wrote my lawyers, even if I didn't get to sign the revised draft.

An uncountable segment of time passed. Pearl mostly concentrated on normally autonomous actions like breathing in and out. When she had attention to spare, she counted her heartbeats. They seemed rather more frequent than usual, and very erratic.

Not promising.

A low rumbling sound intruded upon Pearl's derailing train of thought. The rumbling diminished, then vanished. There was a short, sharp bang. An erratic tapping, staccato and sharp. A shadow came between her and sunlight she hadn't consciously registered until it was gone.

Pearl opened her eyes and fought to focus. A man's face swam in and out of her field of vision. A familiar face, a Chinese face, but not one she particularly liked.

It was a meticulously groomed visage, the brows neat, the hair dark, shining black. Only tiny lines around the eyes and mouth gave away that this was a man in his sixties, rather than twenty years younger. It was the face of Franklin Deng.

Franklin Deng, who resented that the Thirteen Orphans possessed a wealth of lore that he felt should be shared—at least with their Chinese associates, most especially with him. Franklin Deng who, while not precisely an enemy, was certainly not a friend.

Deng was talking to her, switching between English and Chinese. His tone, at first imperious and autocratic, softened. Pearl felt a hand on her wrist, then on her chest. She tried to summon the proper indignation at the familiarity and failed. To her horror, she thought she might even weep with gratitude that if she must die, at least she wouldn't die alone on a strip mall sidewalk.

Pearl heard faint beeping as Deng worked at a cell phone. She heard his faint curse as the phone failed to connect. She heard him speaking to someone.

". . . and put through a call. Not to 911. She'd hate that. Call . . ."

Pearl didn't hear who the other was to call.

The rumble of a car engine starting up, pulling away. Soft sing-song chanting, the words Chinese, sung in a high-pitched nasal register. Following the meaning was beyond her. Cantonese was her fourth or fifth language. Right now, the inflections kept getting tangled up with the Chinese languages that were more familiar to her tired, aching brain.

Breathing didn't seem to be as hard. Was her heartbeat stabilizing? She forced herself to count carefully. Yes! The pain was less. Definitely less.

Pearl didn't know if this was good—except that hurting less had to be at least somewhat good. Or was it? She'd heard that there came a point in dying where the body began to shut down, the pain began to diminish. That was why some people—those white-light-at-the-end-of-the-tunnel types—said it was so hard to come back from death into life. You had to fight back into the pain.

Pearl had never run from a fight in her life. She concentrated, forced herself to attend to what Deng was chanting.

Something about metal, about spirits of metal. Calling on fire, fire that melts metal. About melting metal, forcing away that which dwelled in metal, an entity that hid from fire.

Pearl guided herself through the rhythm of the words, aware now of a new presence—or rather of something that had been present, but concealed from her until Deng had driven it from hiding. An elemental spirt, one of those that anchored itself in metal.

Pearl felt a shiver deep within her soul. The element associated with the Tiger was wood. Wood absorbed strength from earth, but was destroyed by metal. If one was hunting a Tiger, sending a hsien, or spirit, that thrived in metal would be a good choice. She recalled how her car—a metal beast, for all that so many parts were plastic these days—had vibrated, then shook, as if possessed by a will of its own.

"Car," she gasped. "My car."

Franklin Deng glanced down at her, then nodded crisply. He waved both hands expansively in a gesture of warding, then rose from her side and walked over to the town car. Pearl turned her head, the motion taking a terrific amount of energy. Deng placed his hands on the hood of her town car and resumed his chanting.

Gone was the high sing-song note. These words were strident, commanding. Deng repeated them. Pearl caught a few. The dialect he was using was an archaic Cantonese, even more unfamiliar to her than the modern version. Even so, she grasped some of his meaning. A spirit had taken root in her car. Deng sought to force it out.

He was succeeding, but at what cost? The pain in Pearl's head and chest were returning. The hsien was willing to depart, most willing if it could fulfill its mission and take her with it. By urging the spirit to depart as quickly as possible, Deng had inadvertently given it new strength. Unfortunately for Pearl, the quickest way for the spirit to depart would be for it to fulfill its mission, to take its victim. Then the bindings that had brought it to this place would be broken.

Does Franklin Deng know this? Does he seek this indirect way to murder me? He might even be praised

for what he had done, condoled for accidentally con-
tributing to the death of the old woman he sought to
save.

But then, if my death was what he desired, Deng
could simply let the hsien go ahead and finish what it
was about.

A ripping sensation coursed through Pearl's flesh.

Pearl almost screamed in pain and fear, but pride—
pride and a deep fear that all she might manage was a
pathetic squeak—kept her breath within her tortured
lungs. Taking the ch'i she would have expended on a
scream, Pearl strove to fight back.

She became aware of the hsien's hold on her as if it
was centered in five hooks set within her flesh. She
concentrated, focusing in on releasing the hooks.

One. The first hook was set within Pearl's right arm,
a sharp claw shaped like an octopus's beak. The hsien
was unprepared for resistance from its victim, so Pearl
popped the hook free without too much effort.

Two. Left arm. The hsien reset its hooks more deeply,
diverting some of its attention from resisting Deng's
banishing spell, but Pearl had a free arm now. She
reached over and found the hook by touch. Blood ran
hot and wet as she grabbed hold and tore.

Three. Four. Both legs. Not too difficult to remove
these hooks—if your definition of "not too difficult"
included agony akin to adhesive tape pulled off sun-
blistered skin. More blood flowed, ruining her stockings and the trousers of her favorite summer casual
outfit.

Franklin Deng's chanting had taken on a new note.
Pearl heard astonishment, but redoubled purpose as
well.

Despite Deng's holding much of the metal hsien's
attention, Pearl trembled as she contemplated the final

hook set within her. This one was anchored deep within her heart. If she pulled this one out, she would probably die. Yet to leave it in place also meant death.

Metal is destroyed by fire. Wood creates fire. Wood is the Tiger's element. Tiger Bright. Tiger burning bright.

Pearl Bright envisioned her heart as something shaped from the hardest, densest wood—from heart wood. Both the Chinese and the American within her chuckled at the pun. Pearl took the time to make her vision perfect: the heart polished smooth, rubbed with fine oils, the grain visible in complex, circular patterns.

Wood burns. So do hearts, as anyone who has ever loved or hated knows with absolute certainty. Hearts burn. Pearl, with a kindling of hatred and a spark of love, set her own heart aflame.

Now Pearl did scream, loud and shrill. Tears streamed down her face, but their dampness did nothing to extinguish the fire within her. A burning heart aches beyond bearing, but despite the pain humans can live with a heart of fire.

Metal, by contrast, cannot survive within that burning heat. Pearl screamed and wept, feeding the fire within her, bearing the increased pain as her heart grew hot enough to melt gold, hot enough to melt silver, hot enough to purify iron into steel, and beyond that to heats that burn steel into a smoking, viscous puddle and then to ash.

As the final hook was burnt away within her, Pearl swallowed a final scream. Franklin Deng was staring at her, his hands raised in invocation.

"It's gone," he said. His voice was a little hoarse.

"Yes."

"And you owe me."

"Probably."

Pearl looked down at herself. The wounds in her arms and legs were real, the blood trickling from them in a slowly clotting stream, but when she touched her chest all she detected was a residual heat.

Human hearts do burn. And cool.

"Thank you, Franklin," she said.

They might have said more, but at that moment a car—Franklin's car, driven by a Chinese American Pearl vaguely recognized—pulled up and disgorged Dr. Broderick Pike of the Rosicrucian Museum. With him was a severe looking woman Pearl vaguely recognized as a member of the museum's staff.

Both started running as soon as they saw her sprawled, bloodied and battered, on the sidewalk. The driver turned away, and Pearl guessed from the angle of his shoulders he was fighting the urge to vomit.

I must look pretty bad, she thought, relaxing to accept the others' ministrations. For the first time, she became aware of the roughness of the sidewalk, of the cooler patches in shadow as it gave up the heat stored during the day.

Questions were being asked, mostly by Pike, and answered by Deng. Awash with exhaustion, Pearl lay back and let the woman—who seemed to have a good knowledge of conventional medicine—examine her wounds. Blood was washed away, an IV hooked up.

"No drugs," Pearl rasped.

"No drugs," the woman agreed. "Just liquid. You're badly dehydrated. Do you know your blood type?"

Pearl told her. She heard the woman making a phone call.

Dr. Pike had hunkered down next to her. "Pearl, is there anyone staying with you at your house?"

"No."

"Shall I call one of your brothers?"

"Albert Yu."

"Right."

More beeping. Voices. Pearl felt herself being lifted into the backseat of Franklin Deng's car. It was less crowded than she thought it should be, and she heard the woman explaining.

"Dr. Pike is staying to make sure the blood is washed off the sidewalk. He'll arrange a tow for your car. It seems fine, both on a mechanical level and otherwise, but we thought it best not to take chances."

Pearl nodded. She drifted off to sleep. Later, she woke as they transferred her into a building. Not her house. She forced her eyes open and recognized one of the private buildings on the Rosicrucian Museum grounds. She drifted off again.

When next she woke, a new voice had joined the conversational symphony, and her head was much more clear.

Albert Yu saying, "Franklin, I deeply appreciate your saving Pearl—and I'm sure she will, too, but I admit I'm a bit puzzled as to how you happened to be so opportunely present."

Franklin Deng: "I have been monitoring the activities of your cabal. I admit, after being told so very pointedly that I should not interfere, I almost did not. However, after further thought, it seemed to me that what was happening was that someone—or some thing—was interfering with Pearl. Therefore, I was not interfering with you so much as facilitating your progress."

Broderick Pike, very, very dryly: "I admire the logic, and certainly applaud the end result. When I remained to clean up the area around the car, I found no traces of residual mana. The attacker left a faint signature on the vehicle, a psychic footprint. It was already fading out, but I made a recording."

Pike's voice muttering a few words in corrupted

Latin. Then Franklin Deng: "I've seen something like that. Embodiment of the element of metal—much as the dragon can be embodied water."

"Yes," Albert agreed. "I have done some studying of the indigenous Chinese traditions, and my understanding is that these spirits are not at all well known here—not as dragons are, for example."

A slight noise, probably mild indignation from Deng who, as Pearl knew all too well, resented that the Orphans had access to his traditions while he did not have access to theirs.

Albert went on. "But from what I have gathered from talking to Uncle Shen—that is, Shen Kung—and Righteous Drum—one of our allies—the magical traditions in the Lands embrace a much wider variety of supernatural entities. They also have a considerable attachment to elemental magics."

Dr. Pike: "So are you saying you suspect this attack came from your enemies?"

"I do." Albert's tone shifted slightly, containing both amusement and acid. "Not that I do not think Franklin Deng or one of his allies is incapable of such a summoning, but I do not think it likely in this case."

Pearl found herself stifling a chuckle and turned the sound into a little moan, such as an injured person might make upon coming conscious.

"Aunt Pearl? How do you feel?"

"Tired. Home?"

"I can take you to your house. We're next door. Dr. Pike brought you to the museum to give me time to drive from San Francisco."

"Deng okay?"

"Yes. Franklin's fine. He burned quite a lot of ch'i aiding you, but he's recovering well."

"Good. Thank him."

She raised her head slightly from the pillow as she

spoke, but now she let it sag back as if even that small effort had been too much. If she was honest with herself, she would have admitted it almost had been, but she wasn't in the habit of being honest when it came to admitting weakness.

Pearl felt herself being moved, possibly onto the same stretcher that had once carried a battered Waking Lizard. The thought made her sad.

Waking Lizard has gone ahead, she thought. *I wonder when I'll follow. Not quite yet, please heavens. So much I want to do. So very, very much I want to do.*

☆

The evening was warm and pleasant, a breeze from somewhere breaking up the August heat so that the four University of South Carolina students' walk to the coffee house was actually quite nice. The sidewalk wasn't really wide enough for more than two to walk side by side, and so Brenda found herself walking with Parnell.

He grinned at her, his green eyes dancing with mischief. "I guess I challenged him." He tossed his head to indicate where Dermott was walking with Shannon. "I didn't mean to . . ."

Brenda snorted disbelief. "Yeah, right. You flirt with a guy's girlfriend, and you don't think he'll take offense?"

Parnell's grin didn't fade, and Brenda was glad that scattered light from the street lamps hid the blush she could feel burning in her cheeks.

"Parnell," she said, desperately searching for a way to change the subject. "That's not a really usual name."

"Know where it comes from?" he asked, turning that wicked grin on her. "There'll be a prize if you're right."

Brenda thought about asking what prize, then decided she didn't want to risk his answer.

"My guess is Irish history. Charles Stewart Parnell. Home rule. Rumblings of rebellion, all that."

"Charles Stewart Parnell, called by many Ireland's uncrowned king," Parnell agreed cheerfully. "That's the answer. The rebel leader brought low by a woman—or by the Catholic Church. Depends on how you want to look at the situation with Mrs. O'Shea. Really, Parnell's become almost a mythical figure."

"A lot to take on," Brenda said, thinking of the Orphans, of dreams, of a young man with long black hair who didn't laugh quite this easily, but warmed her heart when he smiled. "Being mythic."

"You'd know," Parnell said, "wouldn't you?"

He reached out, and Brenda thought he was going to take her hand, but instead he touched the mah-jong tile bracelet on her left wrist.

"Wouldn't you?" Parnell repeated.

Brenda blinked at him, but she wasn't going to say anything. That lesson had been drummed into her over and over again. You didn't talk about magical things except with those you knew were in on the secret. You didn't e-mail about them. You didn't talk about them on the phone. Despite the eerie familiarity of those green eyes, Brenda wasn't going to break that rule here.

"Shannon," she called, "just where are you taking us?"

"Koffee Klatche," Shannon said. "They're open late and they have desserts—unless your summer in healthy California has made you swear off ice cream."

"Absolutely not," Brenda said. "It has made me very much swear on to desserts. I want a sundae. Butterscotch and hot fudge on pecan chocolate ice cream."

Parnell made a mock expression of horror. "Good thing the euro is strong right now."

Shannon looked surprised. "You're treating?"

"Sure. Least I can do when you and Dermott came to get me from the airport and then agreed to show me about. If you want to hit a pub . . ."

"Not legal," Dermott said primly. "We don't need to get busted our first couple of days back."

"Do we ever need to get busted?" Parnell asked, touching up his brogue just a bit.

Brenda laughed, and Dermott's wooden expression melted away.

"I guess not," he admitted, "but I'll take you up on the treat and thank you for it."

After quantities of ice cream—the two boys decided to compete to complete a massive confection called an Ice Age—they walked for a while, showing Parnell the older section of campus around the Horseshoe.

Shannon had worked that summer as a tour guide for prospective students, and knew lots of cute little facts. They were having quite a good time, but eventually Shannon started yawning.

"Sorry," she apologized. "Long day."

Brenda laughed. "I guess it is. Midnight here is nine at Pearl's. Made Mom crazy that I couldn't seem to adjust."

As if on cue, her cell phone rang. She glanced at the read-out and saw Pearl's home number.

"I guess someone there has forgotten, too. Just a sec."

She stepped a few paces away and answered the call.

"Hello?"

"Brenda, this is Albert."

"Hi." Brenda tried to remember if Albert had ever

phoned her, and decided that he had not. Her pulse quickened and she took a few more steps away from the others. "Have you heard from—"

"The scouts? No. I'm calling because Pearl had an accident tonight."

The way he inflected "accident" made Brenda think he meant otherwise. Remembering the rules about communicating via phone, she quickly sought a way to ask.

"Anything like when she got those thorns—was it twenty-seven or only ten?—in her hand?"

"Something like that," Albert said. "She's going to be fine, but she wanted everyone to know. You know how superstitious she can be. She keeps saying bad things happen in threes."

Brenda doubted that Pearl had said anything of the sort. Despite having spent the formative years of her life on stage and screen, Pearl was probably the least superstitious person Brenda had met.

I guess it comes from knowing what's real and what's not, Brenda thought. Aloud she said, "I understand. I'll be really careful. I have those lucky bracelets she taught me how to make, and I don't take them off."

"Very good," Albert said. "Aunt Pearl is sleeping now, but I'll tell her what you said."

"Thanks, Albert."

The connection went dead, but Brenda stood there for a while, staring at her phone.

Shannon called softly, "Something wrong?"

"A little," Brenda said, sliding the phone back into her purse. "My mentor was in an accident. She'll be okay. Someone called to let me know in case I saw something on the news or on the Web and got worried."

"That's right," Shannon said with a sort of reflected pride, "she's sort of famous, isn't she?"

"Pearl would be the last person to think so," Brenda said. "I bet this won't even make a small line in entertainment news."

"Still," Dermott said. "It's good to be careful. You would have gotten a nasty shock."

"Yes," Parnell agreed, and Brenda had the feeling he was talking about something quite different than merely getting startled by reading the information that a friend had been in an accident. "It's good to be careful. Very wise indeed."

XIII

The scouting party pressed hard, covering the distance between the lake where they had encountered Li of the Iron Crutch and the Lands side of the Ninth Gate in three and a half days.

"I'm always amazed," Des said, dismounting stiffly from Nine Ducks's back and stretching, hands on hips to work the kinks out of his back, "by how much faster any return journey seems."

Flying Claw, who had been acting as their group's cartographer, slid from Loyal Wind's saddle and laughed.

"Is that a sly criticism," he said, "of my desire to stop every few *li* and make accurate notes?"

"Not in the least," Des said, "but I'll admit I was relieved you didn't decide to do so on our return trip."

"I almost wish we had stopped to check the maps," Flying Claw said. "I am certain we traveled further on the way out than we did upon our return."

"We did," Copper Gong said, a trace tartly. Her acerbic temperament had not been improved by more than a week with the Monkey on her back. She had all but thrown Bent Bamboo in her eagerness to return to her human form. "Side to side, over to that ridge to check a rock formation that looks like a palace, but turns out to be a heap of unusually shaped boulders. Sending Bent Bamboo up the nearest tall tree to view the land from above, having Gentle Smoke probe in tight areas to see if we must go around or if we can widen the trail. Widening the trail only to find we must go around in any case because the gorge is blocked half a *li* further in."

"Deviate a fraction and you lose a thousand miles," quoted Gentle Smoke, who had returned from her snake form and was now tucking loose ends of her elaborate two-bun hairstyle into order. "I agree with you, Flying Claw. I also thought the return journey was shorter than even our taking the most direct route could account for."

Riprap, who had been rebalancing the packs Nine Ducks carried, glanced over at Loyal Wind.

"You didn't do anything to speed us along, did you? Like the trick you worked with running on the winds when we traveled to the Nine Yellow Springs?"

"I did not," Loyal Wind assured him. "I was only able to manage that because of the unusual nature of our mounts."

Bent Bamboo, also returned to his human form, scratched his head in a very monkeylike gesture. "If we're all ready, why don't we start back? The others will surely be worrying. We haven't communicated with anyone for several days."

Des frowned. "Because of static or something very like it. You're right. Let's get a move on before we meet a rescue party coming the other way."

Their progress through the Nine Gates went as

smoothly as could be desired. In the warehouse that held the First Gate, Nine Ducks and Loyal Wind again resumed their human forms.

They left some of the gear—tents, bedrolls, and the like—spread to air in the warehouse and loaded the rest into the van. Des pulled out his cell phone. "It's getting on to evening. How about I call Pearl and see if she wants to meet us at Colm Lodge? We can pick up some takeout along the way, and brief everyone at once."

"Takeout," Bent Bamboo agreed enthusiastically. "Pepperoni pizza. Hold the cheese."

Loyal Wind noticed how Des's expression, cheerful when he greeted Pearl, grew suddenly sober.

"That doesn't sound good. We'll come there, then. Right. Be there in not too long."

He tucked the cell phone back into his pocket.

"Pearl wouldn't go into details, but apparently things here didn't stay quiet. Something happened a couple of days ago. On the good side, Righteous Drum and Honey Dream are over at Pearl's house, as is Albert, so we're going there."

"Did she say . . ." Riprap began. "No, of course she didn't. This is Pearl. We're all packed. Let's get going."

The van pulled up in front of Pearl's house in what Riprap commented was something like record time.

"Our luck must be in," he said, sliding open the door to the van and helping Nine Ducks out. "You were going at least ten miles over the speed limit the whole way back."

"Irrational, I know," Des said sheepishly, "but I couldn't help myself. I'll show my infinite self-restraint by taking the van around to the garage. Meet you all inside."

When Honey Dream answered the door, Loyal Wind

noted that although she was dressed in contemporary clothing, she wore her snake fang dagger at her waist.

"Come in," Honey Dream said, opening the door very wide and making shooing gestures as if they were a flock of chickens. "You are all well?"

"All," Flying Claw reassured her. "Des has taken the van around to the garage, but it was easier to unload people out here. Are you well? Your father?"

"We are well. Even Pearl is well, although it was a near thing. Come. We're all sitting in the family room. I have made tea, and Albert has made something called tuna salad."

They were greeted by Pearl, who looked quite pale, even as she assured them that in a day or two she would be "right as rain," and added, "I lost a lot of ch'i fighting that monster, and I'm a bit slow gaining it back."

Righteous Drum rose to greet them, and from how he moved and helped with pouring tea, Loyal Wind could guess that he had been working long hours and practicing using his remaining arm.

This is not one who will be content to let others fight his battles much longer, Loyal Wind thought with admiration.

Over tuna salad sandwiches, potato chips—a delicacy Loyal Wind had already decided was excuse enough for returning from the dead—and various drinks, Pearl, assisted by Albert, related what had happened to her three and a half days before, including the fact that the incident had left the various indigenous magical traditions more anxious than ever for resolution of the question of what dangers might emerge from the Lands Born from Smoke and Sacrifice.

Albert said, "Of course some are insisting they be permitted to 'assist' us in our efforts."

"Franklin Deng, I bet," Des cut in.

Albert nodded. "No takers. Others are less eager to intrude in our feuds, especially after I pointed out that Chinese magic is rather specialized, and does not abide by the rules most of those who have studied within Western magical traditions would know."

"No spirit closely affiliated with metal," Honey Dream said as smugly as if she had invented the idea, "in a culture that does not recognize metal as an element—a culture in which many magical traditions abhor iron."

"So the members of the indigenous traditions are still arguing among themselves," Albert said. "They will have noted your return. Eventually, I will need to tell them something—if for no other reason than to keep them from speculating."

Pearl added, "One good thing has come from this mess. Nissa is telling her sisters that I have had a mild heart attack. They're good-hearted young women. Their protests regarding Nissa and Lani moving here melted into nothing when she presented to them the specter of an ailing old woman living alone in a big house. She'll be back within a week or so."

Nine Ducks said, "Do you have any idea how the attack on Pearl was done? Are you certain it was from the Lands?"

"We are fairly certain," Righteous Drum said, "that the hsien was closer akin to those of the Lands than to here—a summoning, therefore. However, we are still at a loss to explain how the summoning was worked. I have examined Pearl's car, but whoever set the trap was clever. The activation of the summoning was done in such a way as to destroy any physical traces of the spell itself."

Riprap pursed his lips. "Like the way wiping fingerprints leaves a smudge that tells you there were prints there, but you don't have the prints."

Righteous Drum looked somewhat puzzled by this analogy, but Albert nodded crisply.

"Precisely. We know a spell was set on the car, and we know that the person who did so expected someone to look for a trace."

"That's not much," Riprap said dissatisfied.

"It is quite a bit," Albert countered. "It shows that Pearl's attacker knew magic might be suspected—that we wouldn't simply dismiss this as a tired woman who has been under a great deal of stress having a heart attack at the wheel."

"Thank you," Pearl said, "for omitting the 'old.' Honestly, I do feel as if I've had a heart attack—based on how I've heard the after-effects described. I'm willing to bet 'heart attack' is what a medical examiner would have ruled."

"You don't think Deng was responsible?" Riprap asked, his big fists clasping and unclasping. "Trying to get an 'in' with us by charging to Pearl's rescue?"

"Of that," Albert said, "I am fairly certain."

"Fairly."

"Nothing in this world is certain," Albert said in a tone that closed that topic. "Let's move on to what brought you back."

Loyal Wind said, "Go ahead, Des. Tell him. We will help if you forget anything."

Des emptied his teacup, then launched into an account of their meeting with Li of the Iron Crutch.

"We think," Des concluded, "that it's possible that all the humans are within that central area."

"If," Copper Gong said darkly, "they are anywhere at all."

"I prefer," Gentle Smoke chided, "to believe they are."

Righteous Drum leaned back in his chair, but Loyal Wind could see that he longed for action.

"My daughter and I will not give up hope of finding our family. Do you intend to try and learn what is within that series of barriers?"

Des nodded. "Yes. The barriers seem to be oriented around the five elements—incredibly extreme examples of each one. If we're to get through, we're going to need the means to either resist or adapt to each one."

"As the dragon Li T'ieh Kuai told you about could breathe water," Honey Dream agreed, "and so was less troubled by the wall of water. My father and I have spent many of the last several days writing down various spells we thought would be useful in the future."

"And," Albert said, "we have a fairly wide array of amulet bracelets stored upstairs. Before she left for Virginia, Nissa made at least one a day."

"We can't strip you of your defenses," Nine Ducks objected, "especially not after what happened to Pearl."

"Even so," Pearl said firmly, "we can spare some."

Flying Claw reached out and grasped Pearl's hand firmly. "Thank you, Aunt. We will accept your generosity, but several of us have decided that we should also prepare to deal with these challenges in a non-magical fashion."

Loyal Wind felt he should speak up, for the Horse is a commander of troops and well studied in tactics. "As we made our return journey, Flying Claw and I discussed what we might encounter. We speculated that if we were the ones who had somehow banished a collection of the most magical creatures in the Lands— as hsien tend to be—then we would not rely solely upon magical barriers to keep them out."

Flying Claw cut in, enthusiasm coloring his words. "If it were me, I'd find a way to create areas where magic wouldn't work or where ch'i was hard to gather."

Loyal Wind nodded. "I agree. If you know your enemy has many archers, see if you can summon a wind. Riprap and Des had several good suggestions."

Riprap took over. "We'll bring gear from here, things that aren't in the least magical, but might help us to overcome the various obstacles. Little things, like padded footwear for crossing the hard stone of the petrified forest. Bigger things, like waterproofing—maybe even oxygen tanks—for getting through that waterfall."

"We tested," Des said, "and in the Lands, as in the guardian domains, electronics and elaborate mechanical engines don't seem to work. However, simpler mechanics do work. Artificially made fabrics retain their qualities. My nylon tent handled a drenching downpour just as well as it would here."

"I like your plan," Albert said. "You might have to make several trips once you learn what is beyond the fire barrier. 'Metal' might be represented by a wall or a sea of molten iron or something else entirely. Still, you can plan for what you'll need to cross the petrified forest and get through the waterfall. Getting across those burning coals, though . . ."

"That might take magic," Des admitted, "but I was wondering what would happen if we diverted some of that water into the coals. Hoses. Siphons."

"I like it," Albert repeated. "I've my laptop in the front hall. If everyone is refreshed, we'll start planning."

Loyal Wind watched as everyone—except for Pearl, who asked Riprap to turn her easy chair to face the table—took seats around the long table. Honey Dream had a list of the spells she and her father had been working on, and Riprap ran upstairs to make a quick catalog of amulet bracelets.

Voices rang out, quick and eager, the five ghosts contributing as much as the living.

What odd perspectives we bring to this battle, Loyal Wind thought, feeling a surge of pride. *The thoughts of the living and the dead. Experience in peace and war spanning many minds and more than a hundred and fifty years. The strange technological lore of the Land of the Burning combined with the magics not only of the Lands but those which the Orphans developed in their exile. I will admit that, like Copper Gong, I had begun to lose hope, but now . . .*

If I did not wish to be guilty of overconfidence, I might even pity our opponents.

Then Loyal Wind looked at where Pearl sat pale and wan enfolded in the hold of her bulky chair and revised his opinion.

No. Never pity. Those who hunt tigers must expect to be bitten. Our enemies will be awaiting our return.

☆

Brenda called Pearl daily after Albert's report of Pearl's "accident." She was reassured that other than massive ch'i depletion and a few minor cuts, Pearl was doing well. Pearl also told Brenda that the scouts had returned from their "camping trip" and had made some adjustments to their gear before returning to the Lands.

Brenda wanted to know more, but knew that Pearl would not say more over the phone. Gaheris Morris was even less help, but he did add that the scouts had been in San Jose for a couple of days before they had departed once again for the Lands.

He also made it very clear—in the nicest way possible—that what the scouts or the Orphans were doing was no longer any of Brenda's business.

"Study hard, Breni. Figure out what you want to major in. You've done your part and more."

So Brenda tried to distract herself, hanging out with Shannon (with and without the increasingly omnipresent Dermott), meeting up with other friends, buying textbooks, going to her first few classes. Even a few days gave her the distinct feeling that sophomore year, with its pressure to settle on a major, was going to be different from freshman year.

Then there was Parnell. The Irish transfer student had soothed Dermott's bruised ego sufficiently that the two had become buddies. They would often arrive at Brenda and Shannon's room together. Since there always seemed to be a point where Shannon (or Dermott) would "suddenly" remember an appointment or something that had been forgotten or simply get lost in the sort of private gooey talk that makes everyone but the participants nauseated, Brenda found herself more and more often in Parnell's company.

Not all that much time had passed since their initial meeting, but Brenda was beginning to feel Parnell had potential to be a real friend. She wondered if he might want to be a bit more.

Parnell claimed to have kissed the Blarney stone—repeatedly—and the way he said this gave the impression that the stone in question had been quite enthusiastic about their osculatory interludes. Despite his gift of gab, Parnell was very good at encouraging thoughtful conversation, above and beyond the jokes and quips most guys his age thought passed for wit.

It didn't hurt that Parnell was handsome, with his dark honey surfer boy locks and brilliant green eyes, nor that Flying Claw had been "home" and apparently hadn't bothered to leave her a message.

Surely Flying Claw has figured out how to use a cell

phone by now. Surely he could have found time to call if he was in San Jose for several days. I wonder if Honey Dream is working on him again. Of course she is! I wonder if he minds. . . .

It didn't hurt that, when Brenda was in Parnell's company, Brenda found herself on the receiving end of some more or less covertly envious glances.

Most of all, it didn't hurt that wherever Parnell had been brought up, dating was still practiced. Dermott hung around Shannon looking hopeful and possessive—and his behavior was a huge step up from the majority of guys who seemed glad to take advantage of those times when a girl was in the vicinity, but who didn't make much effort to maintain a relationship.

Parnell, by contrast, could be positively courtly. He had the gift for opening doors without making the action seem like he thought Brenda was too stupid to figure out a door latch. He'd treat her to coffee or lunch—and was gracious when she returned the favor. He even brought her flowers once. Wild flowers, true, picked from a landscaped median strip, but the first time any guy had brought her flowers.

Well, other than those funky corsages guys' mothers make them get for prom, Brenda thought.

This early in the term, homework wasn't exactly exhausting. Midterms were comfortably far away, and other than for her German and English Lit classes, Brenda had very little in the way of daily assignments. There was plenty of time for long walks in the evening, when the humid heat seemed comfortable by contrast to the day. The USC Columbia campus had grown large and rambling in its more than two hundred years of existence, always offering another turn, another side street between mostly quiet buildings.

Brenda and Parnell were walking along a tree-lined concourse when Parnell suddenly cut off in the middle of an amusing anecdote he'd been telling about three bottles of beer, five guys, and a set of parallel bars.

"Very well," he said softly, and Brenda wondered if he was even talking to her. "We are alone."

Parnell turned to her, his green eyes serious and seeming somehow several shades darker. "Look, Brenda. I wasn't supposed to need to get into this so quickly, but Pearl's being attacked has changed matters."

"Getting sick," Brenda corrected, but her words were a fencer's sword, raised to block and parry. "Having a heart attack."

"Getting attacked," Parnell said. He paused, his usual glibness completely vanished.

Brenda felt her blood run hot and cold, her pulse quicken, and her breath come shallow. She had remembered Parnell's resemblance to the handsome squire in her dream—the dream that had been interrupted by Loyal Wind's contacting her with the news about Thundering Heaven and Bent Bamboo.

However, there had been no way—especially not within the rules and regulations Pearl and Des had explained bound not only the Orphans but the indigenous magical traditions as well—to raise the point. She simply could not say, "Hey, did I dream about you one night? You were dressed like a squire from a book of Arthurian legends."

At best, that would have sounded flirtatious. At worst, really, really dumb.

"Attacked," Parnell repeated for the third time. "By a spirit—a hsien—with a specific affinity for metal."

Brenda blinked, but didn't admit to anything. Pearl and Albert had, between them, managed to—if cryptically—get across at least that much. She'd needed to go look up what element was associated with the Monkey and the Rooster, but at least what Pearl and

Albert had said would have come across to an eavesdropper as nothing more than Chinese astrology.

I'll listen. I won't volunteer anything, but I'll listen.

Parnell steered Brenda to a comfortable seat next to a spreading oak. The trunk was wide enough that they could both lean back against it, intimate, but not unduly cozy.

Parnell glanced at Brenda, then decided that her silence could be taken as a reply.

"Brenda, before you end up the next target, there is information you should know."

Brenda made a noncommittal sound that might be taken as "Go on."

"Last month, you had several conversations with a woman who—for sake of convenience—I'm going to call Leaf."

He glanced at Brenda, then continued. "Leaf is a relative of mine. She had a feeling that your father was going to try and keep you from getting much more involved in the Orphans' business. Gaheris is probably right to do so. They're involved in some dangerous matters."

"Orphans. Leaf." Brenda heard herself talking even though she'd resolved to stay quiet. "You know?"

"A bit. Enough. Enough to know that you never told the Orphans about your dreams about Leaf. You passed on her warnings, but you never said where they came from."

"Yeah. Well, it's not like Leaf was telling me to ask them to do anything other than what they wanted to do anyhow," Brenda said. "They—we—really didn't need a distraction."

"Fine reasoning," Parnell said approvingly. "Anyhow, what you did for us—for Leaf and all—put a stopper in the business, but it's not over, as you well know. Leaf decided that we owed you a bit of protection, since you wouldn't be living in Pearl's warded domain. I'm that protection."

"You?"

Brenda remembered some of the things Leaf had told her about herself. Her traitor tongue spoke ahead of her resolve.

"Are you sidhe folk?" Spending time with Shannon had made fresh all the Irish myths and legends they both loved. "A member of the Tuatha de Dannan, like that?"

"Sidhe, sure," Parnell said.

A little whisper in Brenda's brain, memory of a joke she and Shannon had come up with last year around exam time, when they'd sat up way too late.

Tuatha de Dannon, the yogurt fairies, cousins to the Keebler elves.

Brenda swallowed a hysterical giggle. She'd gotten used to the Chinese stuff, learned to take it almost for granted. She hadn't had much choice, not with Albert Yu getting brain-raped right before Brenda was supposed to meet him. She'd believed all that stuff Auntie Pearl and her dad told her because it made more sense than not believing.

But Brenda's encounters with Leaf had been dreamlike, and here was the boy of her dreams—quite literally—sprawling on the ground next to her, telling her that he was an elf.

"Sidhe," Parnell went on, considering, maybe wondering about the weird little smirk that Brenda knew was twisting her lips, even though she was trying her best not to giggle. "But not really Tuatha de Dannan. Look, before I get into other matters, I'd better clarify what we are."

"Okay," Brenda managed, letting out the swallowed laughter on the exhalation. "Go ahead."

"When I say we're sidhe, we're not talking all those noble, elfy-welfy Tuatha de Dannan types with their lineages going back to dubious Spaniards and all those interminable battles over cows. Those tales are the result of the later residents trying to supply themselves with retroactive history."

Brenda nodded. "Like those stories that talk about 'real' Irish being descended from Milesius of Spain after he beat all the Formor. Stuff for people who don't want to believe that they're descended from savages who painted themselves blue, or worse, from the savages who came in and wiped the blue people out."

"Right," Parnell said. "You understand pretty well."

"Hey," Brenda said, "I grew up believing I was of mixed German and Irish descent, more Irish than German, but both. You aren't going to find another pair of cultures as fond of creating mythic histories to make them feel better about their ancestry."

"I'm not going to let you distract me," Parnell said with one of those winning grins. "We can debate that later. I'm going to tell you about my own ancestry."

"Go on."

"Like I said, forget the noble elves with their high brows, pointy ears, and fondness for elevated music and poetry. We're talking the underbelly stuff, the Little People who weren't always so little. We're talking the breath and pulse of islands."

"Islands?"

"The United Kingdom: England, Scotland, Wales, and, of course, Ireland. Biggish islands dotted around with some really dinky islands, the whole brimming to the eyebrows with myth, legend, folklore, poetry.

"Islands are weird places, Brenda. Land that belongs more to water than to earth. Ever wonder why the old stories held on so hard there? Why Saint Patrick could banish the snakes but not the bogles? One word for you, chicky: islands. And islands are in you, girl. The blood of islands."

Brenda listened, mesmerized, hypnotized, but she forced herself to protest.

"But Grandma Elaine, she's the one who told me all the old legends. This underbelly stuff isn't what she loved. She loved just what you're sneering at, all the pretty stories: King Arthur, Finn, Deidre of the Sorrows, heck, even Robin Hood. Are you saying those aren't part of the blood of islands, too?"

"They are. Those who know that the monsters are real, can you blame them for dreaming of all the rest?"

Very softly, Brenda replied, "No."

"Even in the pretty stories," Parnell went on, "there are hints of older lore. Gawain playing the beheading game with a knight who keeps growing back his head. Cuchulain's battle transformation from a normal human into something pretty horrible. The Formor, who even the Irish can't seem to decide are monsters or are just somewhat irritating kin of the prettier folk.

"But I'm not here to tell you stories you already know, Brenda Morris. What I want to do is to prepare you for the idea that those stories are real—as real as you are. You spoke of your grandma Elaine, but remember, you inherited from your mother's side as well."

"Oh," Brenda paused, thinking this over. She'd grown so accustomed these last few months to thinking of herself as Gaheris's heir that she'd almost forgotten what came from her mother's side. "Parnell, why is it suddenly so important that I know this now?"

"Because, acushla, when the trouble comes that I think is coming, we're going to need your help. And believe me, Brenda Morris, as much as we want your help to forestall the storm before it can hit us, I think you're going to need our help to keep from being blown away."

"I'm not ready," Brenda said, hating herself for admitting this, but knowing it was true.

"Ready or not," Parnell said, "the trouble will come."

XIV

Between errands to hardware stores, sporting goods emporiums, grocery stores, and even odder establishments, the Orphans still found time to speculate about just how the attack on Pearl might have been worked.

"After all," said Riprap, his big, broad hands surprisingly delicate as he folded bandana-sized pieces of brilliantly colored synthetic fabric into a zip-top bag, "if we can figure that out, we can also figure out how to defend you."

"We don't have much to work with," Albert reminded him. "We know the magic was centered on Pearl's car. That's it."

Riprap shrugged. "Okay. That still helps. Who has access to the car? After all, she keeps it in her warded garage, not parked on the street. That limits access."

Des, who had been making up small packets containing miniature bottles of wine and spirits, freshwater pearls, and tiny vials of perfume, glanced up, his expression concerned.

"Do we eliminate members of the household?" Des said. "All of us who have stayed here have access to the garage and anything in it."

Pearl didn't answer. Albert took over. He looked

uncomfortable. "I was going to eliminate our own automatically, but—"

Pearl, who had been observing all the preparations from her recliner—she was still inclined to get tired—cut in.

"But I insisted we work an augury."

"The results?" Riprap asked, his deep voice gruff, his hands pausing in their work as if he was prepared to spring to his feet and head out after the malefactor the moment he learned his name.

"They were," Pearl said, "undecided."

"Undecided?" Riprap said, the word almost a bark.

Albert frowned. "Yes. Auguries are not perfect, especially if the target has the sense to muddle them in advance."

"I guess there must be ways," Riprap agreed reluctantly. "It's always like that with weapons. Someone invents the perfect solution to a problem, then ten other people get to work on countermeasures. Okay. So is that 'undecided' reading saying that Pearl could have been attacked by someone within our own group?"

"It's possible," Albert said. Pearl could tell he hated even admitting to that option, "but I don't see it as very likely. There are other, much more reasonable solutions."

"Oh?"

"Pearl's car hasn't been in the garage all the time," Albert said. "Given all the people who have been staying in this house, both the car and the van have been out a great deal."

Des frowned. "But would someone have been able to work a complex spell without being noticed?"

Albert made a disapproving sound. "Sure. Put up the hood, pretend to be checking for engine trouble. Slap a prepared amulet down where it would be concealed in the workings. If the spell was meant for Pearl in particular, the casting might have been done weeks ago. She hasn't had much reason to drive lately."

Pearl nodded. "That's true. I rarely drive if I can get someone else to do so."

"Or," Albert continued, "the spell could have been meant to hit any one of the Orphans at a time when he or she was alone in the car. I did some checking. Lately, there have been so many people here that at least two people have gone out at a time—usually more."

"True," Riprap said. "Okay. So the spell could have been done weeks ago. That's no help at all."

"Were we able to learn anything about the nature of the spell itself?" Des asked.

"No," Albert said. "Nothing. Pearl's attacker covered his—or her—tracks carefully there."

Speculation continued, but Pearl tuned out the conversation. She and Albert had been over the matter in great detail earlier. Despite Albert's dislike of the ambivalence of the result of the augury, she found herself considering what that ambivalence could mean.

The unhappy reality was that their most obvious enemies—those who had come recently from the Lands—were now bound to them by very carefully worded treaties, treaties that made such an attack all but impossible.

Pearl found herself wondering if they had been careful enough with Twentyseven-Ten and the other two former prisoners. Her car had been parked at Colm Lodge many times. Meddling would be easy enough for someone there—and with little chance of interruption.

Both Twentyseven-Ten and Thorn were magically adept. Twentyseven-Ten had a considerable amount of both talent and training. Moreover, he was a product of the same hard school that had produced Flying Claw.

And like Flying Claw, Pearl thought uneasily, *his goal was to be the Tiger.*

If Twentyseven-Ten and Thorn had worked the spell in conjunction, they might have been able to find a loophole in the prohibitions against their causing harm, since two parts of a spell done separately would not, in themselves, be dangerous, especially if the third component for making the spell activate was the presence of a person or a certain set of circumstances.

But Pearl didn't raise that possibility. She was tired of debate and wrangling. In the end, very little would be changed. Everyone was alerted now to these new dangers. The scouts must set out again.

And what if the one who placed the spell was one of us? she thought unhappily. *But who? I can't really believe anyone in our number would want to kill me. But perhaps I am becoming naive and trusting in my old age.*

Pearl Bright sighed and let her eyes drift shut in sleep. Sleep, that close kin to death. Death which still prowled in the jungles of her mind, wearing her father's face.

☆

The scouts passed through the Nine Gates, heavily burdened, but cheerful, ready to face a challenge they could see.

"We've been fighting shadows for too long," Flying Claw said as he oriented his compass to find the most direct route to the Center. "I long for an opponent I can touch, a mountain I can climb."

The three ghosts who possessed quadruped animal forms had opted to travel in them so that they could serve as pack animals. Bent Bamboo traveled as a human. Gentle Smoke alternated between her snake and her human form, for the snake could often penetrate where the larger creatures could not. More than once her scouting saved them the need to backtrack.

After several days hiking in as straight a line as was possible, they came to the first of the barriers Li of the Iron Crutch had mentioned, the Forest of Stone Trees.

The Immortal's description didn't do the place justice.

"It doesn't look like a forest," Riprap protested. "It looks like someone set up a bunch of agate pillars at random—sort of a maze without solid walls. Then they stretched a sheet over it to substitute for the sky. Gives me the creeps."

Loyal Wind thought the pillars bore some resemblance to living trees. True, they lacked leaves or branches, but the striations of the multicolored stone did resemble the grain of living wood.

Copper Gong, still in ram form, was sniffing the ground. She looked up, nostrils flared.

"The ground from which these 'trees' spring smells rather like cement," she said, pawing the surface. "Feels like it, too."

"What bothers me," Des said, leaning back, hands on hips, to look at the sky, "is how that white sky starts exactly at the edge of the stone field. Makes the whole thing look like a stage set."

Nine Ducks had cut into the edge with one hoof.

"The same here," she said. "Look. Under the surface, the 'cement' edge is as clean cut as if it had been poured in a mold."

"What bothers me even more," Flying Claw said, consulting his compass, "is how quickly we reached here. I calculated our rate of progress during our prior visit, and again this time. It seems to me that we have found this Forest of Stone Trees too soon. Surely we covered at least as much distance during our much longer, earlier exploration."

Loyal Wind realized that once he would have been automatically aware of such an anomaly, but altered versions of time and space were so much a part of what was "normal" in a ghost's life that he had not noticed.

"You are right to be alert to such oddities," Loyal Wind said. "However, I wonder if somehow our journey was facilitated by the spirits of the Lands. Li of the Iron Crutch did tell us that many hsien found themselves exiled from their former homes. Perhaps word has spread of our desire to set things right, and the Lands themselves are helping us."

Riprap had been unpacking footgear from one of Nine Ducks's packs. Now he paused, his dark features troubled.

"I wonder who else might know we're coming," he said. "I can't help remembering Thundering Heaven's nasty attitude and that odd sword of his."

"And what we encountered at the end of the Tiger's Road," Des added. "Yeah. Maybe the local hsien welcome us, but I don't think we'd better count on everyone doing so."

Flying Claw lowered the binoculars with which he had been sighting out as far as he could through the stone pillars.

"I agree," he said. "As far as I can see, though, there is nothing out there, nothing at all. Are you all willing to continue?"

"Let's camp for the night," Bent Bamboo suggested. "Start in the morning with everyone fresh. That will also give us a chance to scout along the perimeter. Maybe we'll meet someone who can tell us more."

"At the least," Gentle Smoke said, "we can top off the water."

"My aching back," complained Nine Ducks, who carried the water bags, but Loyal Wind knew she wasn't serious.

Bent Bamboo's suggestion was sensible, so, even though Flying Claw was clearly eager to move on, the young Tiger agreed. Flying Claw did, however, insist on being one of those who would scout the perimeter. When he returned, all he brought with him was a fat deer.

"We can eat well tonight," Flying Claw said, dropping the carcass from where he had slung it over his broad shoulders, "and in the morning as well. This doe hardly started when I approached her. I had the impression that she had never seen a human."

Nothing interrupted their rest, and, with first light, they set off across the featureless expanse.

Li of the Iron Crutch had warned them that one of the worst features of this part of the journey was the hardness of the surface over which they must travel. To counter this, Riprap had purchased shoes that would protect the humans' feet. He had also acquired a variety of soft, rubberized materials. From these, he had made hoof covers for the Horse, Ox, and Ram. These had soft padding covered by thick soles that provided traction. Once he got used to wearing his, Loyal Wind had to admit they were an improvement over horseshoes.

Everyone—humans and not—had been provided with head and eye coverings as well. Loyal Wind was certain that his made him look very silly, but after several hours tromping over the featureless plain, the only distraction the wriggling lines of heat radiating up from the stone surface, he was glad to have both. The humans carried umbrellas as well, and from time to time Riprap would hold his over either the Ox or the Horse to provide some relief from the sun.

Copper Gong refused such pampering, saying that her packs were not nearly as heavy as those carried by the others.

Night came, and they were grateful for the chance to rest. They had to do without tents, because there was no way to picket them in the stone, but as rain seemed unlikely, no one much minded.

"I wonder if," Riprap said once they had all eaten and rested, "we should consider continuing after we've had a little sleep. Night would certainly be cooler."

"But we are navigating solely by the compass," Flying Claw reminded him. "Flashlights do not work here, and torches are cumbersome and unreliable. I would hate to discover we had strayed between compass checks."

"We could work a spell for light," Gentle Smoke mused, "but there are creatures that would be drawn to the spell—and we would not be able to see them coming."

In the end, they decided to keep traveling by day. They had packed plenty of water, and unless the structure of the terrain had changed since Li of the Iron Crutch had made his journey, there was promise of water at the end of the Forest of Stone Trees.

Li's report had led them to expect two days of such travel, but it was not until very late on the second day that they saw what must be the wall of water far in the distance.

"At least another half day, then," Riprap estimated. "I can't hear anything."

"I might," Loyal Wind said, twitching his horse ears forward. "A distant rumble, but then I could be imagining it."

Gentle Smoke stretched the length of her snake's body against the stone and begged them all to hold perfectly still.

After a long moment she said, "Perhaps a faint vibration, but like Loyal Wind, I could be imagining it."

It was not until evening of the third day that they reached the wall of water, and since the light was fading, they chose to stop short of the wall itself.

"We can sleep dry," Des said, toweling himself off. He and Flying Claw had insisted on going closer to the wall in order to inspect it. "Even thirty feet out the spray soaked me to the skin."

"And the sound!" Flying Claw added, pressing his hands lightly to his ears. "The sound was like a thousand tigers arguing with the grandmother of all thunderstorms. Thank you, Riprap, for insisting we pack those ear plugs. Even wearing them, I thought my head would split from the noise."

"There's no way," Des said, taking a dry shirt out of his pack, "we're going to cross that without magic—lots of magic. I'm glad we decided not to haul diving gear along. Even if we could breathe, the force of that falling water would pulverize us."

Flying Claw nodded. "And I'm glad we prepared spells in advance. I don't think I could concentrate to cast from memory—and more usual written charms would simply wash away."

He was bending over his pack as he spoke, pulling out a dry tunic and trousers. He had agreed that wearing his armor all day in the heat would be more bane than blessing, because if some monster rose from the plain to attack them, he would be too exhausted to fight effectively.

Loyal Wind wasn't precisely watching, but when he was a horse, he did tend to be more alert to sudden motion. Therefore, he noticed when Flying Claw quickly moved something from the pocket of his wet trousers into the pocket of his dry set.

Whatever it was was purple, a dark lavender shade

that Loyal Wind was certain he had seen before. In a moment he had placed it. . . . Brenda Morris liked that color, and often tied her long hair back with a soft fabric band in that precise shade.

Does the Tiger care for the Rat, then? Loyal Wind thought with the sensitivity of one romantic for the amours of another. *I believe he does, although he is very careful not to show his feelings too plainly. Sad. I think the girl would have welcomed a declaration, and now she is gone. If her father has his way, I would not be surprised if she is gone for a very long time.*

Loyal Wind wondered if, when this new life was over and he had returned to the afterlife, he should seek out the ghost of Water Cloud the Rooster. Although death had reunited them in a common state half a century ago, Loyal Wind had never sought her out, kept from doing so by his anger, resentment, and—he could admit it now—his own self-loathing.

But he had grown beyond that now, and although he wondered just a little why Water Cloud had never sought him out, he had to admit that even if she had, the reunion would not have been a joyful one.

Perhaps she sensed that, he thought. *Perhaps someone even told her what a sorry excuse for a man I had become. I will seek her out, even if only to apologize for thinking so much of myself that I didn't think better of her.*

When morning came, the scouts made preparations, then advanced on the wall of water.

One option they had discussed while in the Land of the Burning had been summoning one or more dragons to help them with the crossing, since dragons not only could breathe water as if it were air, but could extend this power to one or more companions.

However, Gentle Smoke had expressed concern

that they could not be certain that any dragon associated with this part of the Lands would not be in league with whoever had created this strange area.

"We would not wish," she said, "to be in the midst of that maelstrom and find ourselves betrayed."

Gentle Smoke had offered to come up with a solution that would enable them all to breath water and travel in close company. Bent Bamboo had offered to assist.

Now, with considerable pride, they revealed their creation.

"We apologize," Gentle Smoke began, "for not showing you sooner, but we were working on refinements until right before our departure."

She pulled out a slim piece of hollow bamboo, capped at each end, and from it slid a piece of rolled paper. Spread out, the paper revealed an intricate drawing surrounded by various ideograms.

The picture showed a fish rather like a carp except that on the bottom of its body, along with the two pairs of lower fins, were two sets of chicken legs.

"Is that a real creature?" Des asked, obviously amazed.

"It is," Gentle Smoke confirmed. "This is a Zao-Fish. They live in a lake fed by the snowmelt of a particular mountain. In the spring and early summer, the lake floods a considerable area, but in late summer the lake begins to dry up. The legs enable the fish to cross the dry areas to rejoin the larger part of the lake."

"Makes sense," Des said. "In a twisted sort of way. Why chicken legs?"

"Good eating?" Riprap hazarded. Then more seriously, "How can a Zao-Fish, or even a school of Zao-Fish, solve our problem?"

"Like dragons," Gentle Smoke said, "the Zao-Fish can breathe both air and water. Like dragons, they can share this ability with those who are in close contact with them.

"When I was alive, I had a cottage near the lake where the Zao-Fish lived and I grew very familiar with them. What I propose to do is enchant the semblance of a Zao-Fish to carry us on the next stage of our journey."

"Carry us?" asked Flying Claw.

"Yes. We will ride on its back. Our luggage can be carried within the belly."

Bent Bamboo took a box from his sleeve and opened it to display a perfect replica of a Zao-Fish, shaped from clay.

"We made this back at Pearl's," he explained, "and have already set the preliminary enchantments. We will need to activate various spells to give the fish greater size and the ability of independent motion."

What followed was a discussion of how the spell—or rather series of spells—could be worked.

"I'm going to feel really dumb riding on a giant goldfish with chicken legs," Riprap said. "I'd feel pretty dumb even if it didn't have chicken legs. Couldn't you have made a car or even a horse?"

"Cars would not likely function here," Gentle Smoke said calmly, "any more than flashlights do."

"And horses," Loyal Wind added, "don't breathe both water and air."

"Yeah, I know," Riprap persisted, "but this thing we're making won't either, will it? You've infused it with spells for water breathing and all that."

"And the spells will work," Gentle Smoke replied patiently, "because the Zao-Fish can do those things, and we will also be telling the clay figure that it is a Zao-Fish."

"A really big Zao-Fish," Des added, looking at the

clay model in Gentle Smoke's hands. "That one is hardly big enough to have for dinner."

"We will be activating spells of increase," Bent Bamboo said, rather less patiently. "Why don't you go and focus your ch'i? We're going to need a great deal, even with all the advanced preparation Gentle Smoke and I have done."

Loyal Wind decided meditation was a good choice for him as well. Staying in his horse form was no more tiring for him than remaining human, but the transition between forms was draining. Nine Ducks had already returned to her human form and withdrawn to the edge of the campsite.

"I agree with Bent Bamboo's suggestion," Nine Ducks said. "I am experiencing great difficulty in tapping the local ch'i—something I had not expected, since we are effectively upon earth and earth is the Ox's element. However, the currents seem bound into this strange, hard soil, and I can only release them with great effort."

Loyal Wind found it impossible for him to tap the local ch'i at all, not a great surprise given the proximity of vast amounts of water—the element that destroyed his own element of fire. However, he had long experience in enhancing his personal ch'i by circulating it through the various meridians of his body. He sank into deep meditation so that he might focus more efficiently.

When he was brought back into the outer world by a tap on the shoulder from Copper Gong, Loyal Wind found the Zao-Fish neatly set in the center of a small altar. The model was exquisitely detailed, with a long body, the dorsal fin set far back along its spine, its tail short and powerful, its eyes wide set and slightly bulging. Even the chicken legs were sculpted, the lumpy skin similar to yet different from the fish scales, detailed right down to the more polished surface of the clawed feet.

"Nice altar," Loyal Wind said.

"Riprap set it up," Gentle Smoke said, "so that Bent Bamboo and I would be free to meditate."

Riprap shrugged. "I could fetch and carry," he said, "and I'm not good at building my ch'i yet."

"Nine Ducks is right," the Monkey said, stretching in a manner that made his joints pop audibly. "The ch'i here is bound up tighter than—"

He caught a warning glance from Copper Gong and looked abashed. "Really tight. My element is metal, and I couldn't touch either earth or water."

"Then it is fortunate," Gentle Smoke said, "that you helped cast so many of the spells back in the Land of the Burning. Your generous expenditure of ch'i there means that we will need less now—and so have some left over for when we need it."

And I fear we will need it, Loyal Wind thought.

While shaping the model, Gentle Smoke had infused it with a number of stored spells. Now, with the assistance of the others, she activated them. One gave the fish the semblance of a living creature, its dark orange scales lightly mottled with black flecks, its fins translucent except for the continuation of the dark markings.

Another spell gave the Zao-Fish an appetite for luggage. Another made it receptive to carrying passengers—and strong enough to do so with ease. Others assured that it would breathe both water and air, and pass those qualities on to its passengers.

Gentle Smoke had not forgotten to ensure they would be able to see easily while under water, and to bear the pressure of the water beating down on them, for these were both natural traits of any fish.

"We may still get wet, though," Gentle Smoke said. "Zao-Fish like being wet."

The final spell was the one that gave the model its abnormal size. When it had been worked, and the luggage fed into its belly, Loyal Wind was more than happy to mount up and rest.

"I will take my snake form," Gentle Smoke said. "That will give the Zao-Fish a little less weight to carry—and if we need a scout ahead, I can swim fairly well in that form. Snakes are not as powerful as dragons, but I can protect myself from drowning."

"I wonder if the wall of water will also take three days to cross," Flying Claw speculated. "Tigers like to swim, but three days of wet is a bit much."

"We can hope not," Copper Gong said. "After all, crossing through water is much harder than walking over earth. The one only requires persistence, but the other requires a certain amount of ingenuity."

But the wall of water was indeed three days thick, three days of pounding water beating against them until they gave up on modesty and rode naked lest their clothing shred from the relentless pressure. The water was not particularly cold, but it chilled them to the bone nonetheless. Only the fact that the Zao-Fish considered being cold and wet natural kept the situation from being unbearable, for some of the Zao-Fish's attitude passed into its riders.

By the end of the first day, even Riprap and Bent Bamboo had lost the capacity to joke. Since the Zao-Fish was tireless as long as they continued to give it ch'i, they decided not to camp, but to press on.

Gentle Smoke periodically slid into the Zao-Fish's belly and emerged with food to sustain them; drink was unnecessary. The portions of cold meat, fruit, and a few eggs that had been boiled over the last fire were small, because although Gentle Smoke could be a large snake, she had many to feed and lacked hands. Nor could she spare the ch'i to shift form repeatedly.

Somewhat less than three full days later, they emerged from the wall of water into a zone where water and fire fought for dominance, creating a narrow stretch that steamed but did not burn.

"There's the next element," Riprap said, squeezing water from the wool of his hair with hands on which the skin was as wrinkled as prunes. "Fire."

The burning coals stretched as far as the eye could see. The heat rising from them warped the landscape, making any judgment of distance impossible.

"Fire," Des repeated. The force of the falling water had undone his hair from its usual neat braid, and now it fell in bedraggled strands across his naked torso. "I can hardly wait."

XV

Despite Parnell's ominous warning, the young man did not ask Brenda to accept his own claim to a less than normal heritage. Instead, he gave her time to think.

Back in her room, trying to fall asleep while staring at the glow-in-the-dark stars she'd glued to the ceiling over the top bunk, Brenda considered.

After all, what good would I be to anyone if I cracked up under the pressure of believing six impossible things before breakfast? I mean, that habit didn't do much good for the White Queen . . . or was it the Red Queen?

Brenda avoided being alone with Parnell for the better part of the next week. She saw him in classes—

noticing for the first time that his schedule pretty much overlapped her own: not always the same classes, but always in the same floor of the same building. Him walking with her between classes was as natural as could be.

Perfect for a bodyguard, she thought uneasily.

Brenda saw Parnell at the weekly meeting of the Celtic Culture Club, and often at meals in the cafeteria. A few times, she considered asking him to tell her more, but chickened out.

Then Gaheris called. "I'm going to be downstate seeing a client tomorrow. When's your last class?"

"It's over at two-thirty."

"Interested in coming home for the weekend? We could surprise Thomas for his birthday."

Normally, Brenda would have made an excuse; early term was a great time for socializing. This time, she jumped at the opportunity to get away from Parnell and the uncomfortable problem he posed.

"Great! I can meet you out front at three."

Brenda told Shannon, and wasn't surprised to see her roommate's eyes brighten. After all, Brenda being away meant that Shannon and Dermott would have some serious private time. Brenda wondered just how well Shannon's Catholic resolve was holding up under the pressure of Dermott's adoration, but she decided that was none of her business.

Parnell looked momentarily concerned when he heard Brenda was going away, but when he heard she was going home, he relaxed so visibly that Shannon grinned.

Shannon probably thinks Parnell's relief is because he has a crush on me, and everyone knows I don't have a boyfriend at home. I wonder what she'd think if she learned that his relief had more to do with his being my bodyguard, keeping me safe so I can do something the sidhe think is important somewhere down the road.

On the car ride home to Greenville, though, Brenda started regretting her decision. Other than the most general of generalities, Dad would not discuss anything to do with the Thirteen Orphans. He wouldn't even talk about Pearl's "accident" other than to express relief that Auntie Pearl hadn't been seriously hurt, and to confirm that Nissa was going to move to San Jose so Pearl wouldn't be alone.

The weekend home went well. To Brenda's surprise, Thomas actually was glad to see her—and not just because of the tee shirt with the USC gamecock that she'd bought him as a last-minute birthday gift.

Privately, wishing that Dad was being open enough that she felt like sharing the joke with him, Brenda admitted to herself she'd picked the shirt because the jaunty fighting chicken reminded her of Des Lee.

After Thomas's birthday party, Brenda tried to get Gaheris alone, but her dad steadfastly avoided her. Brenda didn't think it was a coincidence when Keely volunteered to drive her daughter back to Columbia on Sunday afternoon.

"Give you some mother-daughter quality time," Gaheris said brightly when Keely suggested it, but Brenda heard his words as "Avoid more father-daughter uncomfortable time."

Gaheris's stubborn silence, combined with Brenda's growing suspicion that he'd issued an ultimatum to the other Orphans, demanding that they keep his daughter in the dark, changed her feelings about learning more about Parnell and his strange heritage.

The last couple of times I've called San Jose, Brenda thought, *I could barely get confirmation that the scouts had returned to the Lands, and that Des had managed to check in when they crossed that petrified*

forest. That's it. Fine. If I can't learn anything from
my so-called friends, maybe I can learn something from
people who at least think I'm worthy of being courted
as an ally.

Of course, now that her resolve was set, when Brenda
got back to the dorm no one was around. She'd phoned
Shannon, giving her an estimated time of arrival, so at
least she didn't catch her friend and her beau in amo-
rous embrace, but she did feel a little hurt that no one
was there to welcome her back.

Shannon came back an hour or so later, Dermott-
less.

"He's playing soccer with some of the guys," she
said. "Boring . . . I have reading to do for English and
History."

Brenda realized she did, too, but as she tried to im-
merse herself in Arthur Miller, she found herself resenting a salesman who couldn't understand where
his own kids were coming from, resenting golden
boys who didn't do what they were expected to do.

Brenda didn't see Parnell until the next day, after
her second class. He ambled up to walk with her to
the cafeteria for lunch. She nearly hugged him, an impulse which surprised her as much as the actual act
would have surprised him.

"I want to know more," Brenda said.

"About?" A teasing light in his eyes.

"You know."

"I do," Parnell said, relenting, perhaps hearing from
the tone of Brenda's voice that she'd had her fill of
witty fellows that last weekend. "But not here, not
now. How about I drop by this evening and offer to
take you for a stroll?"

"I'll be ready," she said.

Parnell was as good as his word, showing up as
twilight was gathering, complaining that American

students took their studies far too seriously and his Irish brain cells needed a rest.

Brenda saw the hope in Dermott's eyes—he and Shannon had been "studying" since dinner—and had to swallow a grin as she said she'd be glad to go out for a while.

Parnell also saw the look the young couple exchanged and was less kind, filling the time that it took for Brenda to grab her sandals and a room key by making comments so loaded with double entendres that they were nearly single.

Brenda grabbed Parnell by the arm, rolling her eyes at a blushing Shannon.

"Sure and begosh and begorrah," Brenda said in a very, very bad imitation of an Irish brogue, "here I am wishing to take a break myself, me lad, and you stand there a-prattling. Will you be interested in buying me a latte and studying the stars rather than dry words on a page?"

"Gladly, fair colleen."

Giggling, they left, but the giggles stopped as soon as they were outside the immediate vicinity of the dorm.

"Okay," Brenda said when they were well away from eavesdropping ears. "Tell me more."

"Better than telling," Parnell said. "If you'll come with me, I'll show you a couple of things that should assure you that I'm not just spinning a yarn, not assuming you're a credulous reader of myth and legend and occasional bits of fantasy fiction who will swallow any tall tale."

"All right, then," Brenda said. "Lead on, MacDuff."

"Isn't it 'lay on'?" Parnell quoted with as wicked a grin as he'd ever given Dermott and Shannon.

"When I say lead," Brenda said, hiding her embarrassment at his double entendre with mock hauteur, "I mean lead."

Parnell took Brenda to one of those overlooked spaces that during the day would be filled by ample foot traffic as students passed back and forth to classes, but at this hour, when even the night classes were over, was deserted.

Parnell paused, turned slightly away from Brenda, scanned the immediate area, appeared to listen. There was something foxlike in his alert demeanor. Brenda found herself remembering her dream meetings with the green-eyed woman of the sidhe she'd come to think of as Leaf.

Leaf's ears had been slightly pointed.

When she was a horse, too, Brenda thought with a suppressed giggle. *I wonder if Parnell's ears are pointed. Hard to tell under those curls. I wonder if that's why he wears his hair so long. I mean, longer hair seems to be coming back in, but it's hardly universal.*

At last Parnell murmured, in a voice so soft Brenda wondered if he was talking to himself, "Right. All clear. Here goes."

He turned toward Brenda and motioned to the lawn beneath the tree. "If you would have a seat upon this grassy sward?"

Brenda lowered herself onto the lawn under the oak, anticipating the slightly prickly feeling of the close-cropped blades, wishing she'd thought to change into long pants. The university kept its lawns in beautiful shape, but that meant hardy strains of grass and frequent mowing, neither of which made for softness.

To Brenda's surprise, this grass was almost as soft as moss. There were tiny flowers growing in it: pale blue with gold centers, the stems as insubstantial as spiderwebs. She lifted her hand, horrified that she might have crushed some of the miniature beauties, but the flowers rose up again as if they had never felt her weight.

She looked at Parnell and realized that she could see him more clearly, his image no longer dimmed by the gathering dusk. Had a nearby streetlight gone on all of a sudden? She glanced around, noticed the surrounding area still cradled the blue-grey threads of twilight. Her heart began to pound harder. Parnell answered the question in her eyes.

"A wee bit of enchantment, yes . . . How can I convince you what I'm telling you is true if afterwards you'll be able to tell yourself you were fooled by the darkness? Don't worry. We're not spotlighted here—the opposite, in fact. I've thrown up a ward around us. To any who pass by, this space under the spreading oak is unoccupied—as in a sense it is."

The last was said with a note of challenge, and Brenda rose to it. "You've moved us a little into somewhere else. That's why the grass is so soft and the flowers aren't all smushed."

"Your experiences as a scion of the Thirteen Orphans have served you well, acushla," Parnell said. "Keep your heart firmly rooted in those memories. Last time we spoke, I spooked you some, I think."

"Well, you *were* talking about otherworldly creatures, and pronouncing warnings of doom and destruction," Brenda said tartly.

"I didn't say you were wrong to be spooked," Parnell replied. "I knew what I had to tell you would not be easy to take, and as I told you then, I had hoped to have more time to work you around to liking me so maybe you'd trust me a bit more easily, but Pearl's 'accident' was too much of a warning to ignore."

"I remember," Brenda said. "So, go on."

"I want to start by presenting you with my bona

fide character as a weird alien creature not in the least human," Parnell said. "That means later you can't get angry at me for holding out on you."

Brenda felt her fingers clutching the turf and forced them to relax and straighten. She gave Parnell a curt nod.

"Okay."

He shifted slightly, bringing his right arm out in front of him, turning the hand so the palm faced upward.

Brenda tensed again, expecting almost anything other than what happened. Parnell took a pocketknife out of his left pocket with his left hand, opened the blade with an ease that spoke either of much practice or ambidexterity, and then, before Brenda could move or protest, cut himself across the ball of his right thumb.

"'If you cut us,'" he quoted, "'do we not bleed?' The difficulty is . . ."

He bent, wiped the knife on the turf, folded it, stood, and slid the blade back into his pocket. Then, with his left hand, he gently squeezed the ball of his right thumb.

Something white as snow, thick as sap or honey, oozed from the cut.

". . . our blood—my blood—is white."

Brenda let impulse carry her past shock. With an almost apologetic glance at Parnell, she gently touched the wound on his thumb. There was no sleight of hand at work here. At even this slight pressure, more of the white oozed forth.

She jerked back her hand, nodded acceptance.

Parnell stuck his thumb in his mouth, a completely natural gesture, one Brenda herself had done dozens of times after nicking herself in the kitchen or on the edge of a sheet of paper.

After a moment, Parnell removed his thumb from his mouth, examined the still oozing wound, and tamped it with a perfectly normal handkerchief he pulled from his pocket.

"One good thing," he said. "My blood won't stain this like yours would."

Brenda was still too stunned to speak.

"You find references to the white blood of the sidhe folk here and there. Most of the time such references are framed in a Christian context—an excuse for the sidhe folk's professed propensity for stealing human children. The legends say we're trying to breed red blood into the next generation so we will be considered human enough to be admitted into the Christian heaven."

"Are you?"

Parnell laughed. "No. If heaven's that picky, most of us aren't interested. We don't even steal human babies. We've rescued a few, but that's not the same at all. Humans are interesting, yes, but it's a wholly human idea that you folks are some pinnacle of creation the rest of us are striving to reach."

Brenda tried hard to find something intelligent to say.

"Is that the only difference between us? Your white blood?"

"Oh, no," Parnell said. "There are many others. That was just the easiest way to show you that I'm as different as some of the people I'm going to introduce you to. . . ."

Brenda held up her hand. "Wait. Is this—" She ran a hand in the air to indicate the green-eyed, honey blond young man who sat comfortably curled on the grass near her. "—how you really look?"

"Right now it is," Parnell said, "and believe me, it's hard work maintaining a full shape-change, so I'm not shifting again. What you're seeing here isn't a mere glamour. I could be x-rayed and every organ would be in its proper place, every bone perfect."

"But if you were hit by a car," Brenda protested, "you'd bleed white goo."

"Actually," Parnell said, "even that detail has been attended to. I made a minor adjustment tonight—and don't be deciding that the whole thing is a trick."

"Don't worry," Brenda said. "I'm not. I never even heard about the white blood thing. You'd have done better to give yourself pointed ears or something if you'd just wanted to fool me."

"Harder," he said. "For reasons I'm not going into . . . And less likely, anyhow. Not all of us have pointed ears. We're not Vulcans or Romulans. Now, are you ready to meet a friend of mine?"

Brenda felt herself biting into her upper lip with her lower teeth and quickly corrected the gesture. She knew it looked really ugly, like she was some sort of ogre with an overshot jaw.

"Uh, sure. Is it Leaf?"

"Oh, no. You've met Leaf, sort of, kind of. I'm going to introduce you to someone else."

"Okay . . ."

Parnell looked directly at the trunk of the oak tree. "Come out, Gall. There's a lady waiting to meet you."

Brenda waited, expecting someone to walk around the trunk of the tree. Instead the trunk of the tree itself began to change character. What she'd taken for a lumpy growth—an oak gall, now that she thought about it—began to move.

Clapping her hand across her mouth to stifle a sudden squeak of surprise, Brenda watched as the oak gall grew—or extruded, she really wasn't sure which—skinny arms and legs. Using these, it pulled itself from the embrace of the tree's bark and hopped down onto the ground next to Parnell.

What stood there had no real head or body; it was just a small lumpy mass the color and texture of oak bark. The entire thing was about the size of a baseball, but not nearly as neatly spherical. It had a face in the way that you sometimes see faces on tree trunks—a sense of eyes, a nose, and a mouth, unevenly proportioned, but unforgettable once you saw them.

Brenda remembered how in her room at home there had been a stain on the paint on her bedroom wall, hardly more than a heightening of shadows. One night, padding into her partly lit room after a trip to the bathroom, she'd suddenly seen it as a demon face, ferocious and evil. Even in the brighter light of day, Brenda couldn't remove the impression that a demon was there and watching her. She'd hung a picture over the "face," but even then she could imagine the evil-seeming, glowering face was still there. Eventually, she'd convinced her mom to let her repaint.

That was how Gall's face worked. It wasn't anything like a face in the proper sense, but once Brenda saw it, saw the eyes bright as beetle carapaces staring at her with curiosity equal to her own, she couldn't ignore that it was really there.

Now that she'd had a moment to adjust, Brenda noticed that Gall wasn't humanoid. He had three legs, rather like twigs, set in a rough tripod around his base. He had at least four twiglike arms.

"So," said Gall, addressing Parnell, "is this a maiden or a hero?"

"Are the two mutually exclusive?" Parnell said. "Who this is, as you know perfectly well, is Brenda Morris. Remember, my lumpy friend, you agreed to come here. Don't pick now to act up."

Parnell's tone was friendly but stern. Brenda was

reminded of her dad talking to one of the boys when he acted in that jerky way boys can when they're nervous.

Nervous, she thought. *Yeah. Well, me, too.*

"This," Parnell said, turning to Brenda, "is Oak Gall—that is, you can call him that until he tells you otherwise. He's not the only oak gall, but there are times he acts as if he is."

Brenda held out a hand, doing her best to act normal.

"Hello, Mr. Oak Gall. I'm pleased to meet you."

Oak Gall walked forward, his gait spiderlike on those three spindly legs, but no less graceful for that. He took her hand—grasping it between two of his own and making a shaking motion. He was stronger than she'd expected.

Why do I expect to know anything? White blood. Walking and talking tree lumps.

Parnell was watching them both carefully, and Brenda realized that this meeting was as much a test for Oak Gall as it was for her.

I wonder why it matters? she thought. But what she said aloud was, "Anyone else lurking about?"

"Not tonight," Parnell said. "I thought two of us were enough."

"And one of you," Oak Gall said. He'd sat down, sprawling by supporting himself on various arms and legs. The more Brenda looked at him, the more she realized that her mind was what had superimposed the idea of arms and legs on the little rounded figure. Structurally, Oak Gall more resembled a daddy long-legs. If it lived in trees, that made a whole lot more sense than humanity's awkward bilateral symmetry.

"So there are Chinese spirits," Brenda said, thinking aloud. "And now I have to accept Irish ones. What else?"

Parnell shrugged. "Just about anything you can imagine."

"Imagine? Then do we give you your shapes through our imaginings?"

Oak Gall made a rude noise that Brenda decided to interpret as a derisive laugh. Parnell sighed.

"No, not really. Sometimes we take on the shapes you have created for us, because that's what you expect, but we aren't creatures of your imaginations."

"What are you?"

"Living, thinking beings . . . The world is full of us if you would just look. Modern humans don't want to look, so they miss a lot."

Brenda flung her arms around her legs and pillowed her chin on her bent knees. After a long moment, while she tried to wrap her brain around all this weirdness, she sighed.

"But what's real?"

"Real?"

"I mean, we've got you Irish creatures. I've met dragons and tigers that are just like what Chinese mythology would have led us to believe in. Right? From what Pearl and Des and the others have told us, there are tons of indigenous traditions, each with their own ideas. So what's real?"

Parnell grinned at her. "I can tell you were raised in a monotheistic, scientifically oriented culture, Brenda. Try this instead. It's all real."

"All? But the various traditions contradict each other!" Brenda unfolded herself and started talking faster, waving her hands as if that would get her point across. "I mean, Christians and Jews and like that say you live and die once. Tons of other religions say you get reincarnated. Some cultures say everything has a spirit in it—even rocks and buildings. Others say that only humans have souls. How can they all be right?"

Parnell grasped one of her flailing hands and gave it a soft squeeze. "Relax, Brenda. Try to think about it this way. Opposites, contradictions, whatever you want to call them, are more real than anything else. In a sense, we know what everything is by knowing what it's not."

"I don't get it."

"What is green? Bluer than yellow, yellower than blue."

Brenda had flinched when Parnell took her hand, but she didn't pull away. To be honest, those warm, slightly rough fingers were a distinct comfort. She forced herself to look at Oak Gall. The craggy, knobby, barky face was studying her. She wondered if she was the first human Oak Gall had ever met, if this was as startling for him as for her.

Parnell went on. "You're like a little bug who lives at the South Pole."

"Are there bugs at the South Pole?" Brenda said, trying hard to sound more relaxed. "Wouldn't it be too cold for them?"

"Don't try to distract me, Brenda." Parnell squeezed her hand one more time, then let it drop. "You yourself are too distracting by far. Now listen."

"Sorry. Okay. I'm a bug at the South Pole."

"You're *like* a bug at the South Pole. All you've ever seen are degrees of cold and ice and snow. Little Bug You judges everything by all this cold. You won't even believe there could be something as impossible as fire. You'll believe in greater and lesser degrees of cold as an intellectual exercise, but not in something as hot as fire."

Brenda straightened slightly, thrust her legs out in front of her. She'd always been like her dad in that she preferred to work through problems. Dithering was not her speed—not for long, at least.

"Okay," she said. "So now Little Bug Me goes out into the world away from the South Pole. Not only do I learn about fire, but I learn that there are places where snow and ice can't exist. I see. So this universe or multiverse or whatever that you're telling me about is like that. Everything, even flat-out contradictions, exists—and you don't need to go elsewhere to find it. It's right here, if you know how to look."

"That's about it."

"Parnell, do you really believe all that? That anything is possible if you know how to look?"

"Believe? Sure." He flashed a grin at her. "Understand? Not really, but I'll take that view over the one that tries to eliminate the contradictions to the point of not seeing what's in front of my nose."

Brenda looked over at Oak Gall. "Like him."

Oak Gall grinned at her. She wasn't sure how she knew, but she did.

"Like you," said the tree-bark creature.

☆

Despite the accident—as everyone had started calling it, to avoid the uncomfortable word "attack"—Pearl had insisted that Nissa stay in Virginia long enough to get her life in order. However, by the middle of the second week in September Nissa and Lani were back.

Pearl had insisted on driving to the airport to get them; she wasn't going to let herself be jinxed by one piece of bad timing. The car had been kept inside a garage since the accident, as had the van. When it must be parked and left, some very interesting wards were set. So far, no one had shown interest in either vehicle.

"I heard from Des," Pearl said when they got into the house and unloaded the luggage. "They've crossed the wall of water—on the back of a fish, apparently. They're working out plans to cross the sea of fire."

"I don't envy them," Nissa said. "I talked to Brenda today. She sounded keyed up, but not cranky. She suggested that Lani and I go ahead and take over her room right away, said that at the rate things are going, she might manage a visit at Christmas, but not before, and maybe not even then."

"She has a point," Pearl said reluctantly. "I don't like Gaheris's attitude, but I do understand. Brenda has her education to think about. Still, I hope she's finding a way to keep in practice with her magic."

"I doubt it," Nissa said. "Brenda's sharing a room with her friend Shannon. I can't see when Brenda would have the privacy to go over the various routines, not to mention that she has classes to take up her time. Honestly, Pearl, in a way Gaheris is behaving almost as badly as his father did. He probably wouldn't have let Brenda get involved with the Orphans if she hadn't been thrown right in the middle of the mess."

"Maybe," Pearl said, uncomfortable with the thought, but unable to deny Nissa's point. "Maybe so."

Pearl's house came back to life with the return of Nissa and Lani. Even the cats, Amala and Bonaventure—who Pearl had assumed had enjoyed the return to their more usual quiet—brightened. Bonaventure even deigned to lower his considerable dignity to chase a ball or piece of string for Lani.

Wang, the gardener, was thrilled to have his little assistant back. Joanne immediately started pestering to have Lani rejoin some of the play groups she'd enjoyed over the summer.

Nissa had decided that she could wait for the spring term to continue her pharmacological studies. Almost before she had unpacked, she resumed her daily amulet making, joined in the daily martial arts practice at Colm Lodge, and began insisting that Pearl start tutoring her in some of the more sophisticated techniques as she had promised.

All in all, life rapidly became very pleasant indeed. Pearl wondered why she could not divest herself of the feeling that this was merely the calm before the storm.

XVI

The scouts would have liked to take a full day to rest after slogging through the wall of water, but such a luxury was beyond their resources.

"At least we don't need to worry about getting fresh water to drink. Or bathing." Riprap commented. "Or making a fire to cook dinner. I'm finally warm again."

Copper Gong was less optimistic. "Enjoy it. When we pass through this sea of fire we'll all be hot and dehydrated soon enough."

Bent Bamboo bopped the Ram lightly on the head with one long-fingered hand. "Give it a rest, woman. You wanted to get back into the Lands. We're here. You should be gloating at your triumphant return."

"I wanted to get back home," Copper Gong said. "This place . . ." She waved a hand to take in the waterfall thundering down to one side of them, the gently undulating sea of molten ooze and ruddy coals on the other. "This place is nothing like home."

Nine Ducks, who was lying back against a heap of bedrolls, resting after working the spell that had dampened the sound of the falling water, looked at her longtime associate with a mixture of sympathy and annoyance.

"Absolutely nothing has gone according to plan since the days when our emperor began to lose his hold on the Jade Petal Throne," Nine Ducks said. "Isn't that so, Flying Claw?"

The young man had been staring gloomily over the sea of fire.

"I agree, Grandmother Ox. Since their creation, the Lands have always behaved in ways that—at least to those from the Land of the Burning—would be considered strange. However, some scholars have long argued that the attenuation of the Twelve Earthly Branches, which began with the departure of the Exiles, contributed to changes the like of which have not been seen in the over two thousand years the Lands have existed."

"We can't," Des said, breaking the silence, "do anything about any of that. What we can do is decide just how we plan to cross a sea of fire. Even if we managed to somehow fireproof our boots, I don't think we can hope to walk."

"I agree," Flying Claw said. "When we first arrived, I thought this was lava, but it is not. There is no sense of earth about it. This is purest fire. What we see as coals are not the husks of burnt material, but the eyes of the element itself."

"You're creeping me out, man," Riprap said. "But I get what you're saying. Is there a creature that lives in fire the way that fish live in water? Can we make ourselves a fire fish or whatever and use that for the next stage of the journey? What about phoenixes? Don't they live in fire?"

Des laughed. "You're thinking of the western version of the phoenix. That's a unique bird that once in a while—five hundred years, I think—lays an egg, then burns itself to ashes. The new phoenix comes from the egg and is hatched by the heat."

"The Chinese don't have a phoenix?" Riprap persisted. "I'm sure they do."

"The Vermillion Bird of the South," Nine Ducks said, "is sometimes called a phoenix by Westerners. So is the feng hua, which, although a mystical creature, has two sexes and is not in the least unique."

"Although seeing one," Gentle Smoke said softly, "is nearly as good an omen as seeing a ch'i-lin. I would not mind seeing a feng hua."

"To see a feng hua," Loyal Wind quoted from an ancient bestiary, "you must have a wu t'ung tree, and I fear there is not a single tree in this place."

"True."

There followed a rather morose silence, as if they had all somehow expected the feng hua to manifest.

"So, no creatures who live in fire," Riprap said, returning to his original point. "How about some version of dragon?"

Flying Claw, who had returned to his thoughtful study of the sea of fire, now turned his attention to them.

"I have been thinking about this problem," he said, "since Li of the Iron Crutch first told us what the hsien had described. When we were in the Land of the Burning, I made some preparations. I also consulted Righteous Drum, since sophisticated magic isn't my province."

"And you're only telling us now?" Riprap said indignantly.

"You and Des were very busy," Flying Claw replied with more mildness than might be expected from a Tiger. "As was everyone else. Moreover, I did not wish to speak until I was certain that there would be no better way for us to make our passage. I am still not certain my suggestion is the best."

"Go on," Riprap prompted. "I'm burning with curiosity."

"Let us hope," Flying Claw said, smiling a little at the pun, "that my plan will not leave more of you than that afire."

Des cut in. "Does this have anything to do with those squares of material you asked me to get for you—and the glue and bamboo?"

"And needles and thread," Flying Claw agreed. "Yes. What I propose is that we make kites to carry us over this sea of fire."

"Kites!" Bent Bamboo said, looking both appalled and intrigued. "You think we could?"

"Heat rises," Flying Claw replied. "We will use kites to carry us above the fire, then summon winds to propel us. Since air is not an element, I do not believe we will find it as tightly bound."

He paused, then added, "Actually, I know we won't. I've tested. The winds are as free as ever we could wish. Since we are west of Center, the west wind will be best—not so much because of how it blows, but because this is the quarter belonging to the West."

"The White Tiger's direction," Copper Gong said, sounding pleased for once. "That should offer us some additional support, since Pai Hu is an ally."

"We'd need a great deal of material," Gentle Smoke said dubiously, "if we are to make eight kites, each large enough to carry a person."

"We have found a way around that problem as well," Flying Claw said. "When I consulted Righteous Drum, he suggested that we make our kites small and then enlarge them magically."

"As we did with the Zao-fish," Gentle Smoke said.

"Yes. Righteous Drum knew of your plan, and told

me of your clever solution to the problem of our needing to carry too much material. Des helped me research the best fabric for making kites, and how to bind it securely to the frame."

Des nodded. "I thought you had some sort of scouting device in mind."

"I didn't wish," Flying Claw said, "to be presumptuous."

Flying Claw is young enough to worry about seeming a fool, Loyal Wind thought, *yet old enough not to run about flapping his lips, bragging that he has a brilliant solution to all our problems. If he lives, this Flying Claw could be quite a formidable Tiger.*

"I remember that fabric," Riprap said. "I packed it. I thought it was part of Des's store of gifts for any potentially friendly hsien we might meet."

He went over to the luggage and dug out a plastic bag containing more than a dozen square pieces of brightly colored fabric.

"There should be a bundle of bamboo rods," Des said, "and a bottle of glue. Oh, and the ribbons for the tails. Get the sewing kit, too. I put in a couple spools of a particularly strong thread the man at the hobby store recommended."

He spoke to Flying Claw, his tone mildly reproving. "I wish you'd told me what you had in mind. The fellow at the store tried to convince me to get some lightweight fiberglass rods as well. Those would have been stronger than bamboo."

"Probably," Flying Claw agreed, "but I think bamboo will serve us very well here. Not only is bamboo one of the suits in the version of magic you Orphans use, but 'Bent Bamboo' is the name of one of our company. Resonance and sympathy are key to strong magic."

"You have a point," Des agreed. "What do we do first? I haven't made a kite since my son and daughter lost interest in children's games."

"I drew plans," Flying Claw said, "and made copies on the machine in Pearl's office. Lani knew what buttons to push, and I figured out all the rest."

He looked proud of himself. Loyal Wind, who had often been confused during his sojourn in Pearl's house, where clerks and servants were replaced by various machines, completely understood.

Flying Claw shook the plans out of a bamboo scroll tube. "These are a workable design for a kite that will carry a single person. My late master was fascinated by the possibilities of flight, and since I had always loved kites, I became his assistant."

"Flying Tigers," Loyal Wind heard Riprap mutter bemusedly, and wondered why Des chuckled.

"Do we make our own kites?" Nine Ducks asked.

"That would be best," Flying Claw said. "I asked Des to select fabric in each of our colors, two pieces each, so that we all have plenty. I will assist as needed."

"Good," Nine Ducks said. "I haven't made a kite since before Desperate Lee was born—and that only counts my life in the body."

Loyal Wind had made kites more recently—at least if he counted only the life of his body. The military used them to carry lines across gorges and kite fighting was considered quite a martial entertainment.

Flying Claw's plans were very neatly drawn. As he reviewed them, Loyal Wind was surprised to see that the end result of his labors would be a simple diamond kite.

"I thought you might have selected one of those kites shaped like a bird in flight," he said.

"My master tried those," Flying Claw said, "and

found that human legs trailing behind were destabilizing. In this design, the entirety of the passenger is contained beneath the diamond. The fabric tail provides balance, just as it would in a more usual kite."

"If you say so," Loyal Wind said, trying to keep the doubt from his voice, but obviously not succeeding. Flying Claw tapped the plans and went on with his explanation.

"This is actually a modification of the diamond kite. There is an additional rod, slightly bent, that makes the kite very stable. We could even do without a tail, but there is no reason we should not permit ourselves the added flourish."

Riprap looked up from his copy of the plans. "This looks a lot like what we call an Eddy Kite. I helped make some when a kite enthusiast came to talk at the Y. You're right. They have lots of lift."

"I thought all you did was play baseball and basketball and sometimes soccer," Flying Claw teased.

"I made basic diamond kites with my kids at the Y every spring," Riprap said. "Can't always play baseball. Kites are a great alternative when the winds are high. Now, do you want us to use glue or stitching?"

"Both," Flying Claw responded promptly. "Oh. That's right. You can't read my instructions. I apologize."

"Yeah, I don't read Chinese," Riprap said with a shrug. "Only speak it courtesy of that spell. Don't worry. Your plans are clear enough for most of this. Are you sure glue will hold?"

"Des provided a glue specifically made to bind this fabric," Flying Claw said. "Then I took it to Righteous Drum and he and Honey Dream ensorcelled it for firmer binding. The stitches are reenforcement. They also provide the means for anchoring the physical elements of the enlargement spells and the target points that will enable you to use the winds not only to move, but to steer. The kite fabric, thread, and bamboo have also been treated to resist heat."

"You seem to have thought of everything," Riprap said admiringly, making a few notes with a pencil on his copy of the plans.

"My late master," Flying Claw said, and there was no mistaking the sorrow in his voice, "was a creative and intelligent man."

Loyal Wind remembered Flying Claw's master well, although as Horse and Tiger they had rarely worked in concert. Both were martial in orientation, but the Horse preferred the herd and the Tiger single combat or stalking.

Well, old friend, he thought, carefully placing the stitches where indicated on the red fabric of his kite, *you trained your student well, although I doubt you had the least inkling in what very odd circumstances your teachings would be used.*

There was no need to place a bridle or a towline string on the kite, since the passenger would both handle the steering and control the elevation.

After checking with Flying Claw and finding that the color of tail streamers didn't matter, Loyal Wind chose a random assortment in all the colors of the rainbow. Once these were securely fastened in place, he went to help Nine Ducks with her kite. The older woman was grateful for his assistance in stretching the yellow fabric over the frame and fastening it in place.

"I can't believe I'll be flying," Nine Ducks said. "I don't know why I'm so astonished. I've done more remarkable things since I died, but now that I have a body again, I am loath to risk it."

"At least we know where we'll end up," Loyal Wind said, "but I have no reason to doubt our young Tiger's plans."

Copper Gong, who was giving her yellow kite a tail of fluorescent orange and lime green streamers, snorted.

"If it was so easy, why hasn't this been done for a thousand years? I hope Flying Claw's master wasn't deluded."

Flying Claw overheard her, but rather than losing his temper as Loyal Wind feared he might, he came and hunkered next to Copper Gong, his own dark green, miniature kite in his hands. He'd made the tail lavender, Loyal Wind noticed, and wondered if he was the only one who realized the significance of this little gesture.

"Sadly," Flying Claw said to Copper Gong, speaking so his voice would carry to them all, "these kites will not work in every situation. My master carefully studied the lifting power of various sorts of air. He was fascinated with how much power is contained in hot air. Moreover, to utilize the kite for flight, the passenger must be able not only to summon but to work with the wind. None but those with training in magic could do what we are about to do. A stored spell might summon the wind, but never control it with the flexibility we will need."

Copper Gong had the grace to look ashamed.

"I'm sorry for doubting, Flying Claw." She grinned, looking almost pretty without her habitually sour expression. "I guess Nine Ducks isn't the only one who fears flying."

Fear or not, within a few hours, all eight kites were completed: three yellow, one green, two red, and two white. Despite their basic similarity of form, each said something about its maker, whether in the color of the streamers or in some other flourish. Bent Bamboo had borrowed Des's pen and drawn a grinning monkey face on the outer surface of his white kite. He had made the tails of his kite from bright yellow ribbons and now he wrote "The Flying Banana" beneath the monkey face.

"I have scrolls with the enlargement spell written out," Flying Claw said, not deigning to comment on this silliness. "One apiece, so please take care. Riprap, I'd better read yours, since you don't read Chinese."

"I'm not in the least insulted," Riprap assured him.

The members of their group separated, walking up and down the narrow "beach" between the wall of water and sea of fire so that they would not distract each other in their casting. When they were done, they all held kites slightly longer than themselves, and pro-portionately wide.

"Looks great," Bent Bamboo said. "What do we do about the luggage?"

"I have made one more kite," Flying Claw said, holding it up, "and will attach it to my own in a train. It will hold the baggage—or what each of us cannot carry on our persons."

"Can you handle two kites?" Nine Ducks asked, her concern evident.

"I can," Flying Claw said. "My master and I experi-mented with this also, since flying in a warrior with-out weapons or armor would be of limited value."

"We've gone through a good deal of the food," Des said, "and some of the supplies. We can cache the rub-berized footwear here, in case we need it on the way back. That will lighten our load."

"We can use the shell of the Zao-Fish to hold what we must leave," Gentle Smoke said. "The ch'i neces-sary to give it motion is exhausted, but the form will remain sound for some time to come."

Rearranging packs, sorting through what was nec-essary and what could be left, took them through to twilight.

"I had hoped to depart today," Flying Claw said,

"but depending on the speed of our journey we may be forced to fly in darkness as we cross the sea of fire. No need to begin with that handicap."

"Yeah," Bent Bamboo said, hefting his kite and looking eye to eye with the monkey he'd drawn on its surface, "especially since I'm getting the idea we're not going to be given a chance to practice."

"No," Flying Claw said. "I am afraid not."

Breakfast the next morning used up the last of the presoaked meat.

"Fill your canteens," Copper Gong reminded them, "and hang them where you can reach them."

"Yes, Mama," Bent Bamboo said, but he said it softly, aware even without the steely gaze of reprimand Loyal Wind sent his way that Copper Gong was talking to cover her own nervousness.

"Put yourself within the shell of your kite," Flying Claw said, demonstrating with his own. "Slide your arms through the shoulder straps and strap tight the chest harness. Make sure the belt at the waist is secured and doesn't get in the way of anything else you're going to want to reach. Once you're in the air, it will be too late to adjust it.

"The kites have handholds and a footrest of sorts. If you need to steer, lean right or left. Press your weight down against your heels to pull the kite's head up and rise; lean your upper body and curl your shoulders to descend. Minor motion, like reaching for something hanging on your belt, will not be enough to unbalance the kite, because most of your weight is centered on the harness. Everyone understand?"

Murmured agreement.

"Good. Now, earlier, I gave everyone a copy of a spell for raising the wind. Riprap, you're going to use one of your amulets, right?"

"Right."

"I'll go first to demonstrate. Des, are you set to launch my train?"

"Set," Desperate Lee assured him, holding up one hand to show he already held the spare wind amulet.

"Good," Flying Claw said. "You'll be surprised how easy it will be for us to talk once we're aloft. It's very quiet up there. Even so, I suggest we stay within a loose formation—not so close that we tangle each other, but close enough to talk without our voices carrying too far."

Much of this had been discussed the night before, but Loyal Wind appreciated that, as a good commander would, Flying Claw was providing a briefing.

"Any questions?"

"How do we pee?" Bent Bamboo said.

"Sadly, without much dignity," Flying Claw said. "Gravity works as usual and the fire below should handle waste disposal. The good news is that if the distance involved is similar to that of the field of stone and the wall of water, we should cross by sometime tonight. Our winds will not need a rest, and will carry us much more quickly than we can walk."

Loyal Wind noticed that all the women looked decidedly uncomfortable about the lack of comfort facilities, but none were complaining.

They are of the Twelve chosen to affiliate with the Earthly Branches, he thought proudly. *I don't doubt they had already considered this matter, and have made plans.*

Bent Bamboo's was the only question, so Flying Claw went to stand a few feet back from the sea of fire.

He bent his head and murmured the activating words for the spell stored on the piece of paper he held in his hand. There was a slight pause, then a wind that touched only the young Tiger and his immediate surroundings began to make itself known. When its intensity rose so that the fabric of the kite belled out, Flying Claw breathed a word of command and leapt up and out— over the fire.

For a horrible moment it seemed that he would fall into the seething red and orange mass. Then the wind caught and Flying Claw rose a good twenty feet above them.

"Now, Des!" came the firm, strong voice of command.

Des activated the second wind spell. The kite carrying the extra luggage rose to follow Flying Claw. Flying Claw adapted his loft so that both kites flew clear, then moved out from the shore a short distance.

"Ox!" he called. "Now!"

Summoned as her sign, not herself, Nine Ducks put her fear aside. She had followed Bent Bamboo's example and borrowed someone's pen. A long, triangular ox's head, complete with a water buffalo's curving horns, adorned the yellow fabric of her kite. The streamers of the tripartite tail were shades of light and dark green, like the grass that is the grazer's favorite food.

The spell was spoken. As the wind gained strength, the old woman rose into the air nearly as gracefully as had the young man. She laughed in purest delight as she moved out to join Flying Claw.

"This is fun!" she exclaimed, slipping her feet onto the rest. "Come on, Loyal Wind."

Loyal Wind had not felt trepidation until this moment, but now as he stood at the edge of the sea of fire, feeling the heat curling the hair of his beard, he wondered what it would be like to fall into that red-hot mass. Would he even know if he burned alive or would he crisp instantly?

But Loyal Wind could not show hesitation, not with battle joined and before him. Perhaps a little louder than need be, Loyal Wind spoke the words to activate his share of the west wind and felt himself rise. Nine Ducks was right . . . rising into the air like this, feeling the gentle tug of the kite against his back, was fun.

One after the other, the rest of the group lofted into the dull violet, heat-seared sky over the sea of fire.

"Now we will rise to an elevation where the heat will still lift us, but not be so uncomfortable," Flying Claw said. "Copper Gong, you take point, as we discussed last night. I will take my train onto the farthest right flank; Loyal Wind will cover the farthest left."

Everyone fell into their assigned places with relative ease. Des and Riprap were immediately behind and to the sides of Copper Gong. Behind them, extending the triangle, were Nine Ducks and Gentle Smoke. In this way, the two from the Land of the Burning—the only true mortals among them and the least accustomed to working magic in difficult situations—were framed by experienced spell casters. Bent Bamboo took rear guard, directly behind Copper Gong but two or so human lengths behind.

Or that was the plan. The reality was less organized, with awkward flyers bobbing in and out, kite tails occasionally tangling and needing to be tugged free. Intimidated by the promise of punishment for failure offered by the red and orange and occasionally yellow flames that flowed beneath them, everyone was very careful. Soon enough their desired order had been achieved.

Looking down from up here, you could forget and think that those burning coals were a field of exotic flowers, Loyal Wind thought, *if it weren't for the heat that touches the skin even here.*

He discovered he rather liked flying. As Flying Claw had promised, the kites were astonishingly quiet. Only the caress of his personal wind reminded Loyal Wind how swiftly they were moving. Wind did not roar in his ears, because his speed was that of the wind. There was no thud of horse hooves, no jingle of harness or bridle. The only constant sound was the slight hum of the wind playing against the fabric of his kite, and this was as much felt as heard.

The conversation of his fellows broke the silence for a time. Then even that dropped away, for the uninterrupted vista of burning sea below and dull violet sky did not inspire idle chatter.

Loyal Wind was starting to drowse—not precisely falling asleep, but letting himself fall into the sort of alert trance that every soldier learns while standing guard—when he was startled from his reverie by a whoop and chortle from Bent Bamboo.

Although Bent Bamboo had proven himself quite a good companion, reliable when needed, still he remained a Monkey. Apparently, to drive away boredom, the Monkey had decided to test the limits of his kite.

"Look at me!" Bent Bamboo shouted, ignoring the fact that to do so most of their company would need to turn out of formation and risk tangling with each other. "I can do flips! This is really flying!"

And flip he did—not just gliding along, covering the maximum amount of distance in the minimum amount of time as they had planned, but dipping and soaring, wobbling the sides of his kite in a fashion that made the ribbons fastened to the tips cavort in a strange, aerial ballet.

Loyal Wind dropped slightly back so he could watch, utterly appalled by this lack of discipline, uncertain whether he should force the Monkey back into formation or wait for this—hopefully short-lived—spasm to wear off.

Bent Bamboo began slowly turning himself over in a somersault, investigating the limits between the motions that permitted the kite to rise and fall.

He was halfway into a turn when disaster hit.

In his effort to turn completely head over heels, Bent Bamboo had forgotten that what gave him the power of flight were not wings, but instead a kite. When Bent Bamboo turned his kite so that his head pointed straight down, rather than at an angle to the wind, that wind, magical although it was, could not drive the kite.

Bent Bamboo began to plummet toward the sea of burning coals, his delighted laughter transforming into a scream of raw terror.

Loyal Wind assessed the situation in less than a breath.

Flying Claw was the most experienced of their number, but he was hobbled by the kite train that carried their baggage. Even if he cut the train loose, valuable seconds would be wasted. The others were farther away. A few, Copper Gong and Gentle Smoke in particular, had been doing their best to ignore the Monkey's antics.

Probably hoped, Loyal Wind thought, angling his kite so that he could enter a controlled dive, *that they could discourage him by seeming uninterested. Since when has that ever worked with a Monkey?*

There was no time, not even to listen to the shouts from the others. Loyal Wind spoke to the wind that drove his kite, telling it that stability could be sacrificed for speed. He shifted his weight, driving the kite down toward the sea of fire, toward the Monkey.

Bent Bamboo had stopped screaming and was wrestling with his kite, trying to return it to its proper orientation. His success was limited, but he had succeeded in breaking the speed of his fall. Now instead of plummeting arrowlike, the kite drifted downward as a leaf would on a breeze.

But the yellow and white kite was still falling. The heat below was increasing. Sweat dripped from Loyal Wind's face, stinging his eyes, running into his mouth, tickling his skin, the irritations changing with every shift of orientation he made. He did not pause to wipe it away, even when the sweat caused his vision to intermittently blur.

Loyal Wind swept in as close to Bent Bamboo and his foundering vessel as he dared. Releasing one of the handholds of his own kite, feeling every move he made shift his weight, the Horse reached out with his right hand and grasped some of the trailing, bright yellow ribbons of one of the Monkey-kite's tails.

Shifting his weight left to compensate for the drag, Loyal Wind took a tight hold. The sweat coursing over him made the ribbons slick and hard to grasp.

Now Loyal Wind ordered the wind to give him as much lift as possible.

Yes, Brother Wind came the faintest of whispers, so faint that Loyal Wind was uncertain he had heard it.

The force lifting his kite increased, enough to stop Bent Bamboo's fall.

But there was not sufficient force for them to rise, not with Bent Bamboo's kite confined to its awkward angle by Loyal Wind's hold on the tail.

He was trying to figure out what to do next when Des spoke from slightly above and to the opposite side of Bent Bamboo's kite.

"Bent Bamboo, balance yourself carefully. I can just get a hold on this other tail."

A soft curse. A smell that took Loyal Wind a moment to place. Burning hair.

He shook his head to free his face from some of the sweat and looked down. They were far closer than he had realized to the sea of fire. Perhaps within a few yards.

Then they were rising as Des and his kite took up some of the burden. Once they were a good twenty feet above the fire—although still too close for comfort—Gentle Smoke and Nine Ducks joined them. Working in very careful concert, they helped Bent Bamboo right his kite so that the wind could once again give it proper lift.

As they rose in unison into the somber violet sky, Loyal Wind felt his sweat drying. When separated into their formation, he saw that the end of Des's long braid had been burnt crisp.

So close, Loyal Wind thought. *Too damn close.*

When he managed a swallow from his water flask, the water was as hot as a cup of tea and tasted of sour leather.

It was the best drink he'd ever had.

XVII

In the days following her introduction to Oak Gall, Brenda met several other of the sidhe folk. None of them were at all what she had expected.

Wasp was prettier than Oak Gall, a sharp-featured, vaguely womanlike creature with wings like a wasp's and a temper to match. When she thought Brenda was being stupid—which was frequently—she spat tiny mud balls at her. Brenda thought it was fortunate that Wasp wasn't much more than six inches long, otherwise her missiles would do more than sting.

Because no one ever seemed to notice her, Wasp most often spelled Parnell when the seeming young man couldn't be with Brenda. Brenda had gotten used to feeling those little mud balls hit her at the weirdest times.

Nettle was taller than Wasp and slimmer than Oak Gall, but, like his fellows, he only resembled something human if Brenda stretched her imagination. He was covered in fine hair that shaded between pale green and paler yellow. Sometimes he wore a tunic made from what looked like two multilobed leaves, and a cap that resembled an elongated oval seed pod. Sometimes he didn't bother with attire, and then Brenda did her best to not look to see if he was more like a man or more like a gangly plant.

Both, she decided. *Oak Gall, Wasp, and Nettle look like both. I wonder, does Parnell look like a plant, when he's not looking like a human? Is he a tree, maybe? A sort of male dryad. That would explain why his blood is white, like sap. Didn't the druids worship trees? And weren't the sidhe sort of associated with old gods?*

Brenda knew she was struggling to find logic where none applied, but she couldn't help herself. Anyhow, the idea of Parnell as the human embodiment of some noble tree was better than thinking of him as something else: a dandelion, maybe, or a shamrock.

"Are you keeping up with your lessons now?" Parnell asked Brenda one evening when they'd taken their books out onto one of the greens to study in the pleasant ebbing heat of mid-September.

"Can't you see I am?" Brenda said, indicating the books spread around her. "My Lit survey teacher seems to think we have nothing to do but read for her class. She's completely impossible. Thank God my accounting elective is all stuff Dad taught me years ago."

"No, girlie," Parnell said with a chuckle, "I don't mean your college classes. I'm referring to the important lore you spent all summer devoting yourself to learning."

"You mean the Orphans stuff?" Brenda asked, knowing perfectly well that he did.

"I do."

"Well, a little. I've been trying to memorize some of the sequences, but it's not as if I can sit and make amulet bracelets."

She touched the two she wore, one on each wrist: a Dragon's Tail for protection, a Dragon's Breath for attack. These two bracelets and her notebook were all Gaheris Morris would let her bring away. When they'd left Pearl's house, Brenda had been too crushed to protest. She wondered if Gaheris had even known about the notebook—such aids to memory weren't usually permitted.

Besides, she thought, *it's not like I really need amulet bracelets, even if I did make a bunch. The other Orphans need them, not me. I'm out of it.*

Wasp spat a disapproving mud ball. "Self-pity. It reeks to the heavens and offends the angels, it does."

"Angels?" Brenda said. "What do you know about angels?"

"That they're with God in his Heaven," Parnell answered for the annoyed Wasp, "or so the stories tell. Don't try to change the subject, Brenda darling."

"I'm not," Brenda retorted haughtily. "And, no, I haven't really been keeping up with my 'lessons,' as you call them. What does it matter? Dad's sent me away. No one at Pearl's talks to me."

A mud ball hit her hand, mute testimony as to what Wasp thought of this excuse.

"And so you're never going to be the Rat someday,

are you?" Parnell asked. "And when you are, you're content to be as useless as if you never knew about your heritage?"

Brenda frowned. "Dad's not all that old. He'll be around for decades. Probably by the time I'm the Rat, all this trouble will be over, and what I know won't matter."

"And who will teach the young ones?" Parnell persisted. "Are you thinking Pearl Bright will live forever? Are you thinking that Shen Kung will, too?"

"There's Des," Brenda said, but she knew this was a weak excuse.

"You're the youngest of the Orphans who has any training," Parnell said firmly. "That gives you responsibilities."

"But how . . ." Brenda heard the whine in her voice, caught herself, and started over. "But I can't possibly make amulets in my room. There's no privacy."

"Do you need the amulets, then?"

Brenda's frown returned. "Theoretically, no, but realistically—yeah, I do."

"Why?"

"Because I don't know how to channel my ch'i, because the sequences don't come to me fast enough. Because Des made it very clear that it's dangerous to play around with the spells without proper wards."

"But if you were not playing, Breni, how would that suit you? I could set wards for you, so you could practice. You wouldn't even need to try the more lively workings. What about getting down the one that lets you see magical manifestations?"

"All Green? I'm pretty good at that one already. Since it doesn't summon anything, I could practice that without heavy wards."

"All right. Then why don't you start with a simple attack, that and an All Green or so. I'll provide wards."

"Well, I don't want to forget everything," Brenda said slowly. "All right. I'll do it."

"Starting tonight?"

"Just as soon as I run up to my room and get my notes."

"I'll be setting up a ward," Parnell promised, "over by the tree where you met Oak Gall."

Brenda started walking toward her dorm. Almost without conscious intention, her pace quickened until she was running.

Her heart felt lighter than it had for weeks, even though her soul was troubled at this latest intimation that, despite the recent quiet, Parnell still dreaded some occurrence and wanted her prepared.

Be prepared, Brenda thought. *That's somebody or other's creed. I guess I'd better make it mine, before I'm left with nothing but regrets.*

☆

"You took what was mine," hissed the whisper.

Pearl looked around. She was sitting in the reading chair in her bedroom. Her book had fallen into her lap, but she didn't think she'd been sleeping.

Of course, she'd been bone tired lately. She might have dozed off. Maybe that voice was from the tail end of a dream.

Drowsily, Pearl reached for the book—a charming little memoir one of her friends had sent her, seeking her opinion as to whether it could be adapted successfully into a movie.

Although it had been many, many years since she had acted, Pearl remained active behind the scenes in the world of film. She was frequently told she had a good sense of story and dramatic timing.

And no wonder, Pearl thought. *So much of my life has been a story, a drama of my own construction.*

"You took what was mine," came the whisper again.

Pearl sprang to her feet, looking about. No one was there. No one behind her chair. No one—she felt foolish as she got down on stiff knees to check—under her bed.

Leaning against the mattress, Pearl got slowly to her feet, her muscles aching, her knees stiff and swollen. Her right elbow—on which she had leaned (the hand was stronger, but still healing)—didn't like her very much either.

I must have overdone it at sword practice this morning, Pearl thought. *Well, what can I expect, exchanging off-hand blows with Thorn, who could be my grandson, great-grandson if I started young enough.*

Pearl moved toward the closet, pushing aside the tidy racks of dresses, the slacks on their hangers, blouses, skirts. Nothing behind them. No indication that the shoes, ordered by style and color on their racks, had been moved.

"Mine. All mine," came the whisper, so soft and hoarse that it was genderless. It quivered with barely contained wrath. "I had a place. A home. A duty. You stole it from me. You took what was mine, and what did you do with it? Nothing! Nothing!"

Pearl moved more quickly now, the stiffness in her limbs forgotten in building fear. Where could that voice be coming from? Her gaze fell upon the door that led into the bathroom.

Someone must be hiding in there!

Her heart pounding hard, Pearl threw open the bathroom door. A small nightlight burned with a soft green glow, sufficient to illuminate the small room. Clearly visible were the toilet, sink with a cabinet beneath it, and shower/tub enclosure.

The room appeared to be empty, but just to make

certain, Pearl pushed back the shower curtain. This was printed with bamboo, and for a moment Pearl felt as if she were pushing through a tangled forest.

Nothing. The tub was empty. The pristine white enamel showed no marks.

Pearl opened the door on the other side of the bathroom. This led into a room only slightly smaller than her bedroom. She had used it as a private living room when she had had interns staying with her.

When the current troubles had begun, back in May, she and Des had converted it into a studio where the three apprentices could make amulets. It also served as a classroom, where Des or Pearl or Albert could lecture on arcane matters without fearing that the gardener or the twice-a-week maid might overhear.

There was no light on in this room. The partial light that filtered in through the windows showed only lumpish figures in shades of grey. Aware that her hand was trembling, hating herself for her growing apprehension, Pearl flipped on the light switch.

Harsh white overhead light transformed those grey forms into a utilitarian table large enough to seat six, comfortable folding chairs, bookcases, and a small table holding a toaster oven. Nothing else. The door into the hallway was shut, and the very basic lines of the furniture offered no concealment.

"Why did you have to be born? What use have you been?"

The whisper came from behind her now. Pearl swung around, looked through the pale green light of the bathroom into her bedroom. She saw nothing.

Purposefully, Pearl switched off the light in the studio and closed the door firmly behind her. Like most bathroom doors, it had a simple lock. She fastened this, assuring that her tormentor couldn't slip through that way without her hearing.

Pearl paced back through the green-lit bamboo-lined jungle of her bathroom, her slippers soundless on the tiny white hexagonal tiles of the floor. Once again, she closed the door behind her.

Her reading light cast an ample glow through her bedroom, but now Pearl moved to turn on the overhead light. Under this brilliant illumination, Pearl scanned the areas nearest to the windows, the joins of floor and ceiling. This time she was not looking for a person, but for wires, for a speaker, anything that might be transmitting those horrible whispered imprecations.

"A waste, a waste," said the whisperer, "and you took it all from me for nothing but this sterile existence, the perpetual playing at pretend."

There were no wires. No tape player. Could there be some sort of mini-spy system? A wireless device? But no. The voice shifted around the room, acid words coming forth harsh and cold. Judgment passed, doom pronounced.

Pearl sketched the glowing characters for All Green. Her wards, both within and outside of the house, were so good that she had not thought magic could be used against her. Perhaps she had been overconfident.

When the spell had transformed her vision, Pearl examined her bedroom once more. Other than her own green characters inscribed on floor and ceiling, doorframe and window frame, there was nothing. She looked again, knowing that if someone . . .

. . . *(Another Tiger, another Tiger)* . . .

. . . had worked the spell the color would be the same; even the handwriting might be similar if the one who had written them possessed a style similar to her own.

. . . *(Old Tiger, Thundering Heaven, teacher, enemy, adored object)* . . .

But there was nothing.

The whispering had continued during her inspection, rising in timbre. Accusations of failure, of theft, of misuse of valued commodities.

Pearl spun in place, twisting and turning, looking over her shoulder, moving fast as she could, trying to see where the whisperer was. Even when she angled herself so that the full-length mirror on the stand in one corner made it possible to see both in front and in back of her, she saw nothing, not the slightest flicker of movement.

Frustrated, Pearl threw her head back and screamed, a raw sound of anger and frustration, the precise opposite of that nasty, niggling, doubting whisper.

"I did not! I did not! I only took what was given! I am not a thief!"

Sobs mingled with the screams, but the only reply was silence.

Pearl collapsed onto her knees, feeling all the stiffness of the years. She felt the ache of the arthritis within her swollen knuckles as she beat her left hand against the carpet.

"I did nothing wrong!"

Pearl? Pearl? Are you all right? Wake up now, honey. Come on, wake up."

Nissa's voice, soft and pleading, so very far away.

Pearl struggled to open her eyes, struggled to make sense of the conflicting signals her body was sending her. She'd been kneeling on the floor, but now she was on her back, the firm softness of a mattress beneath her.

"Pearl? Come on, now. Let me hear you talking to me."

There was a sheet over her, and over that the lightweight cotton blanket Pearl usually pulled up, even in summer. Her head was on her pillow. She was wearing a nightgown.

Memory warred with memory. She'd been sitting up in her chair reading. Pearl knew that, but she also knew with rising certainty that she'd gone to bed around nine.

Pearl remembered choosing a fresh nightgown from her drawer, deciding on the sleeveless one with tiny orchids printed on the soft fabric. The gown was old; the touch of satin embroidery at the neckline made it elegant.

She remembered leaning back against her pillow, thinking about the next day, how she and Nissa were going to watch a "play" at Joanne's little day school. Lani was singing a song, and from her impromptu rehearsals Pearl already knew every word and accompanying gesture perfectly, but she knew how important it was for a child to see familiar, loving faces in the audience.

She'd felt herself drifting off, tired, so unbelievably tired but content.

"Pearl?" Nissa's voice sounded strained.

"I'm"—Pearl managed to open her eyes and saw her bedroom, lit only by the light drifting in through the open doorway from the hall—"I'm awake. Why did you come in here?"

Nissa sat on the edge of the bed and took Pearl's hand between two of hers. Normally, Pearl would have been offended by the familiarity, but she could sense that Nissa needed comfort as much as she was offering it.

"I heard you screaming," Nissa answered simply.

Pearl considered this, her brain moving out of sleep into its usual sharpness.

"How did you hear? I had this suite soundproofed back in the day when my interns could be a little noisier than they thought they were."

Pearl pressed her free hand experimentally to her throat, as always feeling a touch startled by the changed texture of her skin, by the slight looseness and delicacy that had come sometime after her seventieth year.

"My throat doesn't hurt, so I couldn't have screamed that loud."

Nissa looked resigned and a little guilty.

"Pearl, I've something to confess."

Pearl pushed herself up on the pillows, but didn't say anything.

"After I came back, Albert took me aside. He told me he was concerned that you weren't recovering as quickly as you should."

"I did," Pearl said, with quiet dignity, "nearly have a heart attack, even if that heart attack was magically induced."

"That's right," Nissa agreed. "But you didn't have a heart attack. None of the tests Dr. Andersen ran showed any damage to the heart muscle. Albert said he told him that you had a heart like that of someone twenty years younger."

Pearl remembered. She'd felt foolishly proud when she'd heard this, like she was getting a prize for all those mornings she'd eaten right and gone out to exercise instead of making excuses.

"Dr. Andersen also said you should be pretty much back to normal within a week. Pearl, honey, it's been a lot longer than that, something like three weeks, and you're still far too tired, far too run down."

Pearl noticed that second "honey," and tried to decide how she felt about it. Nissa had never used endearments before, but their situation had changed. And Nissa wasn't condescending; she was just treating Pearl like she would have one of her sisters.

Despite her confusion and growing sense of apprehension, Pearl felt pretty good about this.

"So Albert asked you to watch me," Pearl guessed.

"That's right."

Nissa was about to say more, but Pearl, shreds of what must have been a nightmare coming back to her, suddenly interrupted.

"Wait! Don't tell me you've cast a spell in here! Surely, I'd have known. Even if the Rabbit and the Tiger are paired signs, I would have known!"

Panic rose.

If I'm getting so slow that I can't tell if a spell has been set in my own house, maybe that voice was right and I'm useless. . . .

In answer, Nissa got up from her seat on the edge of the bed. She reached down behind the nightstand, coming out with a standard baby monitor.

"No spell. I just put this monitor in here. The base unit is in my room. It has a couple of channels, so I could still keep a monitor in Lani's new room. Albert asked me to learn if you were sleepwalking or something else that might account for your extreme exhaustion."

"And you found that 'something else,'" Pearl said. "Screaming nightmares."

"That's what it sounded like," Nissa admitted. "Want to talk about it?"

Pearl didn't, but she forced herself to do so. Dreams were not something to be taken lightly, not for those who lived with their feet set in more than one world.

Nissa listened attentively.

"You took what was mine," she repeated after Pearl finished her account, "and then wasted it. And variations of the same. Interesting. Unsettling. Tell me, Pearl. Is that honestly how you feel about yourself, deep down inside?"

Pearl hesitated for so long that Nissa gently prompted her.

"Go on, Pearl. I'm not going to tell everyone your deepest, darkest secrets, but if we're going to try to decide if these are dreams or some sort of sending, then we need to, let's say, check into your psyche."

Pearl sat all the way up in her bed and plumped the pillows behind her. She knew her hair must look a mess, and she wondered what Nissa thought of her without her makeup. Even when her house had been full of people, Pearl had never left her rooms without at least some primping.

Then she dismissed such thoughts as unworthy and tried to give Nissa an honest answer.

"You know, Nissa. I really don't think I do feel I've failed."

Nissa's doubt showed on her face, but Pearl held up her hand to forestall any comments.

"Let me explain. I know my father, Thundering Heaven, felt that I failed him, not by anything I did, but first by being born female, then by following my own course, refusing to marry and bear the 'proper' heir to the Tiger's line.

"But that's him. I really didn't feel I failed—well, except in the matter of an heir, and I'll come back to that. I know I've mastered the Tiger's lore. I made certain that several people—Albert and Gaheris in particular—who might have otherwise lapsed received the best teaching Shen and I could provide. I've mentored Des. Stayed in touch with your family. Been friends with Deborah—though that's easy. She's very nice."

"She is," Nissa agreed. "What about the heir thing? Is that alone enough to give you nightmares like this?"

"I can't imagine why," Pearl said. "True, I've done a lot of thinking about heirs lately, what with Gaheris getting controlling regarding Brenda, and watching you decide just how much Lani can handle. However,

I've always felt that the Tiger would provide. I have two brothers. They have children. Now that we've reconnected to the Lands, perhaps my heir is there."

Nissa nodded, and for a moment an image of Flying Claw stood between them, as clearly as if they'd summoned him.

Pearl went on. "So I don't feel guilty on that count, either."

"Perhaps the nightmares *are* a sending of some sort," Nissa said. "Do you think Thundering Heaven is the source?"

"That makes the most sense," Pearl agreed. "I met his challenge and bested him, but that doesn't mean he'll honor his defeat. I believe our shared link to the Tiger might provide enough of a channel for him to reach me, even if he is in the afterlife and I am still living."

"And sleep," Nissa said, "makes one receptive to communications from elsewhere. Look how Loyal Wind was able to reach Brenda, though they had a far less intimate link."

"Precisely," Pearl said.

"It makes a lot of sense," Nissa said, "but is there any way we can confirm our suspicions? An augury?"

"There might be," Pearl said. "It wouldn't be as precise as a fairy tale's three answers from a captive demon or the like, but augury and related subjects were among the arts that Li Szu did not advise Shih Huang Ti to destroy. There are many traditions, including those the Orphans themselves developed."

Nissa glanced at the clock on Pearl's bedside table. "But not now. It's two in the morning, and Lani is sure to get up by seven. Tomorrow is Lani's show, but maybe we can try something afterwards. Lani's sure to be tuckered out."

"Why not?" Pearl said. "I think an augury will only

confirm what we already suspect, but that confirmation will be useful."

Nissa touched the baby monitor. "Do you mind if I put this back?"

Pearl considered. She valued her privacy, but as long as someone might be attacking her, it seemed foolish to indulge herself.

"You may."

Nissa did so, then bent and gave Pearl a very matter-of-fact peck on the forehead.

"Sleep well. Sweet dreams."

"Sweet dreams yourself—and thank you."

Pearl did sleep well, and woke eager and invigorated.

Watching Lani sing and dance energized her further. Pearl felt positively tigerish when, after Lani had been carried up to bed—no need to convince the child to nap—she and Nissa went into her office.

"Are we going to use mah-jong tiles, then?" Nissa asked as Pearl pulled out the leather case with an abstract tiger painted on the lid.

"I thought we should," Pearl said, "since the Orphans did design some interesting variations on standard auguries. I thought we might as well make this an extension of your lessons."

Holding the box containing the Tiger mah-jong set in her hands, Pearl frowned down at it.

"But perhaps," she said, "we should either use your set, or we should use one of the more generic sets from the studio."

Nissa caught on at once. "Because this set is made from Thundering Heaven's bones?"

"Well, we are inquiring after his actions," Pearl said. "If he is able to touch me through our shared link to the Tiger, then he might be able to affect something made with his own bone."

"Good point," Nissa said, and Pearl was pleased to see not even a pro forma shudder of distaste. "I'll get my set. From what you've said about Thundering Heaven, I doubt that my great-great-grandmother thought well of his treatment of you."

"Straw Cymbals wouldn't have had the chance to protest," Pearl said. "She died two years before I was born."

"Straw Cymbals?" Nissa said. "Is that what 'Nao Nao' means? That's what my mother told us her name was."

"Straw Cymbals," Pearl agreed. "When Nao Nao died, your great-grandmother Naomi Nita was already twenty. She was good to me, and because of her kindness I found myself very ready to stay in touch with the Nita clan."

"I'm glad," Nissa said. "Now, let me run upstairs and get my set."

She was down a few moments later, holding in her hands a case on which the Rabbit was painted in a stylized fashion that resembled a form used more commonly in paper cuts. Pearl remembered when those designs had become the "thing" among the Orphans. The second Ram had started it, and soon everyone was clamoring for her to do one for them.

A brighter memory.

Pearl spilled the tiles onto the card table that had become a more or less permanent fixture of her office. Someone was always spilling tiles over it, working out the right configuration for a particular spell.

Nissa helped Pearl arrange all the tiles facedown, then automatically joined in as Pearl began "washing" the tiles, as the gentle mixing of the tiles across the flat surface was termed.

"Now give me a moment," Pearl said, "and I'll concentrate on framing the question."

"And what question is that?" Nissa asked guardedly. "I want to know, and I want you to promise you won't waffle."

"I'm going to ask if Thundering Heaven is the source of last night's nightmare."

"That's it?"

"The more specific, the more likely we'll get a clear answer. We can always ask another question."

"And if we ask something more general like 'who is behind it'?"

"Then we're not likely to get a clear answer." Pearl ran her hands over the tiles. "This isn't a Ouija board."

"Would one of those work?" Nissa asked.

"Probably not for us," Pearl said. "Neither you nor I were raised to think of those as anything other than toys for kids or tools to trick gullible old women."

"I can see that," Nissa said. "All right. Ask your question."

Pearl shuffled the tiles, feeling ch'i channel from her into the bone and bamboo rectangles, almost hearing the echo of reply. Suddenly, she was eager. "Next we build the wall."

"Just as if we were playing a game."

"Right."

Hands moving with quick experience, they took the one hundred forty-four tiles and stacked them into a square two tiles high.

"Now what?"

"Now we deal a hand," Pearl said. She handed Nissa one of a pair of dice. "Roll for who breaks."

Pearl rolled her die. She was unsurprised when Nissa rolled a one, and herself a six.

She rolled both dice, counted around the walls, then handed the dice to Nissa.

"You roll for the actual break," Pearl said.

Nissa obeyed, then counted individual tiles. She lifted two sets out, set them aside, then looked at Pearl.

"How can we deal with only two 'players'?" Nissa said.

"We don't," Pearl said. "We'll just count off the first fourteen tiles, and see what we get. I'm expecting lots of green since that's the Tiger's color."

She counted off the fourteen tiles while Nissa watched, then flipped them face up, almost without looking, but her fingers slowed as the various combinations were revealed.

"I can't believe it," she said. "This makes no sense at all."

Then Pearl looked at the spread tiles again, and a cold wave of purest fear hit her.

"Or maybe it does."

XVIII

The far side of the sea of fire provided a vista of unimaginable loveliness.

Mountains rose from the fiery lake, unblackened, untainted by the heat. The lowest slopes caught the reddish orange light of the coals, giving it back as molten mirrored rubies blending scatterings of dark orange citrine and shimmering yellow topaz.

Higher up the slopes, foliage began. First, there was wispy grass, dry and prickly, but miraculous in growing at all. Higher still, sparse concentrations of stunted shrubs grew in twisted contortions. About halfway up the slopes, where the heat would be no more than unpleasant, the first trees began: sparse-needled cypress giving way to elegant evergreens.

"Steer toward that area to the right," called Copper Gong from her place at the lead. "There seems to be the start of a pass there, as well as a beach where we can easily land."

Loyal Wind spotted the indicated space almost at once, a stretch of silvery sand easily wide enough for all of them and their gear. He wiped his parched lips on the back of his hand, thinking of the large canteens in their luggage. The water would be hot, but even so, it would taste wonderful.

The flotilla of kites moved in the direction of the beach, silk butterflies arrayed in a snowflake pattern against a cinder grey sky that shaded into a hard, unforgiving blue against the peaks of the mountains.

Copper Gong was the first to bring her kite in to land. As her feet hit the shining sands of the beach she yelled out. Recalling the west wind with a sudden blast of ch'i, she launched herself into the air once more.

"Hot!" she called, circling back and upward. "The damn sands are hot!"

"We should have expected that," Flying Claw said, chagrin on his handsome features. "The sands are next to a sea of fire. Of course they are hot."

Des, who had been coming in to land after Copper Gong, and had been brought up short by her warning, spoke as he struggled to get his kite under control once more.

"We didn't run into the same problem on the other side, because the cascading water cooled the shore. Flying Claw, do you think we can take these kites deeper into the mountains?"

"Maybe," Flying Claw replied, "but not for too great a distance. We're relying on the heat from the sea of fire for additional loft."

"So when the heat isn't enough to lift us," Copper Gong said, "the surface below should be cool enough for us to stand. We've got to do something. Even my brief touchdown singed my sandals."

She held out one foot so those below her could see the blackened soles.

"Is everyone willing to attempt to fly farther?" Flying Claw asked. Following a chorus of agreement, he went on, "Let me take point. I'll warn you when I feel myself losing loft."

"What about all that trailing baggage?" Riprap said. "Want to hand it off?"

Flying Claw shook his head. "We will need to come down when the baggage can no longer stay aloft."

He took himself higher, maneuvering his paired kites as Loyal Wind might have a chariot team.

"There's a pass here," he called back. "It's fairly wide. I think you can follow two abreast."

They did so, Loyal Wind taking up the rear behind Bent Bamboo and Nine Ducks. The Monkey had been positively meek since his near crash. Perversely, this worried Loyal Wind more than if Bent Bamboo had been his usual flamboyant self. From the way Nine Ducks rode herd on the Monkey, Loyal Wind knew his apprehension was shared.

They brought the kites down on a wind-scoured stretch of rock. From there, the pass narrowed and cut sharply upward.

Before his feet touched the ground, Loyal Wind had been analyzing the terrain, guessing that this wider area would have been shaped by wind and water pushing through that narrow area ahead. Then the soles of his boots slid on the surprisingly smooth surface and he immediately reassessed.

Holding the kite up, Loyal Wind knelt and struck the ground with his knuckles. It rang like a deep-toned bell muted in layers of felt, the sound dull but undeniable.

"Metal," said Bent Bamboo, rising from where he,

too, had been testing the surface. "We've had a forest of stone, a wall of water, a sea of fire, and now a mountain of metal—molded to boot."

"Molded?" asked Gentle Smoke.

"Why would it ring if it wasn't hollow underneath?" Bent Bamboo said. "At least this portion isn't unduly hot."

Nine Ducks frowned. "Metal. This isn't good. If this is an artificial landscape, we're not going to find food or water here."

"Probably not," Bent Bamboo agreed. "Although we may be able to manipulate this surface to create some water. Remember, according to the ancient laws of elemental progression, metal is destroyed by fire but gives forth water."

"I memorized that progression," Riprap said, "as part of one of Des's lessons, but I've got to say that I've always had trouble with the logic of that. I mean, some of the combinations make sense, like water quenching fire, or even fire creating earth. Why would metal have been thought to make water? From what I've seen, water rusts metal—or at least iron. It isn't good for copper or bronze or silver either."

"Metal is the Monkey's element," Bent Bamboo said, "so perhaps you will permit me to explain."

Riprap nodded. Des, who had been about to explain (and who, as the Rooster, also shared metal as his element), shut his mouth quickly.

Another, thought Loyal Wind, *who has noticed that the Monkey needs to redeem himself. Perhaps playing the pedant will be enough. I sincerely hope so.*

"The ancients observed that under certain circumstances," Bent Bamboo said, "metal appeared to give off water for no apparent reason. For example, a metal pitcher, although completely sealed, will form water on its outer surface."

"Condensation," Riprap said. "Okay. I can see that, but concluding that the metal creates water does seem to be pushing matters."

"Does it?" Bent Bamboo said. "Does any other of the five elements give forth water without the water first being added?"

Riprap thought about it. "No. Mud might, but that's earth with water added. Fire definitely not. Wood, maybe, but sap isn't really water. Okay. I can see the logic. Thanks."

"So maybe we will be able to have water," Nine Ducks said. "Good. I'm parched after our journey over fire, and the idea of husbanding what water we have was not pleasant."

Gentle Smoke, ever diplomatic, said, "Perhaps some of us can test this theory while the rest of you fold down the kites."

"Good idea," Flying Claw said. "I thought to leave one large kite—mine perhaps—intact in case we need to send someone up to scout the terrain. The rest can be broken down and the parts stored in case we need them again."

Loyal Wind, whose element as the Horse was fire, which made him the absolutely worst choice to join in creating a water spell, helped with the kites. By the time the last square of synthetic silk was folded into the bag and the last of the bamboo frames was untied and bundled, the conjurers reported success.

"It wasn't easy," Copper Gong said with satisfaction, "not without a water sign to help. Happily, we had two metal, but even so the summons took a lot of ch'i. Here, as elsewhere in the Lands, drawing ch'i from the surrounding area seems unduly difficult. However, the spring we've started should give enough water to refill all our canteens and water bags. Drink your fill."

Refreshed, the worst of the dried sweat washed

away, they shouldered their packs—and heavy packs they were. Nine Ducks and Loyal Wind had tried returning to their animal forms, but both found their hooves slipped too much on the slick metal. The rubberized boots they had worn in the stone forest had been left in the shell of the Zao-Fish.

Copper Gong's Ram form could get a somewhat better grip, but not enough to encourage her to use that form. In the end, heavy packs for everyone were considered the best answer.

That night, when darkness made further progress impossible, Loyal Wind ate his cold meal—there was no wood to burn—and rubbed his aching calves. They had made poor progress and if this mountain range was of a similar size to the areas they had already crossed, they might be trapped here for weeks. Already, Flying Claw's willingness to take his kite aloft and sort out the maze of passes and dead ends had saved them a considerable amount of backtracking.

As Loyal Wind kneaded muscles that screamed in protest at this slipping, sliding mode of travel, an idea came to him. It wouldn't make walking easier, but it would eliminate the burden of carrying a pack as well.

"Sleds," he said aloud. "I think we could make a sled from the couple of blankets we've kept. It would be clumsy, but dragging our gear would be much easier than carrying it on our shoulders."

"Brilliant!" Bent Bamboo said with a return of his usual enthusiasm. "A very horselike solution!"

"We brought the collapsible stretcher," Riprap added more seriously. "It has aluminum poles. We could use those for side support."

"It's not as if we'll need runners or anything," Gentle Smoke said. "All day I've been wishing I didn't need to carry a pack and so could travel in my snake form. Sliding is not as much of a problem for my scales. With a sled, if we avoid the 'rocks' and 'plants,' we should be fine."

"We're going to need to do that anyhow," said Des, holding up a hand wrapped in a thick bandage, "as I learned the hard way."

He'd made the mistake of grabbing at a bit of brush to catch himself only to learn that the leaves were—like everything else—made from metal. The edges on that particular "plant" had not been sharp, but some of the grasses, although flimsy, held a dangerous edge.

When morning came, they cobbled together two sleds. There was ample rope to make harnesses, and they took turns pulling. Uphill slopes remained a trial, and downhill someone needed to trot alongside each sled to make certain nothing spilled loose during unexpected spurts of speed. Even so, they crossed much more ground than the day before, and even more on the two days following.

Midday on their fourth day in the mountains of metal, Flying Claw brought his kite down from a scouting venture aloft.

"I think I see an end to these mountains," he said, and waved down his comrades' cheering. "However, even with the binoculars I could not make sense of what lies on the other side. There's simply too much mist."

Mist and clouds had begun to appear after the second day of their journey, usually wreathing peaks, but sometimes settling into valleys as well. Uncertain visibility had added to their torment.

"Wood," Bend Bamboo said. "We've had the other four elements. This last area must be dedicated to wood. A forest perhaps: cool, green, and well watered?"

"We could only wish," Flying Claw said, grinning at the Monkey's feigned optimism. "I can't see clearly yet, but I suspect that just as we would never have expected an ocean that burned nor mountains without a trace of stone, so wood has been shaped to some characteristic alien to its nature."

"I can hardly wait," Riprap said, "because when we get to other side, I'm going to find the twisted idiot who created this place and wring his neck."

☆

Over the next few days, Parnell continued to expand Brenda's acquaintance with what he claimed were the sidhe folk. None of them fit her childhood daydreams. More than a few were the stuff of nightmares.

After a mutually uncomfortable meeting with a critter who resembled the love child of a cockleburr and a hedgehog, Brenda found herself ticking these new acquaintances off on her fingers: Oak Gall, Wasp, Nettles, Sluggy, Tangles, and, of course, Prickles.

She and Parnell were strolling back toward Brenda's dorm. Brenda removed her swollen finger from her mouth and stared critically at its tip. She *thought* she had all the stickers out.

"Well, that was fun!" she said with bright insincerity.

"You were the one who offered to shake hands," Parnell said. "Despite ample evidence this wasn't a brilliant idea."

"But I'd insulted Sluggy by refusing to shake hands," Brenda protested. "Or pseudopods or whatever that was. I was just trying not to make the same mistake twice."

Parnell didn't say anything, and Brenda couldn't help but feel she was proving to be a disappointment to him.

"It would be easier if they looked more like people," she said sulkily.

"They do look like people," Parnell replied, a decided edge to his voice.

"I mean the way you look like a human," Brenda

said. "Like Leaf did when I saw her in dreams. Is everyone where you come from, well, so kind of weird looking? I mean, are all the beautiful sidhe just in our heads?"

"What's beautiful, Brenda Morris?" Parnell responded with a smile that seemed just a bit sad. "Trust me. No mother robin would think even you, all the flower of young womanhood that you are, the least bit attractive. As for a human newborn . . . they're so ugly they can even shock their own parents. But that same mother robin dotes on her naked, gape-mouthed chick, even to the point of risking her life for it."

"I guess," Brenda said.

Parnell went on dreamily, "You know, there's a certain resemblance between baby humans and baby robins. Both are naked, screaming, really ugly little creatures— all noisy dependence."

"Are you insulting me?" Brenda said. "Is that wise when you yourself say your people think you might need me?"

"You were insulting us," Parnell replied. "And who is to say that need might not be mutual?"

They stopped in midstride, glowering at each other.

"You're right. You're right. You're a hundred and fifty percent right," Brenda said, voice rising, hands on hips. "I don't know why I even bother to say anything."

"What you mean," Parnell said, his voice low, but his tone no less angry, "is that you think I'm wrong. Why must you pick such an annoying way to say so? It closes any chance of understanding."

"Because," Brenda said, words tumbling over each other, riding the waterfall of her confusion, "you *are* right. I know you are. I'm trying to accept that I'm just a narrow-thinking, close-minded human. I can't help not liking that revelation. But I grew up on stories of the beautiful sidhe folk, and I can't quite wrap my heart around the fact that apparently you all look like spiders or weird plants or slugs. I look at you, Parnell, with your green eyes and flowing honey-gold hair, and I wonder what you really look like, and then I wonder if I want to know."

"I thought," Parnell said, "that you would be more comfortable with truth than glamour. I have tried to give you that truth. Now, I see, I would have done better to bring you fairy folk out of your Shakespeare. Of course then, when the time came that the glamour must come down—or worse, some enemy broke it before I had a chance to explain—then would it be better or would you be standing there screaming at me for lying to you?"

There was a long silence, and Brenda let her hands fall loose to her side.

"Seems like you get yelled at either way," she said, forcing a chuckle. "Lucky Parnell. Okay. You're right again."

But she didn't shout this time. Parnell also relaxed.

"Really," Brenda went on, "you're right. I would have hated to be shocked by a sudden revelation even more than I hate having my childish illusions taken away from me. But, oh . . . It's hard, especially since the Chinese stuff has been so splendid."

"Splendid?" Parnell asked, the surprise in his voice genuine. "How is the theft of memory splendid? Wasn't that how you first learned about your Chinese heritage, when your own kin were attacked? When you learned that the only reason they weren't killing you all was because they feared the consequences—but not the deed?"

"No," Brenda protested, "it wasn't that, not that at all. But they were still human—I mean, they couldn't be related to our ancestors if they weren't. Their stories sort of matched those in the books. It wasn't like what you've shown me."

"Our stories have crept into your books as well," Parnell replied, "but in those stories we are usually represented as the monsters or the enemies. Leave that. What you're forgetting is that the Lands Born from Smoke and Sacrifice are a direct offshoot of your own world. That is why there are the similarities, why there are humans. Places like the Lands—born of the dreams of one race—are very rare."

"So whose dream are you?" Brenda asked.

Parnell shrugged. "Whose dream are you, Brenda? When you have that answer, maybe I'll have mine. For now, let's leave philosophy and try something more practical. Are you up for a field trip?"

"Now?" Brenda's heart quickened, remembering another field trip, that first trip into the guardian domains.

"I was thinking tomorrow after lunch. You're done with classes in the morning, I think."

"I am. Where do you want to go?"

"To the Land Beneath the Hills," Parnell said. "Maybe if you see us where we live we won't seem so odd—or if we do, at least you'll understand us a little better."

"Islands," Brenda said, remembering. "You said it all had something to do with islands."

"Something to do," Parnell corrected softly, "with the blood of islands."

☆

The augury doesn't make sense, Pearl thought. *Or if it does, I don't like what I see.*

Pearl forced herself to examine the tiles spread in

front of her, one hand rising inadvertently to cover her rapidly thudding heart.

These panic attacks are happening far too often, she chided herself. *Where is your legendary courage, Pearl Bright?*

A voice within her answered, *Where it has always been, Ming-Ming, mostly within your imagination. When before these last few months did you ever really face a challenge that required courage?*

But Pearl ignored that doubting, self-critical voice, concentrating on the tiles. There were twelve tiles in which the same sequence of numbers repeated over and over again, then two of the blank tiles that Pearl preferred to use to represent the white dragon.

"Pearl?" Nissa's voice broke into Pearl's reverie: sharp, concerned. "Pearl? What's wrong? Why don't those tiles make sense? Do you need some water?"

"No water," Pearl said. "Just a moment, I'll show you what's wrong."

Forcing her hands not to shake, Pearl rearranged the tiles so that they showed the order it had taken her a moment to perceive. The numbers 4-2-4, repeated twice with tiles from the characters suit, then twice more with tiles from the dots suit. She laid these in sets, then followed them with the pair of white dragons.

"Four, two, four," Nissa said, puzzlement in her voice, "and a pair of white dragons. That's not a limit hand I remember, but it certainly looks as if it could be one. It wouldn't even score mah-jong, because those four-two-four patterns aren't runs."

"No, this isn't any limit hand you would know," Pearl said. "Our ancestors spoke the Chinese of the Lands, and although the pronunciations are not the same, the pun did translate."

"Pun?"

Pearl slowed down, reminding herself that Nissa, like Riprap and Brenda, spoke Chinese only by virtue of a spell. Likely the subtleties of the language did not translate.

"In Cantonese," Pearl said, "four-two-four is considered a very unlucky number. In fact, all by itself, the word 'four' is considered unlucky because four sounds very much like the word 'to die.'"

"Okay," Nissa said. "What makes this worse? Wouldn't four, four, four be worse?"

"It would be pretty bad," Pearl admitted, "but four, two, four is worse. Through a similar pun, it sounds like the words 'to die and die again.'"

"That is bad," Nissa admitted.

"Very," Pearl agreed. "Depending on one's religious leanings, the phrase can be taken as predicting many deaths in one family, or to mean that one is bound on the wheel of incarnations and will never reach nirvana. Either way, it's not a number one wants to see."

"No," Nissa agreed. "And especially not followed by a pair of white dragons, right?"

Pearl waited, interested to learn if Nissa was indeed following her train of thought.

"White is the color of death," Nissa said. "Unlike the red dragon tile, which really has nothing to do with dragons, but means 'center,' or the green dragon tile, which is labeled with a word that means growth or increase; the white tile is simply called 'white.'"

"Des has been a good teacher," Pearl said.

"Well, Riprap insisted that he understand why the 'dragon' tiles didn't have the same characters on them if they were all dragons," Nissa said. "We went over the meanings a couple of times from different points of view."

Nissa frowned and ran her index finger over the

tiles. "All right. I agree with you. These tiles supply a very ominous answer. What question did you ask?"

"The same one we agreed on," Pearl said. "Was Thundering Heaven behind my nightmare?"

"This doesn't seem to be much of an answer," Nissa said, "but it's too organized to be just a fluke. To die and die again . . . I suppose that could mean, 'Yes. He wants to scare you to death repeatedly.'"

"I hadn't thought of that," Pearl said. "That's quite a good interpretation. However, I wonder. The suit most usually associated with the tiger is bamboo."

"Because of tigers in the jungle?" Nissa asked. "Oh! And because the Tiger's color is green, and lots of sets print at least some of the bamboo in green. I see your point. There's not a single bamboo here."

"No," Pearl said. "Do you mind if I break these tiles up? Just looking at that sequence makes me nervous. I was raised within the Chinese culture, and old superstitions die hard."

"Even though your mom wasn't Chinese?"

Pearl nodded and when Nissa didn't protest, she swept her hand through the tiles.

"Even so. Thundering Heaven never acclimated. He ate only Chinese food, and in those days that meant shopping in specialty markets. Since my mother's spoken Chinese was limited, I usually helped with the shopping. A lot of the superstitions of our neighbors rubbed off."

"I can see that," Nissa said. "Even if the message is cryptic, we've learned one thing. Whoever is sending those dreams doesn't mean you well. I wonder . . . You asked if Thundering Heaven sent the dream and we got this cryptic answer. Can we at least clarify if your attacker is from among the Orphans or perhaps connected to one of the indigenous magical traditions?"

"You're thinking of Franklin Deng or his associates,"

Pearl guessed. "You're wondering if they've slipped through my wards somehow."

"I am. I've never been quite happy with Deng showing up to the rescue when you had that 'heart attack.' Maybe he was just keeping track of you like he said, but maybe . . ."

"I don't see how checking further could hurt," Pearl said. "Why don't you make certain Lani is still sleeping soundly while I think about how best to go about it."

Nissa came back a few minutes later, a tall tumbler of iced tea in one hand.

"Lani's out like a light. I don't think she slept well last night. Even little kids can get stage fright."

"I know," Pearl said with a soft smile that hardened at a thought. "And if Lani heard you getting up to check on me, that wouldn't have helped. Let's do what we can to eliminate those nightmares. She, at least, deserves sound sleep."

"Will the auguries answer a simple yes/no question?" Nissa asked.

"Yes," Pearl said, "and, well, no. The problem is very few questions have such simple answers."

"How about 'Do you like pickled beets?'" Nissa asked flippantly. "I could firmly answer 'no' to that."

"Let's use that as an example," Pearl said. "What do you mean by 'like'? The taste, the color, the texture? Would you eat pickled beets if the alternative was starvation? Would you eat them if the only other option was eating dog shit?"

Nissa raised her eyebrows. Like most young mothers, she so habitually avoided crudities or obscenities that she was shocked by the use of them by others.

"All right. I see your point. So if we ask, 'Is the person sending Pearl nightmares one of the Orphans?' and the answer we get is 'no,' that doesn't rule out one of the Orphans working in collaboration with someone else—someone, say, who is actually doing the spell casting."

"Exactly," Pearl said. "Or if one of the Orphans is an unwitting tool of whoever is behind this, then we might get a 'yes' answer, but that might be inaccurate."

"You mean like the time Honey Dream used Gaheris Morris to get into this house so she could try and rescue Foster," Nissa said. "Technically, Gaheris was innocent, but an augury would have shown him as guilty."

"Precisely. So we need to phrase our queries as carefully as possible, and then do a series of auguries to confirm that what we think we read from the tiles is actually the correct answer."

"Sounds as if it's going to be a lot of work," Nissa said.

"It will be," Pearl agreed, "and our sequence of readings will probably stretch out over several days. Doing the auguries uses ch'i, and we don't dare deplete ourselves too greatly when our allies might need us at a moment's notice."

Nissa, who had been reaching toward the mah-jong tiles, froze with her hands in midair.

"Do you think that likely?"

"The last message I had from Des said that they were in the middle of an area he referred to as 'the mountains of metal.' It was a very short message. Had we not prepared in advance, I don't think the message would have reached us."

"That's not good," Nissa said.

"But it is not necessarily bad. Des mentioned no losses, no specific injuries."

"But they're not having an easy time of it," Nissa said. "Okay. I get it. We can't wear ourselves out. Still, we can do at least one other augury today. Where do we start?"

"I would like to see if we can rule out the Orphans," Pearl said. "And after them, if we can rule out our allies who reside at Colm Lodge. I think asking something like: 'Are one or more of the living Thirteen Orphans behind Pearl's recent nightmares?' might be a good choice."

"Maybe we should start even further back," Nissa said. "Can we query whether your nightmares are, well, natural or sent?"

Pearl considered protesting. Hadn't she made clear that she didn't think she was harboring any undue anger or resentment? Therefore, her nightmares must be unnatural.

Ah, Pearl Bright, she asked herself, *but what if you're lying to yourself? That has been done before.*

"Very well. We'll start with that question. Let's build the wall."

By the time Lani woke up, eager to reprise her big day in song and story, Pearl and Nissa had confirmed that the nightmares were indeed unnatural.

Nissa had insisted that she felt not the least trace of ch'i depletion, so they had gone on and confirmed that the source of the nightmares was connected to the incident with the car and to Pearl's near heart attack.

"Not much," Nissa said, reviewing the tidy notes she'd been making. "Will this information be of any help?"

"A little," Pearl reassured her. "At least we know I'm not going crazy."

Just being driven there, she thought. *Sweet heaven. I wish I didn't need to sleep tonight. I wish I didn't need to sleep ever again.*

XIX

The next afternoon, following a very prosaic lunch of bacon cheeseburgers, fries, and sweetened iced tea, Parnell took Brenda away to fairyland.

Or to the land of the sidhe, which was just about the same thing in most Irish legends.

They ambled across campus in the general direction of the Congaree River. At some point, Brenda became unsure of their surroundings. This surprised her. She'd done a lot of walking during her freshman year, getting to know her new home in detail, since this was the first place she'd ever lived on her own.

She'd been so aware of what a momentous event that move had been: on her own, no parents watching over her shoulder. Yet, after the events of the summer, Brenda's excitement—no, she decided to be honest with herself: her sense of self-importance—seemed very trivial.

Now they walked through a small copse of trees, trees Brenda felt she should recognize, but didn't. Then Parnell directed her to a particular tree. With hardly a pause, Parnell lifted one hand, placed it against the smooth bark. The tree did not so much open as slide aside. They walked through the gap, into twilight.

Three steps, four, and then they were in full light. Even had she been so inclined, Brenda would have been unable to deny that they were definitely somewhere else.

"That easy?" she gasped.

The sky above was a perfect blue, the winds herding a few scattered clouds that seemed set against the pale firmament for contrast, like a beauty mark on an old-fashioned belle's face.

The grass beneath Brenda's feet was a rich, living green. A green that gave rise to poetry about "green and pleasant lands," and emerald isles.

In the distance, Brenda could just glimpse a line of what she recognized as ocean, an indigo hue to challenge the paler blue of the sky above, touched with grey and silver. Sea spray played tag with wheeling gulls.

Brenda remembered the Orphans' labors to make their own gate, in a warehouse smelling of cotton candy and animal feed. She remembered the wonder of scribing ornate characters into soft wood and seeing them glow as they took hold.

It had all seemed marvelous at the time—a wonder, a fantasy come true—but compared to this . . .

Push aside a tree and walk a step or two into fairyland.

The Orphans' magic seemed so clumsy.

"Perhaps," Parnell said. "Perhaps. Come see a bit more."

Brenda followed eagerly. Their path wended down the curve of the hill on which she now realized they had been standing and came into a vale. Here there were thick stands of greenery, a forest she hadn't noticed from above. Broad-leafed trees dominated: oaks and elms, maples and ash, even the occasional mitten-leafed sassafras.

Brightly colored mushrooms dotted the shadiest parts. Red speckled with mustard yellow. Blue splotched with green. Orange dotted with even brighter orange.

On one of these sat a damselfly, studying them with too-knowing eyes. Had Brenda not made the acquaintance of Wasp, Nettle, and the rest, she might not have recognized the intelligence in those eyes, but now she did, and inclined her head in a polite nod as Parnell led her along.

The forest was inhabited by more than that damsel-fly. Brenda glimpsed a cluster of knobby figures that might have been Oak Gall's cousins peering out from around the trunk of a white oak. They pulled back when they saw her looking, their long, spidery limbs going this way and that.

Brenda knew laughing would be impolite, and swallowed a chuckle. Next to her, she saw Parnell's teeth flash in a momentary answering grin.

By the time they left the forest, Brenda had glimpsed more of the denizens, enough that creatures part-leaf, part-branch, a bit of insect or something small and furry, no longer seemed particularly odd.

Indeed, had she glimpsed something as normal as a squirrel, Brenda would have taken a second look, the way one does when a mouse scampers across the monkey cage at the zoo.

Although Brenda didn't see any animals, there were plenty of birds, their songs point and counterpoint to the sighing of the wind through the leaves and the occasional tittering from one of the many-shaped, many-eyed watchers.

And then Parnell was guiding her toward the cave. Brenda balked a little, not liking the darkness that waited within a cleft shaped just a little too much like a mouth for her tastes.

Wasp buzzed up at that moment, her sharp, almost insectlike face just a bit scornful. Hoping to avoid mud balls, Brenda squared her shoulders and let Parnell guide her on. She thought he might summon a light, perhaps a glowing sphere ephemeral as a dandelion clock that would provide just enough glow for them to see by.

He did nothing so poetic, but bent down and extracted a pair of tin lanterns from where they had been cached behind a rock. Each held three fat beeswax candles. These he lit with a pack of matches bearing the logo of a campus bar.

"Ready?" he said. "Watch your step. There is a path, but the lanterns will be our only light."

They went down into the darkness, Wasp buzzing along beside Parnell's farther shoulder. It seemed to Brenda that the little wasp woman was whispering something to Parnell, but just walking and making sure the candles didn't go out was enough to demand Brenda's full attention.

Besides, eavesdropping was rude, wasn't it?

So's whispering, said a snide voice in her head.

The path down was steep enough to make Brenda's calves ache, but after the first hundred yards or so, she got enough of a sense of the footing that she could look around. Stalagmites and stalactites, muted grey and muddy brown, reached for heaven, pointed accusation toward the ground. Stone formations that looked like draped cloth or leering faces moved in the flickering candlelight.

Brenda had toured a couple of "tame" caves on family holidays, and was immediately struck by how different everything looked without artificial lighting set artistically about. Her three candles shed sufficient light that she could see well enough to navigate, but beyond the circle of their flames, everything was pure, absolute darkness.

Once Wasp landed on Parnell's shoulder and stilled her buzzing wings there should have been silence, too, but as Brenda's ears adjusted to the quiet, she could hear the erratic dripping of water, and something else. . . .

Voices. Soft, high-pitched, softer, low and grumbling. Mutters, whispers, what sounded much like sardonic laughter. Then Brenda knew that this cave was as full of living creatures as the forest had been. As in the forest, the residents were taking a look at her.

She didn't see them, though, not by the faint candlelight, or rather she thought she did not until a rock formation that looked remarkably like a face with two asymmetrical eyes set above a bulbous nose winked at her.

But it was the nose, not the eyes, that winked, putting the face into a whole new, rather horrific perspective.

Brenda had read somewhere that the human mind has a remarkable ability to see human forms and features where there are none. Now, as she made her careful way along the twisting path that led deeper and deeper into the cave—when did a cave become a cavern? She wished she could look it up somewhere—Brenda began to understand why Parnell had brought her here.

He was showing her how the human mind created human forms, then gave those forms names like pixie or bogle or leprechaun, so thought the creatures understood, classified, and tamed.

But noses winked, and wasps gossiped, and the dark was very deep and seemed to go on forever.

Brenda knew she was under inspection, even as she was doing her own inspecting, and it would be rude to chatter to Parnell as if no one—or no one other than Wasp—was there.

Despite her resolution, Brenda couldn't keep back a little cry of pleasure when she saw a glint of light in front of them, light that resolved with satisfying quickness into an exit from the cave.

She, Parnell, and Wasp emerged into another forest, or maybe just a different patch of the same one. Although Brenda felt as if they had been underground for hours, the sun didn't seem to have moved much.

Parnell smiled at Brenda and took the candle lantern from her. There was praise in those green eyes and Brenda felt very pleased.

"Hungry?" he asked.

"A bit thirsty," Brenda admitted. Then she frowned. "But isn't it unsafe to eat fairy food? Doesn't it make you lose track of time or something?"

"Pure water is safe," Parnell said, leading her to where a stream broke from a rock face, "and this water is about as pure as you'll find anywhere. You can drink it safely."

"Swear?"

"I swear."

Brenda thought about asking him to swear by something he held sacred, then shrugged. She didn't know enough about Parnell to know what he did or didn't hold holy. She'd just have to trust his actions, which had been, she was forced to admit, completely honorable.

The water was icy, and it refreshed Brenda so that she looked about her with new interest. They'd seated themselves on the grass next to the spring, and she amused herself by trying to see who might be watching.

"What's next?" she asked. "Is anyone going to come out and say 'hello'?"

"Not yet," Parnell said. Suddenly Brenda realized he looked more than a little sad. "You see, acushla, while my auntie Leaf and I both think you're the one we've been hoping to find, your, shall I say, 'rather judgmental' nature has raised some doubts."

"Doubts?"

"As to whether you'll be of any use to any—except possibly the Orphans—when the trouble comes."

Brenda felt indignant, but more than that, she was soundly embarrassed. She had been rude, repeatedly pressing Parnell about the nature of his kind, saying without quite saying that she thought those she'd seen weird—even ugly.

So she swallowed her immediate protest, and looked squarely at Parnell.

"What do I need to do to allay those doubts?" she asked.

Parnell rose to his feet, a single, smooth motion that made him seem more like a reed bending than a man.

"Get yourself home," he said. Without another word, he turned and walked into the nearest tree.

Brenda saw a glimpse of the USC campus behind him, heard a faint, mocking giggle that had to be Wasp, and then she was alone.

☆

The eight scouts crossed through the final pass in the mountains of metal with emotions that mingled relief and apprehension.

Scouting ahead had proven to be counterproductive. The footing was too uncertain, the labor needed too demanding for anyone to be asked to cover the same ground twice.

Flying Claw took his kite aloft once or twice a day, but there simply was not sufficient ch'i to keep it up for long—not without additional loft from the heat of the sea of fire.

As they began the descent, what attention that could be spared from watching every step sought to gauge what new challenge awaited them.

"It looks like a forest," Des Lee said. "A normal forest with normal trees, maybe a little overgrown, but just a forest."

"I don't believe it," Riprap said, putting binoculars to his eyes. After intently studying the area below, he let them drop. "It sure looks like a forest."

A little later, when they were below the mist, Loyal

Wind took an opportunity to raise his own binoculars—marvelous devices he would have found a reason to use with less excuse—and surveyed what certainly looked like a vast and spreading forest.

"There are gaps there," he said, "and I think I see smoke, not a forest fire or cook fires. I wonder if there might be villages."

"Maybe," Gentle Smoke said, voicing what they all were hoping, "this is the end of it. Maybe the element of wood simply provides the beginning of human habitation."

"That would be wonderful," Copper Gong said. "We might be able to scout out a village, then go in, ask some questions."

"The villages," Flying Claw warned, "might not be inhabited by humans. Remember how Li of the Iron Crutch told us the hsien had been forced out—squeezed out—of the central region. Perhaps some of the hsien were put here. There have been no monsters or armies for us to combat thus far, but that doesn't mean there won't be any."

Despite this warning, Loyal Wind couldn't help but feel cheered. Even if Flying Claw was correct, monsters seemed almost welcome compared to what they'd faced to this point. One could swing a blade at a monster.

He checked his armor, which he had let hang fairly slack, tightening buckles and straightening seams. He saw Flying Claw doing the same, Riprap adjusting the hang of his wolf's-tooth staff where he could get to it more easily.

Others imitated these martial preparations, but even so the mood as the final mountain flowed out into undulating hills was happy, even cheerful. Bent Bamboo twirled his staff and whistled a few lines from a military march. Nine Ducks grinned at him affectionately.

"Stay out of trouble, Monkey."

"Absolutely," Bent Bamboo replied with a mischievous grin that seemed to say the exact opposite. "I have learned my lesson about causing trouble."

As with the other areas they had crossed, the border between metal and wood was absolute. One step clanged on the surface below, the next sunk ever so slightly into soft earth, grass, and traces of duff.

"Let me turn back into my Ox form," Nine Ducks said, dropping her pack from her shoulders. "I'd rather carry all my gear and most of the rest of yours than have those straps digging into my shoulders for another minute."

"Let's all rest," Copper Gong suggested. "After, I can retake my Ram form and share some of the burden. Loyal Wind, I think you'd better stay human, though. We may need your weapons skills."

The Horse did not protest, and was glad to be relieved of making the same suggestion himself. He'd been worried that if he did, someone might think he was trying to get out of carrying his share. He had been speculating what they might encounter ever since they had spotted what might be the smoke of village fires. Flying Claw might be worried about encountering monsters, but Loyal Wind was old enough to know that human enemies were danger enough.

Gladly they unshouldered their packs and shared around water and small snacks. Loyal Wind was aware of muscles aching and felt a small regret for his life as a ghost. Flying Claw, however, seemed immune to such little pains. He rapidly grew restless, and finally leapt to his feet.

"Let me scout, just a little. I see what I think is the beginning of a trail. I've seen no game, so the trail might have been made by humans—or whatever lives here."

Riprap hauled himself to his feet with a great deal less grace than had the other man. Loyal Wind immediately liked him for this.

"I'll come along," the big man said. "No, don't argue. I'll stay back and let you be as stealthy as you want, but if you get into trouble, someone should be along to back you up."

Other than his initial look of protest, Flying Claw did not complain. He might have a Tiger's essentially solitary attitude toward fighting, but he was not a fool.

"We won't stay away more than a quarter of an hour," Riprap said, synchronizing one of their mechanical timepieces with the one Des now strapped onto his own wrist. "And I promise to holler if we run into trouble."

"Good," Bent Bamboo said. "You're not the only ones spoiling for a fight."

But no cry for help came, and within the allotted fifteen minutes, Riprap and Flying Claw could be seen returning.

"We found a trail," Flying Claw reported, "and a small pool where we can refresh our water. There were tracks on the trail, but I couldn't make out the details—at least not in human form. They were quite old and might have been human."

"Looked human to me," Riprap concurred, "but if there are ogres or trolls here, I guess those could have made them as easily."

"Or bear," Copper Gong said sourly, her voice reshaped by her Ram's nose and throat. "Those leave very human tracks. Nine Ducks and I will be able to check the scent when we are closer."

The woman (now water buffalo) snorted, "So shall we load the gear and be off?"

The luxury of walking without a pack on his shoulders was enough to make Loyal Wind contemplate taking up the song Bent Bamboo had been whistling, but caution overruled the impulse.

The green boughs overhead were shady and welcoming, a wondrous change from the uninterrupted sky that had been their companion since they had left the wall of water. When they came to the area where Flying Claw and Riprap had found tracks, the Ox and Ram lowered their heads and snuffled.

"Human, I think," Nine Ducks said.

"Yes," Copper Gong agreed, "and so old as for the scent to be almost unreadable. Let's get to that pond you mentioned."

The pond was spring-fed and large enough to invite fantasies of bathing. But although the Ox and Ram waded in deeply enough to wet their bellies, no one suggested stopping for a swim. After faces had been washed, and water bottles filled (from a location well away from the sodden animals), they returned to the trail.

Scouting duties were taken over by Gentle Smoke, who slithered out of her shenyi with a certain smugness, since, unlike the other shape-shifters, she didn't need to disrobe to avoid becoming entangled in her clothing. However, although she coursed up the tallest trees, often making forward progress without the need to touch the ground, she saw nothing—or rather nothing human.

There were numerous birds, who either fled at the sight of a snake or scolded according to their nature. Occasionally, they glimpsed smaller fur-bearing creatures. Once Loyal Wind was certain he'd seen a fox. There were plenty of insects as well, an annoyance they'd been spared elsewhere: biting things that harassed and annoyed, but didn't do much harm.

After a time, Nine Ducks raised her heavy head and sniffed the air.

"I smell smoke: smoke with a tinge of rice to it, as if the pot boiled over and foamed into the fire."

Copper Gong snuffled audibly. "I smell it, too."

None of the humans could smell the trace of rice, but when the wind shifted slightly, each of them caught the inviting scent of wood smoke.

"It's coming from the direction of that village we thought we'd seen," Riprap said. "Do we head that direction or away?"

"Away—" Flying Claw was beginning when a strong resonant voice interrupted.

"Neither, I think."

Turning as one, they saw Thundering Heaven emerging from a thick stand of trees a few paces farther down the path.

He was clad in armor very similar to that worn by Flying Claw, but the tiger's face that adorned the breastplate gave the impression of bloodthirsty wrath, whereas Flying Claw's tiger was merely fierce.

In his right hand, Thundering Heaven held the sword Soul Slicer, the blade angled to guard rather than attack. Loyal Wind did not doubt for a moment that the hold could be shifted faster than thought.

Thundering Heaven looked even stronger than he had when Loyal Wind had fought him for possession of Bent Bamboo.

Fought, Loyal Wind thought, *and lost.*

There was also something about Thundering Heaven that indicated that, like the other "ghosts," he too had reclaimed a connection to his mortal life.

And therefore, he is very dangerous, for a ghost cannot usually do physical harm to the living.

Loyal Wind's sword was in his hand, and he found himself longing for his magical steed. He knew how to fight on foot, but beginning a battle that way seemed unnatural.

Flying Claw had also drawn his sword.

"You! I dreaded monsters but—"

Thundering Heaven laughed, a bluff, hearty sound at odds with the menace in his eyes. "But never one of the original Thirteen Orphans. How do you know I have not come to join you, to help you in your noble quest?"

Confusion touched Flying Claw's eyes, but Gentle Smoke, who had taken advantage of the interlude to drop from her tree, spoke from where she now rested atop the packs that Nine Ducks carried.

"Because to this point the price for your help has been one we have not agreed to pay."

"A point," Thundering Heaven agreed almost affably. "A point. Of course, I could have reformed. I could have been impressed by my daughter's courage and creativity. I could have come over to the view that if she could defeat me, she was worthy of the Tiger's stripes."

"Have you?" asked Flying Claw, not quite relaxing, but clearly hopeful.

"Actually," said Thundering Heaven, his affable expression transforming into something very nasty, "I have not."

He motioned slightly, and Loyal Wind felt himself seized from behind. He tried to spin, to get his blade into his attacker, but he could not move. Looking about him, he saw that his companions were also held—and not by any human, but by the limbs and branches of the forest itself. Even Gentle Smoke, relatively small in her snake form, had been wrapped around by vines and lifted from Nine Ducks's back into the air, where she thrashed impotently.

"I heard you speculating as to the nature of the area

dedicated to the element of wood," Thundering Heaven said, his tone conversational, his sword still held lightly even though Flying Claw snarled and strained against the branches a mere arm's length away.

"In each area," Thundering Heaven said, "the element was presented in a fashion somehow alien to its nature. Wood is here permitted something that is usually denied it, the ability to move with the speed and grace of an animal. Of course," Thundering Heaven gave a self-deprecatory cough, "it does so at my command."

Flying Claw had ceased his furious struggle, probably realizing, as had Loyal Wind, that all the action did was wear him to the point that if an opportunity for attack did present itself, he would be too exhausted to take advantage of it.

"So you reign here?" Flying Claw asked. "Is this perversion of the Lands your doing?"

"Perversion? Tut-tut." Thundering Heaven sneered with the magnificent insolence of a cat. "My master will be offended to hear you speak so. No, kitten. I do not reign here. The one who does is the one who created these Lands Born from Smoke and Sacrifice."

"Shih Huang Ti," Des Lee said, his eyes wide with wonder. "The first emperor himself?"

Thundering Heaven shook his head. "Shih Huang Ti but gave the orders that enabled the plan to be carried out. The true creator is another."

"Li Szu," Bent Bamboo said, and there was no wonder in his eyes, only fury at finding himself bound so that his strength and cleverness were equally useless. "He's the one who created this perversion of our home?"

"Li Szu," Thundering Heaven repeated with amused calm. "The one who is setting everything right once more. He has a good many questions for you. Will you come along peacefully, or must I have my servants drag you?"

Loyal Wind spoke quickly, before Flying Claw could offer a challenge, or Riprap, who had not ceased straining at his bonds, could do something even more foolish.

"We will come with you."

"Wise," said Thundering Heaven, "very wise. Conserve your strength, for if you plan to defy my master, as I sense you do, you will need every iota."

He smiled again, the expression slow and mocking. Then he nodded to the trees and the captives' bonds were loosed.

"Come," Thundering Heaven said. "The creator, Li Szu, awaits. He is very impatient to get about his work."

XX

Parnell!" Brenda shouted, dashing over to the tree into which he had vanished and running her hands over the trunk.

She didn't know quite what she was hoping to find, the seam of a door, maybe? Whatever it was, she didn't find it. She leaned back against the tree, sliding down to land with a decided thump as her jeans-clad behind hit the soft grass.

Brenda was aware that she was still hoping to trigger some response by accident. How often had she seen that happen in some movie? The despairing heroine angrily thumps her fist against the wall, accidentally triggering just the right knothole or hidden switch.

Clearly that wasn't going to happen here.

What had Parnell said before he'd vanished? He'd told her that her attitude had raised a lot of doubts about how much help she'd be. And that she had to prove herself by getting herself home.

"Prove what?" she muttered angrily.

Brenda waited awhile, hoping against hope that Parnell would show up and tell her his leaving was just a bad joke. She got a couple of drinks from the spring. When her fury at being abandoned so callously had ebbed enough for her to think straight, she considered her options.

She thought she remembered the basic route she and Parnell had taken to get here. They'd walked down a hill, into a forested valley, then eventually entered that cavern. They'd walked downhill through those dark, damp tunnels for a considerable distance. Then the trail had shifted upward again, finally emerging here.

Can I retrace my steps? Brenda thought. *And even if I made my way through all of that and made it back to that hill, what would I do?*

She remembered her comment to Parnell back at USC when he'd simply pushed the tree to one side and led her through.

"That easy?"

Her face burned hot. Now that she was on the doing side, "that" didn't seem easy at all.

Do I even need to go to that same tree? Parnell didn't. When he left, he did it right here. This time he seemed more to walk into the tree, but I'm not sure how he did it mattered. I'm not certain he even needed a tree. That might have just been a bit of show for my benefit.

She thought a while longer.

Damn!

Her butt was starting to hurt. Soft grass or not, she didn't have quite enough padding back there to really enjoy such a rural seat. She rose and stretched. Might as well take a look around. That couldn't hurt, could it?

For safety's sake, she took one of the ribbons out of her hair (she'd done it up nice because she thought she might be going to the fairy court) and used it to mark the spring. Parnell had told her it was safe to drink from there, and so she'd better not lose sight of it.

Remembering Wasp's somewhat malicious moods, Brenda anchored the ribbon several times, pulling the knots really tight. She hoped that would be enough to keep her marker from being removed. She knew that a more permanent mark would be to score the bark on a tree or break limbs from a bush, but remembering the sort of plantlike nature of many of those to whom Parnell had introduced her, Brenda thought this might not be a great idea.

Then she started exploring.

First, she walked down to the mouth of the cave. It was very dark. As Brenda thought about re-entering, the faces she'd glimpsed seemed creepy rather than evocative or enticing. She wasn't sure she really wanted to go back that way—and she'd feel a real idiot if she walked up to the top of the nearest hill and glimpsed the other side of the caverns.

Besides, she thought, looking at the two candle lanterns, *I don't have any matches, and I can't see in the dark.*

Deciding to check her theory about the extent of the caverns, Brenda walked upslope to the top of the nearest hill. In the distance was something that might be the shadow of the forest, tucked down in a dell, but she couldn't be certain.

She located the sun overhead. Mining some vague Girl Scout memory, she stuck a twig in the ground and examined the shadow it cast. There wasn't much of one.

"Okay," Brenda muttered to herself. "About noon. When the shadow gets longer, I'll have an idea which direction is west. I'm not sure what good knowing the directions will do, but it's something."

Continuing her hike, Brenda soon discovered that she was surrounded by gently undulating hills covered in green grass and ornamented by the occasional tree or copse of trees. No nearby stand of trees seemed extensive enough to be the forest Parnell had walked her through, and there were no wide rivers.

She decided to return and check where "her" spring might lead. Once it overflowed the shallow basin into which it trickled, the spring became a narrow stream for maybe fifty feet before spreading into a pool just about as big as a bathtub. The pool had a rocky bottom, but it didn't overflow, so Brenda guessed that the bottom must be just porous enough to leak down into the caverns below.

Brenda sat down by the pool to rest. Surreptitiously, she glanced around, hoping to see someone—even Prickles or Sluggy—who she might ask for help.

She'd seen some animals—squirrels that dashed up the trunks of trees, rabbits that flashed cotton tails and rocketed off at her approach, a field mouse that scampered by with bulging cheeks.

There were many birds, from a hawk or eagle that was hardly more than a dark speck against the brilliant blue of the sky to hosts of songbirds who only quieted when she came right up to their perches. A couple of times Brenda startled mourning doves or some such bird from where they'd been resting on the ground.

They sprang skyward in a flurry of wings, trilling mild protest.

But, although she looked, Brenda didn't see any of the local residents, not even Wasp. A few times she thought she heard giggling and whispers.

Of course, Brenda thought, *I haven't exactly asked for help, have I? And they didn't hide themselves when Parnell and I were walking through. They didn't exactly come out and beg for an introduction, but I saw a lot of them. Damn!*

She considered a while longer, fragments of almost forgotten fairy tales and more recently seen movies flickering through her mind.

"Goblin King . . ."

"I am Zorro!"

"Once upon a midnight dreary . . ."

"There once was a king who had three sons . . ."

"And the cat said . . ."

"With eyes as big as saucers . . ."

"Three wishes, no more . . ."

"I am Arthur, King of the Britons . . ."

One thing was certain, if nothing else was, no one in fairy tales or real life got anywhere lying around, waiting for someone to offer help. Even the stupid son in the fairy tales got on his feet and walked into the dark wood.

Besides, she was getting hungry, and those same fairy tales kept reminding her of the consequences of eating fairy food.

"Really," Brenda said aloud, mostly because she was tired of hearing nothing other than bird song and the bright plashing of the stream. "Really, the Chinese tradition of greeting someone with the offer of a meal seems very civilized. A cheeseburger—even a bacon cheeseburger and fries—doesn't last too long when you've been hiking."

She found herself wondering about other necessities of life. So far she hadn't needed to pee or worse, but what would she do when the need arose? Here, where people walked in and out of trees—or maybe empty air . . . She squinched her eyes shut, embarrassed at the images that arose.

"Well! I'm just going to have to figure out how to get back, that's it."

Brenda remembered several stories, including a movie she'd really liked, that centered around someone struggling to get something that they could have had for the asking.

"I would like," she said to the nearest moving thing, a robin, who paused in its grubbing in the soil near the base of a tree to turn a bright eye on her, "to go home, please. I wish you would direct me to the nearest route. Please."

The robin looked at her, then went back to grubbing for bugs.

Well, Brenda thought. *If there was an answer there, it was "Dig up your own bugs, lady." Or find your own door. Okay. I didn't really think it would be that easy. Now, should I ask someone specific to help? Wasp was here earlier, and I thought I might have seen Oak Gall. Prickles is actually pretty nice. If he's around . . .*

Brenda considered, then shook her head. No, if this was something someone else could do for her, then why would the sidhe folk need her? Why would she need to prove anything to them?

What did she know that might get her home? A little bit of the Orphans' magic? Brenda was still wearing her usual pair of amulet bracelets, but neither Dragon's Tail nor Dragon's Breath seemed particularly useful in her present situation.

Still, Brenda felt heartened, as if finally she was on the right track. What else did she know?

She was the heir to the Rat. The Rat's direction was north. Its color was black. Its element was water. She'd turned into a rat twice, but the first time had seemed more or less like a dream. The second time she'd had help—and had been in the afterlife, which didn't quite abide by the usual rules.

But, Brenda thought with a breath-catching flash of excitement, *this place doesn't either. Parnell and Leaf both mentioned that the sidhe lands are more like the guardian domains—places that exist because they're between other places that define them. What I know might work more easily here than if I were to try it back at Pearl's.*

A plan began to take shape. She went back to the spring, wondering if she felt more comfortable there because it was her only real landmark and source of refreshment or because the Rat's element was water.

There was a border of silty sand alongside the little stream. Brenda smoothed a surface on which she could write. The twig she'd used to measure the course of the sun—now definitely westering, but still far from setting—made a good stylus.

Pulling off the Dragon's Tail bracelet, Brenda studied the characters. The basic Dragon's Tail called for either a pung (set of three) of dragons or a pung of winds, followed by a run of one through nine in any one suit.

Des Lee had taught them to tailor what tiles they chose to their own sign. Although Brenda was not yet the Rat, that was still the sign he suggested she guide herself by.

Therefore, Brenda's bracelet had a pung of north winds, followed by a pair of red dragons. She'd suggested green dragons, since those stood for increase and therefore strength, but Des had said since the caster stood in the center of the Dragon's Tail for protection, the red dragon tile, which bore the character for "Center," was best. For the same reason,

Brenda had made her run of one through nine in the bamboo suit, because bamboo was both strong and flexible.

Brenda drew a few experimental characters, and discovered that damp sand held the images longer and with less distortion than dry. Then she smoothed out her images. Returning the Dragon's Tail to her wrist, Brenda pulled off the Dragon's Breath and examined it.

The Dragon's Breath sequence consisted of one of each dragon tile, the last of which was paired. This was followed by five pairs in any one suit.

For this spell, which sent a blast of hot fire at an opponent, Des had agreed that the green dragon was the most useful, because it increased the heat and intensity of the fire. The suit he'd suggested for the pairs was characters, because what the elaborate Chinese ideograms actually stood for were the numbers one through nine, followed by the word "wan," or "ten thousand."

In the Chinese tradition, ten thousand wasn't just a specific number; it had dual symbolic associations. The first was with scorpions, because some Chinese lore held that these always appeared in huge hosts. The other association was with the idea of vastness. In fact, some older books translated "wan" as "myriads," rather than as a specific number.

"Rather," Nissa had said, "the way kids say 'lots and lots' or 'billions and zillions.'"

Between the two bracelets, then, Brenda had samples of many of the basic mah-jong tiles. She was missing the dots suit, but that one was the easiest to remember. And she didn't have the other three winds, but she was pretty sure she could do the west wind character without messing it up.

"Note to self," she said aloud, feeling more cheerful, "make a bracelet that, even if it won't do a spell, will show the range of characters. And practice more!"

She considered what sequences she had memorized and wrote them in the sand so she wouldn't get befuddled and forget. "All Green," which let one see magical workings, was one she'd worked hard to commit to memory. Then there was "Knitting," which let you share ch'i with another person.

"And only with someone you trust," Brenda reminded herself.

There were several simple wind spells, mostly good for minor defense or pushing something relatively lightweight out of the way. Still, Brenda made note of them.

Then she paused, reaching deep into herself to see if she remembered a spell that might be her way out of here, one she was afraid she wouldn't remember because she'd only had to do it from memory once—and that time she'd only had to work part of it.

Nine Gates.

To Brenda's relief, memory did not fail her. The sequence called for three ones and three nines in a suit, then one of each tile in a chosen suit. The fourteenth tile was chosen so that it would designate which of the nine gates was being created.

Brenda drummed fingertips against her lower lip, considering her options. She didn't need nine gates—at least she dearly hoped she didn't. She just needed one: one to take her back to USC. Come to think of it, she wasn't sure she could summon sufficient ch'i to make nine gates in succession.

Okay, Brenda Morris, she said to herself. *There's got to be a way you can do this. Parnell's played fair with you to this point. Trust that fair play, even though you're pissed at him for stranding you.*

Something was nibbling at the edges of her mind, something about—She had it!

When they'd made the Nine Gates, only one had been needed to take them into the first of the guardian domains. The remainder had been necessary because of the odd nature of Chinese cosmography.

"And the guardian domains," Brenda said, speaking aloud in her excitement, "and this land under the hills have something in common. Both of them are border lands, lands that owe something of their nature to other places. Because of that shared nature, I shouldn't need more than one gate to get me home, any more than we needed more than one gate to get us into Pai Hu's realm."

Brenda brushed a fresh section of sand smooth and started sketching possible combinations, using arabic numbers and familiar letters rather than the Chinese because they were faster for her.

If she was going to use a variant of the Nine Gates sequence, then her first decision needed to be which suit: bamboo, characters, or dots. Automatically, Brenda shied from using characters because she hated drawing the more elaborate numbers, but something made her go back and reconsider. What was it?

The response came so instantly Brenda knew characters was the right suit to use. Characters were written words—the words for one through nine followed by the word for ten thousand. That the words and numbers were in Chinese didn't change anything. She needed words to get back because USC was a place she went to school, a place, so to speak, of "letters."

"Okay. I've got my suit. Now, what number is best?"

That was easy. One, because this would be her first and only gate.

When they'd made the first of the Nine Gates, they'd inscribed the various symbols on an unfinished pine door Des and Riprap had picked up at a hardware store. Certainly there was nothing like that here.

"But I don't need a door," Brenda said, mostly to encourage herself. "We were making a permanent gate. This one only needs to get me home. In fact . . ."

She considered. The last thing she wanted to do was create a permanent gate between the sidhe's realm and USC. College students saw enough weird stuff without her help.

She was not only going to need to make a gate. She was going to need to figure out how to destroy it as she was using it.

"Fun, fun, and more fun," Brenda muttered.

But she didn't mind. Ideas were flowing fast and furious. For the first time, Brenda intuitively understood the appeal of the abacus the Exile Rat had created to assist him the way Thundering Heaven had created the sword Treaty, or the Rooster had made those nasty Talons Des was so good at using.

Calculation was fun, filled with a thrill that set her blood buzzing in her veins and her thoughts quite literally racing each other to see which would be articulated first.

"Doorways in the sand," Brenda thought, remembering the title of a book she'd read a long time ago, something to do with kangaroos and not graduating college.

Brenda cleared a larger section of sand and sketched a rectangular door on it, complete with a little round circle for the knob. Then she rose, stretched, and did her best to focus.

It wasn't easy. Whereas immediately after Parnell's departure, she'd felt very alone, now Brenda was certain she was being watched by things just out of sight, or that moved as soon as she turned to get a better look.

There was something in the shadows beneath the tree into which Parnell had vanished, something else moving with the light breeze that stirred a stand of wild flowers. She was fairly certain that the butterfly that had lofted by, orange, black, and brilliant gold against the blue sky, had been watching her.

Face by face, eye by eye, unable to ignore the reality of the watchers, Brenda accepted those critical gazes, then accepted those that she had not glimpsed, but that were almost certainly there.

She forced her mind to focus on something far more important: making the character symbols she must inscribe seem more real than anything else. The symbol for "one" was easy—a horizontal line with the character for "ten thousand" beneath it. Brenda wrote this four times in a row.

When she moved to the number "two"—the same as "one," but with an added horizontal stroke—Brenda began to imagine where she wanted this door to take her. Sweat beaded beneath her hairline as she envisioned the copse of trees on campus where Parnell had introduced her to Oak Gall.

Brenda suspected that Parnell kept a semipermanent ward of some sort there, had sensed it in her desire to not look too closely at the place when she passed by during more usual business hours, in the fact that although the towering oak cast some very nice shade, she never saw anyone lounging there.

That tree, then, would be her destination. With the number two, Brenda imagined the place. With three—two with yet another horizontal stroke—she began to imagine the oak glade as close as the other side of her door. Four, which turned the strokes vertical, shorter, and placed them within a box, was the number Brenda used to help her envision her door as more than a picture in the sand.

Five and six were complicated enough that Brenda didn't try to do anything but get them right, but seven and eight were stylized and simplified. Brenda used them to firm up her image of her intended destination.

The beads of sweat had turned into streams, but Brenda didn't do more than blink away the stinging droplets that found their way into her eyes. Nine, the final character, was where she must refine her image, and she did so, feeling growing certainty that she had the spell right.

After she had drawn the last stroke of the final wan, Brenda allowed herself the luxury of wiping her forehead with the back of one arm. Touching the round circle that stood for the doorknob, she could feel the latent power of the spell waiting to be triggered.

The urge to open the door was strong, but Brenda held back. She was tired, but there was one thing more she must do.

She needed something to wipe out her spell in case her using the gate was not sufficient. Winds were the simplest solution, especially since she'd drawn her spell in the sand.

North was the Rat's wind, but she must frame it appropriately. After consideration, she decided on a sequence called Windy Chow. It called for one of each wind, followed by a pair of the wind one wished to summon, these followed by a chow—or run of three—in each suit.

The winds were complicated to draw, but Brenda remembered them pretty clearly. She'd make her chows out of the simpler versions of each suit: a one, two, and three of dots and characters, a two, three, and four of bamboo. One of bamboo was always drawn as a bird. Brenda worried that she wasn't up to that level of artistry when her pen must be a stick and her paper a stretch of damp sand.

Concentration was easier to achieve this time. The watchers had become as much a part of the surrounding area as the splash of the water and the softness of the grass. Brenda was also getting too tired to have attention to concentrate on more than one thing at a time.

With firm strokes, she drew the winds, pleased that she did indeed remember them better than she had thought she did. Then she drew the first two sets of chows. With the third, she instilled not only the summons of the wind, but that it would wait to cut loose its force and smooth out the sand until after she had opened the door and stepped over the threshold.

When she was done, Brenda's limbs ached from crouching and she felt about ten thousand years old. She felt good, too. There was no doubt that both spells were "live." All that was left was to use them.

She looked around the green hills, and felt rather than saw the varied awarenesses that pulled back lest she notice them.

"Maybe I'll see y'all later," she said, letting the lazy drawl of the land to which she was returning color her speech.

Then she placed her hand over the drawing of a doorknob and felt it round and hard in her hand. She pulled, and the door opened. On the other side, just as she had imagined, was that little copse under the spreading oak on the USC campus.

Brenda walked through the door. Behind her, the north wind rose and scoured the damp sand clear of the last trace of her magical workings, eliminating even her nonmagical notes.

The door closed behind her. For the first time, she noticed that it was quite dark. She wondered how long she'd been gone. Realized she was almost too tired to care.

Brenda slid down against the rough bark of the tree trunk and sat heavily on the ground. One of the oak tree's roots caught her at the base of her spine. The jolt of pain woke her up a little, enough to notice Parnell rising from where he'd been sitting cross-legged on the grass. He gave her a small bow, not in the least mocking, very much resembling, despite his casual tee shirt and jeans, the squire of those Arthurian-tinged dreams in which Brenda had first seen him.

"Congratulations," Parnell said. "I never doubted you could do it, and I shall enjoy gloating over those who did. So shall Aunt Leaf."

"What time is it?" Brenda asked.

"About two in the morning of the day following that in which you let me take you into the Land Under the Hill. Dermott and Shannon both doubtlessly are wondering what we have been up to, and, if they are awake, are giggling at the idea that we might be entwined in each other's arms."

Muzzily, Brenda thought that wasn't the worst option she'd ever had, but a better one was falling asleep, maybe right here. The grass felt very soft.

"Take this," Parnell said, opening a sack he'd cached to one side of the oak. "I got you a present."

What he handed her was a large carton of yogurt, the container blazoned with the legend "with extra active cultures."

"A gift from the Tuatha de Dannon," Parnell said, proffering a spoon.

Brenda couldn't have been happier if Parnell had given her a coronet of diamonds.

She grinned at him, accepted his gift, and greedily fell to.

It was even raspberry: one of her favorites.

XXI

Pearl confided the situation regarding her nightmares to Albert. To Pearl's surprise, Nissa insisted that they first do auguries to clear Albert of complicity.

"Remember, Pearl. Albert spent some time not quite in his own right mind. While, according to the terms of our treaty, Righteous Drum and his associates had to remove any and all marks, sorcerous and otherwise, from those whose memories they had stolen, that doesn't mean someone else didn't take advantage of Albert's lapse."

That thought had been chilling, for Albert had been Pearl's student and protegé during his youth, and her trusted friend for many years now. Like her, he shared a semi-celebrity. That had created a bond above and beyond their shared heritage.

Am I losing my edge? Pearl thought. *Not too long ago, I could see everyone's ulterior motives far more clearly than their ostensible ones.*

Auguries had cleared Albert, and, at Albert's insistence, Pearl had told Righteous Drum and Honey Dream about her nightmares—but again only after a series of auguries had ruled out each and every one of the residents at Colm Lodge, separately and in combination, from culpability.

Albert proved to be a considerable help in working the complex readings, adding both his ch'i and his expertise to the process.

"We're going to have to clear everyone," he announced. "We'd better start with those who are currently physically closest. They're the most likely to notice you're holding back something."

Pearl had to admit that this was true. Their reduced group had continued meeting for daily martial arts practice on the grounds of Colm Lodge. Many days, Righteous Drum and Honey Dream would come to Pearl's house to consult the materials in her library or simply to visit.

The other three—Thorn, Shackles, and Twentyseven-Ten—had never established the same level of comfortable intimacy, probably because they were all too aware of their ambivalent position. Unlike the cadre of which Righteous Drum had been a part, they had not been trying to keep an emperor on his throne, but to unseat one.

Given the chaotic succession to the Jade Petal Throne, this alone might not have been enough to create an uncomfortable situation, but the three former prisoners had also been forced to admit—to themselves, as much as to anyone else—that they hadn't really known for whom they were fighting.

Pearl thought that Twentyseven-Ten was a facile enough thinker to work himself around to justifying his actions, whatever they might have been, but the other two were more straightforward types. As a result, the former prisoners conducted themselves as something in between prisoners of war on parole and sinners seeking redemption. Neither attitude made them comfortable houseguests.

When Shackles, Thorn, and Twentyseven-Ten met with the rest to spar and exercise, Pearl was polite to them, but did not press intimacy beyond what they invited, nor go out of her way to make them feel welcome.

She rather enjoyed keeping them a little at a distance. It made impressing them easier.

Even within her more comfortable relationship with Righteous Drum and Honey Dream, Pearl did not like admitting that she was being tormented by

nightmares. It felt a little too much as if she were re-
verting to being a child who was having "bad dreams."

To Pearl's relief, neither of the Landers took this attitude.

"Communication through and attack via dreams
are both well known in the Lands Born from Smoke
and Sacrifice," Righteous Dream said. "Is it not the
same here?"

"I suppose it isn't," Pearl said. "Or at least not so
common that we take such occurrences as matter-of-
factly."

One great advantage of Pearl's confession was that,
with the help and considerable skills of Righteous
Drum and Honey Dream at their disposal, the auguries went much faster. They continued to use the Orphans' methods. Peculiar as they were, it was easier to
teach Righteous Drum and Honey Dream something
of the Orphans' symbolism than it would have been
to re-educate the rest of them. The materials were at
hand, and, as Righteous Drum said when he understood the form, very efficient.

"Easier on the turtles, too," Honey Dream said with
a glint of humor in her eyes.

Pearl recalled how turtle shells had been among the
items used for divination by the ancient Chinese. Apparently this practice had passed to the Lands as well.

Methodically, they set about clearing various of the
Orphans from complicity. They started with Shen
Kung, the Dragon, because they might need his con-
siderable knowledge and ability.

Nissa had offered to have herself checked, and only
smiled when Pearl admitted she'd already done the
necessary auguries.

"That's okay, Pearl," Nissa said. "I double-checked
you, too."

Once Pearl would have been shocked by this, but

by now she'd learned that despite her warm and maternal outer affect, Nissa was quite independent and decisive. Doubtless Nissa had decided that Pearl could not be trusted to be suitably critical of herself.

They had cleared Shen and were working on Deborah when Honey Dream articulated what Pearl knew they all must have been thinking.

"Desperate Lee is long past due for his report. Shouldn't we be checking on him and the others?"

"I'm not certain how we would go about it," Albert admitted. "Righteous Drum, do you have any thoughts?"

"If the Lands were the Lands I have known all my life," Righteous Drum said, "I would have many, but regarding this transformed world of which we have been told, I am as ignorant as the merest apprentice."

"The scouts haven't been out of contact all that long," Albert said, trying to sound encouraging. "Five, six days."

"Six," Honey Dream said firmly.

Albert went on. "Des mentioned that they must cross those mountains of metal. He noted that he expected the passage to be formidable. Perhaps the scouts are still in the mountains. Remember, all their other journeys have been on the flat."

Honey Dream gestured toward the mah-jong tiles spread on the table. "How about those? Can't we use them to check?"

"We could try," Pearl said. "However, we've already found that the further realities are separated, the harder it is to make the tiles respond. The Orphans learned that from the beginning of their exile. They longed to check on the family and friends they had left behind, but they could not."

Nissa bounced in her seat, looking for a moment very much like Lani.

"What about the mah-jong sets, though? I mean the specific ones, the ones that are made from the bones of the ghosts who are part of the expedition. We have their sets. Surely the link would be stronger."

"That's an interesting idea," Albert said, stroking his small beard thoughtfully, "a very interesting idea. We were able to contact the ghosts using those sets."

"But they are not ghosts any longer," Righteous Drum objected. "By the gracious will of Yen-lo Wang, they have been re-embodied."

"True," Albert said, "but we're not looking to summon them, just to make contact."

"It's an interesting idea," Pearl said, "but not one I think we should pursue today. I have a feeling we're going to need all our ch'i."

Righteous Drum nodded, stilling what Pearl had a feeling was an incipient rebellion on the part of his daughter.

"I agree. The guardian domains lie between the Lands and this place, so we will need to bridge not one but two degrees of separation."

Albert said, "The scouts are probably simply occupied with what they are doing, and haven't had the opportunity to accumulate sufficient ch'i to contact us."

Pearl heard the note of uncertainty underlying his words. Judging from the expression in Honey Dream's eyes, so did the Snake.

Looking at how those slim shoulders squared and those dark eyes grew thoughtful, Pearl hoped that Honey Dream wasn't planning to do anything impulsive.

☆

Loyal Wind knew that three days had passed since they had been taken prisoner by Thundering Heaven.

He'd seen the light outside the narrow window that

brought fresh air into his solitary cell change from bright to dark and dark to bright. He'd tracked the changes, scoring them deeply into the wood of the doorframe.

Three days, not counting the day on which they had been captured. They'd not walked far that day. Thundering Heaven had positioned wagons around a bend in the trail. After weapons—and, in the case of himself and Flying Claw, armor—had been removed, the prisoners had been bundled one at a time into those wagons. Their hands were tied behind them, their ankles hobbled. A rope about their waists secured them to an iron loop in the wagon.

The bonds had not been uncomfortable, but they had been restrictive. As further insurance against escape attempts, Thundering Heaven had employed the neat little device of a rope looped around the throat, connected to that which bound the wrists. As long as one did not struggle, the loop around the throat remained no more restrictive than a tight collar. However, if one struggled—as in stretching to attempt to untie one's own wrists or those of another—then the loop tightened, first restricting breath, then strangling.

This was the stick. As a carrot, Thundering Heaven had offered not to gag them as long as they remained perfectly silent.

"I will have soldiers stationed in the back of the wagons with you. If they report a single word, even a suspicious grunt, then the gags will go in. You see? I can be gracious—as long as I am not pushed too hard."

The prisoners had been placed in three different wagons. Loyal Wind did not think it a coincidence that he, Flying Claw, and Riprap—the three most effective fighters—had been separated. Loyal Wind shared his wagon with Bent Bamboo and Gentle Smoke. They had all been warned that they must remain in their human shapes.

Gentle Smoke in particular had been warned of the consequences should she attempt to slip away. Loyal Wind recalled how furious Gentle Smoke had been with Thundering Heaven. She'd even tried to bite him. Funny. Until then, Loyal Wind had never considered whether her snake form was venomous or not. He still wasn't certain, but from how the soldier who had been set to guard them had reacted, that young man wasn't going to take any chances.

No one had broken the prohibition against speech while the wagons were in motion. When they were unloaded well after dark in an inner courtyard of a looming structure that smelled of wet stone and grief, Nine Ducks had ventured a question.

"Where are we?"

"Someplace that would mean nothing to you," Thundering Heaven had said. "A place with sufficient quarters to house you all appropriately."

Those quarters had proven to be cells: stone-walled, stone-floored. The furnishings were minimal: a covered bucket, a heap of straw, and a large clay jar filled with fresh water.

The only light came from a narrow window that ran along the top of one wall. This was the only source of fresh air as well. When rain fell, as it did on the second night, water streamed in to splash on the stone floor before draining through slits set a few inches from the wall.

The cell's door had a slot through which food was passed at odd hours: usually rice topped with some slivers of fish and pickled vegetables. The food was fresh and plentiful. The water was replenished through a hose lowered through the window each dawn. The bucket was emptied into the slits on the floor, rinsed through with water from the same hose. If Loyal Wind worked quickly enough, he could even give himself a shower. This was easy enough, since his only garment was a light cotton tunic.

On the first day of his captivity, Loyal Wind had attempted some magic to improve his situation, but found he could not even summon a small light. He was no Dragon to speculate on what charms must have been used to eliminate drawing even on personal ch'i, but the level of exhaustion he felt after his effort made him think that the charm must divert his ch'i from the spell of his choice, draining more ch'i than he had intended to use, judging from his fatigue.

He decided not to risk ch'i depletion. There were worse things than darkness.

In the three days since Loyal Wind had been put in his cell, no one had spoken to him. He had tried shouting, but no one had answered him. Soon after, the food slot had shot back and a voice had made a shushing noise, then added three words: "Or no water."

The pickled vegetables had made him thirsty. Loyal Wind accepted the warning. In any case, given how carefully all the other arrangements had been made, he doubted that his associates were anywhere they could hear him. He'd had to try.

From what Thundering Heaven had already said, Loyal Wind knew the Exile Tiger's master wanted them alive, wanted to speak to them. Except for their confinement, their situation could be worse. They had come here to learn what had happened to the Lands. Now they would do so.

Once Loyal Wind might have raged at being imprisoned. Stallions were not known for their equable temperaments, nor horses in general for loving confinement.

But Loyal Wind had been dead far longer than he had been alive. When, somewhere in the long years of death, he had slowly begun to let go of the anger and outrage that had led to his suicide, he had begun to distrust his own temper.

Now he sat on the pile of straw that was his only furniture and contemplated the situation. He hoped that Flying Claw or Riprap had not done anything too impulsive, that Bent Bamboo had kept his tendency to make sassy remarks in check. Des was not likely to say anything deliberately rude, but his eagerness to ask questions might be misinterpreted.

The ladies provided less reason for concern. Gentle Smoke was skilled in monitoring her remarks. While Copper Gong could be acid-tongued, the long years she had spent pushing the Orphans to attempt a return to the Lands had taught her something of the value of moderation. Nine Ducks, like her namesake Ox, was very calm unless roused.

Loyal Wind felt a stirring of uneasiness when he thought of Nine Ducks. She—not he—had defeated Thundering Heaven back when they had first sought to rescue Bent Bamboo. Would Thundering Heaven attempt to exact some vengeance? Loyal Wind doubted that Thundering Heaven would stoop to anything as extreme as torture—after all, apparently Li Szu wished to speak with them—but withholding food or water or providing some minor humiliation could serve both to punish her and to provide them all with a reminder that their situation might be far worse.

Such thoughts were troubling, especially as speculation made them seem all the more real. Loyal Wind tried thinking about other things. Foremost among these was Li Szu himself.

Thundering Heaven had referred to Li Szu as the creator of the Lands Born from Smoke and Sacrifice. In a sense Li Szu was, for he was the one who had counseled the first emperor, Ch'in Shih Huang Ti, to burn those books that did not agree with the new empire's policies. This action—combined with the executions of scholars who refused to comply—had created the surge of energy that had given birth to the Lands.

It was a tale every child was told, but, strangely, after that initial act neither Li Szu nor the first emperor had any place in the tales of the Lands. The gods and goddesses of the Lands were those of China at the time of the Burning of the Books, though Buddhism had seeped in and left its mark, just as it had in China.

Sometime on the fourth day, probably about noon given the light—Loyal Wind had long ago established that his window faced east—the food slot in the door shot back. It was too early for another meal. Loyal Wind went from an idle drowse directly to his feet.

He cast about for a weapon, but the lid to the slops bucket was chained on and the bucket itself secured by a short but heavy chain to the wall. Straw would do no good, and both the bowl in which his rice was provided and the water jar were made of clay too delicate to be of any use as a weapon.

"Stand where you can be seen," said a voice without, male, but not, Loyal Wind thought, that of Thundering Heaven. "Put your hands out to your sides."

Loyal Wind did this.

The door opened, swinging out into the corridor.

"Come," said the voice.

After the indirect light of his cell, the area outside seemed very bright. All Loyal Wind could make out was a large shape. When he stepped out into the corridor, he realized this belonged to a guard. The man who had spoken was a much less impressive figure, dressed in the robes of a minor official.

"You are to be prepared," the official said. "If you cause difficulties, you will still be prepared, but afterwards you will not return to such pleasant accommodations. Do you understand?"

"I do." Loyal Wind decided to hazard a question. "Prepared for what?"

"An audience. Follow me."

Loyal Wind did so. Another guard as large as the first stepped out between him and the official, while the first took up the rear—this despite the fact that they were in a corridor without any other doors.

Loyal Wind wondered if this was actually the case. Disguising any distinguishing marks was a very simple illusion, one often done in prisons to keep the prisoners from getting a sense of where they were, so that even if they did escape, they would not be likely to find their way out.

They went down this corridor, up a short flight of stairs, into another corridor, down a ramp, and eventually ended up in an area that smelled very invitingly of musky perfumes. The air held an extra note of humidity, and Loyal Wind was not in the least surprised to find they had come to a bath.

"You will bathe," the official said. "You will permit the attendants to trim your hair, beard, and nails. You will then—when you are dry—garb yourself in the clothing provided. Any resistance will lead to punishment. Do you understand?"

Loyal Wind did, and although he felt humiliated by how meekly he was forced to accept this grooming—feeling rather like a horse being prepared for parade—he decided nothing would be gained by protesting. He even tried to enjoy the scrubbing and the attentions of the skilled attendants, but doing so was difficult.

No one would speak to him. The official had moved away to a bench near the entrance, and appeared engrossed in a scroll he removed from one of his capacious sleeves.

Eventually, garbed in rich red robes embroidered (somewhat hastily, Loyal Wind thought) with a horse on the back and on each of the sleeves, Loyal Wind was ready. The slippers he had been given to wear were a trifle oversized, and he wondered if that was deliberate, to make him clumsy if he should choose to run.

Anything is possible, he thought.

Loyal Wind wondered if he would be taken to a waiting area, if he would find some of the others there, similarly fresh from being bathed and groomed. Instead, the official led the way into an inner courtyard. There their entourage swelled to a dozen guards, most armed with clubs but several carrying spears. The message was unspoken but no less clear. Were Loyal Wind to try anything foolish, he would be beaten down.

Loyal Wind did not expect to be warned again, nor was he.

They left the inner courtyard, passing into a larger, central building. Here the corridors were wider, floored in marble or intricately patterned wood rather than the more utilitarian stone of the building they had just left.

The walls were ornamented with subdued taste. There were four-clawed dragons, but no sign of the imperial five-clawed version. The ch'i-lin, who only appears when the ruler is wise and just, was depicted repeatedly, as were emblems for prosperity and wisdom.

Nothing for happiness, though, Loyal Wind thought. *I guess that says something. Certainly the emphasis on the ch'i-lin does.*

Wide, double-paneled doors led to other, even wider corridors, and these to even grander entries. Despite the vastness of the palace, they passed no one. Corridors were empty. There were no sounds, no smothered giggles from functionaries hurrying out of sight, no hints of distant music, only perfect silence and the matched footsteps of the guards who escorted Loyal Wind and the nameless official.

At last they came to a pair of doors that, although wider than the rest, was devoid of the elegant carvings Loyal Wind had seen elsewhere. It was as if whoever was within did not wish to give anything away about himself or his desires.

The foremost guards rapped on the door with the butts of their clubs. In answer, the doors swung open.

"Enter," the official said, stepping back to let Loyal Wind precede him, "and kowtow most profoundly before Li Szu, creator of the universe, absolute ruler of all these Lands Born from Smoke and Sacrifice, soon to bring justice and order and right living to all lands no matter how far they may be."

Loyal Wind did as he was told, performing the kowtow after the fashion demanded for a reigning emperor. When he was finished, he remained crouched on all fours, but dared to sneak a glance at the man who claimed to be the creator of a universe.

Li Szu was a sparely built man who was certainly at least seventy, and quite possibly much older. He wore his hair and beard cut in the fashion popularized by Confucius—or at least in the fashion that great sage was most frequently shown wearing in art. Li Szu was clad as a Mandarin, with a scholar's rectangular hat, pointed beard, and long hair. Despite his grandiose claims, Li Szu did not wear the robes of an emperor, but rather those of a scholar of the highest rank.

Loyal Wind tried to decide whether this was an indication of modesty or the reverse. In his teachings,
Confucius frequently advocated neither extreme, saying that a man should represent himself as what he
was, no more, but certainly no less.

If I could get a feeling for what Li Szu's game is,
Loyal Wind thought, *I might better know how to plan
the tactics of my approach. For now, I shall treat him
like an emperor, as his subjects do, but include the
grace notes accorded to a scholar.*

"Rise, Loyal Wind," said Li Szu. His voice was as
spare as his frame, but not in the least reedy or shrill.
It was the voice of one who prefers whispers, and who
commands so much power that he has never needed
to shout.

Loyal Wind rose, feeling the skirts of his formal
robes fall into place. Good silk. Heavy, yet densely
woven. Looking at the man before him, Loyal Wind
understood that this had nothing to do with him, nor
with any desire to reflect his own honors and achievements. Those who came before Li Szu would always
be clad as that man thought they should be, no more,
but certainly no less.

We are dolls in a shadow play of his making, Loyal
Wind thought. *But what is the script? My role seems
to be that of courtier and advisor, as I was before the
Exile.*

Li Szu was seated upon a chair set upon a raised
dais. It was not a throne. Rather it was the chair of a
high official who represents the emperor, the type of
chair upon which the governor of a large province
might sit when receiving homage ostensibly for his
ruler, but in reality for himself.

Without letting his gaze wander, Loyal Wind assessed
who else was in the room. Guards flanked the raised

dais, their expressions as emotionless as those of painted Men Shen upon a door. The armor and weapons were elaborate, but from how the edges of the heads of the spears cut the light, Loyal Wind did not doubt that these were more than ornamental weapons.

Clerks hovered just out of the imperial line of sight, ready to assist but not intruding. A few scribes sat at a long table, brushes ready to dip into the ink prepared on the stones, long pieces of paper unrolled and waiting.

Loyal Wind noted that even the least clerk wore the cap buttons of officials of notable rank. Most wore robes reserved for those of higher ranks, with ornaments on their sleeves indicating years of faithful and illustrious service.

Like a general, Loyal Wind thought, *whose assistants are themselves ranking officers, qualified to command large forces. Li Szu's robes say he is but a scholar, but his surroundings say otherwise.*

After giving the command to rise, Li Szu kept silent for a great while. Now he spoke.

"Bring a chair for the great general! Bring him tea and refreshments."

Loyal Wind was surprised to be offered the opportunity to sit in the presence of greatness, but he obeyed when a chair was brought.

Li Szu smiled benignly as a green tea smelling lightly of fresh melons was poured. He accepted a cup for himself from the same pot. A steamer filled with elegant dumplings was brought, and each was permitted to serve himself.

Mute reassurance, Loyal Wind thought, *that I need not fear poison.*

The dumplings were perfect, filled with savory, salty things that went very well with the slightly sweet tea.

Host and guest shared for a time, then Li Szu wiped his fingers and motioned for his cup to be refilled.

"Loyal Wind, you have been an advisor to an emperor, a commander of vast forces."

The statement was not phrased as a question, so Loyal Wind did not reply. Instead he inclined his head slightly, acknowledgment of what had been said, but that was all.

"As one who must make decisions that will guide a great enterprise, I have need of advice."

Somehow I doubt that, Loyal Wind thought, but he schooled his face into impassivity that he hoped would be taken as attentiveness. *The next thing he says will give me some inkling as to what game he is playing.*

Li Szu leaned forward slightly. The fall of his ostensible scholar's robes showed a weight and weave of silk that gave lie to any claim of humility. The worked gold and coral buttons on his cap caught the light and gave it back transformed into bloody red.

"Tell me, Loyal Wind, how would you deal with a thief?"

XXII

Brenda sat tucked into bed, the fantasy novel she'd been reading—something about a woman raised by wolves—set beside her on top of the sheets.

Two days had passed since Brenda's return from the Land Beneath the Hills, a perfectly good weekend spent mostly in bed recovering from massive ch'i depletion. The drain hadn't been as bad as the first time, during the summer. She'd been spared the vomiting and aversion to light, but she'd still been so exhausted that she could hardly raise her head from the pillow.

At first, Shannon had teased her, thinking that Parnell and Brenda had gotten a bit wild. Brenda's usual limit was a couple of beers, and she'd never acquired a taste for anything that involved drawing smoke into her lungs.

When Brenda still looked pretty bad by noon, and turned down anything other than yogurt and ice cream, Shannon offered to run to the drugstore for anything and everything that might ease the symptoms. By mid-afternoon on Saturday, Brenda had been willing to choke down a few aspirin and even contemplate eating something semisolid.

Right about the time Shannon might have grown tired of playing ministering angel, Parnell showed up and offered to take over.

"As you should!" Shannon said, swatting him not quite playfully. "After all, you did this to her."

Brenda saw the look Parnell shot her and gave a minuscule shake of her head.

No. I haven't given away any of your—or our—secrets.

For a moment, Parnell had looked as if he might sass Shannon back, but instead he had looked appropriately contrite.

"And who would have thought an evening of dancing and a stroll on the green would have done this to such a fine lass as our Brenda?"

"Maybe it wasn't the dancing, but the st—rolling," Shannon replied, spacing the syllables of the last word to make it clear she thought a bit of rolling about in the grass on a late September evening might have caused Brenda to catch a chill.

Shannon relented, though. Brenda remembered hearing parts of a soft phone conversation between her and Dermott, making plans to join him when he got back from a soccer tournament: "If Brenda's well enough, maybe I will let you take over."

"Go on," Brenda urged. "I'm probably just going to sleep anyhow."

Shannon let herself be convinced, and Brenda had indeed slept. When Shannon woke Sunday morning to get ready for Mass—whatever she was or was not doing with Dermott hadn't broken her of that habit yet—she'd fussed over Brenda, fetching her fresh water, a book, a container of yogurt (Brenda was beginning to hate the stuff, even the raspberry) from the fridge. Shannon was heading out the door when Brenda called after her.

"Hey. Can you grab me my laptop? I think I feel well enough to check my e-mail."

Shannon had complied, and though Brenda had been too tired to do more than skim, she had reassured herself of two things: Nothing had gone wrong, and the Orphans still remained singularly uncommunicative. There was a chatty e-mail from Nissa with attached pictures of Lani doing some song and dance routine, but nothing was even hinted about the Lands, the scouts, or anything else.

Miffed, Brenda didn't even bother to reply, although Lani had looked amazingly cute, and she was glad that Nissa had promised to link some video as soon as she got it loaded. She was leaning her head back, closing her eyes to rest them, when she remembered a file she hadn't looked at in what seemed like weeks.

Once she'd regained some strength, Brenda pulled it up. It was a collection of photos from her time in California. Many had been taken to e-mail to her mom so that Keely could see what Brenda was doing that summer.

There was Des, wearing a hot pink mandarin hat, wildly stirring various ingredients in a wok in Pearl's kitchen. There was Riprap, leaping in the air to slam-dunk a basketball. There was Pearl, cool and elegant, seated behind her desk, a cup of green tea gently steaming at her elbow despite the summer heat. There were pictures of Nissa and Lani, too, but none of the Landers, with one glaring exception.

Most of the file contained pictures of Flying Claw. The first one was a phonecam picture taken by Nissa soon after "Foster," as they then called him, had lost his memory. That hadn't been the first time Brenda had seen him, of course. That was reserved for a memorable encounter in a parking garage in LoDo, Denver, but Brenda hadn't been in a position to take pictures then.

She'd made up for that later, and while the pictures weren't going to win any prizes, they were enough to set her heart fluttering in a way that made her already woozy head uncomfortably light.

Most of the pictures had been taken in the days right before Foster had been repatriated. Brenda had forgotten how different "Foster" and Flying Claw looked. Physically, they were identical, of course, but without his full memory Foster had been somehow out of focus, like those old-style fashion photos, the type popular in the sixties and seventies, where the effect wasn't realism but something almost painterly.

The underlying edge that would come out when Foster regained his memory showed here and there. In a picture Brenda had taken of Foster and Riprap playing Yahtzee, the hard, competitive light was clear in Foster's eyes. Yet in another, where he was deliberately losing at Go Fish to Lani, the fond smile on his perfect lips was enough to twist Brenda's heart in two.

In the weeks after, when Flying Claw had replaced Foster, Brenda had initially struggled to decide if she felt the same about this man. Eventually, she had decided she both did and didn't. Flying Claw wasn't Foster, but he still played quite happily with Lani—not as a duty, but with the same genuine fondness. Then there was what had happened when they'd traveled together to the Nine Yellow Springs.

Brenda shivered, remembering the feeling of Flying Claw's arms around her as the heat of the passing sun crisped their hair. He'd kissed her then. Not passionately, true, but he had done it, and she'd thought the look in his eyes held more than the fondness he'd shown Lani.

Now Brenda studied the pictures, trying to decide. Had her reaction been any different or had it just been relief that they had survived? There'd been so much going on, hardly a moment to think—well, plenty of time for thinking—but very little for anything else. Then, just when that time had come, when there were weeks of routine scouting, time when they might have talked some evening at the edge of a campfire, her dad had pulled her off.

"And sent me to school!" Brenda said aloud. "To school! As if I can concentrate on literature and history and all that . . ."

She took one more look at one of her favorite pictures, Flying Claw in a fencing stance of some sort. He'd been practicing with Riprap, but Brenda had managed to get just him in the shot. He stood there, intent, focused, a little smile playing about his lips in reaction to a joke Riprap had made.

"Damn!" she said, and closed the file, then shut off the computer. She leaned her head back against the wall. "Damn!"

She was drowsing off when a knock on the room's door roused her.

"Come in," she called.

The door opened, admitting the dark honey-gold head of Parnell. Fresh from her contemplation of Flying Claw's pictures, Brenda looked at Parnell with something of the freshness of a first meeting.

He was admittedly handsome, but in a completely different way than Flying Claw—or Foster. Parnell's wide green eyes seemed innocent of anything but mischief, where Flying Claw's were so dark and brooding that the slightest laughter came as a surprise. Brenda thought that Flying Claw was the taller, but neither man would draw attention for either his height or lack thereof.

Parnell's voice, as so often just slightly teasing, broke into Brenda's reverie. "I saw Shannon at Mass. She's going to brunch with Dermott, so I came by to see if you'll be needing anything."

"No, I'm fine. I could probably have gotten up, but I'm getting used to being lazy."

Parnell gestured to her laptop. "Catching up on your homework?"

"Probably should, but it's hard to feel motivated."

Parnell crossed from the door and stood next to the bunk bed.

"I'm surprised Shannon didn't switch beds with you. Getting down from that when you were so woozy . . ."

Brenda shrugged. "For the first day or so I didn't need to. It was like the ch'i depletion burned everything out of my system, not that I had a heck of a lot left after being stranded for hours in the sidhe."

Parnell didn't look in the least ashamed. "I fed you first, left you with water. You could have tried to eat something. There were berries and all."

Brenda shook her head vehemently, rather pleased

that the action didn't make her head throb the way it would have even last night.

"I've read too many fairy tales. I wasn't going to take the risk."

"Would I have risked you, acushla?"

His tone was so caressing, Brenda felt herself blushing.

"Probably. I haven't forgotten that you and Leaf have some agenda of your own."

"Which isn't to say that it is opposed to yours."

"Maybe."

A long silence stretched out, then Parnell sighed.

"I'm getting a crick in my neck from looking up. I don't suppose I could come up and sit at your feet. There's room."

"I don't suppose," Brenda agreed. "Sit in my desk chair. It has a high back. You can lean and not risk that precious neck of yours."

"Like I risked yours? Brenda, would you believe me if I told you that if you didn't get out through your own actions, I would have come for you?"

Brenda considered. "Probably you would have, but not out of any kindness to me. Shannon would have raised a fuss if I'd gone missing, and you'd have been the likely suspect. Even if you could slip away, there would have been people looking into your background, and some of those might have had the ability to find out what you really are."

"Hard words, Brenda Morris."

"Yeah. Hard words. Hard truths. You say you need me—or hope you can use me or something. But you say that there are those who don't think I can do it, whatever that 'it' is. Then you dump me somewhere, and I get back but then I get to spend my weekend being sick. Yeah. Hard words."

"You're bitter."

"Damn right I am." Horrified, Brenda felt herself choking up, felt tears welling into her eyes. "I'm apparently only good for anything when someone needs me. The rest of the time I get dumped. Dumped here at school by my dad. Dumped in the sidhe lands to drag my sorry butt back—or fail and get hauled back and be discarded all over again."

Brenda snuffled hard, managing to push most of the tears back, swiping at the rest with her forearm.

"Yeah. I'm bitter," she repeated. "I think I hate all of you, every damn one of you."

She'd squinched her eyes shut in an attempt to push back the tears. Now she felt the bed frame shaking. Opening her eyes, she was not surprised to see Parnell standing on the ladder. What did surprise her was that his own eyes were bright with tears.

Leaning into the ladder, he reached out a hand and laid it on her shoulder.

"I'm sorry you're hurting," he said softly, "and I'm more than sorry that I had something to do with it. Let me make amends, Brenda Morris. Let me show you I have more feelings for you than for some useful tool."

Those tears were real. Brenda was as sure of that as she hadn't been sure of much else for a while.

"Teach me," she said impulsively. "Teach me what I'll need to know to be useful. I feel like I'm doing a dance in the dark, and I don't know the steps. I was just getting comfortable with the Orphans' magic when Dad ripped me out of there."

"I promise," Parnell said. "I can't teach you magic, but I can find you a place where you can practice safely. And I'll teach you a bit more about the shapes the universe can take. It's going to be my way of seeing things, and that's going to be different than what you've learned in some ways, but if you're willing to try . . ."

Brenda nodded. "Try to stretch my brain around it? Sure. I'll try. That's only fair."

"Deal then?"

"Deal."

Brenda thrust out her hand. Parnell shook it vigorously. Then, putting one knee on the edge of the bed, he leaned forward and kissed her on the forehead. He had bounced back to the floor before Brenda was quite sure how to react.

The kiss burned on her forehead, but she was pretty sure the sensation was just her own surprise.

Pretty sure.

☆

"Tell me, Loyal Wind, how would you deal with a thief?"

Li Szu's question hung in the air.

Loyal Wind waited as long as he could, trying to organize his thoughts. He knew that the Ch'in dynasty had been very law-oriented, legalistic as opposed to the more paternalistic attitude of the Confucians. However, although the governments within the Lands had varied even as their rulers had varied, the Confucian model had tended to dominate.

Was this because so many Confucian texts had been burned and fed their energy into the Lands, or was it because it was a better way? And how would Li Szu himself feel? He was presenting himself as the creator of the Lands. Did he approve or disapprove of the path that creation had taken?

Loyal Wind answered the question with a question.

"What did this thief take? Why did he take it?"

"Does this matter?"

Loyal Wind decided to plunge in. He had neither the wit nor the temperament for extended prevarication.

"I think so. If a man steals rice to feed his family,

certainly this is different than if he stole the same rice to gorge himself, or to sell to gain money to buy wine."

"So the motive, not the action, is what you see as important?"

"Yes."

"But the rice is still stolen. The owner of the rice still must do without what he has fairly earned. Is he to be robbed without recourse simply because there is some slim merit in the actions of the thief?"

Loyal Wind felt momentarily clever. "Lord, you asked me how I would deal with a thief, not how I would compensate the one who had been stolen from."

"I see. . . ."

Li Szu tapped his chin with his index finger. Loyal Wind noticed that the nail on the finger was long and elegantly manicured. It was not the decadent show-piece the idle rich affected, but certainly it demonstrated that this man had not picked up a writing brush for a long time.

Loyal Wind glanced down at his own hands. Courtesy of the bath attendants, the fingernails were fairly clean and neatly trimmed, but they were short enough that the white moons at the top were invisible. A few days' imprisonment had not been enough to soften the calluses he had earned from their days of travel.

He dared sip from his freshly filled cup. The tea remained excellent, but could not rinse the sourness of sudden fear from Loyal Wind's mouth.

"Would you say, then," Li Szu said after reflection, "that there are times when theft is justified?"

Careful. Careful, Loyal Wind cautioned himself, but looking at his interlocutor, he did not think he could escape a direct answer this time.

"Yes, my lord. I do."

A slight inclination of Li Szu's head encouraged elaboration, and Loyal Wind hurried to provide it.

"Consider a spy for an army."

"Such as you commanded."

"Yes, my lord. Now, place that spy within the enemy's camp. He has managed to overhear what the opposing commander's plans are, and even to see a map of the proposed battle plan. The enemy commander leaves his quarters. Our spy has the opportunity to steal that map—but not time to make a copy. He must take the map. Shall he not do so because it is stealing? I think not. I think the information, and how it would benefit those he is sworn to serve, is more important."

Loyal Wind finished, holding back an urge to sigh in relief at having made a somewhat coherent presentation. A minor lackey seemed to approve of his answer, and offered the dumplings once more. Loyal Wind accepted one, but kept his attention wholly on Li Szu.

"Are you indicating then," Li Szu said, "that it would be better for your spy not to steal the map?"

"Yes, lord, but not because the stealing itself would be wrong. If the original map remained in place, then the enemy commander would not be alerted to the fact that his plans had been compromised."

"Interesting. So you see theft as justifiable, if it is to serve a greater cause: to feed a starving family, to provide intelligence in a time of war."

"Yes, my lord."

Li Szu smiled, and Loyal Wind did not think the expression was in the least pleasant.

"Then you will not feel wronged if I take from you something that is yours, if I do so to serve what I feel is a greater cause?"

Loyal Wind tried not to give away his sudden panic, but he felt his head fling back as might a stallion scenting a rival.

"I might feel wronged, my lord," Loyal Wind said stiffly, "even as you said the owner of the rice might consider himself wronged or the enemy commander would be right to feel indignation. Not feeling wronged and whether or not an act is in itself wrong are not the same thing."

"Panic may make a philosopher of even a plodder like a Horse," Li Szu said, lips twisting in the slightest of sneers.

Loyal Wind knew he had not been invited to speak, but the words slipped out before he could school himself to silence. "My lord, what do I, a prisoner, have that you could covet?"

"Your soul," said the creator of the universe calmly, "or perhaps more accurately that structure about which you have trellised your soul until the support and the soul are virtually inseparable.

"When you left these Lands Born from Smoke and Sacrifice you took with you your affiliation with the Horse. This did not deny the Lands the Horse, but it diluted some of the force. I will reclaim what was stolen from my Lands, and I will unite it with these Lands so that the Branches will be whole once more."

Loyal Wind bowed his head. He had suspected such might be Li Szu's desire, suspected in the depths of that trellised vine that was his soul, but he had not wanted to dwell on the option. Yet, regaining the missing portions of the Twelve Earthly Branches was only too obvious a goal. Doing so had been Righteous Drum's intent when he came from the Lands Born from Smoke and Sacrifice into the Land of the Burning.

There was ample evidence that the new rulers of the Lands shared Righteous Drum's goal. The attack of which Twentyseven-Ten and his fellow prisoners were the only survivors was proof enough that there were those in the Lands who would continue striving to regain the Earthly Branches. Certainly, once Li Szu had learned of the situation, he too would have been eager to regain this lost prize.

Or had Li Szu been involved from the start? Had Twentyseven-Ten and his mysterious commander ultimately answered to Li Szu? If they had, then that would explain a great deal.

And this explains why Thundering Heaven has allied himself with Li Szu. He must have been promised that the power of the Tiger would be returned to him.

Li Szu, perhaps denied the hope that shock would make Loyal Wind blurt out something of value and interest, continued speaking, an edge to his voice. "Returning to the matter of theft, there is a way you could save yourself from losing your affiliation with the Horse, from having your soul untrellised from its support."

Loyal Wind tried to school his expression so that his face would only reveal polite interest. In reality, he had strong suspicions as to what Li Szu's next words would be.

"You could join me, Loyal Wind, as Thundering Heaven has joined me."

Loyal Wind took refuge in the fact that he had not yet been asked to speak to hold tight to his silence.

After waiting expectantly for a moment, Li Szu stripped even that slight refuge from him. "What do you think of that possibility? Would you swear allegiance to me? Tigers are excellent creatures, but they lack the Horse's abilities when it comes to commanding armies."

Loyal Wind considered his words carefully. "I have sworn oaths of loyalty to others. How could you trust me to serve if you knew me as faithless?"

"Is an oath to those who are faithless themselves still binding?" Li Szu countered.

Is he lying or has someone else already accepted his offer? Loyal Wind thought, more saddened than shocked. *If so, who? Bent Bamboo? The Monkey has already shown himself easily swayed by the Tiger's arguments. Perhaps it was Copper Gong. Her goal always has been to return home. Or perhaps Des or Riprap. They might not realize the implications of what they were doing. Their land does not have rulers such as Li Szu. They might not understand how ruthless he could be. Or perhaps Nine Ducks or Gentle Smoke felt that they would do everyone more good outside of a cell, and so chose to change alliances and regain some freedom.*

Loyal Wind even supposed that Li Szu could be lying to him. But whether Li Szu told the truth or lied, nothing excused Loyal Wind from oaths freely sworn, oaths that had enabled him to regain the self-respect he had stripped from himself in the long years before and after his death.

"My oath is not contingent on anything but my own sense of my honor and duty," Loyal Wind replied.

"Then perhaps you should consider that your first duty would be to me, as the one who created the Lands, and without whom you would never have been born."

Loyal Wind held himself silent.

"You could guide me, advise me," Li Szu urged. "In a cell you are no good to anyone, least of all to yourself or your allies."

Loyal Wind remained stubbornly mute.

"I will give you an opportunity to think," Li Szu said. "An opportunity for meditation."

He clapped his hands together.

"Guards! Take Loyal Wind from here and prepare him appropriately to think upon the wisdom of accepting my offer."

Something in the fashion the guards prodded Loyal Wind from the audience chamber warned the Horse not to expect any kindness.

He was correct. He was taken to one of the outlying buildings, where his finery was stripped from him. Any gentleness in the disrobing was clearly out of consideration for the expensive fabric, not for the one who wore it.

Then he was shoved through a waist-high door into what he at first thought was a tunnel. Groping blindly, Loyal Wind realized he was in a chamber so small as to hardly be dignified by the word. The ceiling was too low for him to stand, and the walls too close for him to sit with his legs outstretched. A few minutes' experimentation showed that he could either crouch or sit with his knees bent at various awkward angles.

There was no light, except for the glimmer that leaked in around a small hatch set in the middle of the door.

After a time, this hatch was opened and Loyal Wind was hit squarely in the face with a bucket of stale water.

"Beverages, my lord," shouted someone, punctuating the words with a coarse laugh.

Something else was shoved in after, falling to the bottom of the cell with a sodden thud.

"And food. Enjoy your stay!"

Loyal Wind felt around him. The water had settled into a puddle several inches deep. The "food" proved to be a few root vegetables already gone into slime. Here and there, loose grains of uncooked rice were settling to the bottom of the puddle.

Loyal Wind's joints were already aching. He lowered his head into his hands with a feeling of growing despair.

He knew what would happen if he did not beg for

Li Szu's mercy. The time was not far off when he would befoul this puddle in which he sat. Then would come the time that even tainted water and rotten food would be preferable to raging hunger and thirst.

Loyal Wind understood now the diabolical kindness of the elegant refreshments he had been given during his audience with Li Szu. If he had agreed to cooperate, then they would have simply been a small indication of how generous Li Szu could be. However, if Loyal Wind refused, the salty food and copious amounts of tea would only speed along his humiliation.

Loyal Wind felt hot tears trickling through his fingers.

With the bitterness of despair, he made no effort to stop them.

XXIII

We haven't heard from the scouts in over a week now," Honey Dream said, striding through the door of Pearl's office and confronting Albert Yu. Her father came in behind her, his pace more measured. "Nine days. How much longer do you people plan to procrastinate!"

Head thrown back, long-lashed, dark eyes wild with fear and anger, the young Snake would have been a commanding presence even if she were not physically beautiful—and she was undeniably beautiful. Pearl found herself glad that Albert was not a man to be swayed by a woman's seductive charms.

Albert Yu looked Honey Dream squarely in the eye, but did not bother to rise from the chair in which he sat.

"Would today suit your ladyship? We have not been procrastinating. We have been preparing, reviewing a complex ritual the Exile Dragon designed, but which was probably never used."

Albert's inflections held the cool reminder that no matter how powerful she might be, Honey Dream was the supplicant and Albert—and the Orphans of whom he was the titular leader—held the advantage.

"Today would be fine," Honey Dream said, moderating her tone not the slightest. "How shall we begin?"

"We shall begin," Albert said, rising and bowing politely to Righteous Drum, "with the courtesies shared between civilized people. Have you eaten?"

Righteous Drum bowed in return. "We have eaten."

"Still," Albert said, "I insist you have something to drink and perhaps a few savories on which to nibble. Will you accompany me to the kitchen?"

"Certainly," Righteous Drum answered for both himself and Honey Dream.

Pearl and Nissa exchanged small smiles as they trailed the group into the kitchen. Now, if the rest of today's venture would go so well.

"Where is your little daughter this morning?" Righteous Drum asked Nissa as he settled into one of the chairs around the long table.

"Lani has a play date," Nissa said. "Joanne integrated her into a nice group of younger children whose older siblings are in school. Lani misses her cousins in Virginia, but this mob is shaping up into a good substitute. I'll need to pick her up after lunch."

"By then," Albert said from where, in a very nonimperial fashion, he had just put the kettle on to boil, "we should be done with what we can hope to achieve today."

"With whom shall we begin?" Honey Dream prompted. "With one of the ghosts?"

Pearl admired the young woman's regathering of her scattered poise. Surely Flying Claw, the young man Honey Dream had once openly boasted of as her "beloved," must be foremost in her thoughts.

But perhaps I am unfair to Honey Dream, Pearl thought. *She and Righteous Drum had hoped to learn news of their family weeks ago. Instead what they have learned is that all human populations are missing, and the Lands themselves have been drastically altered.*

Albert glanced at the clock set into the front of the stove.

"It is rising the Double Hour of the Snake. That seems auspicious. Moreover, we have a Snake in our own company, and we have the Snake's mah-jong set."

"Then we will start with Gentle Smoke," Honey Dream said eagerly. "Very good. She is clearheaded and sagacious."

Tea was made and a full pot carried into Pearl's office. By nine, the beginning of the Double Hour of the Snake, all was ready.

The five of them—Pearl, Nissa, Albert, Honey Dream, and Righteous Drum—took up positions around the table. The extra leaves had been put in, so the table quite crowded the area in front of Pearl's desk.

We'll need the space, though, Pearl thought. *I hope we have enough.*

The tiles were spilled from the Snake's mah-jong set—tiles made from Gentle Smoke's own bone.

"We'll build the wall as usual," Albert said, "with one exception. We need to pull the tile for Summer and reserve it. Oh, and let's build the wall along the northern edge of the table. We're going to need space."

Even as his fingers busily sorted through the 144 tiles on the table, seeking the Summer tile, Albert clarified for the benefit of the two from the Lands.

"Each of the Thirteen Orphans has a single tile associated with him or her. Most of these come from the eight bonus tiles—the Flowers and Seasons. The rest are made up from the honors suits."

Nissa nodded. "Pearl was telling me about this just the other day. The Rabbit has a special association with the east wind tile, the Tiger with the flower tile for bamboo."

"The Snake," Albert said, "is associated with summer because the element of the Snake is fire, and reptiles are most lively when the weather is warm."

"I've found Summer," Pearl said, holding up a tile on which a leaping fish was depicted in elegant detail. "When we build the wall, leave a gap in the middle of the southeastern section."

"Because the Snake's direction is south-southeast?" Honey Dream asked.

"Precisely," Albert confirmed.

The wall was quickly built and Albert set the Summer tile in the gap that had been left, exposing the face rather than the blank bamboo back.

"Pearl, you take charge for the next step," Albert said.

Pearl lifted the Tiger mah-jong set from where she had placed it on the floor near her feet, then spilled the tiles out onto an empty section of the table.

"We're going to build another wall so that it abuts on the south side of this one," she said. "We'll reserve the bamboo tile from the flowers and seasons set to place opposite the summer tile."

"I've got it here," Nissa said, holding it up. The carved stand of bamboo was more representational than simple cylinders that represented the suit with the same name.

Doubtless, Pearl thought morosely, *if Des was here he would take this opportunity to remind us that the bamboo suit actually does not represent bamboo at all, but rather a string of coins—of Chinese cash— strung through the hole in the middle.*

A lump formed in her throat, but she reached for the cooling tea in her cup and washed it away. The time for tears would be later.

If we fail.

"One last wall," Albert said when the wall from the Tiger's set was completed. His eyes narrowed as he estimated the room left on the table. "We have room to place it to the east of the Tiger set. Nissa?"

Nissa reached down and lifted up the box containing the Rabbit mah-jong set. She spilled out the tiles onto the southern end of the table, away from the completed walls.

"Does it matter which," Honey Dream asked a trace smugly, "east wind tile we hold out?"

"It doesn't," Albert said, smiling serenely at her. "We'll leave the gap this time in the center of the west wall."

Righteous Drum opened his mouth as if to ask a question, then shut it without speaking and helped shuffle the tiles. He was becoming increasingly dextrous with his one remaining hand. Pearl had spoken to him privately about a prosthetic—Dr. Andersen could be very discreet if the need arose and he was offered sufficient remuneration—but Righteous Drum had refused. "I will need to learn to function first without an arm. Later, when doing so has become second nature, and I can write and cast spells quickly, then perhaps I will consider an artificial arm. Now, though, I think I would come to rely upon it too much, and that would slow my retraining."

Pearl understood; a man of surprising depth and courage, this Righteous Drum. She hoped his wife and other children were still alive and unharmed. She knew that he doubted they were, and admired him even more for going after the truth so fiercely when he could have continued in delusion.

When the Rabbit wall was finished, Albert poured himself tea, then addressed them.

"I did not ask you to concentrate while we built the walls, because setting up the structures is not what is important. What will be is how we bridge them. There are several steps—and I must remind you, this spell is wholly theoretical, designed by the Exile Dragon, preserved in our archives, but, as far as I know, never used successfully. We've spent days going over it and working out the steps, because I suspect we won't get many chances to try it. It uses a lot of ch'i."

Everyone nodded. Albert sipped his tea and continued.

"When mah-jong is played as a game, many people refer to this first step as building the 'Great Wall,' as in the Great Wall of China."

He looked inquiringly at Righteous Drum and Honey Dream. Righteous Drum nodded.

"We have—or at least had—such a wall in the Lands. It was a project dreamt of by Shih Huang Ti, the same emperor who Li Szu convinced to burn the books. The imprint of his works and dreams is very strong in the Lands."

"Good," Albert said. "Then I don't need to explain to you that the mah-jong wall and the Great Wall bear no resemblance to each other."

"No," Honey Dream agreed. "The Great Wall zigzags, partially to accommodate terrain, but also because it was constructed from segments of other walls that were already there. Mah-jong walls are perfectly square."

Nissa interjected herself into the lecture. "Des said that this was because we're not really building the Great Wall, but we're building a universe, and the Chinese thought—or I guess, think, because it's true in the Lands—that the universe was square, or a cube."

"What we have done," Albert went on, "is build three universes. The first represents the Lands, where Gentle Smoke should be. The second, the one we built from Pearl's set, represents the guardian domains."

"More precisely," Pearl said, "the western guardian domains where Pai Hu, the White Tiger of the West, has been kind enough to interest himself in our problems."

"That's why you used the Tiger set," Honey Dream said, nodding approval. "I thought that might be the reason."

"The last square represents this world," Albert said, "what you call the Land of the Burning. We wanted to use the set tied to one of us here. We chose Nissa's because the Cat is a rather anomalous figure—not properly associated with any of the Earthly Branches."

And because, Pearl thought, *we did not want to wait until Shen or Deborah or Gaheris could get here. Honey Dream doesn't realize how hard it has been for us to wait this long, but it seemed wise to give the scouts a chance to contact us, and nine days isn't that long. . . .*

Or might it be too long?

"Righteous Drum, our part in this is going to be easy," Albert said. "We will do what in our system we call a Triple Knitting spell, supplying ch'i for the group effort."

"Our name is not as colorful," Righteous Drum said, "but we have a similar spell. Who is the focal caster?"

"Not any one of us, but rather the tiles themselves. You'll feel they are receptive."

Righteous Drum laid his fingertips lightly on the tiles closest to him. His eyebrows shot up.

"Yes. Almost as if they have a life of their own."

"Not so much of their own," Albert said, "but of our own. Honey Dream, in addition to contributing to the Triple Knitting, you will roll two dice and count off the walls, then two more and count the tiles."

"Yes. I know how this is done."

"Good. When you do the second count, draw the two tiles indicated and place them like this." Albert took the spare tiles from Gentle Smoke's set and stacked them like a short flight of stairs. "Touch them against the Summer tile."

Honey Dream nodded crisply.

"Pearl, you'll do the same within the Tiger square, but you'll need to do the routine twice—once to connect with the Snake, once to connect with the Rabbit."

Pearl knew this. She'd helped Albert review the old spell, but she didn't protest. The explanation was meant for the rest.

Nissa was less patient—or perhaps more nervous.

"And I," she said, "finish off connecting the Tiger and the Rabbit. Then what happens?"

"Then we concentrate on finding Gentle Smoke. We should feel a line of ch'i coursing through the avenue we have created. If all goes right, if the White Tiger of the West aids us as I have implored him to do, then our search should reach the Lands. What will happen there, I cannot say."

"We will find Gentle Smoke," Honey Dream said firmly. "We will. We must."

"Anyone need a potty break?" Nissa asked, sliding her chair back, "because all of a sudden, I do."

Honey Dream looked momentarily indignant at this intrusion of mere biological concerns, but when Nissa left the room, Honey Dream quietly excused herself as well.

On her way to her own bathroom, Pearl stopped to make certain the house phone ringer was off and the machine would take any calls.

When such mundane necessities had been tended to, Albert took advantage of the disruption to move them around the table.

"Nissa and Righteous Drum, if you won't be too crowded, take your seats on the east side of the table. Honey Dream, you start on the north side, so you can reach the wall, but then take a seat on the south, next to your father. Pearl, we'll put you on the west to start, but when you're done moving tiles, go to the north. I'll cover west. That way we'll be in something like the correct order for our signs, and have all four directions covered."

During the break, Albert had lit some incense on the family altar. The light sandalwood scent was soothing, the exotic odor cutting them off from the ordinary world as neatly as the house's soundproofing eliminated the noise made by the early arrivals to the Rosicrucian Museum.

"Everyone ready your Triple Knitting," Albert said. "Nissa, don't be ashamed to use a bracelet."

"I've got this spell down," she assured him.

"Honey Dream, I trust your judgment," Albert said, settling himself into a chair on the western edge of the table. "When you sense that everyone is connected, begin."

Of such little things are alliances forged, Pearl thought, seeing Honey Dream straighten a little at Albert's words. *Far more than any treaty, no matter what my father thought.*

She forced any memory of Thundering Heaven from her mind, and concentrated on building her spell. Around her, Pearl could feel the others slot their own spells into place. Honey Dream was perfectly patient, waiting for the resonance between five such different forces to fall into harmony. Then she began.

Pearl felt rather than saw the fall of the dice, the selection of the two tiles that connected the Snake's universe to that of the Tiger. Honey Dream was settling into her appointed seat on the south side of the table as Pearl tossed her own dice, one pair to select the wall, the second to select the two tiles.

To her delight, she felt a faint growling purr. Pai Hu would assist.

Pearl repeated the process. Without glancing at Nissa, she settled into the empty chair on the north side. Nissa took over, handling the dice without the least diminishment of her Triple Knitting.

Now to seek Gentle Smoke. The Exile Snake had died some years before Pearl's birth, but Pearl had known her heir, had heard stories of the Exile Snake's wisdom and, perhaps even more important, solid common sense. To these Pearl added more recent memories, from the time since the ghosts had come to stay at her house. Ghosts who had accepted a return to mortality—a return that in some cases, as for Loyal Wind who longed for redemption, might have been welcome, but for Gentle Smoke who had died at a relatively advanced age, with daughter and granddaughter, both, to carry on her line, might not have been so welcome.

These were not coherent thoughts, set down in orderly fashion, rather a flow of images, of emotions, of shifting perspective. Pearl's portrait of Gentle Smoke made one cord in a five-strand rope of shaped ch'i, a rope that made its way, snakelike (how appropriate) out of this Land of the Burning, into the facilitating force of Pai Hu, out of the guardian domains, through an opening she knew was the last of the Nine Gates, and . . .

Pearl felt her entire upper body rock back as if someone had slammed a fist toward her face and she had jerked away in self-defense. Her ears heard corresponding gasps from each of her four companions, but she, like them, made no other reaction, every iota of ch'i and attention focused on adapting, adjusting, reconfiguring.

They had penetrated into the Lands. Currents sucked the ch'i from their spell as she would juice from an orange slice. Automatically, she started to pull back, to regroup, but Honey Dream protested. An image of Gentle Smoke flooded through the confusion. Pearl agreed, gave accord, pressed all the force of the Tiger into finding Gentle Smoke, to touching the Snake.

Honey Dream gave their seeking form and focus. In a very real sense she and Gentle Smoke were echoes of the same greater thing, the Sixth Earthly Branch. There were not words for what they sought to do, but it was not unlike looking for a single shape among scattered jigsaw puzzle pieces, the one with two "arms," one "leg," and a lopsided head, printed in the blue of the sky that is also the blue of the sea.

Finding, discarding, finding, almost matching, close, close, doesn't quite work, pushing away options, glancing at the template, finding, finding, and there, there was Gentle Smoke, far, far away, her mind clear, her body was wracked with shrieking pain.

"Taken," came Gentle Smoke's voice, faint as a whisper, vibrant as a gong struck on a still night. "Li Szu. Past the mountains. Forest walks. Taken by

Thundering Heaven. For the Branches. If you come, taken—"

The contact broke—no, was cut—and Pearl knew Gentle Smoke feared what would happen if anyone detected this powerful surge of ch'i in the desiccated place the Lands had become. Flung back into her body, Pearl felt her muscles trembling and gripped the sides of her chair lest she tumble to the floor. Her face was wet, and she realized the wetness was tears.

"Taken," Albert said, and his voice rasped. He, too, wept. "Taken, and although she wished to hide it, I think tortured as well."

Honey Dream's face showed no tears, but not, Pearl realized, because she felt no compassion for her sister snake. She was too furious to cry.

"Tortured," Honey Dream confirmed, "and worse. They know Gentle Smoke does not fear death, so they must make her fear living more."

Righteous Drum was pale, his eyes red. "The branches. They want the Earthly Branches—as we did."

"But they," Nissa said softly, "are far more ruthless."

"Flying Claw," Honey Dream said, her voice low and hot, "had nothing to offer them—and his death would release the Tiger to their use. Likely he is dead."

Pearl found her voice. "We must go after them."

"You cannot go into the Lands," Righteous Drum protested. "You possess what our enemies want: affiliation with the portion of the Earthly Branches that came with the Exiles back into the Land of the Burning. They will be watching for you."

Pearl met his gaze without flinching. "They have Des, whom I have known all his life. They have Riprap, who has become a friend. Despite my unkindness to Flying Claw, he has honored me by calling me aunt. I will either save or avenge him."

Albert nodded agreement, but it was Nissa who spoke. "The Exiles came back to life for us. At least we owe them an honest death."

☆

When he started instructing her, Parnell decided that the root of Brenda's difficulty was that she could not tap ch'i external to her own.

"And when you run out of what you have, acushla, you collapse and get sick. I'm not blaming your teachers, mind. They were trying to teach you and the others, while at the same time struggling to learn who was hunting you all. Those amulet bracelets were a good compromise, but the time has come to move beyond them."

For the last several days, therefore, Brenda had been letting her college studies slide. She still went to lectures and did the bare minimum of preparation for those classes where she had to be ready to respond. Otherwise, she spent her time on Parnell's lessons.

He'd warded a half dozen locations, all near areas where, according to him at least, natural energy was more abundant. The plan was to teach her to tap that energy, then learn to focus it into one of the amulet bracelets.

"Killing two birds with one stone, so to speak," Parnell said cheerfully. "The ch'i, as you call it, won't be wasted, and you'll build your arsenal up a bit."

"The clay is going to get pretty grungy," Brenda protested.

"I don't think that is important," Parnell assured her.

Brenda was coming out of one of the warded areas after a long morning's lesson when her phone rang.

"Breni?"

"Nissa!" The joy Brenda felt at hearing Nissa's

voice instantly faded. Maybe it was because she'd been concentrating so hard on intangibles, but there was a tense note in Nissa's voice. "Is something wrong? Has Pearl had another attack?"

"Well," Nissa paused, "not quite. Actually, I was calling you about that role-playing game we started this summer. You remember, the one about portals into another land?"

She needs to talk about magic and stuff, and knows we're not supposed to over the phone or even in e-mails, Brenda thought.

Aloud she said, "Sure. How could I forget? It took the whole summer, and I had to leave right when things were getting interesting, when we were sending out scouts."

Parnell, who had been walking alongside Brenda, politely ignoring the conversation, now stiffened. Brenda wondered if she should let him eavesdrop, then shrugged. How could she stop him? She had no idea what Parnell was capable of doing. Even if he walked away, he might return in another form, or have one of his little allies listen for him.

Brenda slowed and motioned toward a bench near a spreading maple. Then she held her phone out from her ear, and hoped Parnell could hear.

Nissa was saying, "That's it. I knew you'd remember. Listen, do you want to know what's happened since?"

"I've always wanted to know," Brenda said, "but whenever I asked, no one would tell me anything."

She tried to keep the bitterness from her voice, but suspected it crept in nonetheless. "I figured that since you had another player for my character, you didn't want me to play anymore."

Nissa's Virginia drawl intensified as it always did when she got emotional. "I can see why you'd think that, honey, but that was just one player's choice. The guy who took over your role said that he didn't think you'd want to be distracted—and that he couldn't play if he was worrying about you."

Dad, Brenda thought viciously. *Dad was the one who didn't want me to "play."*

But the momentary anger faded in light of the realization that Nissa now refused to maintain the ostracization.

"Tell me about the game," Brenda urged. "How are our scouts? Did they find the way through the maze?"

"They did," Nissa said. "Took them quite a while. Some of the sections were really hard to figure out. But it might have been better if they didn't make it through."

"Why?"

"It was all a trap. Remember the guy who tried to keep us from getting the Monkey?"

"Yeah."

"He was waiting. They're prisoners."

"Prisoners!"

"We only learned three days ago," Nissa said. "We had puzzles of our own to solve, but we finally figured out how to get in touch with G.S. She's in bad shape, but we don't think her life is in danger."

Brenda's heart was hammering so hard she could hardly hear over the pounding of her pulse in her ears.

"Why not? I mean, I'm glad, but . . ."

"Because we think the people who captured her want . . ." Nissa paused.

Brenda realized that Nissa wasn't just following protocol. She was afraid that someone might tap in, someone who could fill in the gaps on this weird conversation.

Who? One of the indigenous? Dad? Some other enemy?

"Want?" Brenda prompted.

"The same thing everyone seems to want," Nissa said. "Remember earlier in the game?"

The Earthly Branches.

"I do. God! Nissa, what can I do to help? This is horrible. Do you know if the others are okay? Did G.S. say more?"

"She said very little, but I think . . . We can't count on everyone being okay. There's one scout who doesn't have anything they want."

One scout? Brenda mentally ran through the list: the five ghosts, Riprap, Des, and—

"Oh, God! No!"

"I think you've guessed," Nissa said, her voice heavy. "We're not leaving it lie. We're doing all we can. Shen got here yesterday, but even with his help it's going to take time."

"What can I do?"

Nissa let the question hang so long that Brenda thought the connection had been broken. Then she realized that Nissa was honor bound not to ask.

"Hey!" Brenda said. "I've got a great idea. I'm ahead on my classes. Why don't I come out and help you guys? Tomorrow's Saturday. I'll tell my roommate I'm going on a road trip, that I might be away for a few days after the weekend."

The relief was evident in Nissa's voice, but she didn't push.

"Sure you won't get in trouble? Can you afford the tickets?"

"I'll work it out—sometimes you can get some great last-minute fares online. Midterms are ages away. My roommate will cover for me. I probably won't even tell my folks."

"Good. Your dad dropped in for a few days, but he's off again. He's the busiest . . ." Brenda heard "most uncooperative" in Nissa's inflection. ". . . fellow."

"Yeah. I wish . . ."

Brenda let that thought trail off. She was already angry at her dad. Moreover, Parnell was pointing to himself, thumping his index finger against his chest.

"Uh, Nissa," Brenda said, "I'll get right on those plane reservations, but there's one thing. A friend is coming with me."

"Breni? Is that wise?"

Brenda looked at Parnell. His green eyes were bright and determined, and she knew that if she refused to let him come with her, he'd show up anyhow and the explanations she would need to make then would be worse.

"I think it's the smartest thing I can do. He's a great game player, and he might have some clever moves we can use."

XXIV

Loyal Wind had lost track of how many days had passed. His joints—especially his shoulders and knees—never stopped screaming at the odd angles they must hold, but he had grown accustomed to the horrible smell and had even stopped feeling hungry.

Thirst remained, a persistent nagging counterpoint to the ache in his limbs, but the filthy liquid in which he crouched had long ago ceased being anything like water. Occasionally, Loyal Wind gave in to the thirst and sucked a little of the wet stuff up from the palm of his hand. It didn't stay down long, but at least for a short time his mouth stopped feeling so dry.

He itched, and couldn't reach to scratch. After a

while, he couldn't feel his feet. That, actually, was something of a relief.

The cacophonic plaints of his body had settled into a twisted version of normalcy when the slot on the door to the cell slammed open. Light seared his eyes, even though he squeezed them tightly shut in reaction to the first bright ray. He heard the rattling of metal keys, the lock creaking open, felt the change in the air when the door was opened.

Loyal Wind didn't move until hard hands grabbed his upper arms and pulled him out. His legs tried to straighten, failed. He fell forward, unable to move cramped arms to catch himself.

The hands caught him again.

"His feet are swollen. He's not going to be able to walk."

"Drag him, then."

"He stinks!" the first voice protested.

"Hold your breath."

They dragged him. Some sensation returned to his feet, enough so that Loyal Wind felt tender skin, immersed in liquid for so many days, scraping against stone. He felt a trickle of blood grease his passage.

One of the draggers noticed, too.

"Shit! Pick him up. We're going to have to clean this up, and blood stains are a bitch."

"He stinks!" came the protest, but rough hands shifted their hold.

Loyal Wind's joints cried out, but he didn't let a sound past his teeth. If his jailers thought him conscious, they might try to make him walk. Loyal Wind knew he couldn't walk. He didn't think he could even crawl.

He concentrated on what he could do, easing open his eyelids to the thinnest slit. His line of sight was limited to the floor, but after nothing but darkness, the varied shapes and hues of grey stone were quite interesting.

Eventually, they passed through a door, across a gravel path, and into another building. The air felt different here. Moist. Steamy. A strong floral scent penetrated Loyal Wind's deadened sense of smell.

The bathhouse.

The jailers handed Loyal Wind over to the bathhouse attendants. There was little conversation, but forms were signed.

When the jailers were gone, Loyal Wind risked raising his head. His neck hurt astonishingly, but he could see that the two attendants were squat-figured, flat-faced, middle-aged women of the peasant type. They were inspecting him as they might a basket of dirty sheets.

"Clothes no good," one said.

"Cut 'em off. Give him a rinse first."

"Yeah. Otherwise we'll be scrubbing the big tub for days."

That was the extent of the discussion. Loyal Wind's clothing, saturated with filth, rotten where it had sat in the water, was cut from him. In a few places, the fabric stuck and had to be peeled away.

The action hurt exquisitely, but the bath attendants didn't comment when tears rolled down his face.

They laid him facedown on a bench. Without ceremony or explanation, they dumped buckets of tepid water over him. Loyal Wind saw the color of the water that swirled down the drains in the floor. Gagged when he saw it was the brownish-black of raw sewage, highlighted here and there with green and orange that might be fungus.

When the rinse water ran more or less clear, the

attendants turned Loyal Wind over and poured water over his front, even into his face, although one did hold a hand over his nose and mouth. When he whimpered and tried to rinse his mouth, she held a thick pottery cup to his lips, let him drink just a little.

Then Loyal Wind was put into a large tub filled with steaming water. His hair was washed three times, then cut. His beard and mustache were clipped, as were his nails. The attendants never spoke to him, but they did heed his whimpers of pain when they raised an arm or moved a leg too suddenly. They didn't apologize, but handled him more gently thereafter.

When the bath was over, Loyal Wind still could not walk—his feet were hideously swollen—but this time he was not dragged. With impressive strength, the women lifted him out of the water and onto a massage table. Head dangling luxuriously, Loyal Wind submitted gratefully to rubbing that eased his tormented joints. The final step was application of an ointment that smelled strongly of lanolin.

Still naked, he was placed in a chair with wheels on the sides. One of the bath attendants wheeled him into the hallway. Loyal Wind dreaded seeing his jailers again, but waiting for him, forms in hand, was a severe-looking woman of middle age. Her features were finer, even attractive, and Loyal Wind wondered how she had come to be here.

A concubine, perhaps, grown past interest, childless? A spare daughter?

Loyal Wind recognized the return of curiosity as a danger. He had managed to stop caring, to stop thinking. Now with his body no longer in as much pain, his mind was coming alive.

The severe woman wheeled Loyal Wind to a small chamber where she spooned rice mush into him and gave him more water to drink. The quantities were small, but Loyal Wind's shriveled stomach could hardly accept them.

As with the others who had handled him since his removal from the cell, the severe woman spoke only when absolutely necessary.

Loyal Wind didn't care. If he didn't speak, he couldn't betray his fear that they were only doing this to him so that they could put him in the box again.

Next the severe woman took Loyal Wind to a place where he was clad in a light sleeveless cotton tunic that came to beneath his knees. Clothing him even in this simple garment took three orderlies, because his limbs still would not answer to his command.

Their final destination was a small room, hardly twice the width of the cot set to one side. It had a small window, set high, and the now-familiar barred door.

An orderly laid Loyal Wind faceup on the cot. The severe woman gave him more to drink, then indicated a wide-mouthed pot set on the floor next to the cot.

"If you must vomit, try to hit that. If you must evacuate your bowels, call for an orderly. Try not to make a mess."

"Yes, ma'am," Loyal Wind managed. His voice creaked like that of an elderly cricket.

"Hmmm . . ."

The severe woman left, and when she returned she had a bell attached to a length of light rope. The bell was hung from the ceiling over the cot.

"Can you pull that?"

Loyal Wind moved his hand. The fingers were not in as bad shape as his feet because he had been able to keep them mostly out of the filthy water. He was clumsy, but the bell rang authoritatively.

"Good. Rest now. You may also request food or

water, but will only be given small amounts. Do you understand?"

"Yes, ma'am."

The orderly came a few hours later, offered water, silently anointed Loyal Wind's feet with one ointment and his joints with another. This was the routine, day and night, for what Loyal Wind thought was about two days. He couldn't be certain, because he spent much time asleep, and the light from the high window was indirect and faint.

The swelling in Loyal Wind's feet gradually diminished, and on the day he could walk, the orderly took him for a stroll—more like a stagger—down the corridors. There, glimpsed through a window, Loyal Wind saw something that made returning to his former dull, animal complacency impossible.

There was a garden, flower-filled, and in that garden walked Copper Gong. She was alone, apparently deep in thought. Her clothing was simple but of good quality. The brief look Loyal Wind saw of her face showed it to be drawn, but not unduly harassed.

Returned to what he now thought of as his hospital cell, Loyal Wind tossed and turned on the cot, his mind afire with speculation.

Had Copper Gong joined the enemy or was she being exercised much as he had been? Her clothing had not been as fine as he would have expected that of a royal advisor to be, but she had been alone, with no guards apparent.

Had he been meant to see her, or had it truly been the chance glimpse it seemed? Loyal Wind tried to reach out to Copper Gong, tried to touch her through the closeness of their shared House, but as always since they entered this part of the Lands, there was no ch'i for him to tap, and his own body was far too weak to supply surplus.

Loyal Wind's thoughts ran round and round, fearing, dreading, until the orderly came and gave him a soporific.

When he slept, Loyal Wind's dreams swirled with tormented speculation.

Slowly Loyal Wind became stronger. He graduated from rice gruel to solid, simple food, from sips of water to strong tea. His hospital cell, once a welcome refuge, began to seem like a cage, but he never asked to be taken out, only welcomed the increasing frequency and duration of his walks.

He was given a shorter tunic and a pair of simple cotton pants: peasant's clothing, but welcome for the modicum of dignity that came with it. Every day he was permitted to bathe; every two days, an orderly shaved him and trimmed his facial hair.

But although Loyal Wind grew stronger, his mind was increasingly troubled. His sense of the fortification was that it was quite large, but even so, he caught glimpses of his former companions—now fellow prisoners.

Or were they? He saw Copper Gong more than once, usually apparently alone, but once in conversation with a woman who might have been his severe-faced "hostess."

He saw Des Lee, clad in scholar's robes, engaged in what seemed to be heated debate with two men in similar attire.

Once he thought he saw Gentle Smoke, but the Snake was walking away from him, down a flower-lined avenue, so he couldn't be certain.

Another time, through a lattice screen, he saw Riprap, bare to the waist, his dark skin glistening with sweat, stick-fencing with a stocky man similarly attired. Riprap's expression was intent, and although a welt rose from one upper arm, his opponent bore similar marks, so this did not seem evidence of his having been beaten.

Twice, once coming from the bath, another time when being escorted to the garden where Loyal Wind most frequently was taken to exercise, he saw Nine Ducks—perhaps a bit slimmer than when they had last seen each other, but otherwise serene—walking down a corridor. Once she had a scroll in her hand, as if she had been reading.

Since Loyal Wind had been offered no entertainment other than his periodic exercise and grooming, he took this as a sign that Nine Ducks was in good odor with Li Szu. His heart burned with anger, for somehow he had never thought the stolid, determined Ox would be among those to betray their cause.

Flying Claw was the one member of their company Loyal Wind never glimpsed, even fleetingly or uncertainly. This disheartened Loyal Wind more than the apparent evidence that the others might have turned traitor, for he knew there was no reason for Li Szu to preserve the young Tiger, and every reason to destroy him. Dead, Flying Claw's hold on the Third Earthly Branch would be released, and Thundering Heaven could possibly claim it and grow in strength.

With nothing to do but eat, rest, and wait like a pampered dog to be taken for walks, Loyal Wind was left alone with his thoughts and fears. He cursed those who must have betrayed their cause. Forgave them. Hated them all over again.

His nightmares were full of the box, of feeling himself slowly rotting away, of being found stuffed in a box, a skeleton, clad in nothing but shreds of flesh.

Again and again in nightmares, Loyal Wind was carried to the box and screamed protest. Clubbed nearly senseless. Shoved inside. Sometimes his friends came to the window and pleaded with him to join them. Other times, they merely laughed at him for being a fool.

At last, what Loyal Wind had dreaded from the moment he had first been pulled semiconscious from the box cell occurred.

He was taken as usual to the baths. This time, after he had finished anointing himself with healing ointments, he was handed first undergarments, then inner robes, and finally a brilliant red courtier's robe. This last was not embroidered with the Horse, but otherwise much resembled what Loyal Wind had worn in his first audience before Li Szu.

Loyal Wind forced himself not to panic, but his gorge rose. Swallowing bile, he donned the robe, put soft slippers on his nearly healed feet, and carefully combed his hair and beard.

The severe-faced woman met him outside the bathhouse and escorted him to the door of the palace, where he was met by the same official who had brought him before Li Szu that first time. This time there were no guards, and Loyal Wind did not know whether to be offended or not. He hated to think himself tamed, gelded by fear, but clearly Li Szu thought this was the case.

The corridors were the same, the audience hall as grand, but this time Loyal Wind had eyes only for the man in the deceptively simple robes who sat upon the carved chair on the raised dais.

"You have had time to meditate," Li Szu said. "What is your answer?"

Loyal Wind met the cold eyes, and answered simply.

"I will not betray my associates. I cannot join you."

"Then you will go back to the box," Li Szu said. "And this time, I do not think you will come out."

Loyal Wind did not answer, but he found the strength for the slightest of smiles.

He had betrayed a trust once, and tormented himself during the long century and more after his death. Did Li Szu really think he could do worse to Loyal Wind than Loyal Wind had already done to himself?

☆

A nasty note of glee had sound-tracked Pearl's dreams these last several nights, glee combined with a sense of being on a roller coaster. She ricocheted around turns, up and down hills, pulled by a force as inevitable as gravity toward something that felt ominously like her own destruction.

None of the auguries Pearl and her associates had worked had helped them pinpoint the source of these invasive nightmares. They had confirmed that the nightmares were in some way linked to Pearl's association with Thundering Heaven, but since Pearl had suspected this all along, she felt no more secure.

Nissa's shamefaced yet defiant confession that she had phoned Brenda Morris, and that Brenda and an anonymous—"but almost certainly male"—friend were on their way from South Carolina, provided a welcome distraction.

"The only thing I feel certain of," Nissa said as she and Pearl sat discussing the matter over afternoon tea, "is that Brenda has confided at least some of our current problem to this friend, and that is why he is coming."

"You're sure it's not her father?"

"Absolutely. I didn't need to see Breni's face to know that she was pretty unhappy when I admitted that we'd not communicated with her about recent developments at Gaheris's request."

"I wonder," Pearl said, "if we should tell Gaheris that Brenda is coming here?"

"Let him," Nissa said with a definite edge to her voice, "find out by showing up himself."

Shen, who had returned the evening before from New York, bringing with him Umeko's blessing and the promise that his son Geoffrey was prepared to join them if he was needed, entered the family room at that point.

"I agree with Nissa. I'd like to say that Gaheris isn't behaving like himself, but that would be untrue. He is behaving perfectly like himself—at least where Albert is concerned."

Pearl sighed, the sound coming out as a sibilant hiss of which Honey Dream would have been proud. "But this isn't about Albert. This is about Des and Riprap, about our five ancestors, about people who need us."

Shen shook his head. "To Gaheris, this is about returning to the Lands. Returning to the Lands has always meant one thing to Gaheris Morris: Albert becoming emperor."

"But that's crazy!" Nissa said. "Will Albert become emperor? I didn't think that was possible, even likely. Oh, I know Righteous Drum promised his support, but that's a pretty flimsy promise. Righteous Drum can't even get home, much less make anyone emperor."

"I agree," Shen said. "Righteous Drum agrees—we talked about this last night. But I bet if we were able to get Gaheris to honestly admit his motivations . . ."

"Not likely," Pearl admitted dryly. "He is a Rat."

"Then," Shen continued, patiently ignoring the interruption, "he would have to admit that resentment of Albert's birthright as emperor would be central to everything Gaheris has done to this point."

"Maybe," Nissa said. She reached in her purse and jingled a set of car keys from her index finger.

"Pearl, I've got about an hour before I need to pick Lani up from Joanne's. I thought I'd go and get a few extra treats, some of that strudel Brenda likes or something."

"A welcome back," Pearl nodded. "Good thought."

"Then Lani and I will pick up Brenda and Mr. Mystery. We'll be back in time for dinner."

And they were. They came in through the kitchen door, Brenda first, her expression of very real pleasure at being back not completely hiding her obvious apprehension as to how Pearl would react to her bringing someone into Pearl's private domain.

That someone came through the door next: a handsome young man with tousled curls the color of dark honey and sparkling green eyes that looked as if they laughed more readily than they maintained their currently serious and formally polite solemnity.

Pearl had cast All Green when Shen announced that he'd seen the town car round the corner. Through the spell's magical aura, she inspected her latest houseguest for anything unusual.

Parnell maintained no obvious spells, but there was something about him that hinted that all was not as it seemed. As if he felt her critical regard—and he might well have done so, for Pearl had made no effort to mask her own spell—Parnell bobbed Pearl a short, courteous bow.

"My hostess, please accept my promise that I know how a guest should behave. You have no reason to believe me, but I tell you most sincerely that I mean no harm to you or any member of your household—although I cannot say I feel quite the same about all your kin."

Parnell's voice held a pleasant Irish lilt. Gaheris's mother, Elaine, would have been enchanted by the sound of that voice alone. Pearl wondered if Brenda had shifted Flying Claw out of her feelings, replacing him with this attractive Irish lad.

If Parnell's even Irish, Pearl thought. *There's something very odd about him.*

Over dinner, a relatively simple meal of baked chicken, rice, and salad—a concession to the fact that they hadn't known anything of Parnell's tastes when planning the menu—talk stayed general and conversational.

Lani chattered happily, and Pearl was amused to see that although everyone else had long ago become accustomed to Lani's particular patois, Parnell was understanding only part of what the little girl said. However, he was game. The smile Pearl had known must be his habitual expression arrived and set about charming everyone it touched.

After dinner, while Brenda and Nissa were upstairs moving some furniture around, preparatory to Lani's bedtime—Lani had insisted that Brenda have "her" room back for this visit and Brenda had not protested, making Pearl question again the young woman's probable relationship with Parnell—Parnell turned serious.

"I'll need to explain again when Nissa comes down, and surely when the rest of your company arrives later this evening, but I'm not going to be guilty of misleading my hostess one moment longer than need be."

In a few brief words he explained his heritage, and pricking himself with a pocketknife, demonstrated the reality of his strange, white blood.

"So," Parnell concluded, "if you're not wanting me beneath your roof, I understand, and will go without hard feelings or delay. I've gotten Brenda here safely, and although I'm eager to help you in the trials to come, I'm not going to force myself in where I'm not wanted."

Pearl swallowed an appreciative grin, wondering just how long it had taken this fey youth—although he might not be a youth at all—to decide that frankness would get him further than deception.

Pearl glanced at Shen and found her old friend looking bemused.

"Sidhe folk," Shen said. "Well, I can't say I never suspected your people of tampering here and there in human affairs. One doesn't live in New York as long as I have without having good reason to wonder. Do you plan to explain why you've involved yourself in our business?"

"I do and I will," Parnell said. "The short form is that your enemies are a threat to the sidhe, as well as to you. We'd rather have the battle fought in lands other than our own."

"And Brenda? Why did you fasten yourself to her?" Shen persisted.

"Beyond the fact that she's as sweet a colleen as one might wish?" Parnell grew serious again. "Brenda drew our attention because, although you think of her wholly in terms of your concerns and your heritage, she has links to us as well. Her grandmother, Elaine, made sure of that when Brenda could hardly walk."

"Did Elaine know what she was doing?" Pearl asked. The more magically sophisticated of the Orphans had long suspected that Keely McAnally, Brenda's mother, brought more with her into her marriage with Gaheris than met the eye.

"Elaine did and she did not," Parnell said. "That is, she believes in the sidhe folk with all her heart, as faithfully as she believes in God the Father, God the Son, and God the Holy Ghost, in the Virgin Mary and the choir of saints. Elaine would be a bit surprised, though, if one of us came knocking at her door."

"As doubtless she would if Saint Patrick showed up

to drink the beer she pours him on his feast day," Pearl agreed. "I understand. Fervent belief, perhaps a touch of the Sight, but nothing more."

"There might have been more," Parnell said, "if there had been training of it, such as the training you've given to our Brenda, but the time for such teaching is before the brain knows so much that it forgets what is real."

Pearl nodded. "We have found that as well. We were lucky with our three most recent apprentices that events they each witnessed gave them reason to believe the unbelievable, even though each was past the age of easy acceptance."

"So," Parnell said. "May I remain, or shall I make my farewells to Brenda and depart? Brenda only let me accompany her on the terms that I be frank with you and obey your decision."

Pearl saw the smile that twitched the corner of Shen's mouth. He, at least, approved of this strange addition to their numbers.

"Stay," Pearl said. "You'll abide by our rules and not abuse my hospitality?"

"I promise," Parnell said. "You can trust me."

Albert arrived with Righteous Drum and Honey Dream shortly after Nissa and Brenda came down from putting Lani to bed.

Over dessert, coffee, and tea, Parnell once again explained his true nature. Albert had a few questions, but catching Pearl's signal that she and Shen thought Parnell had something to offer, did not push overly hard.

Righteous Drum and Honey Dream had some questions of their own, but they were less aggressive than might have been expected. Once again, Pearl had to remind herself that in the Lands other worlds were accepted—not as a matter of speculation or faith as was the case here—but as a reality as definite as the history of their own world.

And not as an origin myth, Pearl thought, *such as that of P'an Ku, or Prometheus, or even that of God creating Adam and Eve and the Garden of Eden, but as fact harder, drier, and more real than current scientific speculations about the age of the Earth. Honey Dream and Righteous Drum know how their world came to be, that it is an offshoot of this one, so why shouldn't there be other worlds sharing some strange linkage with our own?*

"Is this all of us, then?" Brenda asked. "Will Deborah be coming back?"

Unspoken was: And what about my dad?

Albert ignored the unspoken question. "Deborah hopes to join us, but she can't for at least a week. She caught chicken pox from one of her grandchildren."

"Oh!" Brenda said. "That's not good for old—"

She caught herself and corrected, "Older people, I mean. Is it?"

"It's not great," Albert agreed. "Deborah's doing all right, but she certainly shouldn't travel while she's still possibly infectious."

"Lani," Nissa said, "hasn't been vaccinated yet. I'd been waiting until she was a bit older. My sisters raised a huge fuss. Now I wish I had ignored them."

Now, Pearl thought, *when your attention is going to be needed elsewhere. Now, when you couldn't sit at her bedside or be with her while she soaks in a tub of cool water and cornstarch. I agree. . . . Childhood illnesses have their place, but not now.*

"Okay," Brenda said, when it became apparent that no one was going to clarify Gaheris's status. "Then what are we going to do? Nissa filled in me and Parnell a bit while we were driving back from the airport.

Somehow our scouts have been captured and it doesn't sound as if their captors are very nice. I think Nissa said something about Li Szu being involved, but I admit I can't figure out how that's possible."

"Li Szu," Honey Dream echoed with a shiver. "The creator of the Lands Born from Smoke and Sacrifice, the ruthless one who did not hesitate to order the murder of both scholars and wisdom if that would simplify the task of establishing empire."

"Li Szu," Parnell said, his Irish brogue a marked contrast to Honey Dream's light, clipped words. "Li Szu who is more of a threat to this universe and others than you seem to realize."

"What," Albert said politely, "does one of the sidhe know of a Chinese official from the time of the founding of the first empire?"

"I'll tell you," Parnell said. "I'll be glad to have it said. It has been a weight on me, a heavy weight indeed."

XXV

Brenda stared at Parnell. "You knew Li Szu was our enemy? Before we did, I mean?"

Parnell nodded. "I cannot pretend otherwise, acushla."

Brenda saw the surprised expressions that crossed the Orphans' faces at this endearment, so casually employed. Nor did she miss the look of calculation that flickered across Honey Dream's to that point carefully neutral features.

Of course, the translation spell would politely decide to translate from the Irish, and now Honey Dream

has heard Parnell call me "darling." She's figuring
I've transferred my affections and Flying Claw is fair
game.

Brenda's face got hot, but that moment of embarrassment made her only more determined to find out what Parnell knew. After all, Flying Claw was the one to whom Li Szu offered the greatest danger. Whether Flying Claw loved her or Honey Dream or neither of them hardly mattered if he was imprisoned . . . or dead.

"Why didn't you tell me?"

"I feared you would not believe me. As Albert Yu has said, why should a member of the sidhe folk know anything of a Chinese official from long ago?"

"And why should you?" Albert asked.

"Because Li Szu proves a danger not only to this world and the Lands, but to our world as well. Indeed, Li Szu is a greater danger to us at this point, because we do not fit into his conception of what the universe should contain."

"Let's back up," Shen suggested. "Parnell, do your people have any idea how Li Szu came into power?"

Righteous Drum added, "I have wondered about this since Gentle Smoke's message came to us. Li Szu is very important to the creation of the Lands, but in all our history, he has never belonged to the Lands."

Brenda thought she understood, but she figured she'd better make sure.

"You mean that even though Li Szu's advice to Shih Huang Ti led to the Burning of the Books and the death of all those scholars, Li Szu himself was never part of the Lands?"

"That's right," Honey Dream said, and Brenda winced at the familiar snap of disdain in the Snake's voice. "After all, the reason Li Szu advised the books be burned, the scholars slain, was to eliminate them from the ideal Chinese empire he wished to help Shih Huang Ti create. He was not among those who died—well, not until somewhat later."

"I remember asking my father about what happened to Li Szu," Pearl said.

Pearl paused. For the first time since her return home, Brenda noticed how tired Pearl looked. Nissa had mentioned that Pearl had been having horrible nightmares, but this looked like something more. Pearl looked somehow attenuated, stretched out, as if even when awake she wasn't quite able to focus on what was going on around her.

"Thundering Heaven said," Pearl continued, "that regarding Li Szu the histories of the Lands were unclear, even contradictory. In most records, Li Szu vanishes after the death of Shih Huang Ti in roughly 207 BC, six years after the Burning of the Books. However, Thundering Heaven also said that he had heard one tale wherein Li Szu was among those who oversaw the building of the first emperor's tomb. You all recall that Shih Huang Ti was obsessed with immortality?"

They nodded, and Nissa added, "Shih Huang Ti is the one who ordered all those terra cotta warriors made, and not just warriors, but representations of other types of people, too. They've found statues of musicians and acrobats and jugglers and all. And chariots, with dead horses to pull them."

"The tomb," Pearl continued, "has never been fully excavated, because if the contents are even half as grand as the legends say, modern archeology does not have the technology to preserve what would be found."

"Does this have anything to do with how Li Szu ended up in the Lands?" Honey Dream asked acidly.

"It may," Pearl said. Brenda had to admire how well the Tiger kept a civil tone, for Honey Dream's had definitely been challenging. "From what Thundering

Heaven told me, one tale said that Li Szu arranged to have himself interred along with his emperor. However, unlike Shih Huang Ti, Li Szu did not die before entering the tomb."

"You mean," Nissa said, her voice shaded with fascinated horror, "he had himself buried alive? Has he been alive all these centuries?"

Parnell, who had listened patiently through this, now cleared his throat.

"My people did some investigating. Li Szu has been not quite alive, but not entirely dead, either. In death, spirits usually lose interest in the matters of this world—unless there is something to hold them to it."

"An unfulfilled oath," Righteous Drum said, "or a suicide clinging to the life he rejected."

"That's right," Parnell agreed. "Li Szu had unfinished business. He was determined to continue overseeing the empire he had helped create. Events, however, did not work out precisely as he had planned. The greatest shock for Li Szu was that, although in life he had known nothing of the Lands Born from Smoke and Sacrifice, in death he became aware of them."

"He must have been fascinated," Shen said, "but horrified as well."

"Horrified?" Honey Dream said indignantly, immediately defending her homeland. Then she nodded, "Yes. I understand. The Lands were created from all Li Szu wished discarded, destroyed. What he discovered was that he had perpetuated—strengthened, even—what he thought worst about Chinese history and culture."

"That's about it," Parnell agreed. "But although Li Szu brooded over the injustice of these circumstances for centuries there wasn't much he could do until . . ."

Parnell paused and looked very uncomfortable. Albert Yu rubbed a hand along the line of his beard.

"I'll guess," Albert said. "Until our ancestors, the original Thirteen Orphans, were exiled from the Lands Born from Smoke and Sacrifice, and decided to exploit a loophole in their exile to retain their links to the Twelve Earthly Branches."

"That's it," Parnell said. "In taking with them their affiliation to the Branches, the Orphans weakened the inherent magic of the Lands. Exploiting this weakness, Li Szu was able to regain a life of sorts in the Lands."

Brenda had been listening intently, her mind sifting through the implications, sliding possibilities back and forth as one might beads on the wires of an abacus.

"Li Szu," Brenda said, her voice indicating she was open to correction, "is dangerous not because he's the ruler of the Lands, but because of the type of person he is. He doesn't believe in anything except what he thinks is right, and what he thinks is right is pretty limited."

Parnell nodded. "That's how my people see the situation. A quirk of fate or possibility or whatever you choose to call it put a monomaniac in control of not merely a world, but a universe. We fear that Li Szu will not be content with reshaping the Lands, but that when he has done so, he will extend his reach elsewhere."

"Here?" Nissa said.

"And into the sidhe," Parnell said. "Perhaps the sidhe first. The clay of which the Land Under the Hills is made malleable. While that has advantages, in a situation such as this, that malleability makes us very vulnerable."

"But to go against the creator of a universe, on his own grounds?" Shen asked. "Do we have a chance?"

Parnell nodded, perhaps a bit too intensely, Brenda

thought, as if he must convince not only them but himself.

"I think so. We have several things in our favor. One is that Li Szu is bound by the rules he himself has made—in which he himself believes. Most importantly for us, Li Szu believes he needs the full power of the Twelve Earthly Branches in order to reshape the Lands."

"Does he?" Brenda asked. "I mean, from what the scouts reported, Li Szu has already done a lot of reshaping."

"I don't know if he is correct," Parnell said. "What is important is that Li Szu clearly believes this is so."

"What I am most worried about," Righteous Drum said, "is that the taking of our scouts is an elaborate trap. Li Szu must be behind the attack that cost me my arm, the attack that brought Twentyseven-Ten, Thorn, and Shackles here. At that time, they crossed the guardian domains by means of a dormant spell set in Waking Lizard. I do not think our enemies will find crossing the guardian domains again easy—if at all possible."

"No," Pearl agreed. "The four guardians are allied with us."

She looked narrowly at Parnell. "I wonder if Li Szu could use another land that shares some of its nature with our own to invade us?"

Parnell shrugged, and his grin was distinctly saucy. "I won't say we of the sidhe haven't worried about this possibility. In many ways, the sidhe is more like the guardian domains than it is like this world."

"Another reason, then," Pearl said, "that you would wish to aid us. I approve. I prefer enlightened self-interest to altruism, no matter how carefully that altruism is presented."

"An elaborate trap," Righteous Drum repeated. "But how do we save our allies without being taken ourselves? Li Szu must be waiting for us. We have what he most desires—not only the remaining Branches, but I am the creator of the spell that permits the Branches to be separated from their host without passing on to the Orphan's heir."

"He'll be watching for a rescue, all right," Parnell agreed. "So we need to be where he won't think to look."

☆

Loyal Wind was suspicious, but not terribly surprised when he was let out of the box cell perhaps twenty-four hours after being stuffed in again.

He'd suspected this might happen. They'd clean him up again, maybe let him regain a little strength, then threaten him with reimprisonment.

So he wasn't surprised by the bath and massage or the clean robes. He was a little surprised by the sumptuous meal he was served, but not too much. Food fantasies were a horrible stage of fasting. This elegant meal would doubtless haunt him in the days of starvation to come.

For Loyal Wind was determined not to give in to Li Szu.

Once again, Loyal Wind was escorted into the deliberately unostentatious throne room that Li Szu seemed to favor. Here he did encounter something that startled him out of his detached contemplation.

Unlike his other audiences with the despot creator, this time he was not alone.

A half circle of chairs was arrayed before the dais upon which Li Szu was seated, and in these chairs waited Loyal Wind's companions.

No. One was missing. The one Loyal Wind had

feared would be missing. Flying Claw was not present—
nor was there a chair set for him.

As Loyal Wind exchanged formal greetings with Li
Szu and accepted a seat in the last empty chair, one in
the center of the semicircle between Bent Bamboo and
Copper Gong, he studied the three women and three
men who had arrived before him.

They all looked healthy enough—but Loyal Wind
knew not to trust that impression. He didn't doubt
that to external observation he himself looked fairly
healthy. He suspected that his meal had included some
drugs to help him bear the pain of his tormented joints,
for he had been able to walk without undue stiffness.

*And, yet, perhaps I should trust appearances. Li Szu
implied that several, if not all, had betrayed our cause.
Perhaps this is a final attempt to sway me to their side.*

Yet Loyal Wind wondered. The semicircle was tight
enough that he could not study the others without
showing deliberate discourtesy to Li Szu—something
he was not prepared to do. However, he could see the
two at the opposite ends of the crescent without moving more than his eyes.

At first glance, Des Lee seemed much as ever, well
groomed after the peculiar fashion he favored, his
forehead shaved high, his mustaches neatly trimmed.
But Loyal Wind thought the color on Des's head was
too light, as if he had only recently been shaved. Des
had always been slim, but there was a new gauntness
about his high cheek-boned features.

And Gentle Smoke . . . The Snake was neatly attired, her hair shining with cleanliness. Yet there was
something in how she sat in her chair, a stiffness to
her bearing that Loyal Wind recognized all too well.
He might have missed it, but she was jittery as well,
jumping when a servant with a tray holding green tea
and various small savories came up beside her.

Loyal Wind could not inspect the others without being too obvious. Conflicting emotions warred within him—hope with anger, triumph with despair, for the very things he was relying upon as evidence that his fellows had not betrayed him was also evidence that they had been treated as harshly as he. . . .

His rage against them as he crouched in his dark cell, believing himself betrayed, had been in itself a betrayal.

"I am certain that all of you are pleased to see each other once more," Li Szu said, a new note in his voice making Loyal Wind focus his attention. "But I am certain that you all have noted the absence of one of your number."

He paused provocatively, and Riprap, less schooled in proper court behavior, or perhaps simply beyond caring, spoke with rough aggressiveness.

"Flying Claw! Where is Flying Claw?"

The big man seemed about to say more, but perhaps cued by the shocked expressions that flitted across the faces of the servants, he drew in his breath and held back.

"I have made no secret of what I want from you. You—or in two cases, your ancestors—took with you some of the force of the Earthly Branches. I wish this returned, but the provisions you made that upon your deaths the Branch would pass to your heir has made this difficult for me. I also have not been able to learn the precise nature of the spell you used to create this perversion of the natural order."

"I told you," Nine Ducks said flatly, "the Exile Dragon crafted the spell. None of us know the details, only our part in it."

"Convenient, convenient," Li Szu said. "I've heard the same from others. I'm not certain I believe it. However, we were discussing Flying Claw."

He paused and sipped delicately from his teacup. Defiantly, Loyal Wind drained his own, drinking from the dainty bit of nearly translucent porcelain as he might have from a leather water flask in the field, and holding the cup out for more.

What did he care if he pissed himself? He knew what was coming, and might as well enjoy what little pleasures he could before the return of humiliation and pain.

Li Szu's gaze had traveled over them all, daring another outburst. There was none, but not, Loyal Wind thought, because they were all cowed. Rather, faithful or traitor, each wanted to know what had happened to their young Tiger.

"Flying Claw," Li Szu said at last, "was a different matter. His affiliation was to a Branch of the Lands. Traditionally, in the Lands, simply willing a release can permit the Branch to pass on. In some cases, this is to a designated person, in others to someone who wins a contest or challenge."

The means of passing varies with the Branch, Loyal Wind thought, *as we know far better than do you. Stop showing off how much you've learned about this world you created by merest accident and let us know the worst.*

He hadn't missed the use of the past tense. He didn't think the others had either.

"However, Flying Claw proved stubborn. Despite promises of considerable reward, he refused to pass the Tiger on to the one who should hold that affiliation."

Thundering Heaven, no doubt.

"Of course, without the impediment offered by your very annoying spell, death would be sufficient to free the bond and permit someone else to claim the affiliation. However, that would have robbed us of a useful resource, a means of impressing our sincerity upon you all—especially those of you . . ."

Here Loyal Wind was certain a particularly harsh gaze was directed at him.

". . . who continue to oppose our will. Would you like to see Flying Claw?"

Bent Bamboo snapped, his usual good humor completely vanished. "You know we would! Please, do us the honor."

Perhaps, Loyal Wind thought, feeling again that curious mixture of hope and despair, *more of us have held out than I thought. Those were not the tones of an obedient lackey—unless, of course, Bent Bamboo was schooled for that line. Monkeys are good actors.*

But hope held up the balance against despair, at least until Thundering Heaven led out, from behind one of the screens that separated the throne from the dutiful clerks, a shambling figure, clad in nothing but a rag about his hips.

Flying Claw was no longer beautiful.

Loyal Wind had never been a man drawn to men, but nonetheless he had been aware that the young Tiger was exquisitely handsome. Now, the most logical reaction upon sighting the man who stood slumped before them would not be instant attraction, but a scream of horror.

Loyal Wind heard Nine Ducks stifle a sob, heard sharply indrawn breaths from the others. No one quite screamed, but then all of them had been through hell—and he was certain that none wished to add to Flying Claw's torment by their rejection.

"Flying Claw insisted on being the Tiger," Thundering Heaven said, "so I decided to help him achieve his goal. Hold up your head so everyone can admire my handiwork."

Flying Claw did, and this time someone did utter a short, shrill scream.

Flying Claw's nose had been broken, the nostrils slit and peeled back, creating a travesty of a cat's broad nose. Dagger slices above and below his eyes—cut straight through the lids—created the illusion of vertical pupils. Whiskers had been carved on his cheeks. His upper lip had been slit in two. His ears had been hacked into points.

The ear mutilation was easy to see, for Flying Claw's long, midnight-black hair had been cropped short. Patches had been shaved close to the scalp. In these places, the skin had been razored raw, blood contrasting red-orange against the black of Flying Claw's remaining hair, a garish parody of tiger stripes.

His body was striped, too, but this striping had been done with a whip, one with multiple lashes, and those tipped with something that had torn the skin in ragged gashes.

"I haven't figured out how to give him a tail," Thundering Heaven said affably, rather like an artist discussing a work in progress. "I was thinking that if I flayed some of the skin from his back, then braided it to hang over his butt, that might work. What do you think?"

No one answered. The servants had stopped circulating with refreshments. Even the clerks whose brushes had provided a skittering backdrop were frozen in horror.

Into this silence, Li Szu spoke. "Flying Claw's resistance is really quite idiotic. We can get what he so valiantly protects by slicing his throat. All he has done is serve to demonstrate how much we can do to you without killing you."

"It's worse than that, really," Thundering Heaven

said. "I told him that if he gave in I would repair his injuries. A Tiger respects courage in another—even when it is foolhardy. Yet still he resists."

Loyal Wind had forced himself to look past the ruin of Flying Claw's face, seeking to see how much intelligence remained within the young man's eyes. He had expected insanity, or perhaps the dull resignation of pain. What he found shocked him: anger, raw anger, the focus pure and absolute.

"So," Li Szu said, turning his attention from Flying Claw so entirely that Loyal Wind had to fight the feeling that the young man had been led from the room. "Some of you have not yet seen your way to cooperating with me. Shall we discuss your options?"

XXVI

And how," Honey Dream said sharply, "do you expect us to get into the Lands without their creator being aware of our coming?"

"I expect," Parnell said, "that Li Szu will know of our coming, sooner or later. What I'm thinking is that we may be able to confuse him by coming in from at least two directions."

Pearl had not particularly liked the idea of waltzing through the Ninth Gate and into the arms of whoever—quite possibly her father—Li Szu had waiting. Now she laughed aloud as she guessed what Parnell was suggesting.

"You think you can get us in through the sidhe?"

"I can't, but I think—and my aunt Leaf thinks—that Brenda can. Brenda bears the blood of both heritages, and has already proven that, if pressed, she can create a useful gate."

"What?"

The outburst was general, and Brenda—who was beginning to look very tired, and no wonder, given she had admitted earlier that she'd been too worried to sleep much, even on the long flight west—roused herself to explain.

"But that," Honey Dream protested when Brenda had finished her account, "is not the same as making a gate into the Lands."

"Haven't I been telling you," Parnell said, "that the Land Under the Hills is more like what you call the guardian domains than it is like either this world or the Lands?"

Honey Dream nodded. "Still, I—"

Nissa interrupted. "How many of us can Brenda take through?"

Parnell looked a touch uncomfortable. "Well, now here's the problem. There are those in the sidhe who don't like the idea of strangers coming through."

"Even if these strangers are passing through in order to help you?"

"Not everyone believes we need the help," Parnell said. "Why should we sidhe folk be more rational than any other people? Aunt Leaf has—after considerable arguing, mind—managed to get permission for Brenda to take one other of the Orphans with her into the Lands via the sidhe. Gaheris Morris would be the most logical choice since—"

"No!" Brenda said with blunt force. "I don't think so. I love my dad, but he has no respect for me. He's tried to shut me out. I couldn't . . . He'd be standing there, making suggestions. I'd get nervous."

"Wait!" Shen interrupted. "Parnell, that touches on

something that's been niggling at the back of my head. Why didn't you go to Gaheris with your offer? He's Elaine's son, after all."

"But although Elaine is attuned to us," Parnell said, "and is the one who 'introduced' Brenda to us, Brenda's mother's family is the one that is fey."

Pearl cut in before Shen could bring up that the Orphans had indeed been aware of this, that Albert had in fact resisted Gaheris's marriage to Keely on the grounds that they shouldn't confuse the Orphans' heritage by blending it with indigenous magical traditions. Brenda had enough conflicting demands on her without that old history coming up.

"Parnell," Pearl said, "you can take one other in addition to Brenda into the sidhe?"

"That's right. If Brenda won't have Gaheris, then Shen would be best. I smell a hint of our islands about him. . . ."

Shen looked startled. "My grandmother was English. Is that what you mean?"

"That might be the connection," Parnell agreed. "And you're sophisticated in magic. My people respect wizards—or at least have the sense to fear them."

Brenda cut in. "So, Parnell, what you're figuring is that you and me and Shen go into the Lands via some sort of back door?"

"You and me and Shen and . . ." Parnell paused, and Pearl could almost hear a drum roll, "some of my friends: Oak Gall, Wasp, and the like."

"You're planning to invade the Lands yourself," Honey Dream said heatedly, "with Brenda Morris as your lackey. Don't think I haven't noticed how men unaccountably fall for her dubious charms. I won't . . ."

"Honey Dream," Brenda said tiredly, "shut up. The friends Parnell is talking about are really weird little creatures. They might annoy people, but they're not going to be able to take over the Lands. Anyhow, even if Parnell was bringing through Oisin, Finn, Cuchulain, and all the great heroes of Irish legend, if the Lands are in such bad shape that they could be conquered, then there's nothing much your whining will do about it."

Honey Dream blinked. Pearl was surprised by Brenda's tone. She'd actually thought the young women were getting along better. Brenda seemed to remember, too.

"Honey Dream, I'll swear on anything you like that I won't cooperate with letting your homeland get taken over by anyone I help through. We can't afford to delay while we worry about each other's motivations. Flying Claw . . ."

Brenda's voice quavered. She stopped speaking, swallowed hard. "Flying Claw may already be doomed, but we know Gentle Smoke was alive a few days ago. Some of the others might be, too. We owe them a chance."

Honey Dream nodded. To Pearl's astonishment, she reached out and patted Brenda's hand. Her dark velvet eyes were bright with unshed tears.

"I am sorry, Brenda. I'm so afraid. . . . Not just our scouts, but my mother, the little ones. My friends. I apologize."

"And the world ends," Albert said. "Okay. Let's get back to making plans. Brenda's right. Time is short."

"And the world ending is all too real a possibility," Parnell said seriously. "But so is our making a mistake if we continue planning while tempers are short and bodies are crying out for sleep. We do no one but our enemies any favors if we make mistakes."

"I agree," Righteous Drum said. "If someone will take Honey Dream and me back to Colm Lodge, I will do my best to assure that Thorn, Shackles, and Twentyseven-Ten will aid us in this matter. I will tell them about Li Szu, and how the Lands have been re-shaped. That may move them to genuine cooperation, rather than acting because we coerce them."

"Sounds like a good tactic," Pearl said. "They were quite unsettled when they realized they had been mis-led by their commander. Knowing the nature of the puppet master may give us their good will, not simply their obedience."

"Shall we reconvene early tomorrow, over break-fast?" Righteous Drum asked. "I believe we should skip our usual morning martial arts practice."

"I agree," Pearl said. "The time for practice is over. The time for action has come."

Despite her own stirring words, Pearl's feet were heavy as she went up the stairs. Nissa, who had been mount-ing to her own room a few paces ahead, paused on the landing.

"Are you going to be all right? Would you like me to make you some chamomile tea?"

"Thank you, Nissa, but if I drink any more, I'll trade the restlessness of worry for trips to the bath-room. Dr. Andersen gave me some powders when I injured my hand. If I can't fall asleep after an hour, I'll take one."

"Tiger's promise?" Nissa said. She tried to put laugh-ter into the words, but failed utterly.

"Tiger's promise," Pearl said. "My promise."

So when an hour had gone by and Pearl had listened as one by one the various sounds of the old house had settled to silence, she rose and went into the bathroom.

She mixed the sleeping powder with water and drank it off.

She slept, and sleeping, nightmared.

Feet playing percussion on hardwood stage. Face

fixed in a bright smile, eyes focusing unfocused. Re-membering what she's been taught. "Ming-Ming, let all of them think you're smiling at them individually. . . ."

From the expressions she glimpses over the foot-lights, she's doing it, too. They love her. All but one face, dour, set, arms crossed over a broad chest.

Ba-Ba. Daddy. Thundering Heaven.

He's the only one without a smile for Ming-Ming, star of screen and stage.

Ming-Ming is used to it, and glances to his right where her mama always sits. Mama will have a smile, a smile as bright as Ming-Ming's own, a warm, loving smile that never fails to ease the pain.

But Mama isn't there. Where Mama always sits is another woman, a Chinese woman. This stranger woman's hair is skinned back tightly from her fore-head, lacking even the ornament of a part. Her lips are pursed in a disapproving frown, her eyes downcast. She wears a plain, high-necked tunic, sewn from matte black cotton, over equally ugly loose pants.

What shocks Ming-Ming most of all is that for all her meek posture, the woman's hand rests with quiet possessiveness on Thundering Heaven's thigh.

Ming-Ming's feet falter in their flawless rhythm. She misses one dance step, then another. Now the stranger looks up. There is a smile on her face, a cruel smile, and the words she mouths are crueler still.

"Failure. Disappointment. Useless waste of your life and mine."

The woman rises, and tugs at Thundering Heaven's sleeve. They leave their seats. He follows the stranger woman from the theater. Ming-Ming hurries after, danc-ing fast, the beat set by her wildly pounding heart.

The band playing in Ming-Ming's heart screams protest, plays cacophony, but Ming-Ming doesn't hear.

She follows her father and the stranger. They walk briskly, but without hurrying, down narrow streets bordered by the walls of tall buildings. The walls are almost entirely covered by ragged flyers printed in English and in several dialects of Chinese. Random fragments of those written words tug for Ming-Ming's attention, but she will not let herself be diverted.

She dances after, feet tired now, but unable to stop.

They have come to a river. Thundering Heaven stands, water gushing from a hole in his chest.

The woman kneels by the water. She is weeping, weeping. Ming-Ming senses that the woman's tears feed the river, and that the river's wellspring is anchored in the deepest soul of Thundering Heaven.

The river waters run fast, salt congealing on the banks, forming crystal sands.

The woman is lying in the river, facedown. Wisps of hair have come loose from that ugly braid. Her body is drifting aimlessly. Swelling, bloating.

Ming-Ming dances and her tap shoes crunch flat notes on the tear-salt sands. The stranger woman is drowned, surely drowned, buoyed up into a semblance of swimming by those racing, tear-saturated waters. The current moves her, making her corpse swim an ungainly water ballet.

Is she waving? Ming-Ming moves closer, closer, her feet dancing in the salt sands, the rushing water a susurrus of sound. Ming-Ming looks.

The drowned woman rolls over in the waters. Her round face is bloated. Something has been chewing on the flesh of one cheek. But her lips are entire, and she smiles a sad, wistful, angry smile.

"Come to me, little thief, useless child. Come to me, ruination of hope and love and laughter. Come to me. Come to me. We will be a family. A family of three."

And Thundering Heaven is there in the waters,

*one arm around the woman, the other open to wel-
come Ming-Ming as she was never welcomed by him
in life.*

*"Come to me," repeats the woman. "Come to me,
and be drowned."*

Pearl sat up in bed, her head heavy with the thick
feeling that told her the sleeping drug had not yet released its hold. Staggering to her aching feet, grabbing
at the bedpost to steady herself, Pearl dragged herself
toward the bathroom.

She'd splash some water on her face. That would
wake her up. She could wash the salt off, too. Her mouth
was so dry, so very dry.

Although the effort was tremendous, Pearl managed
to raise a hand and touch her face. She expected to feel
salt encrusted against the skin, but her fingertips met
nothing but the usual soft texture of her carefully maintained skin, nurtured with the latest developments in
sunscreens and moisturizers.

"Dream," Pearl said, and heard her voice thick and
muddled. Her tongue and lips felt fat and swollen, but
she forced them to work. "It was only a dream."

Only a dream, Pearl thought. *Why do people always say that? Dreams are the most real thing there is.
Dreams are what drive us to take action, to plan, to
persist. Dreams might make a man . . .*

There was an insight there, but her heavy mind
could not hold it.

Pearl passed through the bathroom door and knelt
to run water into the tub. She leaned heavily against the
smooth, hard porcelain, then dipped her face into the
water. The cool wetness felt so good. It was washing
the salt away, the salt of that horrible river. The salt of
the tears of dreams lost, dreams aspired to, dreams never
fulfilled.

Pearl wondered what breathing the water would feel like. Cool, probably. Soothing. Washing away all this thickness and heaviness. So much nicer than air. Air wasn't really there. Air wasn't even an element. It couldn't do anything for you. Water was an element. Water would wash away her cares. Water was there, right there, just below. . . .

"Pearl!"

The scream was high and shrill. Rough hands jerked Pearl back with such force that she slipped and would have fallen. Those same hands managed to adjust, to catch her.

Pearl shook her head. Through the muzziness that slowed her thoughts, she saw Nissa, half soaked, water plastering her nightshirt to her full, round breasts, gaping at her in horror.

"Pearl! What were you going to do? If Lani hadn't . . ." Nissa motioned wildly, as if she couldn't manage the words. "You would have drowned!"

Brenda was standing framed in the doorway.

"Oh, God! What can I do?"

"Help me get her to her bed. She's heavier than she looks."

Two sets of hands moved Pearl to the bed. A little voice, grubby with sleep, spoke.

"Mama? Wha's wrong?"

"Auntie Pearl slipped in the bath, Lani. Please go to bed. Everything is going to be all right now."

A little hand, gripping Pearl's own very hard, so hard the healing bones ached a little. Being lifted. The soft firmness of her mattress underneath her. Lani's voice, determined, perfectly awake now.

"I'm staying. Auntie Pearl had a bad dream, yes?"

"Yes. Probably." Nissa's voice, coming from the bathroom now. Softer. "Geez, Breni. It looks like Pearl tried to drown herself in the tub. I hear someone moving around upstairs, probably Shen or Albert. Don't let them in, okay? Pearl would just die if they saw her half soaked and her hair all over. Let me get her decent."

"She looks like she nearly died already," Brenda said in soft, shocked tones. "I knew she didn't look right when I got here. I didn't want to say anything, but she looked nearly transparent. I thought it was just those bad nights."

"Go watch the hall," Nissa persisted. "We'll talk later."

Nissa's hands on her, competent, steady. Hands that had dressed and undressed many less cooperative than Pearl. In the background, the gurgle of water running from the tub, Brenda's voice, tight, but in control, explaining. Someone's feet moving down the stairs.

There would be tea, soon. Tea to wash the taste of salt tears from her mouth.

Pearl's head was losing its muzziness. Perhaps the dream was wearing off. Perhaps the drug was wearing off.

"Nissa," Pearl said, and her voice was closer to her own. "Thank you."

"I nearly didn't make it in time," Nissa said, and her voice held shocked practicality. "I was so tired I didn't hear the water running. Lani did. Lani woke me up and asked who was taking a bath so late."

"Lani." Pearl squeezed the little hand that had never let go of her own except when the logistics of getting her dry and into a clean nightgown demanded. "Lani, thank you."

"It was the dead lady," Lani said. "Wasn't it?"

Nissa gasped, but Pearl was beyond being shocked.

"I think so. Have you seen her?"

"When I'm sleeping, yeah. She's not nice. I thought she was just a bad dream. Scary."

"So did I," Pearl said. "But I think I know who she is now. And now that I know, I don't think she can scare me anymore."

Pearl hoped with all her heart that she was right.

☆

Brenda knew Pearl must be in worse shape than she looked—and she didn't look very strong—because the next morning's conference was held in Pearl's bedroom.

Nissa and Lani sat up on Pearl's bed while the rest of them—Albert, Shen, Parnell, Honey Dream, and Righteous Drum—crowded on chairs squeezed into the available space. Brenda herself sat on the windowsill.

"I believe I know," Pearl said, "who has been attacking me—and why those attacks have been able to get through my wards."

"Ghost lady," Lani said, lowering her sippy cup and looking very serious.

"That's right, Lani," Pearl said. "Ghost lady. I wonder how you knew?"

"Seed her," Lani said seriously, "when I was sleeping."

Pearl looked as if she wanted to ask more, but Brenda saw her shake her head slightly, as if reminding herself that there would be plenty of time to talk to Lani—or rather, there would be plenty of time if they won against Li Szu.

And no time at all if we lose.

Pearl continued, "I believe my attacker was the ghost of my father's first wife. I can't remember how old I was when I learned my father had been married before. I may well have been as young as Lani. Later,

I learned that Thundering Heaven's first wife had been Chinese, that he had married her after the Orphans came to the United States, and that he divorced her because she could not bear children. I never even knew her name."

"Tea Rose," Shen said unexpectedly. "My grandfather mentioned her a time or two. The name stayed with me, because it was the same as a woman made famous by Genthe's photographs."

"Tea Rose," Pearl said softly. "Well, if my vision of her last night is anything to go on—and we know it may not be—this Tea Rose was never as lovely as Genthe's model. She was, however, a good, solid Chinese woman. I think Thundering Heaven might have even loved her."

"You base this upon?" Righteous Drum said stiffly.

"The fact that I believe he visited her grave after she committed suicide by drowning," Pearl said, "and that then her kuei seized hold of him."

Honey Dream said, "Kuei. Yes. That is quite possible. The ghosts of suicides are especially potent, and those with magical power are particularly vulnerable to manipulation. I see. Thundering Heaven was not a fool, so he would not have visited her grave unless he cared for her."

"Or was asked to identify the body, perhaps," Albert said. "Let's not get too carried away."

"I am not," Pearl said. "I saw how he looked at her."

"How do you know she died by drowning?" Parnell asked into the uncomfortable silence that followed.

"Because," Pearl said, "she tried to drown me last night. Kuei are potent ghosts, but they are not known for great imagination."

Pearl sighed and looked down at her folded hands.

"I am not trying to justify Thundering Heaven's actions—not now, not when I was a child—but I believe that the ghost of Tea Rose must have infiltrated his spirit. I also believe that she used the guilt Thundering Heaven felt over divorcing her, over choosing the Orphans' cause over his own desires, to manipulate him."

Shen said quietly, "You do realize, Pearl, that understanding Thundering Heaven makes him no whit less dangerous."

"Oh, I know," Pearl said. "It may make him more so. It's always harder to fight someone who is not merely a faceless villain. And I do plan to fight—and to use the advantage they have given me."

"Advantage?" Albert said. "I don't understand."

"Tea Rose was able to attack me through my connection to Thundering Heaven. I believe I can attack her—and him—through that same link. I may even be able to use it to physically make a bridge into the Lands—a bridge that would carry only me, true, but, as Parnell explained so eloquently last night, we need to slip in under Li Szu's radar."

"I didn't put it exactly that way," Parnell said with a grin. "I don't know much of your magic, but my gut tells me you're right. You could slip into the Lands that way, but it's going to be very dangerous for you—even if you win."

"I know," Pearl said, "but I have a very bad feeling about what's happening to our scouts. I don't think Tea Rose's ghost would have had such power if Thundering Heaven wasn't ascendant."

And there's only one way he could be "ascendant," Brenda thought, her heart twisting. *And that's if he's reclaimed the Tiger of the Lands, and the only way he could do that is if Flying Claw has given it up. And I don't think he'd do that if he was still alive.*

Her vision blurred with tears she didn't try to hide, but neither did she let her grief take over. Time enough for that later. Time enough when the fight was won.

Time enough when they had a body to bury.

Righteous Drum was speaking. "Pearl, are you certain you're strong enough to try to fight this kuei?"

"No." Pearl looked at him straight on. "I'm not, but what I am certain of takes precedence. No one but me can even try this, and we need all the advantages we can get. Therefore, I must try."

No one disagreed, and if Brenda had needed any further persuading as to the seriousness of the situation, that would have convinced her.

Dad, she thought. *We're going to need you, too. If Albert doesn't suggest it, then I guess I have to.*

Righteous Drum rose from his chair and moved to the right side of Pearl's bed. "If I might examine your hand?"

Pearl lifted it. "It's mostly healed. Dr. Andersen said I was lucky that the break was in the bone. A dislocation or torn tendons would have actually taken longer to heal, and needed more rehab after. Still, it's not as strong as I'd like."

"I may be able to help," Righteous Drum said. "If you would permit me to use some ch'i to probe?"

Pearl blinked, stiffened, then visibly forced herself to relax. "Very well."

Righteous Drum nodded, then grasped Pearl's hand between the fingers of his remaining hand. Sweat beaded on his forehead.

"Pearl," he said, his voice strained, "please, stop fighting me."

"Sorry," Pearl said. "Habit."

She leaned back against the pillow and closed her eyes. The muscles of her face relaxed, then her neck and shoulders. She sagged gently back, looking older as lines that had not been evident were suddenly visible.

Righteous Drum let his eyes slide shut as he muttered something rhythmic and cadenced. He ran his hand up and down Pearl's fingers, touching the bones of each finger, then the hand, then the wrist.

Opening his eyes, and politely letting Pearl's hand rest on the counterpane, Righteous Drum said, "I can help. If the bone was still broken, that would be beyond me as I am, but the break is knit. I can strengthen that knitting and widen the vessels that carry blood so that the circulation will improve. At the same time, I can give you additional ch'i, since your own is dangerously low."

"I accept your very generous offer," Pearl said, "but can you afford the ch'i?"

"I can," Righteous Drum said, glancing at Honey Dream to forestall any protest on her part. "I believe you will be entering battle long before I can."

"That raises," Albert said, "the tactics of our approach. We have a small force going in via the sidhe, and now Pearl—if she can exploit this peculiar connection. What will the rest of us do?"

"Distract," Righteous Drum said firmly. "Honey Dream and I discussed the matter with Twentyseven-Ten, Thorn, and Shackles last night. Li Szu will look for an invasion along the same route the scouts took. After all, as far as he knows, that is the only way we know to enter his barricaded Center. If we do not approach, then he will be left wondering why."

"Then those of us who cannot go in through 'back doors,'" Albert said, "will provide a distraction."

"Only until we cross the barriers," Honey Dream hissed. "Then I plan to do a great deal more than distract."

"We have settled how," Albert said, accepting Honey Dream's declaration as what it was: empty bravado, "and the groups are defined. That only leaves—"

Brenda interrupted, afraid that if she didn't, she'd use any excuse to avoid saying something.

"Albert, we need all the help we can get. There's one Orphan we could have and you haven't called him."

Albert looked at her, and for a moment Brenda could have sworn his confusion was genuine. Then he nodded.

"You mean Gaheris." A strange little smile quirked the corner of Albert's mouth. "I don't know what's wrong with me. I keep thinking of you as the Rat. You're right. We need to call Gaheris, and we will. I will explain why you are involved."

"I can face him," Brenda said. "Even if he's pissed."

"I believe you," Albert said, "but some responsibility should come with all the honors I get for being the Cat. I'll talk to him first."

What honors? Brenda thought. *A lot of expectations, a lot of scorn. I haven't seen many honors.*

"Gaheris," Albert said, "is certain to show up more quickly if I can tell him we've set a time for our departure. Does anyone have any suggestions?"

Righteous Drum said, "I will need several hours to work on Pearl's hand, and on restoring her ch'i. She should have several hours after that to adjust to the changes I will have made. Tomorrow would be best."

"Tomorrow?" Albert considered. "All right. Even Gaheris can't complain about tomorrow."

He turned and squeezed his way from the crowded room, reaching for his cell phone as he did so. Shen turned to Righteous Drum.

"May I help with your 'surgery'?" Shen asked. "I know a little of healing magics, but mostly of the 'first aid' type. My grandfather's interests were more arcane."

"I was going to ask if I could at least watch," Nissa added. "Pearl keeps telling me that the Rabbit is associated with the healing arts, but I really know very little."

"Both of you may assist," Righteous Drum said. "That will free Honey Dream to write some amulets for us. If the ch'i of the Lands is as tightly bound as we have been told, then we should bring in what we can."

Lani hopped down from the bed. "I'll go, too. Wang is coming today."

Brenda left her seat on the windowsill. "Righteous Drum made a good point about our needing to bring in some of our own ch'i. I'll go make an amulet bracelet, one of the Twins, I think."

Pearl roused herself from what looked like the beginnings of a drowse. "Breakfast first, Brenda. I noticed you've only had coffee. Get something solid into you. This is not a time to forget the basics."

XXVII

Someone was screaming. A woman, Loyal Wind thought, but he had been on enough battlefields to know how shrilly men could scream.

He was back in his box, stuffed in by guards who had seemed not only indifferent but flat-out impatient, as if better things were going on elsewhere, and they wanted to be there.

Now Loyal Wind had an idea of what those "better things" might be, and he shuddered to think what kind of men might hurry to be present at torture.

Another scream, this one higher, suddenly smothered as if by a heavy weight.

Or rape.

Loyal Wind listened, trying to discern whose voice was the source of those cries of pain and torment. He couldn't be certain. One moment he was sure it was Nine Ducks. Another time he thought he caught the somehow foreign inflections of Riprap.

Of only one thing was he absolutely certain. The sounds were perfectly genuine, too erratic, too ragged to be faked.

Unaware even of the growing ache in his legs, Loyal Wind crouched in the box, listening with every fiber of his being, as if his bearing witness could somehow give value to the victim's suffering.

As Loyal Wind listened to the screams, a steady cadence beneath the cries reached his ears. It took him a moment to identify the sound of boots on the stone floor of the passage.

They were coming for him next.

☆

Pearl Bright awoke to dawn glow and the first staccato notes of birdsong feeling physically stronger than she had for weeks.

Righteous Drum's ch'i manipulation had removed from the healing bones of her hand a lingering ache she had not even realized was there. Sleep had enabled her body to assimilate the ch'i he had given her, digesting it so that she could draw on it as automatically as her muscles drew upon the food she ate.

Yet, despite this care, Pearl was aware of a sense of impending dread.

"My doom is come upon me," she murmured.

Who'd said that? Of course, Tennyson's Lady of Shallot.

"A loser," Pearl said aloud, "if ever I heard of one."

"Pearl?" Nissa's voice, anxious, from the other side of the door. "Are you all right?"

Pearl remembered the baby monitor. Poor Nissa, ever watchful. Well, after today, that particular vigil should be over.

"I'm fine," Pearl reassured her, going to the door and opening it. "I was thinking about how Tennyson's Lady of Shallot was a wimp."

"Was she? I think I read that poem in high school, but I don't really remember it."

A strong, very familiar male voice cut in, speaking up from the base of the stairs.

"Never let my mother hear you say that, Pearl," Gaheris Morris said. "You know she all but worships Tennyson's version of the Arthurian tales."

"Wimp," Pearl said firmly. "Up and dying because a mirror cracks. When did you get in, Gaheris?"

"Three A.M. red-eye," came the reply, almost triumphant. "I took a cab over and phoned Albert. He came down and let me in. I decided that meditation would do me more good than sleep, so I've been in the front parlor storing up my ch'i."

"We're glad to have you here," Pearl said.

She turned to Nissa, noting that the young woman actually looked less than perfectly pleased. Well, a nurturing Rabbit would not particularly care for a self-centered Rat.

"Nissa, thanks for checking on me. I'm going to shower, then I'll be right down. Did Lani get you up too early?"

"Not really," Nissa said. "Well, a little, but I feel fine.

She understands that she's going to stay with Joanne, possibly for a few days, and seems to be taking it well. She's downstairs with Albert."

"Children," Pearl said, "can be astonishingly wise. Lani certainly was last night. Ghost Lady. We're going to have to be very careful how we raise her."

A certain tension around Nissa's eyes melted away at those words. "We. Good. You're not giving up then, not going on some suicide mission?"

Pearl shook her head. "My mirror is perfectly intact, but if I don't wash up and get some makeup on, I will probably look frightening enough to break mirrors. I'll be down shortly."

All the household was gathered downstairs by the time Pearl made her descent. Unlike previous ventures through the Nine Gates, robes and other such elaborate forms of dress were not in evidence. The team entering via the gates was going to try to move as quickly and decisively as possible.

Quantities of food were already laid out, most prepared the day before while Pearl had been recuperating in bed. She helped herself to a hearty portion of the egg, cheese, and green chile casserole that Des had made a staple of the household's table over the summer, added several slices of whole wheat toast, and joined the group already at the table.

"Pass the green tea," she said. "Good morning."

Various greetings passed around the table.

"I've called Colm Lodge," Albert said, "and told them to expect us within the hour. Pearl, are you certain you're all right with being left on your own?"

"As we discussed last night," Pearl said, "there is really no good alternative. I would prefer to attempt my approach from here. If I am only capable of a spiritual transition, I want my body safe in bed, surrounded by the best wards I can make. If our enemy's observers are good enough to notice that I am not with you, then they will merely think that I am serving as backup, or perhaps waiting for Deborah and other reinforcements."

"Very well," Albert said. "Pai Hu did say that he would deign to inform you when we had crossed the Ninth Gate."

"And I will hold my attempt," Pearl said, "until he does so. That way, your team will provide a distraction."

Albert turned to Brenda, "You okay with your part in this? No dishonor if you choose to back out."

Something in Albert's inflection made Pearl suspect that Gaheris had insisted on this as a condition of his permitting Brenda to participate.

"Absolutely," Brenda said. "I'm the only one who can make the passage out of the sidhe into the Lands. Our friends are in trouble and there's no way I'm not going to try to save them. No way."

Those last two words were spoken directly to Gaheris, who nodded acceptance, smiled slightly, and reached for the mustard.

"Fine," Albert said, and his tone made the single word an accolade. "Parnell will set up his gate into the sidhe from the same warehouse in which we set the First Gate."

"There won't be interference from two such different gates so close to each other?" Gaheris asked.

"Parnell, Righteous Drum, and Shen worked through the details yesterday, after Righteous Drum finished with Pearl," Albert said, and this time his tone added, *as you would know if you had been here.* "There should be no problem, and the warehouse is already well warded against outside interference."

A long silence, broken only by chewing, followed this statement. The doorbell rang and Nissa sprang up.

"Come on, Lani. That will be Joanne."

Lani got up slowly but obediently. Her round face was preternaturally serious as she dragged her new pink daypack with its brightly stenciled array of manga-style bunnies from under her chair.

"Bye, everybody," Lani said blowing a general kiss. She went over to Pearl. "Don't worry about the Ghost Lady."

Pearl kissed Lani on one fresh cheek. "Can I have a kiss for luck?"

Lani threw her arms around Pearl and hugged with surprising passion. Then, almost as an afterthought, she bestowed the requested kiss. Smiling now, Lani scooped up her pack and bounded down the hall.

"That's one great kid," Gaheris said.

Nissa, coming back into the room and dabbing at her eyes, nodded. "She is that. She's just about the best."

☆

The warehouse looks astonishingly mundane, Brenda thought as Albert pulled Pearl's van into the covered loading area. *I wonder if all the magical areas of the world are like this. Warehouses. Factories so boring you don't even look at them except as eyesores on the landscape. Office buildings. I wonder what all those people who want to dance naked at Stonehenge and old Indian ruins and places like that because they're sure that's where the magic is would think if they realized that a real gateway into another world can be found in the middle of the city.*

"Not bad," Parnell said, looking around him, "for an industrial park. Green lawns. Trees. Neat. I've seen far uglier. I like the bramble roses. Nice touch."

"Pearl," Gaheris said, his voice warm with the appreciation he reserved for the financially savvy, "has an excellent eye for real estate. Learned it from her mother."

Brenda had to admire her dad. Short of sleep, doubtless less than happy about being here, and especially about her being here, still he could summon up the charm.

"Well," Albert said. "Here's where we separate. Good luck, Brenda, Shen, Parnell . . ."

He looked as if he was about to say more, then he shook his head. "No. No speeches, not when we'll meet later and share tea around Pearl's table and chatter about how this all worked out."

Nissa came over and hugged Brenda tightly, hesitated, then hugged Parnell and Shen, too.

"Luck."

"Luck," Brenda whispered around a sudden lump in her throat.

Dad came over and hugged Brenda as he hadn't done since she was much younger.

"I like the new boyfriend," he whispered in her ear. "Grandma Elaine will, too. I'm not going to wish you luck. You don't need it. You'll do great."

Brenda hugged him back. This was *not* the time to explain that Parnell wasn't her boyfriend.

Gaheris thrust his hand at Shen. "Later, Teach."

He grinned at Parnell. "Take good care of my little girl."

The five from the Lands stood to one side, obviously impatient to be away, but equally aware of the importance of these small exchanges. Brenda was surprised when Honey Dream gave her an honestly warm smile.

"We'll be moving as fast as we can, Brenda Morris. We'll see you in the Center."

Then, one by one, Albert leading, they passed through the First Gate.

The air in the warehouse somehow felt different when they were gone. Brenda turned from watching the glow fade from the ideographs inscribed on the pine door and found Parnell kneeling on the floor, running his hands over the concrete.

"I'm having difficulty," he said, "finding a 'live' connection. I thought I might, but I didn't want to start everyone worrying. Shen, do Pearl's wards extend out to the fenced area?"

"They do," Shen said. "More than ever since the trouble we had a few months ago. Do you want to make your gate there?"

"I think I'm going to have to," Parnell admitted. "Either there, or back at Pearl's, and I don't think she'd fancy an active gate at one of her houses."

"She wouldn't," Shen said.

"Then let's step outside," Parnell said.

Once there, he walked directly over to the tangle of climbing roses. They were in bloom again, pale pink flowers flowing over green foliage almost as they had in the spring, the one difference being that here and there shreds of spent roses could be glimpsed, and the leaves looked a bit tired, as if they wouldn't mind the quelling that would come with cooler weather.

I wonder if roses ever really die back in California, Brenda thought as Parnell reached into the curtain of roses and swept up a cluster of canes as if they were a curtain.

"Brenda? Shen? If you would . . ."

Brenda looked beyond the greenery, and saw not the fence and the street beyond it, but vaguely familiar rolling green hills. Shen gasped softly, but Brenda managed to find what she hoped was a confident smile as she walked forward.

"How do you manage not to get scratched by the thorns?"

"I convince the roses," Parnell said with a seducer's smile, "that for me they have no thorns."

Brenda's foot fell on soft, dense grass. Two more steps, and she was standing beneath a blue sky ornamented with perfect woolly clouds. She moved to clear the gate and a few moments later Shen joined her, then Parnell. For a moment, an irregular patch of sky was ornamented with pink flowers. Then even that vanished.

Shen sniffed the air. "Bracing. Invigorating. All right, Brenda, now your part. You told us that you plan on using Nine Gates."

"That's right," Brenda said. "A variation on the variation that creates the first gate." She handed him a piece of paper. "Here are the tiles I selected."

Shen looked it over, considering. "Good. Nicely calculated."

Brenda felt embarrassed by the pleasure that spread through her at this praise, so casually offered. She covered by turning to Parnell.

"I'd really like it if you'd call your associates first, before I make the gate." She tried to sound matter-of-fact, not unsure. "I don't know how long I'll be able to hold it open."

"Or what opening it might bring," Parnell agreed. "They should be gathered already, but some of them are going to be a bit on the shy side. You'll probably sense they're here, but not see them right off."

"I can live with that," Brenda said. "Shen, are you all right about not getting a bunch of introductions?"

"As long as they are comfortable with omitting them," Shen said, "I think we'd be better off not wasting time with formalities."

Brenda thought about fairy tales, thought about the purposes served by formalities in fairy tales, and felt a twinge of warning.

"Since we're going into the Lands," she said quickly, unslinging the light daypack she wore over her shoulders and unzipping one of the side pouches, "I'd at least like to abide by Chinese manners. Parnell, can I pick a leaf off that white oak, or will I offend someone?"

"Go ahead," Parnell said. "What are you about, acushla?"

For answer, Brenda plucked the broadest of the leaves she could find, and set it on the ground a few paces away from where she intended to set up the gate.

"In Chinese culture," she said, "you always ask if someone has eaten. Good manners. How can I not do the same here?"

Feeling rather as if she was playing tea party, as she had as a child in the woods near her home, Brenda spilled out the contents of a small package of trail mix onto the leaf platter.

"There," she said, and raised her head to address the still-hidden sidhe folk. "Have you eaten? If you are hungry, please accept our hospitality while I prepare the gate."

She turned away quickly, so as not to frighten any of the shyer sidhe folk. Behind her, she thought she heard the distinctive buzz of Wasp's wings, Oak Gall's now-familiar chuckle, but she didn't let herself be distracted.

"Shen, I don't have a door as such, but we're not looking to make a permanent gate here. In fact, we don't want one that's permanent, or we'll be putting Parnell's home at risk."

"Kind thought," Parnell said, "but while you're casting your gate, some of us will be setting up wards.

If you can create a gate that will last at least a day or so, that would be useful."

"Useful?" Brenda said, then something on his face made her understand. "In case we need a fast retreat. Right. Okay, then, something that we can move if we need to 'close' the gate temporarily."

Brenda cast back and forth, looking at the scenery with new attention. "It should be smooth enough that I can write on it, since I'm not up to just envisioning the ideograms that make up the spell. There!"

She pointed to a smooth slab of rock that lay on the ground near a jumbled heap of stone. Originally, it had probably been part of the formation, but some act of weather—maybe ice, if they even got ice here—had split it away.

"That will do, if I stand that up against the other rocks. Parnell, is that rock somebody's house or can I move it?"

"It's no one's house," Parnell said, "but I don't know if you can move it. Let me help."

Moving the slab of rock, half cemented to the ground as it was by moss and grass, did take both of them, but once it was free, it proved to be only about an inch thick. Given that it came up to Brenda's waist and was about two feet wide, it wasn't exactly light, but they arranged it against the other stones so it could be "swung."

Shen now spoke. "You have your spell, Brenda, and your door, but have you considered that we're not going to want to come in just anywhere in the Lands?"

Brenda *hadn't* considered that, but now she nodded.

"You're right. I guess I thought intention would count, but we shouldn't leave that to chance. What do you suggest?"

"Are there any of our scouts with whom you have a particularly close bond?" Shen asked.

Brenda immediately thought of Flying Claw, but Flying Claw might not be . . . She forced herself to think it bluntly, coldly. Flying Claw might be dead. She couldn't afford to waste ch'i on—she swallowed a horrible nervous giggle—a dead end.

"Nine Ducks," Brenda said aloud, and was shocked at how clinical she sounded, "is the Ox, and the Rat's partner in the House of Construction. Loyal Wind is the Horse, and the Rat's direct opposite. Loyal Wind used that link of opposition before, when he needed to get in touch with me. Maybe I should see if the reverse will work."

"Sounds like a good plan," Shen said. "I'm here if you need me, but I want you to follow your own impulses, Brenda. I think they're going to be sounder than anything I could advise."

Brenda nodded, simultaneously pleased and startled by the blanket trust both men gave her.

"I hope you don't mind," she said to Shen, a little shyly, "if I use a crib sheet. I didn't want to get stuck because I couldn't remember something."

"Good thinking," Shen reassured her.

Parnell nodded. "Remember, you have permission to draw on our local energies. Do you remember the training we did?"

"I do," Brenda said. "I guess I'd better get started, shouldn't I?"

"Do," Parnell said, looking up into the blue sky as if he could read omens in the clouds. "The sooner you start, the better."

☆

The oddest thing about the flow of one's own blood, Loyal Wind thought, is that it takes a moment to feel it against the skin. Perhaps this is because skin and blood are the same temperature, and the liquid motion of blood is almost frictionless. Perhaps it is because flow is the natural state for blood, and so there is no contrast of ch'i.

But when the blood cools, when the skin has been sufficiently abraded that the slightest caress of air is anguish, then the coursing of blood across that open wound is perceived. By that point, the sufferer does not feel the sensation as pain, for pain has ceased to be isolated.

Pain is what one has become.

Loyal Wind was becoming pain when he felt the first painting of a one of characters upon stone etch itself upon his soul. The shape of that simple, graceful line, and the tentative contact he felt through it brought him back into a focus he had lost.

When the whip again touched his back, Loyal Wind screamed with a new awareness of the wet leather ripping through skin into muscle.

His ears, which had long since been unable to hear beyond the rasp of his own breathing, the erratic rhythm of his heart, heard a man's voice speak casually.

"See? He wasn't as bad as you thought. Faking it. These warrior types have incredible stamina, and they do say this one has already been dead. There's some question as to whether he can die."

Loyal Wind had wondered the same thing himself. Reincarnated by the grace of Yen-lo Wang, could he die? Or could he only suffer?

The lash stroked over Loyal Wind's shoulders, across his upper back, agony exploding through his skull as leather touched exposed bone.

Yet horrifically overwhelming as this pain might be, as pervasive, was the awareness of ideograms being shaped upon stone, upon soul. The hand that shaped them was unsteady, uncertain, but the force of ch'i that flooded through the link was as a striking bolt of lighting: sharp, jagged, incredibly focused.

In the afterglow of that strike, Loyal Wind knew whose hand shaped those ideograms: Brenda Morris.

He saw her, looking out through the ideograms she was shaping to bridge the gap between them. She knelt before a piece of stone, a pen in one hand, the other hand braced to hold her steady.

Long, straight black hair, tied back from her face. A touch of lavender ribbon just visible when she moved her head up and down, checking her drawing against a small piece of paper. Little earrings, tiny drops of jade and onyx, shaped like flowers.

Brenda's dark brown eyes were narrowed. In their intentness, in their shape, Loyal Wind saw Brenda's great-grandfather, who had been his friend, his companion.

Exile Rat, who, by his cowardice, his selfishness, Loyal Wind had betrayed.

Pain ripped through Loyal Wind's body once more, felt acutely, as he had not suffered for many whip strokes.

Loyal Wind understood through his gut. His intellect was still not fully his to command.

Unintentionally, in working this spell, a spell doubtless meant to help effect Loyal Wind's own rescue, Brenda Morris was feeding ch'i into him. The ch'i gave him strength, but not the sort of strength that would enable him to struggle or to fight. His tortured body was long beyond anything other than hanging by the leather bonds that tied Loyal Wind to the whipping post.

Unknowing, while trying to save him, Brenda Morris was granting Loyal Wind strength enough to suffer.

Loyal Wind screamed, sensate horror giving nearly

articulate meaning to sounds that had long ago dete-
riorated until they contained less sense than the insane snarls of a rabid dog.

Freed by suffering from the realm of thought, now
once again Loyal Wind knew what was happening to
him, what would happen to him. He passed back to
where dread adds its spice to sensation, giving pi-
quancy to the torturer's art.

Another ideogram was shaped. Another thin channel of energy flowed forth to sustain an intellect that
wished nothing more than to descend into the maelstrom of unconsciousness.

Loyal Wind began to throw himself from side to
side, seeking to break not the bonds upon his wrists
but the bindings upon his soul. He could not bear it,
could not bear feeling, thinking. Could not . . .

Or could he? Could he?

Loyal Wind dropped limp once more, so limp that
he was only vaguely aware of the attempts of his torturers to ascertain whether or not he lived.

One rough voice argued that he must, for the blood
that flowed from his open wounds still moved with
the pulsing of a heart. The other said he could not be
alive. Surely that frenzy had been the brain or heart
giving way beneath the demands of the whip.

Li Szu would be angry, the torturers whispered nervously. He had not wanted his prisoners to escape
him, especially into death.

Argument stilled the whip. With this small relief,
Loyal Wind struggled to shape the coherent thought
that he had sought to banish breaths before.

He could not bear it. Could not bear the pain.

If he broke this link—whether by forcing his death
(if he could die) or by forcing unwelcome ch'i back
along the silk-fine fiber that connected him to Brenda

Morris's spell—then once again Loyal Wind would have surrendered to cowardice. To betrayal.

If he could bear it, bear the pain, bear the even worse awareness, then . . .

He resolved.

Loyal Wind's head had fallen back against his bloodied shoulders, but in imagination the Horse shook his mane and snorted challenge to his enemies.

They could ride him to the ground, rupture proud heart and lungs, break his back, and strip his sides with spur and whip, but he would never give way.

Never.

Cruel callused fingers pinched Loyal Wind's nose, held his mouth shut, trying to see if he still breathed.

Never.

Convinced there was breath and heartbeat, rough voices shouted at him, bellowed so close to his ears that his bones felt the vibration.

Never.

Offered Loyal Wind surrender. Surcease. Rest.

This tempted. He could feign surrender. Surely they would not call him to account immediately. Brenda would finish her spell, but . . .

Never.

The whip snapped beside his earlobe, ripping a new hole in soft flesh. Blood flooded from the wound, pooled in his ear, clogging, yet somehow failing to deafen the demands that he surrender. Give way. Confess that he'd been wrong in what he'd done all those years ago.

Never.

More threads. More clarity. More pain.

Brenda's hand, steadier now, continued drawing the characters on the stone. The ch'i she fed into her spell was alien to Loyal Wind, a green ch'i, a bright ch'i, whereas the ch'i of the Lands was red and yellow and golden. . . .

As that green ch'i fed him, Loyal Wind experienced the input of his senses more acutely, although he grew no stronger. He wondered if any of those who were witnessing his degradation could see the alien hue that tinted his blood.

The whip fell again, this time across a patch of thigh, virgin and unspoiled until now. Fell again, across the sole of his foot. The pain was sharp, fresh. He howled or tried to howl, but his throat was thick from screaming, and what came out was choked and rasping.

Never.

How many ideograms had she drawn? How much more must he bear?

Loyal Wind strove to count back, touching the silken threads.

One. Five. Seven.

With the next stroke, black and red pain thundered through Loyal Wind's entire body. He nearly lost the count.

Nine. Twelve.

Never!

Thirteen.

Fourteen.

Loyal Wind slumped as a green-gold light cut through a dimness of which he had long since ceased to be aware.

Blackness. He felt himself falling.

Never.

XXVIII

Rough as the rasping caress of a cat's tongue, Pai Hu broke into the chaotic stream of Pearl's thoughts.

"The Ninth Gate has been crossed. Brenda Morris has vanished into the sidhe."

Pearl listened, but there was nothing more. Well, she hadn't exactly expected the White Tiger of the West to pause for a chat.

She'd been sitting in her favorite easy chair, listening to music and letting her thoughts wander over a long life fully lived.

She had already dressed for the confrontation to come: tailored slacks of raw silk dyed buff, paired with a coordinating top adorned with a broad center stripe in a green slightly darker than mint. Sensible—but not clunky—shoes, a clasp to hold back her hair. Emerald earrings. A selection of amulet bracelets. The sword Treaty.

Now Pearl walked briskly through the house that had been her home for so many years, checking the status of both locks and wards. All were in place. Her revised will sat on top of a stack of essential paperwork beneath a blown glass paperweight set in the precise center of the desk blotter.

Pearl had prepared a delayed e-mail to be sent to Dr. Broderick Pike of the Rosicrucians. The computer would send it if she or one of the other Orphans did not return within a week. The e-mail directed Dr. Pike to query her lawyer, who in turn held a letter. The letter explained the complex details of the situation, and suggested actions that the indigenous magical traditions might need to take.

Deborah Van Bergenstein, the Pig, would get a copy of the same letter.

Hopefully unnecessary preparations, but Pearl and Albert had both agreed that matters had escalated to the point that nothing could be left to chance.

Resisting an urge to check the wards and locks once more, Pearl returned to her easy chair. She had learned to meditate when she was very young, but, even so, sliding her mind into the familiar space from which she could touch regions not normally accessible to the waking mind was not easy.

Forcing herself to forget how very much might depend upon what she was attempting, Pearl tried again.

To the untrained, the realm of dreams is as untouchable as thought. Even the adept finds entering dreams difficult, and Pearl had never been one to live in dreams when reality offered more than enough to hold her interest.

However, what Pearl sought now was not precisely a dream, but rather something masquerading as a dream. That something did not come from without, but from within, twisted somewhere within the tangles of past experience that was the foundation upon which Pearl had built her present life.

Pearl searched. After what felt like an eternity, she found the alien trace snaking through the convolutions of her mind.

She colored it pale pink, the shade she associated with the tea rose. Without touching it, she looked to where it had made its entry. As she had expected, the rose rooted within the Tiger. What she had not expected was that the parasitic growth seemed unshaded by the Tiger's deep green.

Tea Rose was riding the Tiger, but the Tiger was apparently unaware what clung to its shoulders.

Pearl felt a breath of relief. She had not realized

before this how deep her sense of betrayal had been. For many years now, since Thundering Heaven's death certainly, but even earlier, when she had been determined that she would become a fit heir to her peculiar inheritance, Pearl had identified with the Tiger. The thought that it had betrayed her had been a thorn in her paw.

Pearl claimed a courage she had not known she lacked, assured that she could challenge the invader without ripping into what had become the center of her own soul.

Or so, at least, she dared hope.

Moving with elaborate care, Pearl set one hand on the rose pink tendril. It would have been easier if her goal had only been to destroy the invader, but since she wished to use Tea Rose, Pearl must instead control her.

And from that first touch, Pearl knew this was not going to be easy.

Despair. Choking. Thick as fog over San Francisco Bay. Deadening sound. Deadening. Merely, purely, deadening.

Staggering from a post office, a piece of paper in hand. Printed at the top in both English and Chinese is the name of a prestigious legal firm. The listing of names and titles is longer than the text of the letter. This states simply, without elaboration, that her divorce from Thundering Heaven Ming is final.

There is nothing further, nothing to evoke how she had wept and pleaded, wept that surely she was not barren, that someday they would have the children Thundering Heaven so desired. Nothing to show how she had pleaded for him to at least consider adoption. Nothing, even as she had become nothing in the eyes of the man she had elevated as her lord and god on this earth.

Staggering. Placing a phone call. Empty bells, empty. Realizing that pleas will do her no good. Nothing will do her any good. Fate leaves her two choices. Of them, death is preferable.

The river. The cold water. Feeling it in her lungs. Longing for dissolution. Two horrors, inextricably intertwined. She is dead. Her body is dead. So, within it, is the body of the child, a tiny thing, not even vaguely human in shape. The boy child. The son. Fruit of the humiliating encounter when she had all but raped the man who had already declared her no longer his wife, who had thrown her out the door in furious disgust; his semen still wet against her bare thighs. . . .

If despair had been horrible, this is worse. Clinging to the cold, colder, coldest corpse and the dead thing within. Clinging, because if only she can crawl back inside, crawl back in and animate the lifeless flesh then she will be able to bear the child, carry it to her lord, her master, redeem herself. Win him back.

And he comes and stares, he, her lord and master, he the light who had kindled her in the last, only to throw her away, and she reaches up and grasps and holds. And holds. And holds . . .

From this day forth, as man and wife, never to be separated, she the whispering voice in his nightmares, the force that renders his eventual fatherhood sour, his many long decades of warmth and breath empty until death itself seems a welcome release.

But she will not release him, not even then. Not ever.

The force of hatred and malice was so intense that Pearl gagged, retching, flung forward in her chair, hands balled in her stomach. She struggled until the force of her will was equal to Tea Rose's bitter and malicious memories. Although her grasp slipped, Pearl did not let go.

Another might have answered hatred with love, rejection with compassion, malice with forgiveness.

Pearl was Pearl, and offered sorrow. Sorrow for the child who had never had a soul. Sorrow for the mother who had never been, for the wife who had been and could not be. Sorrow for herself, rejected at the moment of conception, sorrow for Edna Ming who had never known that she was wed to twinned misery, not to a man. Sorrow for the young sons, brothers to a rejected daughter, rejected because they would not be sororicides, even in their thoughts.

Sorrow was Pearl's weapon as she pulled herself hand over hand along the pink trace of Tea Rose's soul: a po soul given hun intellect by its insertion into the liver and mind of the man who had been called to identify the body of a suicide, and had permitted himself the luxury of regret.

And because Tea Rose had shaped herself of sorrow (as well as of anger and despair, of malice and bitterness), sorrow cloaked Pearl as she pulled herself along the trace anchored at one end within her own mind, at the other within the mind of the man who had been her father.

Pearl hauled herself along that trace, glimpsed how Twentyseven-Ten—almost a Tiger and as nearly filled with malice and a desire to blame as was Tea Rose herself—had been manipulated to set certain characters onto the engine block of Pearl's car, how he had convinced Thorn to complete the spell using compulsion and a touch of agile rationalization.

These events were as a maze into which Pearl might have been lost, but she fought the desire to delve into that wrong. Past was passed. Her need was to affect the present.

Sorrow served Pearl as a cloak and a good one, too. Even so, Pearl wondered that Tea Rose did not sense her coming and react. Seeking to understand, to sense whether Tea Rose might be feigning indifference, lying in wait, Pearl became aware that events were working in her favor.

Thundering Heaven was deeply involved in some action, an action that had Tea Rose so distracted that she no more felt Pearl moving as a dream of sadness through her soul than Pearl had realized who manipulated her sleeping self.

A maelstrom of hatred, a riptide of anger, shook the strange firmament through which Pearl forced her way. Brilliant crimson slashes of wrath raked the skies. White explosions of fury shook the earth. They made Pearl's bones shake, her internal organs vibrate within her body, but she did not release her grasp.

The rose pink trace on which Pearl was traveling was wider now, wide enough that Pearl swung herself aboard like an acrobat mounting a tightrope, no longer pulling herself hand over hand, but running, sensible shoes slapping down on the hard, rubbery surface.

Pearl ran hard, urgency penetrating her being as glimpses of what events so distracted Tea Rose. Anger's crimson light illuminated the present in which Tea Rose and her host resided, where they were bent over the body of a young Tiger, a young man they wished to slash free of everything that made him worthy of being a Tiger. . . .

Pearl had run hard. Now she ran harder, ribs aching, lungs gasping, drawing her sword, praying to whatever gods might listen that she not arrive too late.

☆

Initially, Brenda was acutely aware of Shen and Parnell standing a few paces in back of her, of them and of the not-quite-silent watchers who lurked just out of sight. Her hand shook a little as she drew the first of the sequence of characters. She felt her control of the ch'i shaking also.

Steadying the flow of energy, channeling it into the black lines upon the grey stone, drew Brenda into the spell. She breathed deeply, permitting herself access to the tingle of brilliant golden green that was the ch'i of the Land Under the Hills. It flowed at her command, passing through her, entering the ideographs sketched on the stone.

Awareness of those standing in back of her faded as the gate took on dimension, the surface of the stone shimmering like a heat mirage. Brenda found she didn't need the crib sheet after all. The logic of the tiles she had selected guided her from one to the next.

She was halfway through the sequence of fourteen when a violent jolt of pain flung her back on her heels and nearly broke her hold on the spell. Only an equally violent determination not to waste what she had done thus far kept her concentration from failing—that and an awareness that beneath the pain there was something, someone, familiar.

She recognized Loyal Wind with the next burst of pain, and knew that on some level he had recognized her as well. Recognized both her and her intent, and found a new will to fight against the blackness that sought to claim him.

With a lavish hand, Brenda flooded ch'i into her spell, hoped that some of it would sustain Loyal Wind, for if he lost consciousness, she would lose her anchor. Her gate might still open in the Lands, but that opening could be far away from the beleaguered Horse. Brenda was determined that they weren't going to give him hope only to abandon him.

Voices spoke, but she was not certain whether they were on Loyal Wind's side or her own. She refused to let anything distract her. The echoes of Loyal Wind's pain were almost too much for her, roaring along her nerves, firing her brain, threatening to burn out her eyes.

Ninth tile. Tenth. Eleventh. Twelfth.

The pain growing worse and worse; her hands began to shake and Brenda had to press hard against the stone to ensure that lines that should be straight were straight, those curved were curved.

Thirteen.

She nearly botched that one although the final nine of characters was an ideogram she had practiced hundreds of times.

Something was wrong with her wrists. They were throbbing, the amulet bracelets around them suddenly too constricting, too binding.

Brenda forced herself to ignore the ache in her wrists, carefully writing the fourteenth and final character, focusing on each stroke and line so that it would be perfect.

She lifted the pen from the stone.

The heat mirage wavering shone brilliantly, the light blending the green-gold of the sidhe with her own Rat's black.

"It's open!"

Shen's voice, triumphant, but with an undertone of shrillness.

Parnell's words next.

"Brenda, acushla. By our Lord and Lady and all the spirits of field and stream, are you all right?"

Rocking back on her heels, Brenda pushed herself up from her knees and nearly crumpled. Her back was alive with pain, her back and wrists both. Catching herself on the edge of the rock, she saw blood leaking out between the tiles of the amulet bracelets.

"I'm fine enough," she said. "It's Loyal Wind . . . Let's go!"

Brenda did not wait to explain. This was not a time for waiting, nor a time for defense nor for anything but motion. She swung open the door and breathed a foul musk combining blood, urine, feces, sweat, and rank terror that made her gag.

Brenda didn't let this slow her, but darted through the gate, moving to one side to clear the doorway even before her eyes had adjusted to the dim light from the guttering torches set high on the walls of the stone-walled room. Her foot slid on something noisome.

She caught her balance even as she fumbled for the lead bracelet on her "attack" wrist and slammed it to the ground.

Dragon's Breath blossomed in her veins. Brenda held out her arm, palm extended, at one of the two hulking figures that only now was realizing that this closed and locked room had been invaded.

The force of the fire caught him squarely in the face. His eyebrows flared and flamed before the skin on his face caught and began to burn.

Brenda caught a smell not unlike burning pork chops and heard a choked scream that turned into coughing as fire coursed through the open mouth down the throat and into the lungs.

Nightmares later.

The thought was hardly formed, for in the flare of her spell, Brenda had seen Loyal Wind.

The Horse was naked except for a shredded bit of blood-soaked rag about his hips. At first glance, he seemed to be standing, but then Brenda realized he was hanging from his bound wrists. These were tied to a post high above his head.

She understood her own blood-soaked wrists now,

and reached for a second Dragon's Breath amulet without hesitation.

"No!" Shen's voice. He didn't wait for her to obey. Without needing to resort to the intermediary of an amulet, he sent ch'i rocketing forth from hands extended, linked by joined thumbs.

The second torturer—for he could be called nothing else—toppled forward like a felled tree, hitting the slimed stone floor with a satisfying thud and crack.

Brenda looked back toward the man she had flamed, knowing that Dragon's Breath did not last unduly long. She had been surprised at her spell's intensity. Now, seeing the color of the flames, she realized that she'd fueled the fire with some of the surplus energy she'd brought with her from the sidhe.

Parnell was bending over the burning man, wiping his sword on the torturer's loose trousers.

Better than he deserved, Brenda thought viciously. *He should have choked to death on his own lungs.*

Her feelings did not change as she reached up to cut at the blood-soaked leather bonds that held Loyal Wind's wrists to the whipping post. Parnell came and held the Horse's unconscious body against his own, slowly lowering him to the stone floor.

Shen, meanwhile, had moved to check first the man he had felled, then to listen at the door.

"No sign anyone noticed," Shen said, his voice harsh and bitter. "The lack of screams, rather than any commotion, is more likely to bring someone to check."

"We should have some time," Parnell said. "They must be used to having their victims pass out, if they treat them all as they have Loyal Wind."

"Is he alive?" Shen asked.

"He is," Parnell said, "and if he doesn't bleed out is likely to remain so. Brenda, how do you feel?"

For the first time, Brenda had a chance to inspect

her own injuries. Sliding back the amulet bracelets, she found stigmata matching the wounds she had seen on Loyal Wind's wrists. She didn't doubt that her back bore a few stripes as well.

She shrugged off her daypack, wincing at the sharp bite of fresh wounds. The pack's fabric was marked with blood.

"Angry," she said, ignoring the pain as she transferred a few spare amulets from the pack to her wrists. She'd have to leave the rest behind. "Impatient. Parnell, can Loyal Wind be taken back through the gate? Can some of your friends tend him?"

"Yes. You go with him," Parnell urged. "You're hurt, too, and with the gate made, there's no need for you to be risking yourself further."

"I'm going on," Brenda said. "No one beat me. This bleeding, it's just echoes of what they did to Loyal Wind. The wounds will probably stop hurting as soon as the link between us fades."

Privately, Brenda doubted this. The cuts on her wrists were quite vivid, but there was no way she was going to be put to pasture.

"Will your people care for him?" Brenda repeated.

A voice so gentle Brenda hardly recognized it as Wasp's spoke near her ear. "We will. Honey is a good antiseptic. I have cousins who will clean him, and others who will wash him, and yet others who will guard him until our return."

Parnell looked as if he would protest, then visibly bit back whatever he had been about to say.

"Very well," he said. "I'll carry Loyal Wind through. Don't leave without me."

"We won't," Shen said. He was crouching near the second torturer. "I felled this one with a sending of sleep. He hit his head when he fell hard enough to knock himself out. He's coming around. I can compel him to tell us something of this place, where we can find the others."

"Not too many questions," Brenda said, straining her ears for any other sound. "As you said, it's silence, not screams, that will bring the guards. We got to Loyal Wind just in time. I don't want to be too late to help the others."

When the three of them stepped cautiously out into the corridor, Brenda had both an All Green and a Dragon's Tail up. The All Green didn't help much in the dim light—the infinitely distractable part of her brain made a mental note to ask Des if there was a spell that allowed the user something like night vision.

Des. The thought of him chattering away about some esoteric aspect of Chinese culture or sitting down to his breakfast of congee and pickled vegetables made Brenda's heart feel funny.

They had ample evidence, first from their slight contact with Gentle Smoke, now from Loyal Wind, that the prisoners had not been treated at all well.

Loyal Wind was a soldier, and might be expected to hold up under torture, but Des? Des Lee was a part-time movie consultant, a model who sold expensive men's clothing. He might be fairly solid on theory, even pretty fast with those Rooster's Talons, but under a whip?

The burning of the welts on Brenda's back and wrists, secondhand though those injuries were, made her doubt she'd manage to do anything more heroic under torture than faint.

The guard Shen had questioned hadn't known precisely who was being held where. However, he knew the layout of this cellblock perfectly, and had been pathetically eager to share his knowledge with Shen, especially with Parnell standing just within the torturer's line of sight, looking way too familiar with the sword he kept shifting restlessly from hand to hand.

Doubtless it didn't hurt that Parnell's fair-haired, green-eyed appearance must look demonic to the Chinese.

The cellblock was arranged so that each cell could be isolated from the others, double doors deadening the sound of the screams. These doors led into a long corridor that, Brenda noted as she stepped out into it, would make a great amplifier if hearing what was happening to the guy—or gal—next door would make the prisoner more eager to talk.

Right now that corridor was very silent, but that was because—so the torturer had explained—Li Szu had felt that letting the prisoners each wonder if he or she was the last holdout was more effective than hearing the others' suffering. Comfort, even a sense of solidarity, could be found in knowing one wasn't alone in misery.

That Li Szu is a nasty creature, Brenda thought. *He'd be nasty enough if he just depersonalized his victims, but it's like he gets into their hearts and souls, knows exactly what they're feeling, and doesn't care.*

Parnell was on point, or rather Wasp was, buzzing ahead, then fluttering back to mutter her report in Parnell's ear. Brenda appreciated the sidhe woman's attentiveness, even though it wasn't exactly necessary at this point. They knew where they were going.

Stopping in front of the third door to the right and across the corridor, Parnell motioned for Brenda to come forward. She did so, the ring of keys they'd taken from the torturers tight in her hand.

Parnell had offered to go first, but Shen had pointed out that none of the scouts knew who he was and explanations would waste time. So Brenda was to open the locks while Parnell stood ready to deal with any trouble and Shen kept watch on the corridor behind.

With her magically enhanced vision, Brenda watched the lock carefully as she worked the key, remembering stories where a warded lock had given everything away, but the dull metal showed no indication of being anything but a normal lock. The key turned the tumblers with a solid, perfectly natural, metallic click.

No need for fancy wards here, Brenda thought, carefully checking the short length of stone-lined corridor before stepping in. *We're in the cellar of a heavily guarded building in the heart of a walled city, in the heart of a walled country. Even if a prisoner got out, where would he go?*

Her heart lifted a little at the thought of Loyal Wind, safely gone, and of the contingent of fierce-faced sidhe folks who now guarded the gate. They had orders to close it rather than let it be used against them, and Brenda felt certain that anyone trying to challenge those weird little people would be thoroughly surprised.

She pushed the door open quickly, for if any enemy was inside, they might have heard the lock tumble, and stealth would only give them opportunity to prepare. She had a Dragon's Breath bracelet ready on her fingers, but there was no need to use it.

The room was empty except for two men, naked but for cloth wrapped around their hips, slumped against the chains that bound them to rings on the walls.

"Des! Riprap!" Brenda kept her voice soft, but against the bareness of that contained area the sound echoed.

The better to hear you scream, my dear, she thought, anger flaring in her breast and making her breath come short.

Des had moved slightly at the sound of Brenda's voice, so she hurried to attend to him first.

The key ring contained the means for opening the shackles, but Brenda could see a problem right away. Des was not standing, but was suspended against the stone, his feet off the ground. At best, his feet would be numb, and he would be certain to fall.

"Parnell! I need you."

He understood immediately, and hastened forward, sheathing his sword as he did so. For the first time Brenda was struck how, despite the fact that Parnell still wore the jeans and casual tee shirt that had been his college uniform, there was more about him of the green-eyed squire of her long-ago dream.

"I'm unlocking the leg shackles first," Brenda said, kneeling. The floor smelled strongly of pee, and she guessed the prisoners had been there a while. "Be ready to catch him."

Parnell didn't say anything, but shifted his stance so he was closer.

As with the door, the locks turned easily. In four snaps of the key, Des was free. He fell forward into Parnell's hold, and Brenda heard rather than saw Parnell move to lay Des on a cleaner spot of the floor.

She was moving to inspect Riprap. For a horrible moment, she thought the big man wasn't breathing, then she heard him. The breaths were shallow and erratic, but they were there.

Parnell was back, and they repeated the procedure, Brenda assisting with moving Riprap over by Des.

"I wish Nissa were here," she said, feeling useless.

Parnell had rocked back on his heels and was inspecting the two men. "I don't think they're anywhere as badly hurt as was Loyal Wind. The marks from beatings are older, and something like a cane, rather than a whip, was used. Let's try giving them some water."

They did. Des drank almost at once. Riprap let it dribble over his face, but then seemed to suddenly become aware. He drank greedily then, and Brenda, very conscious of how strong he was, leaned down and spoke.

"It's me, Brenda, Riprap. Des. We're here to get you out. We've got Loyal Wind already, and we think we know where to find the others."

Des's eyes flickered open, bloodshot but holding intelligence. Only one of Riprap's eyes could open. The other was sealed shut with as nasty a black eye as Brenda had ever seen.

"He fought," Des wheezed, "when he saw Flying Claw. . . . You came."

There was wonder in his voice, despite the fact that he could barely shape intelligible words.

"And you're going," Brenda said. "We have a way out."

"We'd better carry them," Parnell said. "I've sent Wasp for some help."

Des's eyes widened at the sight of the unfamiliar young man with the honey-blond hair, but Brenda had prepared an explanation she hoped would work.

"Indigenous tradition. Absolutely trustworthy."

Des seemed willing to accept this, but Riprap's one open eye narrowed as if he wished he had the strength to ask questions.

He licked his lips as if trying to form words, but at that moment Wasp and her reinforcements arrived.

Brenda had already learned that the sidhe folk were often much stronger than their size would indicate. What Wasp had brought with her were some variety Brenda hadn't seen until she'd started taking lessons in the sidhe. These six creatures resembled a cross between short squat men and tree stumps with arms and legs. Head, neck, and chest seemed all of a part, while legs and arms looked as if they could merge back into the whole more easily than they managed independent movement.

Despite their rather frightening appearance, Parnell had assured Brenda that these were some of the creatures who had helped give rise to legends of brownies or bogarts or house goblins—essentially mild, more helpful than not, creatures. Only their relatively large size—they were almost three feet tall—had kept Parnell from assigning a couple to Brenda's rotating entourage. That, and the fact that they were almost congenitally shy.

The Stumplings looked anything but shy now. They looked equal parts angry and apprehensive, with a dash of fierceness for garnish. Under Parnell's direction, they lifted up the injured men, three to a victim, and started trotting toward the gate into the sidhe like mobile stretchers.

Shen was keeping watch, but spared Des and Riprap a horrified glance before returning to his vigil with added alertness.

Once they were in the room with the gate, Brenda hurried to explain the situation to Des and Riprap, finishing, "So you'll be safe and cared for while we get the others out. Please trust us."

Riprap had been trying to get some words out, and now he managed.

"Come with us," he said, his voice thick. "These bad to men, but real bad to women."

Brenda shivered, knowing what Riprap was hinting at.

"All the more reason I need to stay and help get them out," she said.

Riprap seemed to understand. "Careful."

"I'll be careful," Brenda said. Impulsively, she kissed each of them quickly on the forehead, then stood back as they were passed through the gate.

Parnell was waiting in the corridor, and pointed toward another door, farther down.

"That one next," he said.

Before they could move, the sound of many shod feet moving in cadence stilled them in their tracks.

From somewhere out of sight there was a pounding, then a deep voice shouted, "Thundering Heaven, open in the name of the lord!"

XXIX

Feet hitting hard against memory and malice, Pearl Bright pushed herself to where Thundering Heaven was raising his sword, stooping toward Flying Claw, who lay facedown on the floor.

Like Athene born from the forehead of Zeus, although with no Hephaestus to act as midwife, Pearl sprang forth, fully adult, armed with a sword. Seeing the weapon Thundering Heaven held in his right hand, she realized she was seriously lacking in the way of armor.

Pearl took advantage of Thundering Heaven's moment of stunned surprise to remedy this. She cast a prepared Dragon's Tail amulet to the floor where it broke into powder. This was a more complex variant of the spell, permitting easier attack out of the dragon's protecting tail than the one they had taught the apprentices, but otherwise it was the same—a simple barrier, best against hand-to-hand attacks, less effective against anything else.

Pearl didn't wait for the spell to finish taking hold, but shifted her stance so that she stood protectively between the nearly unconscious youth sprawled in a pool of blood on the stone floor and his tormentor. One of her feet slipped slightly in the gore, but then the sensible soles, constructed to compensate for old women far less sure-footed than Pearl, caught hold.

Thundering Heaven had overcome his moment of shock and redirected his attention to her. He was taller than Pearl—although not unduly so—and much more massive. He was also younger, a vital fifty, the age, Pearl now realized, when he had divorced Tea Rose in his quest for an heir.

"You!" he growled, anger and consternation mingling in his voice. "You! Get out of my way . . ."

Then a slow smile bled onto his face, and Pearl saw two people looking out at her from his narrowing eyes.

"Or, rather, die!"

The blade Thundering Heaven held was Soul Slicer. With amazing speed, he lashed out at her with it, but Pearl—assisted by Treaty's sense of offense at promises broken—was faster. Treaty blocked Soul Slicer, and began to hum in barely contained indignation.

Pearl heard the message in Treaty's song. Thundering Heaven had renounced claim to the Tiger, first when he died still bound by magic of his own creation that passed the affiliation on to his heir, again when Pearl defeated him in their challenge bout some two months before.

Yet here Thundering Heaven was, trying to force Flying Claw to release his own bond with the Tiger.

And not through any fair challenge fight either, Pearl thought. She had not been able to spare much attention for Flying Claw, but the glimpses she had caught showed where at least some of that blood had come from. *What is the weight of a soul? I have no idea, but Thundering Heaven seems to believe it has substance enough that it can be cut away like any other organ.*

Treaty sustained Pearl as Thundering Heaven strove to bear her down by means of his greater weight and mass. He broke the clinch and stepped back a pace, assessing the situation.

Pearl studied him. She'd cast an All Green before seeking to use dreams as a gate. Through this she could see that Thundering Heaven wore no defensive spells, nor did she see the gathering of ch'i that would indicate he was about to cast one.

Well, why should he have had protection up? Pearl thought. *It wasn't as if he expected a fight.*

She spared a quick glance down at Flying Claw. She was fairly certain the young man was alive, for bleeding stopped when the heart did, and blood was trickling from a series of small cuts.

The cuts follow the pattern of the energy meridians. It looks as if Thundering Heaven has moved from mere torture to something like surgery. I wonder if that tactic would have been any more successful.

Thundering Heaven was studying her, of two minds as to how he should proceed.

Literally of two minds. Pearl could see the shifts in the aura of the man who stood before her. First Thundering Heaven, then Tea Rose dominated. It looked like a very heated argument. Pearl wondered if Thundering Heaven was aware he was possessed.

And with that thought, she realized what she must do. She watched, waited for Tea Rose's aura to dominate. Then, lunging forward, she struck out with Treaty, leaving herself wide open, trusting in the Dragon's Tail to offer some protection.

Long years of training came to Thundering Heaven's

aid and he parried easily, adjusting his stance so that he could take advantage of the tempting opening she had offered. Perhaps if Tea Rose had not been vying for domination, Thundering Heaven would have been more cautious about taking advantage of that opening. Then again, he might have struck anyway. Tigers were not known for calculation.

Pearl did not try to parry. Instead, adjusting her own stance, she struck along the line of Soul Slicer's blade, running parallel with her own strike, bringing Treaty in and along to bite deeply into Thundering Heaven's wrist.

Soul Slicer hit the Dragon's Tail, jolted hard, and was knocked from Thundering Heaven's loosened grip.

Pearl felt the Dragon's Tail falter, far more drained by that single blow than it should have been, but retaining enough strength that its protection should last just long enough.

She darted to where Soul Slicer had fallen and grabbed the sword with her free hand, though she feared that the weapon would attack any but its holder. However, the second sword settled into her grip, as cold and indifferent as if it were no more magical than a length of rebar.

Thundering Heaven ran up behind Pearl, his aura flashing madly back and forth between his own dark green and Tea Rose's frosted pink. He was bellowing something inarticulate, two minds seeking to use the same mouth, snarling at each other with every breath.

The confusion wouldn't last. Pearl thrust Treaty back into its sheath and tossed Soul Slicer into her right hand. Thundering Heaven was no longer bellowing. He was swinging around, heading back to where Flying Claw lay in the pool of his own blood on the stone floor.

His intent was clear. Flying Claw could be both hostage and weapon. Thundering Heaven was gambling that Pearl would not have come all this way just to kill the boy.

Pearl snarled. She'd been running on adrenaline and fear to this point, but now she was beginning to feel the first hints of exhaustion. Her joints were beginning to ache, the weight of two swords dragging her down.

Raising Soul Slicer, feeling it as dead metal after Treaty's ferocious sense of intent, Pearl ran forward. Thundering Heaven was bending, bending, reaching for Flying Claw, grabbing at the youth's arm, twisting the torso around as if that arm was nothing more than a convenient hold. The younger man was screaming, his eyes rolled back, showing nothing but the whites.

Pearl tried to push herself faster, but each motion felt broken into distinct elements, stuttering like the frames of an old movie. Pearl forced herself to speed the film, to move more swiftly.

Thundering Heaven had exposed his back. His movements were stuttering, too, but he was moving, aura shifting rose to green, rose to green, as he hauled Flying Claw up. In a moment, Thundering Heaven would turn and that screaming wreck of bloodied flesh would be imposed as a barrier between them.

Pearl struck, reserving the blow for that moment when green was shifting to rose, directing Soul Slicer to cut not just flesh, but soul from flesh, flensing Tea Rose from the body in which she had anchored herself all those years ago.

The moment came. Pearl struck a wide slash along the meat at the back of one strongly muscled shoulder.

Blood splashed. Thundering Heaven's scream sounded like that of a woman. Flying Claw was dropped to the floor hard, but no sound came from him. Thundering Heaven turned heavily.

His aura was wholly green now, but his eyes held no less malice. He spread his arms wide, fingers curled, and Pearl saw that claws were coming forth from the tips. Thundering Heaven's face was changing shape, far more rapidly than Pearl had dreamed possible. Black and orange fur was sprouting, fangs distorting his open mouth.

In a moment, she would be facing six hundred pounds of furious, wounded Tiger.

Pearl didn't hesitate, but brought Soul Slicer down in a two-handed strike, slashing into her father's open, exposed chest. The heavy blade went through muscle, jolted against bone, the force reverberating up through Pearl's arms, making the bones of her barely healed hand ache and creak as if on the verge of breaking.

Thundering Heaven did not scream, did not snarl, just fell back in terrible silence. His partly transformed foot slid in Flying Claw's blood, in his own blood, and he struggled to find balance.

Pearl raised Soul Slicer again, finding the blade easier to wield now. Maybe it liked her intent, maybe having taken one soul from this overpopulated body, it was eager to do so again.

Pearl didn't much like the glee she could feel coming up through the weapon, but she certainly didn't have time to switch back to Treaty. Thundering Heaven had come back from the dead once. She was going to make damn certain he didn't do it again.

Her second cut, low through the gut, met resistance only when the blade grated against the spine. She drew the sword back, shifting for another blow, but although Soul Slicer was willing, Pearl saw there was no need.

Blood still gushed from the body of Thundering Heaven, but it did not pulse, merely guttered out like cheap wine from a plastic jug. A new pool spread to touch, then merge with, that which surrounded Flying Claw.

Thundering Heaven was dead. Hopefully this time for good.

Pearl sagged. She wanted to drop Soul Slicer where she stood, but couldn't bring herself to be disrespectful to a weapon that had been helpful, even if she found it somehow disgusting.

"Thanks for your help," she managed to say, then laid it on a cabinet top, next to a whip, a pair of branding irons, and an assortment of sharp knives.

Exhaustion, nausea, and something like sorrow all vied for her attention, but she didn't have time for any of that.

Pearl hurried to Flying Claw. As soon as she ascertained he was still breathing, she tried to think what to do. There was no going back via the route by which she had arrived. Tea Rose was gone, hopefully to get a stern talking to from the Yama Kings. The road her malice had carved into Pearl was gone with her.

Brenda, though, Brenda should have created a proper gate. When Flying Claw was stabilized, Pearl would need to leave him just long enough to find Brenda and her allies. Maybe she could use a spell to facilitate finding them. Shen was with Brenda, and they had come up with some tricks long ago—the equivalent of passing notes in class.

Maybe something like that would work.

As she thought, Pearl's hands were busy. She was no doctor. Nissa had far more training, but Pearl knew enough first aid to do a basic triage.

What Pearl saw both appalled her and gave her hope. Flying Claw had been horribly mutilated. It would be a long time—if ever—before the sight of his face made a girl's heart leap with anything but horror.

But although he was nearly bled out, most of his wounds—aside from the mutilation of his face—were actually superficial.

There was no froth of red in his saliva, nor did she smell the stench of ruptured organs on his breath. It was possible that Thundering Heaven had actually sought to keep his victim alive, perhaps so he could cause him to suffer as much as possible.

She took a peek under the rags about Flying Claw's hips and relaxed slightly. At least Thundering Heaven hadn't gone that far.

Pearl wasn't strong enough to lift Flying Claw, but she could get him out of the pool of blood. This, she now realized, was somewhat less extensive than she'd thought. Part of the stain was old, although there was ample new.

She dragged Flying Claw, forcing herself to ignore his involuntary whimpers of pain, then propped him up against the cabinet, since being upright seemed to make it easier for him to breathe.

In the cabinet Pearl found some bandage fabric and several containers, one of ointment, two of water, one of a weak rice wine. Using these, she cleaned and bound the worst of the wounds, stanching the bleeding. When Flying Claw began to moan, she soaked a rag in water and nursed a little between his mutilated lips.

He sucked and winced, sucked and winced, eager need and acute pain warring so visibly that Pearl felt tears start in her eyes.

But Pearl wasted no time on pity either. Allowing herself a slug of the rice wine, she assessed her own condition. Her first Dragon's Tail was down, so she cast another. Then, because she would not be able to defend Flying Claw when she went to find Shen and Brenda, she broke another amulet, setting the Tail it contained to protect him.

Crossing to the heavy door that seemed to be the only entrance or exit from the room, Pearl listened. Not surprisingly, the heavy, metal-banded door was built so that sound would not penetrate. There was a jailer's peephole, though, and she eased that open.

What she heard was less than reassuring. Footsteps, rapid and purposeful, were coming down the corridor. Many footsteps, whose matched cadence announced without words: "military."

Pearl laid a hand on Treaty at her belt. Then she closed the peephole and stood to one side, where she would be out of direct sight when the door was open, but not blocked from action by its opening.

There was a thudding on the door; a deep, muffled voice shouted: "Thundering Heaven, open in the name of the lord!"

Pearl did nothing, hoping against hope there was only one key, that they would leave.

That hope was nearly instantly dashed. There was a sharp click, and the door began to open into the room.

Pearl raised Treaty, focusing hard on her promise to protect Flying Claw, knowing Treaty would fight better if in defense of a promise.

A voice, cold and perfectly measured, spoke from the corridor outside the door.

"I see Thundering Heaven. It seems I heard his call too late to bring him aid, but perhaps I am not too late to avenge him."

At the cold precision of that voice, Pearl took an involuntary step back, then another, moving rapidly to stand near Flying Claw.

Two soldiers, armed and armored, entered, then two more. They fanned out, seeming unmoved by the carnage within the room.

A man in court robes followed them. Protection spells shimmered around him in a rainbow aura.

"I am Li Szu," he said formally. "The punishment for patricide is death."

☆

Without discussion, Brenda, Shen, and Parnell turned toward the shouting. Wasp, always fierce, grown fiercer since the discovery of how the prisoners had been treated, flew ahead to scout the route, saving them innumerable turns down blind alleys.

Palm upraised, strange, multifaceted eyes bright, Wasp mimed just peeking around the corner, then cupped one pointed ear to indicate they should listen.

Brenda sneaked forward and crouched low, figuring that if anyone did glance in this direction, they were likely to focus at standing height. Down the corridor a few paces was a heavy door.

A man wearing light armor—a breastplate, greaves, and a light helmet—was inserting a key into the lock. Behind him stood three other men, armored much as he was, and behind them a man in understatedly elegant robes. This man shimmered with magic, protective, Brenda thought, but she wasn't sure.

Behind him stood several more armored men. Most looked eager and intent, but one or two looked a little scared.

The guard with the key pushed the door open, then stood so that while he blocked it, the man in the robes would have a clear line of sight into the room.

"I see Thundering Heaven," said the man in the robes, his impassive face becoming, if possible, more impassive. "It seems I heard his call too late to bring him aid, but perhaps I am not too late to avenge him."

He made a motion with his hand and the guard with the key, followed closely by three others, entered the room, drawing swords as they went.

The man in the robes followed them, moving, Brenda

noted, at an angle that meant he would stand behind those protecting ranks.

"I am Li Szu," came the cool, precise voice. "The punishment for patricide is death."

Pearl's voice, astonishingly steady, answered, "Death, I am sure, is the punishment for many crimes. The Legalists made that mistake before. When the punishment is death, what reason is there to surrender?"

But Brenda wasn't waiting to hear the reply. She'd felt warmth as Parnell and Shen moved up beside her, heard faint, dry ticking on the flagstone floor and suspected that some of the sidhe folk had also joined them.

A plan would be nice, but it was pretty clear that Pearl was alone in there, and against all those armed men even that Lady Tiger didn't have a hope.

Brenda touched the offensive bracelets on her wrist and chose two that held Winding Snakes. It wasn't as nasty a spell as Dragon's Breath, but she wasn't sure where the backwash of flame might go in this contained corridor.

These, though . . . She held them up so Shen and Parnell could see them. Shen nodded. Parnell looked puzzled, but nodded for her to go ahead.

Brenda cast the amulets against the floor and directed the force of the spell against the guards. Cued by her motion, Shen smashed a pair of amulets of his own. Brenda felt their force go past her as she started running in the direction of the guards.

Shen's spell flashed red. Brenda blinked as a bright light put spots in front of her eyes. The four corridor guards were clutching at their eyes; two were tottering as her Winding Snakes began to bind their legs.

Behind her, Brenda could hear Parnell and Shen, but she had the lead. What she'd do with it would depend on if she could squeeze by the guards who remained in the corridor. They might be temporarily blinded and unsteady on their feet, but they were still pretty big.

Clanging of metal against metal was now coming from the room. The cool voice said, "Keep at her. Her protective spell is not very strong."

That made Brenda mad somehow, like not only Pearl but all the Orphans' carefully hoarded lore was being dismissed. When she got to the doorway and saw a narrow gap between a blinded guard and one who was not only blinded but uncertain on his legs, that anger gave her courage to act when otherwise she might have hesitated.

Aiming low, trusting her Dragon's Tail to pad her from the worst impact with the stone floor, Brenda dove through the gap. She came up on the other side, sliding in a foul-smelling puddle of still-sticky blood. Thundering Heaven's body lay almost directly in front of her, close enough that she saw the gaping wound in his chest and the blue-grey loops of his intestines spilling out from a cut in his abdomen.

The Dragon's Tail could cushion Brenda from impact with the floor, but it couldn't do anything about the spears of pain from the stigmata on Brenda's wrists and back. Nor did it stop the cold blood that now saturated her clothes.

Brenda didn't care. As she had suspected, Pearl was being attacked by all four guards. The robed man was right; Pearl's protective spell was giving way under the onslaught, and only the speed of her parries was keeping her from being wounded.

Still half laying on the floor, Brenda grasped for the strongest of the offensive spells she had brought: two sets of the Twins—the Twins of Sky and the Twins of Earth.

The Twins were yin and yang, male and female,

clad in elaborate costumes more indebted to Chinese opera than to any real battlefield. Those of Sky wore white and pale blue, the dominant theme in their embroidered designs clouds and suns. Those of Earth wore brown and bronze. Their embroideries evoked growing things. Their long hair was bound with strands of rough gemstones.

They materialized armed with swords and spears. They had bows, too, but the room was too crowded for these to be effective.

"Help Pearl," Brenda commanded, the words less necessary than her mental image of her desire. "I'll distract Mr. Rainbow."

She didn't know how she was going to manage that. The robed man was standing within the most amazing aura of protective magics she could imagine. With the knowledge gained in her recent training, Brenda could see that these spells were powered directly from the ch'i of the Lands. Apparently, Li Szu had no trouble tapping what for everyone else was a diminished flow.

Shouting from the corridor—human voices mingled with the shrill inhuman chitters and squeaks of the sidhe folk—told Brenda that reinforcements had arrived. Behind her where the Twins and Pearl fought the guards, everything sounded very busy. The Twins were good, but they were only a spell, and lacked the innovation of a human warrior. At best, they might defeat a couple of the guards, but even at the worst, they should be providing Pearl with a breather.

Brenda wished she felt braver. She wished she wasn't soaked in evil-smelling blood and gore. She wished her dad hadn't sent her off to college, that she'd been studying fighting techniques instead of history and literature.

But wishes weren't going to get her anywhere. Something in how the cold glower in Li Szu's eyes had gotten positively glacial when Brenda had cast down the Twins and sent them to Pearl's aid gave Brenda courage.

Brenda hauled herself to her feet and moved toward Li Szu. He had made certain to stand far away from the spreading pool of blood, so after a few tacky steps, her footing was steady.

What she saw appalled her. Li Szu was ignoring her. His lips were moving slightly, his eyes were hooded. Brenda guessed that he was working on a spell of some sort, trusting to his protective spells to keep him safe.

Brenda knew that if she broke Li Szu's concentration, it was likely his spell would also break. She didn't think any of her spells could get through his personal ward. She didn't have any weapon, but she did have herself. Her Dragon's Tail was still at nearly full force. So, taking a few running steps, Brenda threw her arms wide and flung herself directly at the lord creator of the Lands Born from Smoke and Sacrifice.

Her idea had been to grab him in a sort of bear hug and shake. The Dragon's Tail acted as sort of a full body boxing glove, after all, and why hit with a fist when you can hit with a whole person?

What happened wasn't exactly according to plan. Brenda leapt and felt her Dragon's Tail hit solidly against whatever it was Li Szu had wrapped himself in. There was a flash of multicolored light, and Brenda felt herself thrown back. She sailed through the air until she hit the stone wall all the way across the room. The impact did for what remained of her Dragon's Tail, and she felt the bruising impact along every inch of her already tormented back.

She screamed. She couldn't help it. Pain ripped the

sound from her lips, even though in that moment of flight, as she balled herself up as best she could so her head wouldn't hit, she'd resolved not to make a sound that might distract Pearl or the others.

But she screamed.

She heard someone—Parnell, she thought—yell, "Brenda!" but when she tried to call, "I'm okay!" she didn't have the breath.

Staggering to her feet, Brenda fumbled for another Dragon's Tail, early lessons in the need to defend first all the more acute after recent events.

As she smashed the bracelet to the ground, Brenda tried to assess the situation. She saw segments that her mind struggled to arrange into a whole.

Pearl was still facing off against the guards, but there was one fewer guard and another one looked very ragged. The Twins of Heaven were gone, but the Twins of Earth were still fighting, although chopped at around the edges.

At the door, Shen stood, head bent, muttering fiercely, a cluster of amulets in one hand, preparatory to being cast down to release the spells they contained.

There were still sounds of fighting from the corridor, but Shen seemed confident, so Brenda guessed that someone was covering his back.

And between where Brenda had hit the wall and a rough wooden cabinet, a nearly naked creature was taking a sword from where it rested on top of the cabinet. It looked like a demon from hell, flesh reddish brown and bloodied, the face a horrible parody of something feline, its ears pointed, its hair carved into stripes.

It moved stiffly, but with some remnant of grace, and even as Brenda started to raise her voice in warning to Pearl, to shout, "Watch out, behind you! A monster!" by this grace she knew him.

Flying Claw.

He did not spare even a glance for her, but wrapped fingers that didn't look as if they should be able to move around the hilt of the sword. His gaze was locked on where Li Szu—unmarked even by a smear of blood from Brenda's failed attack—was once again muttering a spell.

Brenda knew Li Szu couldn't be permitted to finish it, and with a flash of insight understood what Shen must be doing, and that someone had to be ready to take advantage of it.

She had one Dragon's Breath still hanging on her wrist. Her other attack amulets were in the pack she'd taken off because her tortured back couldn't bear the pressure. Sure, she'd stuffed a few more amulets into her pockets, but it would take time to get them out.

She had to make this one pay.

Flying Claw was moving now, moving faster than Brenda thought was possible. She did her best to live up to that example, forcing herself to trot when she hadn't thought she could even walk.

Li Szu, absorbed in his own preparations, confident in his protections, did not make any move to avoid the two battered figures who approached him. Not until Shen roared out a short phrase in Chinese, a phrase Brenda's ears heard as "Release and combine!" did he seem to acknowledge he could be in danger.

Shen's spells burst forth in a torrent that stripped the spells of protection away from Li Szu, layer by layer, rainbow hues dimming as they were swallowed by the golden light of Shen's magic.

Brenda ran forward and cast her Dragon's Breath, willing it to burn this horrible man, to melt that smug expression from his face once and for all.

All her fire did was burn against the remnants of the last fragments of protective magic, turning them to jeweled ash that heaped at Li Szu's feet.

But Flying Claw was there, and his ravaged arms were strong and steady as he swung the heavy sword toward Li Szu's chest. Brenda saw Flying Claw faintly haloed in green light and knew that for this moment he was as much the Tiger as he was the young man she had thought she loved.

Flying Claw's ferocity was terrible. The blade passed through the layers of silk that wrapped Li Szu as if the protective charms embroidered on them were nothing more than twists of thread, although they spat sparks in an effort to defend their wearer.

"Be gone!" Flying Claw snarled, his voice so rough as to be hardly recognizable, but the words perfectly understandable. "We are what you rejected. How dare you set yourself up as our god! Be gone!"

Li Szu had said nothing to this point, his lips still shaping his spell even as Brenda's fire burned away his shield, then, when the first sword blow hit him, paralyzed with shock.

Now, his voice no longer cold, but shrill with fear and anger, he began to yell. Brenda felt the power coming up from the Lands in answer to that yell. Without thought for her own safety, once again she dove at him.

This time she took him out at the ankles.

Flying Claw's sword came down and sliced off Li Szu's head.

Even when the head rolled free, still the lips tried to shape words, but the phrase was never finished. Li Szu was beyond drawing breath.

And Flying Claw, bringing down the sword once more, split Li Szu's skull in two, just to make sure.

XXX

Resolution did not come at once, although when Pearl carried the pieces of Li Szu's shattered head into the corridor the emperor's forces had surrendered. That surrender cascaded slowly throughout this stronghold, and was reported as flowing out through the Lands.

Conquest by violence was probably the most traditional way the Jade Petal Throne changed hands. The people of the Lands were, if not quite like the people of China in anything else, as sincerely attached to tradition.

It did not hurt that Li Szu had been an unpopular ruler, not content merely with reigning, but determined to restructure the Lands to suit his peculiar personal vision—a vision in many ways the antithesis of everything the Lands were.

Flying Claw's words as he struck down Li Szu had been heard by many, and were repeated as the news of the coup spread.

Despite Li Szu's death and the prudent flight or abject surrender of his major advisors, there was still some question as to who, precisely, would sit on the Jade Petal Throne. There was no doubt that Flying Claw was the official slayer of the emperor, but he had declined the throne, saying he lacked both the training and the temperament to be emperor.

What Flying Claw did not say was that he looked like a monster, and that even though his wounds had been treated, he was in very bad shape, both physically and mentally. So, to varying degrees, were the other scouts.

Des and Riprap had come through the least scathed

of the eight. Des had explained the reason for their less violent treatment: "Li Szu was fascinated that the five 'ghosts' had been permitted to come back from the dead. I think he was curious to see whether their hold on life was stronger because of that. In contrast, Riprap and I were mere mortals, and had to be handled with a little more care lest we die and the affiliations he was after flee to our heirs."

Loyal Wind felt Des's claim that he and Riprap had received more mild treatment was admirable, because, despite this greater "care" not to do them damage, both men were severely injured. Moreover, their injuries were peculiar enough that Pearl had felt that not even her tolerant and underinquisitive Dr. Andersen could be expected to treat them without comment. Therefore, once the Lands were secured, all the injured had been brought back from the sidhe into the Lands for care.

Then Brenda had closed the gate into the sidhe, although her blond cavalier, Parnell, and the small, fierce spirit called Wasp had remained in the Lands in some vaguely defined diplomatic capacity.

The chief physician who came to tend to the wounded proved to be one of the bright spots in this dark time, for she was Flying Claw's elder sister, the sage and healer, Joyful Promise.

Despite fears that they might have been executed, the families of Righteous Drum, Flying Claw, and the late Waking Lizard were all discovered to be alive. Their property had been confiscated and given to supporters of the new regime, and the "village" to which they had been relocated was little better than a concentration camp. However, no one had been slain or even too roughly handled, probably because of their value as potential hostages.

Joyful Promise was a healer of considerable merit,

employing both mystic and purely medicinal remedies. Released from captivity, she had requested—insisted— that she be permitted to use her skills to relieve the injuries of those who had risked all to overthrow Li Szu.

Her skillful hands and interesting ointments had done a great deal to relieve the pain of Loyal Wind's whip-torn body. However, one day as she worked energy manipulations to assure the mending of some of the worst of Loyal Wind's lacerated muscles, she had confessed that healing her younger brother's extensive mutilations was beyond her abilities.

Tears bright in her eyes, Joyful Promise had confided that perhaps—but not certainly, for nothing was certain in the Lands—healing Flying Claw was beyond anyone's ability.

The three women—Nine Ducks, Gentle Smoke, and Copper Gong—also had injuries that nothing but time could heal, for rape had been among the torments to which they had been subjected. Joyful Promise said that none were pregnant, but that was small relief.

Loyal Wind felt guilty gratitude that he—and apparently the other men—had been spared rape, although from something that flashed in Flying Claw's eyes when the topic was raised, Loyal Wind wondered if the young man, so beautiful before Thundering Heaven had taken knife and razor to him, had indeed been spared.

He wasn't about to ask, and Flying Claw was not talking, not about that or anything else. He did brighten when his sister came to him, and again later as she told him details about various family members, but he did not become talkative, even when Brenda—fiercely refusing to leave the Lands, though everyone knew she could do so with honor—came and sat for long hours beside him as he pretended to sleep on his cot.

It was Brenda who burst into the suite of rooms that served as an infirmary with the good news that Righteous Drum and Albert Yu and all the others who had entered the Lands via the Ninth Gate had finally arrived.

Their journey had been substantially shortened, for after the death of Li Szu the ch'i of the Lands had resumed something of its normal intensity. With the easier use of magic, the layers of obstacles Li Szu had set around his "perfected" Center had become much more passable.

Shen had established communication with Albert and Righteous Drum, reassuring them that the change in the ch'i flow that they had already detected was not a sign of some new disaster, but the precise reverse.

Further speeding their arrival, various of the local denizens who had been pushed out of their places in Li Szu's reordering were eager to return to the Center. Several dragons had offered their services in gratitude for what had been done. Li of the Iron Crutch and two of his immortal companions had shown up, still looking for their island, and were happy to assist those who had gotten rid of what the ever irreverent Li persisted in referring to as "that inconvenience who has polluted my name."

The entire expanded group had arrived with a flurry of questions and a great deal of enthusiasm. Righteous Drum and Honey Dream had been reunited with the family they feared lost. Then they had applied themselves with almost indecent enthusiasm to negotiating just who would rule these reclaimed, but considerably more chaotic than usual, Lands.

Only one person did not seem precisely happy about

the arrival of the last part of their small army, and that was the person who had announced it so joyfully.

But then Brenda Morris was the only one of them still with a fight on her hands, and Loyal Wind knew she wasn't at all certain she could win.

☆

"Breni." Dad's voice caught up with Brenda as she was leaving the infirmary. "Wait. I want to talk to you. Privately."

Brenda went to the infirmary every day to keep the invalids company. Okay, especially to be near Flying Claw, but she spent time with the others, too, playing board games with them as they sat or more often lay awkwardly propped up with pillows and rolled blankets in whatever position gave them the most relief. All the ghosts were badly hurt. Although technically they had living families, they had been dead to those families for more than a hundred years, so there were none to visit them.

Of course, Brenda thought, turning to acknowledge her father's call. *There are times that being dead to your family would make life a lot simpler.*

"Dad," she said, and motioned down the hall to where a series of suites had been set aside for their use, "why don't we go into my room?"

"Brenda," Gaheris said as soon as they were in the room and settled onto the silk brocade cushions of two elaborately carved chairs. "It's time we talked about getting you home. You know that Righteous Drum and Shen opened a gate that will link this Center to the Ninth Gate. Nissa went back right away because of Lani. I think you should go back, too. I'll be coming in a day or two. I've let business drag without me for too long."

"Dad," Brenda said, drawing in a deep breath. "I'm not sure I'm ready to go home."

"You're missing school," he reminded her.

"I am seriously considering," Brenda said, taking in a deep breath, "dropping out of school, at least for now."

Gaheris Morris started to say something, but Brenda held up her hand and, miracle of miracles, he shut up.

"There's a lot I need to know," Brenda said. "A lot that has nothing to do with American History and British Literature and all that. I thought I wanted to major in political science or maybe economics or accounting. Now, now I think I *need*—" She stressed the word. "—to major in magic and swordplay, and I can't learn those at USC."

"Brenda," Dad said patiently. "It's over. Completely over. The Thirteen Orphans have fought their final battle. The Exiles are home—or as home as they'll ever be. For us, it's over."

"For you, maybe," Brenda said, "but I'm not sure it is for me. I've made friends, Dad. I'm not about to walk out of their lives, like I'm closing a book after reading the last page or after watching the final episode of some really good TV show. They're my friends. Real friends."

"Who are your friends?" Dad countered. "Honey Dream, who you bitch at most of the time? Righteous Drum? If you mean Flying Claw, get real. He's not your type. He was never your type. He's even less that now. Or have you fallen for that green-eyed Irish fairy? He's pretty enough, but you . . ."

Gaheris Morris stopped talking, maybe seeing the anger Brenda felt flooding her face. She stared at her father, feeling her expression grow as hard and cold as Li Szu's had before they'd broken through his rainbow and taken him down.

"Dad. This has nothing to do with Flying Claw or

Parnell. And everything to do with all of them. Damn it. This may be over for you, but it's not for me. I've changed, Dad. Can't you see that? I've changed. I've slid in blood. I've fried a man with fire so hot that his face melted. I've been tortured—secondhand, but I know how much even that hurts. I can't go back and pretend that it's going to matter to me how many people the Celtic Culture Club can get to come to a clog dancing show or whether USC wins homecoming. I can't. And I won't."

Dad played a new card. "And your mother? Do you expect me to explain to her that my weird family heritage is corrupting her one and only daughter?"

"I'll talk to Mom. Me. By myself. As you say, she knows a bit about the Orphans' heritage already. I think Mom's going to understand, maybe even better than you could."

Brenda didn't feel like pulling punches, although arguing made her feel weak and tired now that her initial adrenaline was ebbing.

"Mom has always been better at listening than you, and a whole lot better at seeing people for themselves, not as pieces in some grand scheme. I think she'll understand."

Dad now turned what, for him, was his trump card. "And who do you expect to pay for your year or years of self-discovery? Me? Seems I'm already going to be out the tuition and books and dorm fees I've paid for this year."

Brenda had been ready for this, at least, but she knew Dad was going to hate the answer.

"I've talked to Albert. He'll hire me. He says the fact I'm 'exotic' looking will be an asset. I'm not going to be a counter girl, either. He's going to train me to handle setup and act as a liaison for those big events he does. Best of all, I can do most of my work for

Your Chocolatier electronically, which means I can stay at Pearl's and save rent. She'll teach me and Nissa both."

"And the tuition?"

"Pearl's loaning me—loaning, not giving—the money. I'm going to pay her back weekly, and pay some room and board."

"So you've got it all planned."

Gaheris Morris's face grew thin-lipped with anger, those lips turning white, but when he continued speaking his voice was very, very even.

"Well, do what you want, young lady, but I'll expect an apology when it all goes sour. Tell me this. Why do you think you'll be able to visit with your new friends here in the Lands? Didn't I tell you the days of the Orphans are over?"

"You did," Brenda said, "but I figured you meant that wrongs were righted and like that."

"I meant," Gaheris Morris said, getting to his feet, "that there is a very real chance that we'll be returning to the Lands what our ancestors took away. Returning our affiliations with the Earthly Branches. Ask Pearl what she's been negotiating these last several days. Ask Shen. Ask these 'friends' you're so loyal to. Ask them what they want to do to us all."

☆

The group of sages and mages filed from the room. Most were grey-haired and wrinkled, as fit expectations, but unlike what one would expect if traditional China was serving as your model, they were almost evenly split between male and female.

That's one good thing Li Szu did when he burned the books, Pearl thought. *Many of the texts of which he disapproved were Taoist, and the Taoists always valued individual merit more highly than accidents of birth.*

She was thinking about something else Li Szu had done that was proving to be useful in a manner he surely had not intended, when Brenda Morris burst into the room through a side door.

"Pearl! Shen!"

Her outburst drew a few mildly disapproving looks from the final group of sages, and Brenda visibly calmed herself until they had finished their dignified exit.

"Pearl! Shen! Dad says you're working on a plan to take the Earthly Branches from the Orphans."

Pearl and Shen, who had been politely standing to either side of the main door to thank their departing visitors, shared a worried look. Then, shutting the door after the last of the departing guests, Pearl motioned for Brenda to take a seat on one of the several vacated benches while she and Shen resumed their own chairs.

"You could say that," Pearl admitted, "or you could say we're working on a plan to strengthen the Lands against further exploitation."

Brenda was sitting on the edge of her chair, her entire body tense, but when she spoke her voice was soft and under control.

"But doesn't that undo everything we've been working on? I mean, from the start, when Righteous Drum and all came to our world, they wanted the affiliations. We fought like crazy to keep them. Now you're just willing to give them up?"

Pearl sighed and rubbed her hands over her eyes and cheekbones.

"Willing? No. Able to accept that what our ancestors did seriously hurt the Lands? Yes. Willing to accept that the Lands remain vulnerable for as long as the force of the Earthly Branches remains split? Yes."

Shen cut in. "Brenda, we were going to talk to all the Orphans later today, but we were trying to get enough information together that we could anticipate most of the questions."

"I'm not surprised," Pearl said, "that Gaheris found out. We haven't exactly been keeping this a secret. I am a little surprised he spoke to you."

"I think," Brenda admitted, "I pissed him off."

"You told him about your plans not to go back to USC."

"Yeah." Brenda fell silent, then visibly shook herself. "Can you tell me what's going on?"

Pearl nodded. "Here's the short version. In Chinese cosmology, the underlying supports of the universe are the Twelve Earthly Branches and the Ten Heavenly Stems. Righteous Drum's conjecture that the Earthly Branches were severely weakened when the Orphans retained their affiliation when they were exiled from the Lands has been confirmed."

"Are you sure?" Brenda said. "I mean I've gotten to sort of like Righteous Drum—Honey Dream, too— but that doesn't mean they don't have an agenda of their own."

"They're not the only ones saying this," Shen said. "Their faction was overthrown fairly soon after Righteous Drum brought Honey Dream and Flying Claw to our world. Li Szu learned of Righteous Drum's theories and immediately set a group of scholars to work researching the problem. Those are the people you saw leaving here just now. I'm not going to go through everything they told us, because much of it was nearly too esoteric for me. . . ."

"And would be completely over my head," Brenda said good-naturedly. "That's fine. So you've decided to cave in, that the good of the Lands means more than your own good? What's this going to do to you?"

Pearl smiled dryly. "First, we haven't 'caved,' as you put it. We're still discussing the matter. However, we cannot ignore that something our ancestors did has severely harmed this universe. Moreover, it's likely that as long as the Lands remain in a weakened condition, they're going to be vulnerable to further invasion. We're not sure, but it seems likely that Li Szu had allies, allies who have made themselves scarce, but who know about this weakness, and who may attempt to exploit it again."

"I remember," Brenda said, "what Waking Lizard said, and later how Thorn and Twentyseven-Ten and them said that the captain who led their attempt on us a few months ago wasn't someone they knew. Okay. Still, it doesn't seem right that you guys should give up so much, something that you've fought so hard to keep."

"Sometimes," Pearl said, trying hard to hide how much the idea of renouncing the Tiger distressed her, "life isn't fair. That's just the way it is."

☆

"There's only one answer," Loyal Wind heard himself saying as Shen and Pearl finished briefing them on the situation regarding the Earthly Branches, the Lands, and the Exiles' role in what had caused this corruption of their place of birth.

Loyal Wind thought that especially Pearl and Shen tended to forget how intimately the five former ghosts were involved in the situation. After all, except for Nine Ducks, all of them had reincarnated so that they appeared younger than the Orphans' Tiger and Dragon. That made it easy to overlook that when Pearl and Shen spoke of choices the "Exiles" had made, that five among the number they addressed were, in fact, those very Exiles.

Loyal Wind didn't think they overlooked this consciously, but emotionally, separating the five people who had become their allies—even their friends—from those distant and revered Exiles whose adventures had been the stories told to them in their childhood.

But the Exiles and we "ghosts" are one and the same, Loyal Wind thought, even as he continued to speak.

"The Exiles did the damage. The Exiles must take the first steps to repair that damage. We five should give up our affiliation to the Earthly Branches and accept whatever occurs as a result of this."

His statement met with nods of agreement from the other four Exiles. Copper Gong's crisp nod indicated that Loyal Wind had anticipated what she had been about to suggest herself.

"A good beginning," agreed Nine Ducks. The Ox sat upright in her padded chair, but still looked far from her usually robust self. "I remember how we all laughed over our cleverness—over how we were going to trick those who had thought to render us inconsequential. Now, with the passage of years and evidence of what happened to the Lands through our actions, what we did seems less clever than petty. I agree with Loyal Wind. It is our place to begin setting things right."

The meeting had been restricted to the Thirteen Orphans alone. Deborah still did not trust her health, and so had not been able to come, but Nissa had returned via the Gate. Now Gaheris Morris—something tight around his eyes indicating that he'd probably come to this gathering straight from another argument with Brenda—spoke.

"Noble suggestion," Gaheris said, a dryness to his tone indicating that he wasn't thrilled that Loyal Wind had capitulated so quickly. Clearly Gaheris had been planning to argue against any relinquishment of the Branches. "Let's say—and my willingness to speculate doesn't indicate I agree that this is the best course of action—we do as Loyal Wind suggests and do our best to break our affiliation with our Branches. How do we go about it?"

Shen Kung said, "I've consulted with Righteous Drum. The spell he worked out—the one that separated the Branch from the holder—should still work."

Loyal Wind noticed that Shen looked rather uncomfortable as he said this, nor did he wonder why. Shen had been among those whom Righteous Drum had successfully attacked, and the end result had been such vague behavior that his wife and son had been led to believe that Shen was suffering from some form of senile dementia.

Pearl also looked less than happy, but she expanded on what Shen had said with the same courage that she'd shown in her battles with Thundering Heaven.

"Righteous Drum also says that he thinks he can adapt the spell so that it will not remove memories—or at least not as completely. We've spoken with various sages, and they think that it might be possible for each of us to retain a small sliver of our affiliation, just enough for us to continue much as we were."

"'Much as,'" Gaheris Morris echoed caustically. "I spent over three decades of my life studying to be the Rat. I'm not sure I like the idea of my reward for hours of study and more hours of practice boiling down to 'Thanks a bunch. Go back to selling key chains and inflatable novelty items. We don't need you anymore.'"

Albert, who, as Loyal Wind understood the situation, had devoted even more of his life to the Orphans' cause, who had, directly and indirectly, lost his father and grandfather to the strain of being the Cat, and whose mother was crippled as a side effect, showed little patience with Gaheris.

"What do you want, Gaheris? A medal? A statue? Naw. You wouldn't want anything so noble. A bag of gold and a box of jewels would be more your speed."

Gaheris lurched to his feet, but Riprap, the stiffness of his movements not reducing the power contained in his muscular body, rose and stepped between the two men.

"Grow up, Gaheris," Riprap said in much the tone he would have used for the young men he coached, "and calm down. We've got a world at stake here—a universe at stake. We've got to do the right thing."

"Why?" Gaheris Morris asked. "Why? This is the universe that threw our ancestors out, remember? Would someone remind me why we owe the Lands anything?"

Gentle Smoke, her delicate features shadowed with grey lines of pain, said softly, "We are those ancestors, Gaheris. At least we five . . ." She motioned with a hand on which the nails were broken and torn. ". . . are. You are correct. We were thrown out, but we never accepted that exile as permanent. We never disavowed our homeland. We left rather than do it considerable harm and hoped to someday return home."

Des Lee said, his tone almost teasing, "As I see the situation, Gaheris, the Exiles are rather like people who cut down all the trees because they needed fields for planting crops, and didn't think about what removing the trees would do to the very soil they wanted to use."

"Or," Bent Bamboo said, clearly getting into the spirit of analogy, "people who dumped all their sewers into a river, never figuring that someday the river dragon would get fed up and refuse to clear the stuff out."

Des grinned at the Monkey, but his gaze remained fixed on Gaheris's face. "So, Gaheris, by your logic, just because a mistake was made, a mistake made through all the best intentions—"

"Well," Copper Gong interrupted, "we were very, very angry. Blind with fury, if you must know the truth."

"Okay." Des waved her down. "But you had no idea that what you were doing would affect the very fabric of this universe. Therefore, a mistake was made. The larger consequences weren't taken into account." Des adjusted himself in his chair, winced slightly as some half-healed injury pulled, and went on. "Now we have the opportunity to correct what was done. Should we refuse to replant the trees or clean the river just because we personally weren't the source of the problem?"

"Sorry, Des," Gaheris said, "but your analogy— while doubtless accurate regarding what's happening to the Lands—doesn't answer my objection. As I see it, we're more like Jews or Japanese after World War II. We were sent off to concentration camps. Now that the war is over we're told, 'Not only can't you have any restitution for your lost property, or any compensation for the pain suffered by yourselves and your descendants, *but* . . .'"

Gaheris paused, one finger held high in the air. "'But would you also accept a radical lobotomy in return?'"

His features softened so that he looked almost a boy again, his eyes wistful and pleading. "Look, I'm not happy about what you want to do because of how it might change me. I'll admit that, but from what everyone tells me, I didn't change too much when I was separated from the Rat. Albert apparently got a whole lot less uptight. I'm thinking about Shen and Pearl. They've given their entire lives to this farce. I can't accept a situation that asks them to be rewarded for seventy-some years of faithful service by being mind-raped."

That final word hung in the air, but Nine Ducks, who, from what Loyal Wind had been able to gather, had found the women's ordeal particularly horrible, was the one who chose to break the uncomfortable silence.

"I understand, Gaheris, but your noble feelings on behalf of your old friends and teachers doesn't change the fact that unless we do something, the Lands are going to continue to be threatened, and that through the Lands your own home may be vulnerable."

"Nine Ducks raises an important additional consideration," Pearl said. "Gaheris, do you want to go home and explain to the various indigenous magical traditions that the threat from the Lands isn't ended, only maybe a little delayed? I assure you, old enemies and ones we don't even know exist will shout for our power being hobbled—and they will be much less kind than Righteous Drum's spell would be."

Before Gaheris could speak, a new voice, one with an irreverent lilt that Loyal Wind had been told was typically Irish, broke in.

"I know I wasn't invited," said Parnell, walking through a wall and sliding through the crowded room to perch on the edge of the table, "but since this matter of the Land's deterioration concerns me and mine, I've invited myself."

A murmur—amazed, angered, annoyed—rose from a dozen throats.

Parnell raised a hand, stilling protests. "Wait. I've intruded because I'm here to help. I've been listening politely to your deliberations, but I had to step in. You're all too close to the problem. You're missing an alternative that might answer all your difficulties—or at least minimize them. Loyal Wind and his associates among the reincarnated Exiles have agreed they must return what they stole, right?"

He waited until the five former ghosts had nodded.

"Then let us permit them to do the Lands that honor. Then why not reassess the situation? Perhaps their sacrifice will strengthen the Lands just enough to get by until—"

Parnell again interrupted himself to consult the five former ghosts. "Am I correct that you can undo the binding that you and your associates put on the Earthly Branches, the one that passes the Branch down a line of physical inheritance?"

They all nodded. Gentle Smoke looked as if she might be willing to elucidate the point, but Parnell continued his facile flow of words.

"Of course you can. That's what you did when you needed to take over the five Earthly Branches from your less than faithful living kin. Well then, here's what I suggest. You five ghosts do what you've already agreed to do. Give back what you have stolen. However, before you do take that step, recraft your original spell so that at the death of the current holder, the remaining Earthly Branches return to the Lands, rather than getting passed down the line of inheritance."

"It might work," Bent Bamboo said, his big grin filling his face for the first time since they had been taken by Thundering Heaven. "Would returning five Branches shore up the weakness? Shen? Righteous Drum? You're the students of magic. Do you think Parnell's theory has any validity or is he just seducing us all with that agile tongue?"

"It's possible it could work," Shen said with the hesitance of one who sees a reprieve and doesn't want to seem too eager to take it. "The deterioration happened over time. The return of almost half of what was taken should help a great deal. And as Parnell has suggested, we don't need to go on theory alone. We can test after the five Earthly Branches have been—as you might put it—repatriated."

"Realistically," Pearl said with that unflinching courage Loyal Wind admired, "we can also accept that you and I, Shen, aren't going to live much longer. It will be something of a miracle if we live another twenty years. Therefore, within twenty years—possibly much sooner—the Lands will regain two more Branches."

Albert was nodding. "We'll need to do some analysis, talk with Righteous Drum—"

"And others," Gaheris cut in. He still didn't look exactly happy, but he did look less unhappy. "Maybe even some folks at home. Righteous Drum has too much of a vested interest in the Lands for us to rely solely on him."

"Fine, Righteous Drum and others," Albert said, "but this could work."

Nissa said a little sadly, "Then Lani won't ever get to be the Rabbit, and she was so looking forward to it. Still, I agree. This seems like a good solution."

Pearl leaned forward and patted Nissa's hand. "Don't worry, my dear. Lani already sees ghosts. I think you're going to have your hands full with her, Rabbit or not."

Pearl laughed, the sound bright with relief. "To think, before I met Flying Claw—Foster as he was—I sometimes wondered why the auguries would never give me a clear assessment as to who my heir would be. I thought this was because I refused to bear children, and so confused the Tiger's path, but perhaps the Tiger's eyes saw more options than I dared imagine."

XXXI

Brenda's head was spinning as Nissa related what had gone on at the meeting.

Brenda had been thinking about herself—about how this meant she'd never be the Rat—when Nissa said softly: "Of course, what no one is saying flat out is that this means that soon the five Exiles are going to die all over again."

"But why?" Then Brenda understood. "Yen-lo Wang only let them come back so they could fix things. I remember."

Nissa nodded, not bothering to dab at the tear that trickled down her cheek. "What a reward for their courage—returning to life in order to be raped and tortured—and just when things are getting better, then they have to die? It's not right."

Brenda remembered what Pearl had said to her. "Sometimes things aren't right or fair. That's just the way it is."

She shook herself. "And here I've been letting myself regret I'll never be the Rat. What good did being the Rat do my dad or granddad or great-granddad? Maybe I'll be the first in four generations to learn how to be less of a self-centered idiot. Are you going to tell Lani?"

"Later," Nissa said. "We're going to continue living with Pearl, whatever decision is made. Pearl seems to think that Lani is like you—that she has a few gifts that have nothing to do with affiliation with our Earthly Branch. That means she may need some training."

"Does Pearl think you have any hidden gifts?" Brenda asked.

Nissa shook her head. "No. She, Shen, and Righteous Drum did some tests, and anyhow, Pearl knew my dad and granddad. It's likely that Lani's gifts come from her father's side."

Brenda wanted to ask about this mysterious never-mentioned man, but the expression in Nissa's bright turquoise eyes all but dared her to do so. She decided that, for once, she could keep her mouth shut.

"When do you go back to Pearl's?" Brenda asked instead.

"Pretty much immediately," Nissa said. "I'll be back for the final ceremony, of course. I wanted to fill you in first because the meeting wiped Des and Riprap out, and the five 'ghosts' are going to have too much on their minds. The others rushed off to start arrangements."

And you knew my dad wouldn't tell me, Brenda thought, *or wouldn't tell me everything. Or at least if he did he'd give it a spin of his own.*

Aloud she said, "Let me walk you to the gate, then."

As they walked, they talked about how they'd agreed to rearrange rooms at Pearl's when Brenda moved in.

"You do still plan to come, right?" Nissa said.

"I do," Brenda said firmly. "I may never be the Rat, but I'm not ready to go back to USC and pretend none of this happened. Maybe next year I'll start my sophomore year all over, but right now . . ."

"Good!"

They hugged, and Nissa vanished to begin her journey back from this gate through the Nine Gates and home again.

Home, Brenda thought. *I wonder where that is, now.*

She didn't have a chance to get morose or even philosophical. A male voice called out her name.

"Brenda Morris!"

She turned and saw Bent Bamboo. Of all the former scouts, he seemed to be healing most easily, even more easily than Des or Riprap, both of whom claimed to have been more gently treated. Did Monkeys have healing gifts? She couldn't remember.

"Bent Bamboo, what are you doing out and about? I thought Joyful Promise only agreed to permit her patients to attend the meeting on the grounds that you'd all rest afterwards."

Bent Bamboo gave a mischievous grin. "I will rest. If you would do the honor of stepping into a vacant parlor, I will begin immediately."

There were plenty of vacant parlors—or at least unoccupied rooms neatly furnished with comfortable chairs. The palace complex was operating well short of the usual contingents of servants and minor officials. Until they definitely knew who their allies were, the Orphans and their associates weren't taking any chances. Even those they had reason to treat as allies—such as Twentyseven-Ten, Thorn, and Shackles—had been carefully watched, but so far had given no reason to suspect them of anything worse than opportunism.

Brenda and Bent Bamboo chose a neatly appointed parlor a few doors down from the gate room. Bent Bamboo closed the door before settling into a chair.

"I know I have a bad reputation with the ladies," he said, "but I assure you that I reformed before my departure from the world. You are safe with me."

Okay, Brenda thought, but she was still glad she had a couple of amulet bracelets on each wrist. Bent Bamboo was being perfectly polite, but he had a lecher's grin.

"I think," Bent Bamboo said, "Joyful Promise—if she knew what I was doing—would approve. You see, I'm here on her brother's business."

"Flying Claw?" Brenda was astonished. "He sent you?"

"He, well, he did and he . . . No, I suppose if I were to be perfectly honest, he didn't, but I'm here on his business nonetheless."

"What do you mean?"

In answer, Bent Bamboo reached into his sleeve and pulled out a battered and stained twist of lavender fabric. He held it out to her, and Brenda stared at it uncomprehending. Then she recognized it as one of the wide, fabric-covered bands she put around her hair when she pulled it into a ponytail.

Bent Bamboo dropped it into her outstretched hand.

"I have a confession to make."

"What?" Brenda was still astonished by Bent Bamboo having one of her hair ties, and trying to figure out what this had to do with Flying Claw. "I'm completely confused."

"Let me unconfuse you."

Bent Bamboo leaned ostentatiously back in his chair. In a moment, Brenda realized the significance of this.

"You . . ."

"That's right. I wasn't treated nearly as harshly as were my associates. I don't know if you believe me, but in a small way, that was its own form of torture. You see, the reason I wasn't beaten bloody was because Li Szu believed I could be turned by more intellectual means. He thought," Bent Bamboo's voice was bitter, "I was the most likely traitor, and that if he could prove I had come over to his side, then the others would give up as well."

"Oh . . ."

But Bent Bamboo wanted no sympathy. He spoke quickly now.

"You see, Thundering Heaven had swayed me once. In my own defense, I will say that Thundering Heaven didn't give me anything like the full story. However, I guess that Li Szu thought that my having been swayed once meant either I was a gullible idiot or that I was a good friend of Thundering Heaven. I think the latter, because I was often put in Thundering Heaven's company as he went about his business, and his business usually had to do with Flying Claw."

Brenda nodded, her fingers involuntarily tightening around the hair tie.

Bent Bamboo went on. "Now I like Flying Claw, and more than just liking him, I owed him a considerable debt. Flying Claw helped to save me when I was a complete idiot and would have burned to death in the sea of fire. More importantly, he never once reminded me afterwards of how stupidly brash I had been, not even by a glance. I kept waiting for him to say something, and because of that I kept an eye on him. That's how I noticed he had a lucky piece, a talisman, perhaps a lady's favor."

Brenda held up the bit of lavender fabric. "This. I didn't give it to him, if that's what you mean. He must have borrowed it."

"Not to hold back his own hair," Bent Bamboo said with a slight chuckle. "Flying Claw never wore that hair tie, but kept it tucked away—on his wrist if he was wearing long sleeves, inside his tunic otherwise. He was very careful we not see it, but he also couldn't help but touch it occasionally. I bet I'm not the only one who noticed."

Brenda felt herself blushing, although whether for herself or for Flying Claw, she wasn't sure. Maybe for both of them. She'd thought she loved Flying Claw. She'd hoped he might care for her, but this quiet devotion made her heart hurt, and all her confused love and longing well up afresh.

But who was that love for? For the Foster she'd first met? For the Flying Claw she'd come to know? For the mutilated stranger who would hardly speak to her—or to anyone? Did she love him? Had she ever loved him? If Flying Claw had loved her, did he still, or had Thundering Heaven cut any capacity for love from his heart?

Bent Bamboo kept talking. "One day I saw what had to be Flying Claw's belongings sitting in a heap. They'd been thoroughly picked over, but apparently no significance had been attached to that little fabric talisman. Remembering how Flying Claw had valued it, I picked it up and hid it away. I don't know what I meant to do with it—I just wanted to keep it for Flying Claw, in case by some miracle we all lived through this. I wanted to give him back something he valued. Even more, I think I wanted there to be one thing Thundering Heaven couldn't take from him."

"I think I can understand that," Brenda said. "I do. That was kind."

Bent Bamboo brushed her compliment away with a gesture of one long-fingered hand as if it were a physical thing. "I'd planned to wait until Flying Claw was stronger, until he had more of his confidence back. Then I was going to return it to him and give him a stern talking to. However, I probably won't be here to do that, so I'm going to have to leave it to you."

"To me."

Bent Bamboo smiled at Brenda, and there was only grandfatherly tenderness on his monkey face. "I'm not asking you to fall in love with the boy, Brenda Morris, just to be kind to him. Can you promise me that much?"

Brenda bit into her lower lip in a futile attempt to stop the tears that were welling up in her eyes—tears for her and her confused heart, tears for Flying Claw and his maimed body, tears for Bent Bamboo, who knew he was going to die and had kindness to spare for someone else's pain.

"I promise," she said. "I absolutely promise."

☆

The day when the five ghosts were to keep their vow came all too quickly.

The spells that had all but severed the Twelve Branches from the Lands had been undone the day before, each of the Orphans speaking with greater or lesser enthusiasm the words that renounced, on behalf of their descendants, this intangible inheritance.

Parnell of the sidhe and his small entourage had left before the magical rituals commenced, Parnell saying with mischievous politeness that while he had quite liked helping them solve their problems, he was enough of a diplomat to know when he would not be wanted.

The hour for the ceremony of return and reuniting had been set for noon. Returning to his room to prepare, Loyal Wind found a new set of robes, elaborately embroidered with the Horse, awaiting him.

As he inspected the robes, Loyal Wind noted that in addition to elegant renditions of the Horse in his varied attitudes, the robes were also embroidered with signs for luck and happiness. The emblems associated with wealth, prosperity, and longevity were conspicuous in their absence.

Well, Loyal Wind thought, letting Thorn, who had been assigned to wait upon him, assist him into the robe, *I suppose that wealth, prosperity, and longevity*

*are rather much to expect the gods to grant at this late
date.*

Shortly before noon, they assembled in the throne
room where the Jade Petal Throne stood on its dais,
conspicuously empty. Li Szu's coup had changed the
very structure of the Lands Born from Smoke and
Sacrifice. Finding one who could be elevated to the
role of emperor was not proving easy.

But the succession will not be my problem, Loyal
Wind thought, and realized that his regret was tem-
pered with some other emotion he could not name.

All of the remaining Thirteen Orphans—even Deborah, her face still lightly marked with the remnants
of the chicken pox—were present, clad in their finest
regalia.

Brenda Morris stood slightly to one side, of and yet
not of, the Orphans' number. Her attire consisted of a
long, fitted skirt and brocade tunic styled in such a
manner that they evoked both the fashions of her homeland and those of the Lands. Brenda's tunic sleeves were
short caps, rather out of keeping for the chilly hall, but
then Loyal Wind noted the tattered bit of lavender fabric Brenda wore intermingled with the amulet bracelets
on her right wrist.

Loyal Wind blinked when he recognized this strange
adornment. Then he caught the slight, satisfied smile
that lit Bent Bamboo's features, and thought he knew
how Flying Claw's charm had reached Brenda Morris.

Loyal Wind wondered if Flying Claw, standing defiantly straight and tall, clad in embroidered robes of
the Tiger's green, had noticed Brenda's quiet declaration. The young Tiger's face was less raw but still a
ruin, and its altered character gave nothing away.

As the Tiger, Flying Claw stood at the head of the
small group that represented the remnant of the Lands'
Twelve. Righteous Drum stood next to Flying Claw,

Honey Dream beside him. A few of the sages and soldiers who had proven themselves reliable—including Twentyseven-Ten, Thorn, and Shackles—stood with them, a pace back.

To Loyal Wind, who had seen this throne room teeming with the court of several emperors, the room seemed very empty. Their footsteps as they crossed the polished floor echoed despite the tapestries hung from the walls.

The basics of the ceremony had been designed by Gentle Smoke and Honey Dream. The participants had been briefed on their roles.

First the Thirteen Orphans made a circle, Albert at their center. They joined hands. On his right, Loyal Wind grasped Gentle Smoke's slim fingers; on his left, Copper Gong's more robust digits. They moved a full rotation to the right, then repeated the action to the left, stepping with slow, measured movements. In the center, Albert Yu also turned, but in the opposite direction—the contrary Cat, part of them, but ever separate.

Albert Yu extended his hands in a gesture of welcome, then spoke the first words.

"In the name of my grandfather whose life you saved, and in the name of my father, who you cared for and taught, I thank you for the sacrifices you made to assure that the line of the emperor who you had sworn to serve would not be wiped from the memory of the Lands.

"You have striven beyond life to keep your promise. Now I release you from that promise. In the name of the emperor you served, I ask that you graciously return what you took, so that the Lands may be strong once more."

This was the cue for the five former ghosts to drop the hands they held and step forward. Each did so without hesitation. The remaining Orphans drew back, making a line in front of the Jade Petal Throne, standing solemn and formal, their hands vanished within the wide bells of their sleeves.

Tears stood bright in the eyes of many who wished them silent farewell.

The five inclined their heads to the remaining Orphans, then to the other who stood witness. Finally, in many cases still moving very stiffly, they lowered themselves into the crouched position of the formal kowtow.

Beating their heads upon the polished stone of the floor, they chanted as one.

"We sought to do only right and have learned we did wrong. We sought to preserve our emperor, and so damaged the Lands. We beg forgiveness, and pray to give back that which we took, when thinking ourselves clever, now knowing ourselves fools."

Albert was saying something, and Loyal Wind knew it must be the formal response they had all agreed was appropriate. However, he could not hear the words.

Hoofbeats were sounding in his ears and the trumpeting cry of a stallion in battle drowned out all other sounds.

Raising his head, Loyal Wind saw the Horse running somehow through him, but not from him, going ahead as guide and comfort, leading the way into the crowded official court of Yen-lo Wang.

The great judge sat upon his throne, beckoning with one long-nailed finger for them to rise and come before him.

As he did so, Loyal Wind saw the Horse galloping into the distance, but he felt no terrible loss.

Yen-lo Wang was smiling faintly. Water Cloud, the

Rooster, stood to one side of the judge's throne, arms outstretched, her face bright with welcome.

☆

Pearl was trying hard not to cry, but tears blurred her sight as Nine Ducks, Gentle Smoke, Loyal Wind, Copper Gong, and Bent Bamboo kowtowed before the Jade Petal Throne, begging forgiveness, asking to right a wrong they had not intended.

Was it the tears in her eyes that made the air above those bent figures shimmer and become momentarily solid?

Above the five curved backs the Ox, Snake, Horse, Ram, and Monkey had reshaped the air. Somehow, although wholly animal, each bore some resemblance to their human selves: a twinkle of a smile, a knowing look in an eye, a proud bearing to a head.

The five incarnations of the Earthly Branches reached forth and touched the still kowtowing humans. Between one breath and the next, each fell still. No one needed Honey Dream's spontaneous cry of pain and grief to tell them that their friends were dead.

Pearl removed her hand from her sleeve and dashed the tears from her eyes, watching steadily as the five incarnations faded into smoke and memory.

An odd honor, she thought, *giving death for good service, but a high tribute nonetheless, coming to see their hosts off on this last journey. Perhaps they didn't need to come far, perhaps they were there all along. Do I become the Tiger or does the Tiger become me?*

Pearl laughed quietly at herself. *I guess I won't know until it's too late to share that particular bit of knowledge.*

Across the room, Honey Dream—who had been honestly shocked when she felt Gentle Smoke's death

and the Snake's return to fully bond with the Lands—
was sobbing in her father's arms. A few of the nascent
imperial court were gathered near, murmuring soothing comments. For the first time since her arrival, Pearl
felt out of place.

Pearl gathered her friends to her with a glance.

"Come on," she said. "They need time to adjust, and
I for one could do with a nice cup of tea."

"We'll come back, though," Brenda said, anxiously,
touching a bit of ragged lavender fabric that hung from
her wrist.

"I think so," Pearl assured her. "I think so."

*If not in life, then in death, we will certainly return,
at least a part of us, the part that belongs to the Lands.*